Praise for the w

Heaven Sent: Hell

"Exciting and sexy this book quickly catches the readers' attention through the strong personalities of its characters. Readers will find themselves emotionally involved in this heart touching story as this group of musicians make music and fall in love."

— Anita, *The Romance Studio*

"Jet Mykles portrays incredibly loveable, but imperfect characters that will keep you hot and bothered and at the edge of your seat."

— Sabella, *Joyfully Reviewed*

Heaven Sent: Faith

"Jet Mykles is an amazing author... Her latest release is another emotional and sensual masterpiece. Ms. Mykles is a star in this hot genre. Her books should be on any romantic fans must have list."

— Kimberley Spinney, *Ecataromance*

"I am one of the fans who eagerly anticipated the release of this story and can honestly say I am thrilled with *Faith*. It is more than worth the wait. Jet Mykles definitely knows how to write erotic romance!"

— Robin Snodgrass, *Romance Junkies*

Loose Id ®

ISBN 978-1-59632-623-1
HEAVEN SENT 2
Copyright © 2007 by Jet Mykles

Cover Art by P. L. Nunn
Cover Design by April Martinez

Publisher acknowledges the author and copyright holder of the individual works, as follows:

HEAVEN SENT: HELL
Copyright © April 2007 by Jet Mykles
HEAVEN SENT: FAITH
Copyright © July 2007 by Jet Mykles

Printed in the U.S.A. by
Lightning Source, Inc.
1246 Heil Quaker Blvd
La Vergne TN 37086
www.lightningsource.com

Contents

HEAVEN SENT:
HELL

Dedication

Alvin, JL, Ally, Willa, Luisa, Kim, Maura, Raven, Nik and, most especially, Katrin. You all got me through this when I wasn't all that sure it'd really happen.

Also for my very patient musician boyfriend who helped to supply the appropriate mindset for a certain guitarist.

Prologue

Earlier this year...

He clutched the headboard, sweat sticking his curly black hair to his face. He had his forearms wedged between his head and the heavy wood to avoid getting his skull cracked as his body rocked helplessly, driven to insanity by Luc pounding into his ass. His breathing caught on a moan as the orgasm started in his spine, pulsing, rolling, burning Almost there.

Luc groaned, hands on his hips tensing in a familiar way, almost there as well. Luc fell forward, arms sliding around his torso to clutch him close, back to chest. He turned his head aside, struggling to breathe, and some of Luc's blazing auburn hair fell over his cheek.

"God," he gasped.

Luc slammed hard, angled just so.

"Fuck yeah!" he shouted, tossing his head back into Luc's shoulder and bracing against the headboard as the redhead loosed the pleasure that burst from his spine. It tunneled down his groin and shot through his cock into the sweaty, rumpled white sheets beneath him.

His spent muscles shook, ready to collapse, as Luc barreled into him, chasing his own orgasm. Luc's groan turned into an almost sob, and if he hadn't been listening for it, he wouldn't have heard the name "Reese" sigh past Luc's lips as he came.

Brent's watery knees didn't stand a chance of bracing them both as Luc's dead weight collapsed heavily on his back. He went down to the mattress in a huff beneath the heavier man, face buried in the pillows and belly on the wet spot of his own making.

Lifting his head, Brent licked dry lips. "I heard that."

Luc grunted. He rolled off Brent to sit up against the headboard. Harsh lamplight failed to diminish the elegant planes of his chin and throat as he threw his head back, sable eyes closed. Sweat glistened on his pale, bare skin. Brent waited, but there was no answer. After a moment, Luc sighed, then busied himself with removing the condom, tying it off and depositing it into the wastebasket on his side of the bed.

Brent sighed, pushing to his side, facing Luc as the redhead sat back against the headboard with a pack of cigarettes from the nightstand. "So Are you going to talk to him at the wedding?"

Luc grimaced, plucking two cylinders from the pack. He placed both at his lips and cradled the lighter before him. "I doubt he wants to see me"

Brent accepted when Luc, without looking, handed him one. "You don't know that." He groaned, gingerly pushing his sticky, aching body to sit up. Damn! If nothing else, Luc certainly could fuck like a demon.

"No. I don't."

"You could probably call Reegan and ask her."

"Oh, *fuck* no. I don't even know if he told her about it."

"Mmm, true." Brent sucked in smoke, staring at the ceiling. He closed his eyes, enjoying the after-tingle of sex as they spoke. "From what I remember, the kid was aching for you."

"That was six years ago."

"So?"

"So he's probably got a boyfriend or something," Luc muttered, moodily staring at the slowly burning ember at the end of his cigarette.

Brent turned toward the nightstand and the mostly full ashtray. *Damn, have I had that many tonight?* "So you break them up. Or, hell, you at least find out if there's still something there. We should take Garth's offer and go to the bachelor party. Maybe you can see him there." When Luc didn't respond, Brent sighed. "So you just gonna keep fucking me every time you want to pretend you're fucking him?"

Luc growled but didn't look at him. "You complaining?"

"Not entirely." He ran a hand through the smeared spunk on his belly. He'd have to go wash up soon. He'd finish his smoke first. "I'm used to being a stand-in."

Luc sighed, running his hand through his hair. "God, man, I thought we talked about this..."

Brent waved a hand in the air, turning to bend his knees over his side of the rumpled bed. "Take it easy. We did. Experimentation and all that"

"Speaking of which, when's the last time you experimented?"

Brent snorted, stabbing out his cigarette in the full ashtray. "What does it matter? I'm not the horn dog here."

"I'm not a horn dog."

"Give me a break."

When no comeback sounded, Brent peered over his shoulder. Luc was staring at the teetering tower of ash that balanced atop the filter he held before him. Obviously Luc's thoughts had moved on.

Brent sighed. "So we go home, you see him, and you get him back." He stood "How hard is that?"

Luc nabbed his ashtray and abandoned the burned cylinder. "Damn it, Brent. I shoved him away."

Brent had to watch. It was a rare thing to see Lucas Sloane as anything but self-assured. Even Brent, his best friend, had only seen it once or twice in the twenty-odd years they'd known each other. *It must be love.* "That was years ago." He turned toward the bathroom. "You're a big rock star now. How could he resist you?"

Luc laughed mirthlessly behind him.

Brent sighed, knowing he wasn't really good at this. He turned at the door. A sweaty lock of his silky black hair fell over his left eye. "Joke, man. Joke. So you use the wedding as an excuse to go back, and you apologize. If he's receptive, you fuck him into next year." He shrugged, tossing his head to clear hair from his face. "What's so hard about that?"

"What if he doesn't want me?"

Brent snorted. "You turn on the Lucas Sloane charm. How could the poor guy resist?"

Luc gave him an evil smile. Brent had always known the man was gorgeous, and only rarely did Luc not get what he wanted. That charm and attitude had helped to get Heaven Sent where they were today. The same would get him the man he loved. Reese didn't stand a chance.

Chapter One

Now...

Brent stepped up beside Luc, dangling a tumbler of Jack Daniels over the railing. "I don't believe it."

Luc started, twisting his head toward Brent. He frowned. "What?"

"The mighty Lucas Sloane has fallen." Brent waved a hand to indicate the full dance floor beneath them as well as the packed balconies along the walls of the nightclub "See before you a sea of sensuality with warm Italian bodies ripe for the plucking, and the magnificent Lucas Sloane is standing here in the corner nursing his drink."

Luc glared. "Fuck you."

Brent chuckled, raising his drink to his lips. "Nope. Can't do that anymore. Reese would mind."

"Reese would mind if I partook of this so-called sea of sensuality."

"Indeed he would." Brent smacked his lips, enjoying the burn of the alcohol as it slid down his throat. "Not to mention the fact that I would rat your sorry ass out in a heartbeat."

"Gee. Thanks, buddy."

"Don't mention it."

They stood for a while, watching the crowd below. Bright, multicolor lights flashed in tune to the throbbing techno beat that spurred the mass of humanity on the dance floor below. Brent tried in vain to find Darien among the sea of bodies. Heaven Sent's drummer was down there somewhere, but Brent couldn't pick out his dark blond head.

Joke as he might, he was actually impressed with Luc's resistance. A year ago, Luc wouldn't have been caught dead alone on a balcony. He would have at least had a lover or a prospective lover with him, female or male. But here he stood, on his own, Brent's threat to rat him out aside. Brent now had no doubts that Luc was in love. His behavior since his week reuniting with Reese and fucking him silly had confirmed that. For the two months in Italy that followed that fateful week, if Luc hadn't been talking music, he'd been talking Reese. The mere possibility that he might have ruined his chance with Reese had made him nearly unbearable outside of work. Brent, Johnnie, Darien, and their producer, Paul, had begun to lay odds on how long it'd take him to bring up Reese in any given conversation. They had practically *sent* Luc back to the States after Reese, just to get a little peace. Brent just hoped that now, after Reese had spent a month in Italy with them, Luc wouldn't go back to mooning just because his lover had returned Stateside.

"So," Luc began, swirling his glass to clink the ice, "forget me. What about you?"

Brent adjusted the dark sunglasses he wore despite the fact it was evening and they were in a nightclub. "What about me?"

"Why aren't you partaking of the sea of sensuality?"

Brent shrugged. "Not in the mood."

Luc snorted. "When was the last time you were in the mood?"

That would be the last time with you, Brent thought, but didn't say. Luc didn't need to know that. "I'm not the horn dog here."

Luc snorted. "You should pick yourself up a nice little piece of ass and get laid. I'll even take you to a late breakfast in the morning so you can brag about it. I need to get some kind of thrill with Reese gone, even if it is vicarious. Let's see..." He tucked errant auburn locks behind his ear and looked around. The two of them stood in the balcony VIP section, away from the press of most of the crowd. The others in the section with them weren't at all interested in the conversation between the two rock stars. "What's your poison? Male or female?"

"Neither."

"C'mon, Brent." Luc waved toward the bar below, plainly visible as it was lit with striking blue. "There's a curvy little number down there almost wearing a black dress. She's been looking up here a few times."

Brent turned to put his empty tumbler on a table behind them. "You noticed?" He slid an ashtray closer to where they stood.

Luc rolled his eyes. "I'm taken, not blind."

Brent dug in his shirt pocket for his Camels, refusing to look toward the bar. "Regardless, she's probably looking at you, not the skinny guitar player."

"You don't know that."

Brent snorted, tapping a cylinder from the pack.

Undeterred, Luc gestured with his long chin. "Hey, how about the guy in the mesh shirt? He's got jeans on with see-through pockets in the back."

Brent flipped open his Zippo and lit up. "Just the description of the clothing means no."

"You like 'em flashy."

"There's flashy and there's tacky."

Brent checked his watch, pleased to find that it was almost ten. The show they'd come to watch would start any moment now, halting the need for conversation.

Luc proceeded to point out more choice members of both sexes. Brent actually looked at a few. He had to admire his friend's taste. All said objects of scrutiny were beautiful. But Brent really wasn't interested and tried to convey that. He just wasn't into picking up someone who just wanted to sleep with "the rock star," and he knew better than to think that he could find someone interested for any other reason.

"Brent?"

"Hmm?"

"When *was* the last time you had sex?"

"Hey, there's Darien." Brent brought his fingers up to his mouth and whistled through the thundering music. With any luck, Luc would think he hadn't heard him.

The notes he whistled were distinctive and loud, and Darien actually heard. He lifted his head and waved, then went back to concentrating on getting up the spiral staircase to the second level.

"Brent?"

Brent turned back to Luc, his oldest and best friend. He'd known this man longer than anyone outside his family and trusted him more than anyone. He tilted his head down so he could look over the rims of his glasses into Luc's sable eyes and let his gaze go stone cold. "Drop it."

Luc's eyes narrowed. He wanted to ask, Brent knew. He wanted to push. But as well as Brent knew Luc, Luc also knew Brent. When he was paying attention, Luc almost knew him better than he knew himself. Luc should know by the tone alone that Brent was done discussing it.

The redhead shrugged and turned back to the railing, digging into a pocket for his own pack of Camels. "You think they'll ever start this show?"

Brent handed his Zippo over without being asked. "You know those damn musicians. Can't count on 'em to be on time for anything."

Darien bounded up to them. Paul Thrombone, the producer for Heaven Sent's latest album, was right behind him. Paul was about Darien's height, therefore shorter than either Brent or Luc. His short, snowy blond hair was gelled back from his face, and he wore a flashy dark orange blazer over a white button-down and artfully torn jeans. The roots of Darien's straight blond hair were wet with sweat from dancing, and dark patches marked the collar and underarms of his gold silk shirt. Wide brown eyes matched his grin as he landed at the railing. "This place *rocks*. You guys shoulda come down."

Luc smiled. "You get lucky?"

Darien's grin turned into a smirk. He grabbed the railing and leaned back, swinging slightly side to side, like a kid. "The night is young, my friend. I'm sticking around after the show."

Luc turned back to Brent. "See? Maybe you should stick around."

Brent flicked his still-lit cigarette at him.

"Hey!" Luc shouted, jumping back. He brushed off the gleaming white of his shirt, glaring at Brent. "What the fuck?"

"Shut your damn trap."

Darien frowned from one to the other. "What gives?"

"*Signori e signore*," an announcer's voice cut into the fading lines of the dance track. The lights began to dim.

Luc and Brent still stared at each other.

The announcer proceeded to say more in Italian. Luc, Darien, and Brent didn't care enough to get a translation from either Paul or one of the bodyguards who hovered toward the back of the balcony. The further dimming lights told them the performance was starting.

"Hey, guys?" Darien asked.

Luc stubbed his own cigarette out in the ashtray.

Brent stomped out the cigarette on the floor, then turned to the railing. Luc could just butt the hell out of his love life -- or lack thereof -- for once.

Luc turned to the rail as well, leaving Darien between them, with Paul, silent and watchful, on Brent's other side.

The drummer frowned, then heaved an exasperated sigh. "Fine. Fuck both of you."

Brent disregarded him, seething. Luc may be his oldest and best friend, but it also meant that Luc knew exactly how to piss him off.

Was it Luc's business who Brent had slept with last? Even if it was him? He'd just jump to all sorts of wrong conclusions if he found that out. He'd likely think that Brent was mooning over him, which simply wasn't true. Brent hadn't slept with anyone else because he hadn't put forth the effort to find anyone. It was actually a normal thing for Brent. He'd only slept with Luc because Luc had pressed the point, and, well, Brent had been curious and receptive. It's not like they'd been exclusive, although Luc had done far more experimenting than Brent. But now Luc was all Reese's, and he wished them well. Truly. But Luc might not see it that way, at least not at first. No one would. Which was why Brent just didn't want to talk about it, damn it!

The lights went out. The announcer spoke up, but Brent only recognized the name of the performer they'd come to see through the Italian: Heller Witting. Yet more people packed onto the already crowded dance floor, facing the stage in anticipation as a soft electronic pulse filled the air. This was Heller's niche, and he was quite popular in it across Europe. He played sets in dance clubs in lieu of a disc jockey and, from all accounts, kept people dancing sometimes for hours.

Brent was too far away for his eyes to adjust enough and allow him to see the performer walk onstage. He had to wait until the lights trickled up, synchronized with a wobbling piano passage. The first thing Brent noticed was the hair. He reached up to tip his glasses down, just to make sure that he saw the color he thought he saw. He did. The figure that stood behind racks of keyboards had a wavy mop of short, vivid lavender hair. Lavender. Like an Easter egg. He was enough in profile that Brent could see a thin, long tail of darker purple extending from the nape of his neck down the back of his shiny, sleeveless white overcoat. He looked small and young, but he took command of the racks of keyboards like a pro.

Brent smiled. Paul had supplied some MP3s of the man's music, but Brent hadn't gotten a visual yet. Luc had looked him up on the internet and had, so far, claimed that he was "cute." Now Brent knew what he meant.

So this was the man Paul thought could be a welcome addition to Heaven Sent? Brent watched, his anger at Luc draining away as the keyboardist's haunting, heartbeat melodies and tickling electronic overtones washed over him.

The MP3s had been good. His live show was better. Heller Witting definitely had promise

Brent flipped open his Zippo and lit up. He used the accustomed movement to help put his mind back to rights, gradually recovering from the terrific performance he'd just seen. The last strains of Heller's final song were still in his mind, fifteen minutes after the man had left the stage. He couldn't help but imagine new tracks with other instruments laid down with what he'd heard, making for a pretty spectacular sound.

"Damn," Darien muttered, plopping down on the padded seat of the booth beside Brent. "The kid's good."

Brent nodded, exhaling as he set the lighter down on the glossy tabletop and reached over to slide the ashtray closer to him.

Paul, seated backwards in the chair he'd pulled up to the table, grinned. "I told you. Would I steer you wrong?"

Luc slid into the booth opposite Darien. "That's why we hired you, Paul. You're the best."

Paul laughed, grabbing the back of the chair and leaning back. The loud orange of his jacket gleamed in the nightclub's wavering lighting. He waited until the waiter came to deliver the fresh round of drinks they had ordered before speaking again. He eyed Brent. "What do you think?"

Brent sucked smoke into his lungs, thinking. As often happened when a group decision needed to be made about the sound of their music, they looked to Brent. Yes, they all contributed to the sound and they were all necessary, but for whatever reason everyone looked to him as the lead musician. It was a role he accepted gladly and never acknowledged. Johnnie was the face of the band; Luc was his dark, mysterious counterpoint; Darien was the heartbeat; and Brent was the musician. They all took their roles rather naturally.

How would someone new fit in? But even as he thought it, those imagined tracks filled his mind. He could easily hear versions of Heller's strains complementing some of the rough cuts the band had been working on for the past few months. Musically, Heller would probably be a great fit.

Personally...?

He exhaled, nodding without speaking. If he spoke, he'd likely start gushing about the electric sizzle of the keyboardist's performance. Since he didn't want to do that, even among friends, he settled for the smile and nod. His dark glasses would hide any excitement that might show in his eyes.

Paul grinned and cocked his head, his eyes darting around the table. "So, you guys think he's good enough to play on the album?"

"Oh, yeah!" Darien's typical enthusiasm shone through.

"Is he willing?" Luc asked. "Looks like he's got a pretty good gig right here."

Paul nodded. "Oh, he's interested. He's got a moderate following in Europe, but it's limited to a few clubs like this. He'd love to tackle the States. Plus, he's a big fan. He knows you came to see him tonight."

Luc sat back in the booth. "You didn't make any promises."

"No way. You guys needed to see him for yourself."

Brent nodded. "He's good." He exchanged glances with Luc. "Really good."

Paul nodded, enthusiastic. "That's what I'm thinking. First time I heard him, I thought he *sounded* like you guys. It's like a perfect fit!" He leaned forward. "You want to meet him?"

"Yeah!" Darien piped up.

Brent took another drag of his cigarette, staring at the ashtray. He shrugged.

Luc nodded. "Sure, why not?"

Paul grinned, standing. "I'll be back in a flash."

Darien barely waited until Paul had left before leaning in across the table. "Man, you guys *did* think he was good, didn't you? I mean, that one song, what was it? The one with the --" He mimicked the nasal sound of the strings passage that had filled Brent's mind as well. Darien grinned as he broke off. "That was awesome."

Luc twirled his drink idly over the table. "I kind of liked the one that went…"

Darien and Luc commenced a discussion of the finer points of the keyboardist's performance. Brent knew from long experience that he only needed to clue in to the gist of the conversation and could otherwise tune out. Which was all well and good. Brent needed the time to brace himself before he saw the performer. For whatever reason, the thought of actually talking to the pixie he'd seen onstage made him nervous.

But the twenty minutes it took Paul to bring the up-and-coming keyboardist back to their table in the VIP section of the club proved not to be enough time at all.

Paul and Heller stopped on the opposite side of the table from Brent. Brent was thankful for his dark glasses as well as his practiced control that allowed him to keep his face in an almost bored expression, because if he didn't have both of those, his jaw would have dropped and he probably would have started drooling. As it was, his eyes widened, and he couldn't take them off the thing of beauty that was Heller Witting.

Brent would be surprised if he was more than five foot five and guessed it was more five foot three or four. The top inch was all hair, a fluff of chin-length curls that were lavender under the bright stage lights but could have been mistaken for platinum blond in the dim light of the candle on the table. A single, much darker braid that was about the diameter of Brent's index finger grew from the nape of his neck and was draped over the left shoulder of his sleeveless white overcoat with a flashy rhinestone band on the end dangling at his waist. Brent couldn't see colors very well in the dim lighting, but he thought Heller's big, luminous, kohl-lined eyes were probably a dark blue. His face was round, his nose pert and upturned, and he had an adorable mouth with an upper lip that had one of those elegant, defined curves to it. He looked exactly like some of those characters in the Japanese anime that Johnnie was always trying to get them to watch.

Heller smiled, and Brent was enchanted by the innocent exuberance of it. Luc had told him that Heller was in his early twenties, but Brent would have pegged him for a kid of sixteen. *Maybe* seventeen or eighteen.

Paul stood aside and waved a hand toward Darien. "Hell, this is Darien Hughes."

Darien stood and took the hand that Hell extended. Now Brent had confirmation that Hell was a little shorter than Darien's five foot six. Darien pumped Hell's hand with his accustomed enthusiasm, despite the fact that the excitement of meeting was supposed to be the other way around. "Nice to meet you, man."

"It is nice to meet you," agreed Hell, his smile wide and genuine.

Brent puzzled at the slight accent to the words as Paul turned to gesture at Luc. "And Lucas Sloane."

Luc stood and shook Hell's hand, his height not seeming to bother the cherub at all.

Then Paul turned the man toward Brent, and he forgot everything else.

"And this is Brent Rose."

Was it Brent's fancy that Hell's smile kicked up a notch? Probably. Yeah, had to be. Those eyes were fixed on the stark black lenses of Brent's glasses, likely seeing the reflection of his own pale loveliness. Brent stood partially and extended his hand across the table to take Hell's Long, delicate-looking fingers closed around his palm in a surprisingly firm grip. He wore a thick gold band around the middle finger that was linked to two chains that extended over the back of his hand before linking to a heavy gold bracelet surrounding his slim wrist. Very feminine, but somehow right on that hand.

Brent smiled as he tried not to drown in those big eyes. Blue? No, maybe not. But in the lighting he couldn't quite tell. "Nice to meet you."

Long, dark eyelashes blinked once, slowly. "It is entirely my pleasure, I assure you."

German! Brent remembered it as Paul gestured Hell into the booth to sit at Luc's side. Heller was native German, thus the source of the accent.

"Dude!" Darien enthused just as Paul resumed his seat across from Brent. Darien leaned forward, his blond hair falling into his face as he focused on Hell. "That performance rocked!"

Hell beamed, briefly batting those eyelashes again. But this time it looked to be in surprise. "You enjoyed it?"

"I loved it! We heard some of your MP3s before, but, man, that was awesome! How long you been doing this kind of stuff?"

At times like this, Brent adored Darien. The drummer was rarely tongue-tied, although he often spilled things that he shouldn't. But there was no harm in this. They all knew what this little meeting was for. Brent, Luc, and Darien had agreed to come with Paul to see the keyboardist play while Johnnie was back in the States, helping Tyler with some legal matters regarding the new hotel they were opening in New York. Recording of the album was probably about three quarters finished, but the entire band and their producer were aware that something was missing. Their music had matured past the early style of their first two albums. They were itching to show what they could do now that they had the time and the resources. When Paul suggested adding a keyboardist and recommended one, it seemed prudent to check it out.

Hell and Darien talked over the table with Luc and Paul commenting occasionally. Hell proved to be as garrulous and bouncy as Darien, and the two barely took a breath when the waiter came to ask about drink refills. Hell's English was flawless, his accent subdued but obvious, heard more in his inflections rather than the actual words.

"I am a big fan of your music," Hell admitted after Darien had regaled him on some of the early Heaven Sent days. Those big eyes came around to fasten on Brent. "Paul will tell you, I was thrilled to hear that you would even come to hear me play."

"We're looking for a new sound," Brent said. They all turned to him, and he realized it was the first he'd spoken since Hell sat down. He focused on keeping his voice calm, staring at the fingertips he had braced on his empty tumbler to keep them from trembling. "We need something a bit…more, y'know?"

Hell nodded, lavender hair puffing around his round face. He leaned forward, bracing bare forearms on the glossy table as he gave Brent his full-on attention. His sleeveless overcoat left his pale, virtually hairless arms bare. Brent's gaze trailed over the defined muscle of his biceps, not bulging but toned. "Yes, yes. Tell me more."

Brent swallowed. "We can't make any promises, you understand" He groaned at himself. He sounded like one of those awful big shots talking to a rookie, seeking to put the rookie in his place. That wasn't what he was trying to do. "Johnnie will need to agree."

"Of course! I would very much like to try. I would be thrilled to spend even a day in the recording studio with you."

Brent stared. Hell's eyes were fixed on him. By "you" he'd meant the band, of course, but the weight of his stare gave Brent other ideas. *Down, boy.*

"Johnnie's due back next week," Luc pitched in, leaning in on the table. "Why don't you come out and jam with us."

"Oh, yeah, man!" Darien beamed. "You've got to see this place! It's so cool! We've never done this before. We got this gi-normous place that's like a manor house. There's like acres of the estate to walk around, and we're up on a hill so you can even see the ocean in the distance. You'll love it!"

Hell's mouth fell open. "Amazing! I've never been to such a recording studio."

"Nah, it's an exclusive..." Darien went on to tell Hell about the estate's history.

Brent exchanged small smiles with Luc. To judge by Darien's reaction, he and Hell were already fast friends.

Chapter Two

Brent scribbled furiously, determined to get the gist of what they'd been playing down before he forgot it. This was *great!* He hadn't had this much fun writing in a long time. Oh, he enjoyed it when the band was all together, but recently there were always the inevitable interruptions. Even though they'd gone to Italy to isolate themselves, his band mates still managed to find reasons not to stick around for the hours on end Brent found necessary to write a proper song. Then again, he'd been accused of being a perfectionist when it came to their music. Whatever. It suited them and it worked, so they could just suck it up.

But now they weren't even in the studio. He was on a jet plane, of all places. Luc, Johnnie, and Darien were stretched out on the plush couch and recliner seats at the far end of the cabin, while he and Hell sat at a little table having a grand time with just his acoustic guitar and the little Casio keyboard Hell traveled with. A glance at his watch showed they'd killed more than half of the ten-hour-plus flight back to the good old US of A.

In the last four months during recording, Brent had found, to his extreme delight, that the cherub shared his same work ethic in regards to music There had been a number of nights where the two of them had stayed up late after the others had gone to bed or off somewhere. In those late nights, they'd discussed nothing but music. It had been fabulous!

"It's all here," Hell murmured, flipping a few switches on the Casio. He'd recorded all of what they'd done.

"I know." Brent waved the hand with the pen, without looking up. "Call it habit. I feel better having it on paper."

Besides, scribbling gave him a reason not to look up. Not to look into those fathomless violet eyes. Yeah, violet. Hell had eyes like Elizabeth Taylor, luminous and gorgeous and fucking purple! Even his eyebrows were dyed purple. Brent had yet to see him without mascara, so he didn't know if the eyelashes were dyed too. "Cute as a button" was a perfect description for him.

And when, exactly, did cute become so damn sexy? Brent wondered, not for the first time.

A strain of the last harmony they were working on reached his ears, and Brent glanced over just enough to see Hell's elegant fingers float over the keys. Didn't even look like he touched them. Brent was a pretty good piano player, if he had to say so himself, but Hell put him to shame. The kid was simply gifted. Gold rings on both hands and the odd ring-and-chain thing Hell wore on his right hand shone in the harsh light of the lamp over the table.

Brent finished writing, then sat back, staring at his scribbled version of what they'd come up with. It wasn't notes exactly, but long practice had taught him a way to write music that would make sense to him later on. He fiddled with the pen, thinking. "Y'know, maybe we should change that third part back."

"No. We should do it again" -- Hell reached over the table to point with one manicured finger at the blank space toward the bottom of the page -- "here."

Brent raised an eyebrow, surprised Hell knew what the scribbles meant. But the suggestion set off the sounds in his head. Lost in the music, hearing the unwritten part in his head, he frowned. "But..."

Hell brought his hands back to the keyboard and quickly played the part in question, easily progressing into the next stanza. "See?"

Brent glanced down as he listened, lips pursed. Slowly he smiled. Damn. The cherub was right. "Yeah. Okay." He dropped the pen and took up the pick he'd left on the table. Out of the corner of his eye, he saw Hell yawning. He turned so that he could properly cradle his guitar and bent over it. "You can go get some sleep if you want," he said, not looking up as he applied pick to strings. "You don't have to stay up with me."

"No, no, I'm fine. I'm enjoying myself with you."

Brent glanced up to see Hell smiling at him and felt his own shy smile in return. He missed the shield of his sunglasses, but they were stashed with his stuff next to one of the recliner chairs, and it would be too obvious to go get them. Embarrassed, he bent back over the guitar. "You've gotta be tired, though. It's, like, four a.m. for us."

"What about you?"

Brent shrugged. "I'm not tired."

"Then I'll stay up with you." When Brent looked up, Hell smiled. "I don't want to miss anything good." His slight German accent gave his speech a bit of a susurrus, like silk on skin.

Brent laughed, trying not to feel the tingle. "Not much chance of that. You've improved everything that I've come up with."

"That is not true. Your stuff is excellent! I've only suggested a change here and there."

"Ha. You're being modest. How long have you been playing?"

Hell's fingers danced over the Casio, producing only a ghost of a sound since he'd turned the instrument most of the way down. "Since I was a small child. My mother loves music. She teaches."

Since Hell's focus was on his fingers, Brent felt free to look his fill at what he could see of the cherub's face. He stole glances at Hell way too often and probably should stop, but damn, the man was beautiful! "Ah, that explains it."

Hell nodded, some of that soft pastel hair caressing his cheek. He lifted one hand to tuck it behind his ear, revealing the five gold rings that rimmed the delicate shell. "My father is a percussionist."

"So it runs in your blood."

Hell smiled. "It does. My sister teaches, as well."

"Whoa. That's better'n me."

"Not so. Being self-taught is an amazing skill. To have picked it up yourself is amazing."

"Yeah, I didn't really start playing until I was twelve, though."

Hell nodded. "Yes, I know." His grin was impish and maybe just a touch shy. "You taught yourself, and then you taught Luc."

Brent snorted. "So you've read the bios."

"Is it true?"

"Oh, that part's true. Luc didn't want to learn, though. He used to hate it that I'd sit in my room all day or all night and not want to hang out. Wasn't until we were fifteen before he figured out the girls really *liked* the guys in bands. Then he was *begging* me to teach him, and we *had* to get a band together. Not that he ever needed the help getting girls." Brent shook his head, chuckling. "Lucky for him, he's got a knack for it."

Hell stole a glance at the sleeping redhead, who couldn't hear them thanks to the ear buds plugged into the iPod nestled in his lap. He turned back to Brent, cocking his head. "Girls?"

"Don't let recent events fool you," Brent said, bending over the guitar again. "He's firmly bisexual. He's had a thing for pretty girls since I've known him. There's really only one guy he's ever been into."

"Reese."

"Yep."

"But they have only been together a few months."

Brent shook his head. "We knew Reese way back before we broke big."

Hell fanned his fingers on the smooth surface of the table, sitting up in surprise. "Has it been a secret this whole time?"

Softly strumming a subconscious melody, Brent smiled. "No. Luc didn't want to be gay back then, so he ran from Reese. Bad mojo. Years later, he changed his mind." Brent nodded. "He had to work at getting Reese back, too."

"But he has slept with other men, yes?"

Brent watched his pick drag over his strings. "Yeah. All substitutes." He knew that firsthand.

"It's the same for Johnnie?"

"I don't really know if Johnnie's always been like that, to be honest, but as long as I've known him he's been just as much into guys as girls." He snorted. "He's the one that got the rest of us curious."

"So you have slept with men?"

Brent's hand started to shake, and his blood chilled as it dawned on him belatedly that he didn't want to continue with this discussion. "Yeah."

"And which do you prefer? Men or women?"

"Uh, I dunno." He shrugged, keeping his face averted. "Depends on my mood at the time, I guess." *Oh, yeah, smooth.* Why couldn't some of Luc's poise have rubbed off on him through the years?

"But you have slept with men?"

"Yeah."

"Have you slept with Johnnie or Luc?"

"Y'know, I don't think I want to talk about this anymore." Brent grabbed the neck of the guitar and leaned forward to get out of his chair. Where he was going he had no idea, since the jet's cabin wasn't big enough to really avoid Hell, but he had to get away.

The cherub reached over and grabbed both hand and guitar, stopping him "I'm sorry. Please. I didn't mean to offend you."

Brent settled back, but only on the edge of the chair. He stared at the blackness of the window opposite him as he tried really hard not to react to the warm fingers closed around his. "You didn't offend me."

"I have. And I am sorry. I'm just so very curious about you."

Brent frowned. He had to look at Hell to figure out what the heck that meant. "Huh?"

Hell smiled widely. "I've told you, I am a huge fan."

"Yeah, you told us that."

"No. Well, yes, the band, but I'm mainly a fan of *yours.*"

Alarm bells clanged in Brent's head, and he felt his eyes go wide. "Of mine?"

Hell nodded, still smiling. Slowly, he unclasped Brent's hand, but he didn't relinquish eye contact. He folded his arms calmly on the table between them. "Your licks are fucking incredible. I've never heard anything so incredible. I've been wanting to work with you for years."

"You're kidding."

Hell shook his head. "No."

Brent couldn't take his eyes off Hell's gorgeous little face, reluctantly drinking in the quiet adoration he saw there. The cherub was a fan of *his?* That was a switch. "Uh, thanks."

Hell chuckled. "I've embarrassed you."

"Yeah, sorta."

"I'm sorry for that. But I must thank you. I've had marvelous time working with you."

Brent smiled. "Me, too. *Us*, too," he hastened to add, waving his free hand toward their sleeping cohorts. "We were kind of worried before you came that the album wouldn't come out right. But you've added a lot to it. Stuff that we couldn't have done without you. That's why we asked you to join the band. You're amazing."

Hell blushed, ducking his head. *How amazingly cute is that?!* "Thank you."

Now he felt awkward. He had no idea what to say to the cherub and couldn't for the life of him tear his eyes away from the full, pouting curve of Hell's lower lip.

Hell looked up and caught him staring. That perfect pink mouth fell open slightly, providing Brent a peek at straight white teeth and the point of a tongue just visible between them. The tongue further captivated him by extending out to wet that full, bottom lip. Gold flashed in the corner of Brent's eye as Hell's hand reached toward him. "Brent --"

Before the touch could land, Brent snapped back to himself. Hastily, he backed away as far as the chair would let him. "Y'know, I think I will get some shut-eye."

He stood, managing to get his eyes to meet Hell's. He smiled, hoping he didn't look as panicked as he felt. Heavy lids half hid violet irises as Hell studied him, frowning slightly.

Then, like a veil lifting, the cherub smiled and the frown evaporated. "Perhaps you're right." He stood. The top of his head just barely cleared the height of Brent's shoulder. "We should get some sleep."

Brent nodded and turned to place his guitar on his chair. He really had to get away from Hell, if only for a few minutes. As casually as he could, he walked down the short walkway, past Darien spread on the couch and between the seats at the back in which Johnnie and Luc reclined.

When he was in the relative safety of the lavatory, he finally took a big, shuddering breath. Stifling a groan, he reached down to press the erection Hell's talk had sprouted in his pants. That just proved that his reaction to Hell was already out of hand. Now the cherub had to spring the whole "I'm a big fan" routine on him? Now?! When they were on the way to New York to announce that Heaven Sent had a new member. This was *not* the time to find this out! He wasn't sure he could handle it. He was *so* not good with the whole fan worship thing. Never had been. A few disastrous episodes with early groupies of Heaven Sent had shown him that they were never as sincere as they seemed and more often than not just wanted *any* member of the band, not really him. When given the chance at either Johnnie or Luc, they always left Brent. No, the whole fan and publicity thing was Johnnie and Luc's forte. They did it well enough that he rarely had to bother. But Hell's fan confession rattled him like none before. Hell was different. He was now a coworker. He was a fellow musician. And he was a fan of Brent's?

Brent stared at himself in the wide, clear mirror. After all, there was nothing special about him. He was okay, not ugly or anything, but he wasn't insanely gorgeous like his band mates. His hair was shiny black and curly, but it wasn't Luc's striking auburn. It was chin length and not Johnnie's waist length. He was tall and had a metabolism that kept him on the very skinny side, especially since he tended to forget to eat and ate lightly when he did. His eyes were almost black, but they weren't that smoky sable like Luc's, and they certainly weren't striking gemstones like Johnnie's emerald or Darien's dark puppy dog eyes. Or Hell's amethyst.

He groaned, leaning heavily on the edge of the sink. Hell. Beautiful Hell. Kewpie doll cute, but Brent knew him well enough now to know there probably wasn't an innocent bone in his body. From what he'd told them of himself, he was a world traveler at the age of fifteen and a professional musician playing paid gigs by the time he was twenty-one. The album with Heaven Sent was his first true recording, but he was no stranger to being up on stage.

What the heck was someone like that a fan of *his* for?! No one wanted Brent. Not really. From the father who'd left their family when he was very young, through high school in Luc's shadow, and even to superstardom as a member of Heaven Sent, Brent had had it proven to him time and time again that the real Brent was fatally flawed and no one truly wanted him. At least not as a long-time lover. Hell wouldn't be any different.

Unable to come to any conclusions, he used the facility, taking his time, giving his heart a chance to slow down to normal and letting his blood cool. Nothing to do for it now. He'd just have to deal. Maybe he could keep his distance from Hell for a while He'd be willing to bet as soon as the Heaven Sent glamour and publicity settled on Hell's shoulders, he'd forget all about Brent. After all, with his looks, he'd have his own army of fans in no time.

When he opened the door, the cherub was there to set his blood boiling again with a wide smile. But Hell said nothing, just waited until Brent left the room to go in himself.

Admonishing himself for his reaction, Brent took himself to one of the cushy chairs and sank in. He sat for a moment, eyes closed, muttering to himself.

He jumped when a hand nudged his shoulder. Twisting his neck, he saw Luc's chin propped on the back of the chair. "What?"

Luc grinned. "He likes you."

Brent scowled at him. "What are you, a twelve-year-old girl?"

Unrepentant, Luc's grin turned wolfish. "This isn't about me. He likes you."

"He likes the music."

Johnnie's voice came from across the aisle. "He likes more than that."

Brent leaned sideways in his chair and turned halfway to see the singer. Johnnie's ear buds were still in, but obviously the iPod was not on. His green eyes were slitted, and his grin matched Luc's.

A glance at Darien showed his eyes were cracked open too, with a third version of the grin.

Terrific. Brent rolled his eyes. "Jesus, you're all twelve-year-old girls."

Darien giggled, just proving his point.

Johnnie shrugged, closing his eyes and calmly folding his hands over his belly, his thumbs trailing over the tail of the braid that coiled there. "He wants you. Bad."

"You don't know that."

"*I* do," Luc declared, chin still propped on the back of Brent's seat. He brought his arms up to hug the headrest.

Brent sat sideways, one knee up against the back of his seat. Nervously, he eyed the closed lavatory door behind Luc. He was pretty sure Hell couldn't hear anything. He hadn't been able to hear when he was in there, but then again no one had been talking. At least, he didn't think so. He glared at his best friend's grinning face. "You've talked to him about it?"

"No. But it's obvious."

Brent snorted. "You don't know anything."

"Hell and Brent, sittin' in a tree..." Darien sang softly.

"Oh, fuck you, asshole."

The three of them erupted in laughter.

"But seriously, though," Johnnie murmured once the laughing had died down. His eyes opened fully and focused on Brent. "Is this going to be a problem?"

Brent stared back. "Why would it be a problem? It'll pass."

Luc grunted. "Be honest, man. You want him, too."

Fuck! Brent flicked a look back toward the lavatory. His gaze came back to land on Luc, his mouth open, but the denial he had ready died on his lips. Luc's dark eyes saw the truth. They always did. "Fuck," he grumbled, glancing at the other two to see that they knew it, too. "Okay, fine. Yes. He's fucking adorable. Don't tell me none of you thought about it."

"I didn't," Darien muttered.

They all ignored him.

Johnnie leaned forward, plucking the ear buds from his ears as he braced elbows on knees. "I'm not saying you shouldn't sleep with him." His glance at Luc, then back at Brent, spoke volumes. Johnnie and Darien were among the select few who knew he'd slept with Luc. "But you need to be careful if you do. We've got a good thing going with Hell, and I'd hate to lose him."

Brent drew in a breath, seeing the uncommon seriousness in Johnnie's gaze. He glanced at Darien, who was now watching somberly, then at Luc, whose gaze was sympathetic but equally serious. Brent let out the breath and nodded. "Yeah. I know. Don't worry. I don't plan on sleeping with him."

"That's not what I said."

Brent waved at Johnnie, his eyes averted as he sat frontward in his seat. "Yeah, yeah, I know. I'll handle it. I'm good."

He busied himself pulling out his own iPod from the bag he had stashed beside the seat. When he sat up, he felt Luc's hand reach out to squeeze his shoulder. He nodded without looking back, and the hand slid away. He heard Luc's seat sigh as the bass player sat back.

When Hell finally emerged from the lavatory, Brent was lying back in the recliner seat, eyes closed in feigned sleep.

Chapter Three

The limousine couldn't muffle all of the sounds of the screaming fans that crowded the street. Brent sat back in the buttery leather seat, gazing through the double protection of tinted windows and opaque sunglasses at the girls who wiggled past the bodyguards and police to pound the sides of the long white car.

What do they think? That we'll just see them and jump out into their waiting embrace? Don't they know they're downright scary from this angle?

These were not new questions in his head. In fact, they were the same ones that occurred to him each time he was in such a situation. But being safe in the limousine was *far* preferable to the times when they actually had to wade through the crowd.

He shivered and turned back to face forward. Best not to think of it.

Across from him sat a much better sight anyway. The little man with the cherubic face and the purple hair was a welcome pastime for the eyes, and Brent took full advantage of the fact that his eyes couldn't be seen and looked his fill. He'd been worried that things would be odd this morning. They hadn't gotten much of a chance to talk after landing in the wee hours of the morning, nor on the way to the hotel. Well, that wasn't fair. Brent had actually avoided being near enough for Hell to speak to. He hoped he hadn't been too obvious. He'd managed to stay in his room until Gretchen, Heaven Sent's manager, had summoned him to a band meeting in the afternoon, and there hadn't been a chance to talk since then.

Hell didn't seem bothered. He sat across from Brent, bemused by the mayhem outside of the car. His hair shone in the muted sunlight, and the single braid was draped over his shoulder with the rhinestone-banded tail curled in the lap of his pristine white slacks. He had smiled and greeted Brent very normally during the afternoon hubbub and hadn't done anything weird or "fan-ish" like trying to always stay by Brent's side. Not that he had ever done that.

Gretchen leaned forward from her seat between Brent and Luc. "Hell."

Pastel bangs fell partially into his pale face as he turned from the window. He raised a slim, beringed hand to casually brush them aside. "Yes?"

"Are you ready for this?"

Hell smiled, and Brent had to suppress a sigh. He'd developed an unwitting obsession with the cherub's mouth. "I am," Hell assured her.

"You do realize that most of the questions are going to be directed at you. Are you sure you wouldn't rather sit this one out and let us handle the announcement?"

His smile broadened. "I will have to get used to it sooner or later You have schooled me on what to say. I'll be fine."

"They are definitely going to ask you about the gay thing."

He didn't seem at all worried. "So you have said."

"Don't worry about it," Luc said, reaching over to slide a reassuring hand over her back. "Hell'll be fine. He's a natural at this."

Gretchen nodded, but stayed leaning forward, her elbows propped on the knees she kept primly pressed together. She didn't look convinced. "Hell, if you feel at all uncomfortable, just let Luc or Johnnie do the talking for you, okay?"

Brent rolled his eyes but said nothing. Luc and Johnnie were, after all, the natural choices. They loved press conferences.

Brent, on the other hand, wanted a cigarette. "Are they going to let us smoke in there?"

"Can't you give your lungs a rest for an hour?"

"I've been without a cigarette for an hour," he pointed out. "Not to mention close to twelve hours yesterday on the plane."

"Didn't you make up for that this afternoon?' she growled.

"Not nearly."

"Don't play on my last nerve, Brent," she warned, sitting up and smoothing back her immaculately curled red hair. "We need to get through this press conference."

"I don't see what you're worried about. Word's already leaked that we've got a new member in the band."

"I *know.*" She was clearly still pissed about it. "And that's what worries me. If we'd kept it quiet, they wouldn't have questions all ready to fire at Hell."

Brent shrugged. What was done was done.

Hell leaned forward to put a hand on one of Gretchen's knees. The leather of his long white coat whispered softly as he moved. "It will be fine."

She stared into his violet eyes. "I'm glad you're calm."

He grinned again. "I could not be happier. We are about to announce that I have become a full member of my favorite band. What could spoil that?"

Brent glanced at Luc over Gretchen's back, and they exchanged a chuckle. The keyboardist had proven a natural fit in the band, musically speaking. All indications showed that he'd be a good fit publicity speaking, as well. Nothing seemed to faze him.

Gretchen reached out to smooth a hand over Hell's cheek. "I hope you feel the same way after this conference."

The thump and squeal of rabid fans died away, and the lighting dimmed as the limousine finally entered the underground parking structure. On one hand Brent was relieved to escape the throng, but on the other he was scared because they were closer to the press conference. Actually, it was more a paparazzi event. Even worse.

The stretch car stopped beside an open loading dock. From the dock to the open loading doors was a line of people busy at...various tasks. Brent had been doing this for five years now, and he still hadn't figured out what all of the people backstage at one of these things did. But they always seemed to be really busy.

"All right, gentlemen," Gretchen said, reaching over to grab Brent's hand and squeeze.

He glanced at her and saw her encouraging smile.

He grimaced. She knew he hated these things.

Her smile said that yes, she knew it, but no, he couldn't be excused.

Luc unfolded his long legs out of the car and got out, the tails of his overlarge green velvet shirt trailing behind him. He turned to lend Gretchen a hand in getting out.

Hands on Brent's knees startled him, and he looked up to see Hell leaning forward, face just about a foot away from his. "Are you well?" the cherub asked.

Brent's heart leaped into his throat. *Calm!* He warned himself. "Yeah. Why?"

"You're pale."

He laughed. "More than usual?"

Hell cocked his head to the side, birdlike. "Yes." His eyes were frickin' *huge.*.

Brent smiled but knew it was pathetic. His nerves were too jumbled for him to smile properly. "I'm really bad with the press and public stuff."

Hell's cupid's-bow mouth opened in a silent "ah." Then he smiled wide, showing white, even teeth. The fingers of one of his hands curled over Brent's. "I'll hold your hand, if you like?"

Brent snorted and snatched his hand back. "Get out of here, Hellion," he growled, using the band's favorite pet name for their newest member

Hell laughed gaily as he took himself and the long skirt of his suede jacket with him out the door of the car.

Brent sat there, flexing his fingers, wondering at the smoothness of the man's touch.

Gretchen poked her head back in. "Yes, Brent, you do have to come. Now."

He grimaced and leaned forward. "I'm coming." He reached into the inside pocket of his leather jacket as he went, fingers fishing for the box and lighter he knew were there. "But I *am* having a cigarette."

He stood on the pavement in the small circle of quiet the bodyguards and entourage afforded him and lit up while they waited for Johnnie and Darien to emerge from the second car. Blessed smoke filled his lungs, and he tipped his chin and exhaled directly up into the weird scaffolding-like shit crawling over the cement ceiling, to avoid offending anyone.

Fingers tapped the back of his hand, and he held up the cigarette in his fingers without even looking, knowing it was Luc. When he brought his chin back down, Luc's hand hovered before him, handing back the cigarette.

Luc grinned at him, lifting his hands to smooth auburn hair back toward the tail at his nape. Didn't work, of course. The curly tendrils of fiery red always wanted to come back to frame his face. "You'll be fine."

Brent rolled his eyes and took another puff. They always said that. Luc. Johnnie. Gretchen. Even Darien on occasion. He never was, but they thought it was comforting.

Johnnie and Darien strolled up. The first was dressed in a white cashmere sweater and deep green slacks. The second wore an ice-blue silk shirt and black slacks.

Aren't we all dressed up? Brent thought. But then, they had to be. Official announcement and all. What a fucking circus. *Just let this be over. Why can't I just play music?*

"Let's go, gentlemen," Gretchen called, leading the way. "Brent, put it out."

He pulled another lungful and handed the cigarette off to Luc, who filled his own lungs, then dropped the cigarette to the pavement and ground it out under his shiny green-banded boots. Then they followed Gretchen, Johnnie, Darien, and Hell into the mouth of -- he laughed at his thoughts -- Hell.

They'd barely passed the pipe-and-tarp barriers masking backstage before the flashbulbs started going off. As usual, everyone started talking at once. Brent kept his eyes on Hell's back -- not a difficult task -- and refused to look to the side even when the photographers started calling out to members of the band. He trailed Hell's white coattails up a short flight of rickety stairs to a platform that put Heaven Sent up above everyone else. The artwork for the new album was projected on a screen behind them, and a sea of press crowded the floor before them.

Gretchen stepped up to the podium to introduce the band and instruct the members of the press how they'd handle the questioning. The band would stand up here first and answer what was thrown at them; then they'd come down and conduct two hours' worth of various interviews that had been scheduled with key members of the media. When she was done with her spiel, she stepped back and Johnnie stepped up. The remaining four of them spread out behind him. Obediently, Brent stood so he could be seen. He didn't *like* doing this stuff, but in five years, Gretchen and the others had forced him into proper habits for posing for the cameras.

"Greetings, everyone." There was a reason Johnnie was the lead singer. The man had a voice like chocolate mousse, rich and decadent. He leaned against the podium, perfectly comfortable with a dozen microphones perched before him and countless cameras snapping. He looked damn good with his ridiculously long brown hair loose and flowing over his shoulders to his waist. "Thank you all for coming. As you all know, we're in town for a performance to mark the grand opening of the White Tiger nightclub in the Weiss Strande East Hotel. The venue and the hotel are rather close to both Luc's and my hearts since I'm a part owner in the hotel and he's a part owner of the nightclub." Brent snorted at the pride in Johnnie's voice. Some reporters started shouting Johnnie's name, blurting out questions, but the singer ignored them and continued. "Both the performance tonight as well as the one tomorrow night will be filmed to be part of the video for the first single off our new album, *The Charm*." More flashbulbs went off, and the reporters again pelted him with questions. Johnnie smiled for the cameras, but still didn't acknowledge the questions. "But what you might not know or what you might have heard through the grapevine is that Heaven Sent is proud to announce that our quartet has expanded to a quintet."

Excited murmurs. *Huh, so some of them hadn't heard. Gretchen will like that.*

"While we were recording *The Charm*, our producer, Paul Thrombone, introduced us to an amazing keyboardist. We invited him in, and much to our delight, he not only helped us with the few songs we'd originally proposed to him, but the entire album. We've even done some remixes of our older songs, which will be released as extended singles later in the year. In the end, we just couldn't see not keeping him." Johnnie grinned. "Luckily, he agreed to be kept. So please allow me to introduce you to Heller Witting, otherwise known as Hell."

More murmurs and flashes as Hell stepped up beside Johnnie. Quite pointedly, he dropped down a half-foot-tall block beside the podium and stepped up onto it. The audience chuckled to see that it put the top of his head about on eye level with the tall lead singer.

Johnnie put his arm around Heller's shoulders and squeezed. "And he's cute, too."

Minor roar and blinding flashes as the picturesque moment was captured on film.

Hell leaned into the podium, his lavender hair shining in the bright lights. "Thank you. I cannot tell you how excited I am to have this opportunity. I have been a fan of Heaven Sent for years, so this, for me, is a dream come true."

"Heller! You're a fan of the band?"

Hell's long fingers curled calmly around the edges of the podium as he shifted most of his weight onto one foot. "Yes, I have been since I first heard them on the internet."

"How long have you been playing keyboards?"

"Most of my life."

"How old are you?"

"Twenty-three."

Johnnie leaned in, some of his wealth of brown hair caressing Hell's back. "Hard to believe, isn't it?"

Laughter.

Reporters pelted more questions at Hell, and Brent was proud of the little guy for taking it so well. Brent himself kept his hands shoved in the deep pockets of his jacket to disguise the trembling. And he wasn't even in the spotlight.

"Do you really prefer to be called Hell?"

"Yes. It's quite dramatic, don't you think?"

"What's your real hair color?"

Brent couldn't see him from behind, but saw him jerk back dramatically. He reached up to finger one of the curls that brushed his chin. "This *is* my real hair color." The smile could be heard in his voice.

"Hell, are you gay?"

Ah, the question we've all be waiting for.

Hell cocked his head to the side, his purple braid slipping off his shoulder and around his back. "Does it matter?"

That stumped one reporter but not the next. "The gay thing is quite an issue, after all, given that Johnnie and Luc are now in committed relationships with men. Couldn't you tell us whether you prefer men or women?"

Hell spread his hands, palms up. "I haven't decided yet. I'm hoping to catch some, how do you say, pointers from my band mates." He was playing up the accent. He spoke better English than anyone else in the band.

"So you're into both men *and* women."

"Oh, that sounds like fun, doesn't it?"

"That doesn't answer the question."

Hell shrugged. "Doesn't it?"

The questions continued, but Hell and Johnnie managed to never *quite* confirm that Hell was gay. The most that the reporters could get was bisexual references without the word actually being said. It was a game the band played with the press, a game Hell had willingly -- eagerly -- consented to play when he'd agreed to join. No member of the band would declare outright that he preferred men or women. Each of them would hug the middle, giving ample clues in either direction. True, Johnnie and Luc had rather tipped their hands when they'd hooked up with Tyler and Reese, but Tyler let Johnnie continue to escort lovely ladies to various functions he was unable to attend, fueling rumors of an open relationship between the two men. Reese had agreed to let Luc do the same, but their relationship was so new that they'd barely been apart yet.

Before the questioning got too out of hand, Gretchen stepped up and suggested that the line of inquiry be changed. Everything after that was pretty standard.

After most of the questions had died down, the podium was taken away, and the five members of the band had to stand in a tableau to allow a million pictures to be taken. Brent thumbed the engraving on his lighter and endured, mustering what he hoped were natural-looking smiles.

The pictures were bad enough. Once Gretchen pronounced those were done, then he had to follow Darien off the platform. He hit the floor, and Gretchen's assistants pounced. Each band member had their own babysitter. That's not what Gretchen called them, but that's what they were Brent was thrilled to see Theo Foster, the same guy who'd been his babysitter during the last tour. Theo had short blond hair, laughing green eyes, and a wicked smile.

Brent and he got along great, and he already knew all of Brent's quirks.

"Hey, man," he greeted as Theo led him toward the back. "Long time no see."

Theo grinned. He was a few years younger than Brent, and although he was enthusiastic, he managed not to be bubbly. "Hey. How you been?"

"Okay. Gretchen didn't tell me if you'd be back."

Theo kept hold of his arm as he led Brent through the crowd toward cordoned-off areas. "Are you kidding? I wouldn't miss it."

"You'll be around for the gigs?"

"Absolutely."

"Awesome."

They reached a seating area, and Brent tried not to balk at the sight of the little stool that was obviously his destination. It sat before a soft green-and-purple backdrop with bright lights aimed just so. A camera was set up, and a reporter was talking with the cameraman. They both smiled at his approach.

Brent took a deep breath and mustered a smile. At least Gretchen knew him well and had assigned him the reporters from the music magazines. No *Entertainment Weekly* or *People* magazine for him. No teen mags, either. He got reporters from *Creem* and *Guitarist.* So, even thought he was scared to death and probably sounded nervous, he got to talk about playing guitar and making music. These, at least, were subjects he could be semi-intelligent about.

Chapter Four

Brent stood in the parking garage with Theo, waiting. His few interviews were long over, but he wasn't allowed to leave until Gretchen gave the go-ahead. Brent didn't mind this so much. The worse part of the day was over. Ahead was a sound check just before the irritating but bearable process of hurry-up-and-wait that was getting ready for the performance at the White Tiger.

Theo had just offered to go get him a Coke when Gretchen slid through the crowd into the covered parking garage.

With Hell in tow.

Brent frowned as the pair approached. Gretchen was scowling, but Hell didn't seem upset.

Gretchen saw Brent near the first car and headed for him. "I knew you'd be here." She turned to Hell. "You two should go back to the hotel."

Brent's heart skipped. *Alone?* "What gives? Something wrong?"

"Nothing I can't handle," Gretchen assured him, glaring back toward the doorway. "I just don't like how they're hounding Hell."

Hell smiled, laying a hand on her arm. "It's understandable, isn't it?"

"Yes, but..." She shook her head and reached out to smooth a hand over his smiling cheek. The two of them were of the same height. "You're a living doll to put up with that crap, Hell, but we have months ahead of us to deal with this. I think you've done enough for today. You and Brent go on back to the hotel. We'll give you guys a call when we're back."

The cherub looked at him and smiled.

Crap! Brent was still trying to process the fact that he was going to be alone with Hell. After last night, he wasn't sure it was such a good idea, and he wasn't ready to talk about Hell being a fan again. His reactions to the man's looks were just too potent. *He wants you.* Luc's voice rang in his head, but he still couldn't bring himself to really believe his friend or what he was seeing in Hell's own actions. *Maybe Theo --*

"Theo, I'll need you to stick around here." Just like that, Gretchen dashed his hopes. "I'm sure Brent can get up to his room okay. Tyler's got the hotel security all set, so there shouldn't be a problem." Gretchen turned and smiled up at Brent. "Thank you," she said, squeezing his arm.

He mustered a smile. She always made a point of thanking him for doing any kind of publicity, because she knew he hated it. She really did look out for them. It was one of the things that endeared her to the band.

Brent couldn't think of a valid reason not to get into the car with Hell. He watched the cherub's white-clad back disappear into the limousine and noted that the view of his butt was sadly obstructed by the tails of his coat.

Quit it! he admonished himself. He took a deep breath and got in.

Hell was rummaging in the little refrigerator as Brent settled. "Would you like something?"

Brent adjusted his glasses and sat leaning against the far door, hoping he wasn't being too obvious in trying to put as much space between them as possible. "Is there beer?"

Hell produced two Heinekens. "No, but there's Heineken," he declared, sitting back with a grin as the car took off.

Brent chuckled. "That's beer."

"No, this is not beer. This is slightly flavored water." With a slight grimace of distaste, Hell popped both caps, then handed one bottle to Brent. "There *is* no such thing as beer outside of Germany."

Brent laughed and sat back, facing front rather than watching the mouth of the bottle hit those sweet little lips. "You're prejudiced."

"Have you tried German beer?"

Brent thought about it. "Can't say that I have."

"When you do, you will know what I mean and agree with me."

Brent chuckled again and settled in with his beer.

"Are you all right?"

Out of the corner of his eye, Brent could see the cherub twisted to face him. "Huh?"

Hell gestured with his bottle behind them as the limousine started to leave the parking garage. "The press. You said you're not good with it. Are you all right?"

Brent glanced over to see huge violet eyes focused on him in what looked like true concern. It touched his heart. Not to mention lower portions of his anatomy. He sipped his beer. "Yeah. It's over. I'm okay."

He stared out the window as the long car reached the screaming fans. Eager hands slammed on the sturdy glass; faces pressed in. Instinctively, he flinched back. "Shit!" He jumped when Hell put a hand on his shoulder.

Big eyes blinked as the hand fell away. "This really bothers you."

Brent laughed, facing front and nursing his beer as they passed by the last of the fans and finally got onto the street. "Yeah."

"Have you always been this way?"

"With the crowds? Pretty much."

"How have you managed?"

Brent smiled. "Are you kidding? With Johnnie and Luc as front men for the band, I rarely have to do this stuff. They want Johnnie or Luc or Darien because they're interesting." He tried a joking smile, feeling better now that they were in normal traffic. "They'll love you."

Hell snorted. "There are *plenty* of fans who look at you."

Brent stared at the empty leather seat across from them and the backs of the heads of the two men who sat in the front seat, before the glass partition. "Maybe a few."

"More than a few. The musicians know that you are the truly talented one. *I* think you're terrific."

Brent's hand froze bringing the Heineken back up to his lips.

Hell chuckled. "And I've embarrassed you again."

Brent scowled, keeping his focus on the mouth of the green bottle. "No."

"Yes. I have. I'm sorry if what I said last night put you on edge."

Brent shook his head as cool liquid slid down his throat. "It's not your fault. I just..." Brent shrugged. "I'm not good at the fan thing."

"How do you avoid it? Fans must be after you all the time."

Brent chuckled, sucking at his beer. "Not really. Not me."

"I don't understand that."

"Nothing to understand. I'm not the exciting one. Offstage, at least"

"I don't agree."

Brent shrugged. "Thanks, I think"

Leather sighed, and a sideways glance at Hell showed the cherub sitting back in his seat, pulling on his beer as he stared out of the opposite window. Brent could only wonder what was cooking in that agile little brain, but didn't tempt his luck by asking. He stared out of his own window and was thankful that if traffic was with them, it was a relatively short drive.

"Is that why you wear the glasses?" Hell asked suddenly.

Distracted by wandering thoughts about the layout of New York City, Brent jumped. "Huh?"

Hell turned to face him, bringing his knee up on the seat between them "The glasses. To hide your eyes?"

"Nah. I wear 'em 'cause they're super cool."

Hell didn't fall for his joke. He laughed but shook his head. "You hide behind them."

Brent shrugged. "We all do what we gotta do."

"The press bothers you so much?"

"Just big gatherings of them. I'm usually okay one-on-one."

"What about the fans?"

"Same thing. I mean, I know they're the ones that got us here, and I love 'em for it. But I don't want to *be* with them."

"Did you have a bad experience?"

Brief flashes of memories he'd rather not dwell on flitted across his inner eye. Tongue-tied and looking stupid at one of their first press conferences. A few mass interviews where he'd been unable to respond to direct questions. Quite a few times when he'd nearly drowned in a sea of screaming humanity that seemed to want to tear him apart. He shivered and shrugged, looking back out of the window. "I've just never been good at it, is all."

"I've seen pictures of you at parties."

Brent nodded. "Strangely enough, I'm okay at parties, but I tend to stick to the sidelines."

"I've seen you dancing in those pictures.."

So? Irritated, Brent sank down in the leather, propping his booted feet on the seat in front of him. "Dancing I can do. You don't have to talk when you're dancing."

"Ah. So it's conversation?"

"I just don't know what to say half the time, and I usually don't *want* to say what reporters want me to say."

Hell nodded. "That makes sense."

"Does it?"

"It does. Having to watch what you say can be tiresome."

Brent snorted. "You don't seem to have a problem with it."

Hell beamed. His hand landed on Brent's knee and squeezed. "I enjoy talking."

For a moment, Brent didn't hear him. His brain scrambled at the heat of that small hand on his leg. Then he finally interpreted Hell's words. He mustered control and turned toward the cherub, tilting his head forward so that the man could see the skeptical look in his eyes over the rim of his glasses. "Now *that* I believe."

Hell laughed, a joyous sound that wasn't unlike some of the melodies he coaxed from his Roland.

Brent's heart leapt into his throat when Hell's hand slid further up his thigh. He stared at the elegant spread of those fingers, watched the gold chain over the back of Hell's hand glimmer as those fingers slid toward a tickle that was burning now in Brent's testicles.

"Brent."

He shivered at the sultry note in the cherub's voice. *Oh, God! Say something. Stop this!* But, for the life of him, Brent couldn't do anything but watch that hand slowly massage its way higher.

The cherub shifted closer. "I --"

The sound of the window between them and the driver distracted them. Brent looked up as the tinted glass slid down. Hell snatched his hand back, but he remained kneeling on the seat, facing Brent, turning only his head toward the driver The bodyguard in the passenger seat -- Russ was his name -- twisted around to look at them.

"I hate to say this --" he said.

Brent's heart sank.

"-- but we just found out that the back entrance to the hotel has been blocked by an accident. We're going to have to take you guys through the front."

Brent froze. The front. Immediately, he conjured up the sight of the front of the hotel when they'd left that morning. What seemed like hundreds of Heaven Sent fans had been camped out on the sidewalk. There had even been police tape and officers present to help make sure that traffic kept flowing. This morning was the worst crowd yet since the fans knew for a fact that the band was playing at the hotel that night. "You're shitting me."

Russ shook his head. Brent noticed that he had one of those Bluetooth receivers in his far ear. He tapped it. "Got it." He looked back to Hell and Brent. "We've notified security at the hotel that we're just a few blocks away. They're going to get the police to help them clear the way, but we need to go through the front."

"Can't we just drive around for awhile?" Brent asked.

Hell's hand returned to Brent's knee and squeezed. "We'll be fine." He spun his head around to meet the cherub's gaze. Calm and centered and too damn beautiful for words. Brent could see that even in his panic. "It's only a few meters."

Brent collapsed back into the leather seat, eyes closed. "Fuck."

"Mr. Rose?"

He didn't respond. He pushed fingers up under the lenses of his glasses to rub at his eyes.

"Mr. Rose, should we drive around?"

He snarled. He knew damn good and well that it would make him look like the pussy that he was. Like Hell said, it was just a short way. "No," he snapped. "Let's just get this over with."

He remained tucked back in his seat as they approached the hotel. Yep, there they were. Milling bodies, mostly teenagers, filled the sidewalks. The traffic was crawling. Brent cursed the people who'd gotten into the accident at the back entrance. He cursed Gretchen for sending them home too early. He cursed Johnnie and Tyler for buying a hotel right where someone was going to have a fucking accident. He creatively cursed anything and everyone he could think of as the teenagers discovered the limousine. A number of them swarmed the street, surrounding the car. They didn't even know who was in it. They just assumed that a limousine meant one of the band members. Whose idea had it been to actually stay at the Weiss? It was such easy deduction that, if they were playing there the next night, Heaven Sent must be in residence.

"Will you be all right?"

Brent spun around and was again lost in huge purple eyes. Eyes that had widened in concern. For him.

Shit. Brent tried to pull himself together, but it was useless. Photo shoots were bad. Press conferences were worse. Interviews were agony. But this? This was…well, this was Hell of the fire and brimstone variety.

Brent rubbed a hand across his forehead, through the sweat that now beaded his hairline. *Shit..* "Yeah. I'm fine." A little louder, "Are we there yet?"

"Almost, Mr. Rose."

"Fuck."

Long, warm fingers threaded through his other hand, and he froze, eyes wide and on the hand that was now entwined with Hell's.

"They're only people," Hell murmured.

Brent barked a laugh. "Save your breath, Hell," he advised, thinking he should extricate his hand but somehow not doing it. "They've all tried to get me through this. Nothing works."

Hell nodded, accepting that. "We'll run."

"Oh, fuck *yeah*, we'll run. At least *I* will."

Hell squeezed his hand, then let their fingers slide apart. "You'll be fine."

Brent really wished everyone would stop telling him that.

The limousine stopped at long last in front of the hotel. Brent stared in agony at the revolving glass doors that stood back from the sidewalk. Security and police had cordoned off a narrow walkway. A *very* narrow walkway. Brent wasn't going to get through that one without someone touching him.

"Should I go first?" Hell asked.

Brent gulped, staring.

"Brent?"

"Yeah." Brent heard his voice, very soft, very trembly. "Please."

Strong fingers squeezed his shoulder.

Up front, Brent heard Russ talking but couldn't make out the words. Outside, he watched three security guards trot down the narrow aisle toward the car.

Then the screaming started.

Brent winced.

Hell squeezed his shoulder again, hard enough to make him gasp. His eyes went wide as Hell surged over him, pushing him back into the seat. "Hell, what --?" But his confused words were cut short by warm lips slamming up against his. Too shocked to close his eyes and enjoy, he stayed stock still as Hell's tongue swept his mouth briefly before the cherub pulled back.

Gaping, Brent stared as Hell shone with an impish grin.

The guards reached the door and opened it.

Hell climbed over Brent and out the door. Brent felt the surge of cool air from outside, heard the cacophony of screams, but his entire focus narrowed down to the waft of lavender that settled over him in Hell's wake. He even *smelled* like lavender?

"Mr. Rose."

The guard's voice snapped him back to reality. *Oh, shit! Did anyone see?* No, the door had been closed. Hadn't it?

"Mr. Rose?" The man stuck his almost bald head into sight, eyeing Brent. He held out a beefy hand to wave Brent out of the limousine.

Brent closed his eyes and counted to ten. He turned and stuck his foot out the door, raising his gaze to see Hell a few feet ahead of him, laughing, reaching out to touch the hands that groped for him. A solid, tentacled wall of humanity surrounded him. God, they didn't even *know* him yet. The announcement was just today.

I can do this, Brent told himself. The litany that he always had to tell himself when in this situation.

With one more breath, he pushed out of the car, the security guard's hand at his back to help him stand.

"Breeeennnnt!" He knew it was a lot of different voices screaming, but they all seemed to synchronize on his name.

The guards moved in on either side of him.

Brent forced a smile as he stepped onto the pavement.

Up ahead, Hell disappeared.

Brent blinked, not immediately understanding what had happened. Then panic set in when he realized that the fans had pushed through the cordoned-off area. Police officers and security guards were shouting for them to get back, but it was like trying to push back a flood of water after the dam broke.

Hell was in the middle of it! Were any of the guards with him? Were the police? He was so small; surely *someone* was looking out for him!

Panic took Brent forward a few steps, surging through the crowd. He barely heard the cries and the screams. He distantly felt the fingers groping at his jacket and legs.

Four steps, and Hell was in sight. He was smiling and laughing as two police officers tried to usher him forward.

He was safe.

Which brought Brent's attention back to himself.

Fingers caught at his hands. He looked aside to see crying, scary teenage girls. And not a few boys as well. A lot of them resembled the bald-headed guy in that painting *The Scream*. Amazed even as he was terrified, Brent felt hands pull him down and automatically pursed his lips to kiss upturned faces. Fingers grappled at his sunglasses, and he was horrified when they came off, but managed not to lash out in terror. He very nearly screamed himself as the glasses were whisked away, but the scream cut off when one of the security officers hauled him forward into a quiet spot Even better than quiet, it was the revolving door. He'd reached safety.

He came through the other side and very nearly stumbled into Hell. The cherub caught him by the arms and stared at his face. Brent blinked at him, shell-shocked to be staring into those vivid violet eyes without the shield of his glasses.

Hell squeezed his arms, scowling. "Let's get you upstairs."

"Brent! Hell!"

Brent blinked and looked up at the familiar voice. *Tyler!* His savior. The blond had never looked more like an angel than he did now in his crisp gray suit. He stormed forward, concern evident in his huge, angry blue eyes. Four security guards and two bodyguards trailed in his wake. Before he reached them, he was waving them forward. "This way. We'll take you directly up to the suites."

Brent allowed himself to be led. He followed Tyler with Hell at his side and a handful of security guards at his back. Once in the elevator, he very nearly collapsed. As it was, he sank against the back of the elevator, letting his skull thump against the brushed chrome.

"God, Brent, I can't tell you how sorry I am." Tyler stood before him, hand on his shoulder. Brent didn't suppose Tyler had ever seen him like this firsthand, but someone -- probably Johnnie -- had told him about Brent's quirk. "I would have done anything I could have to spare you that."

Brent nodded, running a trembling hand through his black hair. "I know, man."

"Are you okay?"

"Not yet."

He shut his eyes, and thankfully, neither Tyler nor Hell chose to speak. They stood in silent support to either side of him, and he appreciated it more than words.

When the elevator door opened, Tyler led the way out. Only then did Brent realize that only the three of them were in the elevator.

"I had some food sent up when I heard you'd left the press conference," Tyler was saying. "Gretchen hasn't called to tell me the others are on their way, so you should be able to relax for a while." He used his own key to open Brent's door and stood holding it while Hell led Brent inside.

Brent felt much better now that the crowds were behind him. He took a deep breath, eyes closed, head back. Then he realized that Hell was still holding his hand. *How long?* He wondered, but didn't ask. He took another breath and pulled away gently. "I'm okay, guys."

"Are you sure?" Hell asked.

He dragged a hand through his hair "Yes." He was a bit wigged to not find the sunglasses perched on his nose He recalled the feel of hands at his face, ripping them off, and shuddered. "I just...let me chill out for a while."

Tyler nodded from the doorway, a skeptical frown on his face. "Can I get you anything else?"

Brent managed a smile. A real smile for him. "Nah."

Tyler shook his head. "I'm sorry."

"Wasn't your fault, man. It's a hazard of the job. I know that."

Tyler nodded. "Okay. You've got my cell number if you need anything."

Brent waved his hand, stepping up to the wet bar. A drink was definitely in order. "I can call room service. You've got enough on your mind."

"Call *me* if you need anything," he insisted. "Either of you."

"You're the best, man."

"Thank you," Hell said.

Tyler left.

Brent placed a glass on the bar and reached for the ice bucket. He saw Hell out of the corner of his eye. He found a laugh for the serious look. "Seriously, man, I'm okay."

Hell didn't look convinced. He stepped up to the bar and splayed the hand with the gold chain thing on the surface. "Perhaps I should stay. You need company."

A sudden, vivid picture of making out with the cherub filled Brent's head. Soft lips, silky hair, lavender scent, and all. Yeah, that'd make him feel a lot better.

Oh, God!

He shook his head violently, turning back to the ice bucket. "No. I just need to be alone for a while."

Hell looked like he wanted to protest, but didn't. He nodded. "Okay. You call if you need me. I'm right next door." It was a statement, not a question.

Brent concentrating on dropping ice into his glass. "I'm not an invalid. I was just shaken. I *have* done this before. I'm better already."

"Has it been like this before?"

Brent grabbed a tiny bottle of vodka and twisted it open. "Actually, yeah. Like this and worse."

"Why do you do it?"

He smiled and poured. "Except for that and the press, it's the best job I could ever hope to have."

Hell took a step toward him. "Brent..."

Instinct had Brent stepping back away from the bar, away from Hell. It was either step back or grab him, and he was determined not to do the latter. "Hey, Hell, please just leave me alone right now." He stared hard at the empty bottle in his hands, keeping himself from looking at the cherub.

He heard a sigh. "All right. I'll see you tonight."

He nodded, still not looking up. He stayed exactly where he was until he heard the door close safely behind Hell.

Chapter Five

The sound check that afternoon was a hurried affair. Brent showed up a little late on purpose, hoping to time it so that he arrived just as the others were ready. He was almost on the ball, but he still got there before Luc. Luckily, there was plenty to do and enough people to deal with that he didn't have to really talk with Hell.

But he watched him. Trying to be casual about it, he kept an eye on the cherub who stood on the platform behind Brent's accustomed spot onstage. Both he and Hell were located to the audience's right, Brent manning the front of the stage and Hell raised about three feet above him. The main keyboard faced roughly center stage with four others mounted around him. The amplifiers provided a dark background, perfect for what Brent was sure would be a flashy outfit worn that night. Now, however, Hell was dressed rather simply in an oversized blue button-down shirt and jeans. He looked deadly serious as he adjusted knobs and talked in low tones to his roadies.

Brent tore his gaze away and concentrated on his own instrument when the sight of Hell biting that lush lower lip made his cock stir. *Get the cherub out of your head*, he admonished, turning to face front and playing a few licks to warm up his fingers. It didn't do any good to think about Hell or that kiss. Nothing was going to happen And his sound was off anyway, so he went to find his own roadies.

Luc arrived and they had the sound check, after which Luc and Johnnie immediately disappeared. Darien, bless him, started talking to Hell, so Brent slipped away and found his own way back to his room. One of the perks of staying in the hotel where they were playing was that he got to shower and change in his own room rather than one shared with the other guys. Tonight, he counted that as a blessing.

In the privacy of his own shower, he realized that he'd probably have to talk to Hell. Explain that things just wouldn't work out between them. Hell was a smart guy. He'd understand. It wasn't that Brent didn't find him attractive -- he most certainly did -- it was just that any kind of relationship, even if it were only sexual, would just spell problems for the band. And those were to be avoided at all costs.

Hell would agree, and he'd get over it quick enough. In no time, he'd have his own following and would forget about any kind of interest he had in Brent. Brent knew it would happen.

It always did.

Back in high school...

"Luc doesn't stay cooped up in his room all day."

Brent kept watching his hand at the neck of the guitar, determined to get the fingering right. "I'm not Luc."

"You've got that right."

He ignored Sue as she threw herself down on the couch next to him. A cloud of the cheap, flowery perfume she bathed in settled over him.

"I'm bored."

"Yeah."

"Let's go to the mall."

"You go ahead."

"You come with me."

"No, thanks."

"Luc's there."

"I know."

He heard her growl. "Why can't you be more like your friend?"

"If you want him so much, why don't you go find him?" He knew the answer, of course. She couldn't have his friend. Not at the moment, anyway. Luc had a supposed girlfriend Rosanne was not only built, but she was also sixteen with her own car. And she put out. She'd taken Luc's cherry, which had earned her Luc's undying devotion for at least a few months.

"Nancy lied to me," Sue pouted. "She said you'd be fun."

Nancy. Luc's ex-girlfriend, who *didn't* put out and had ended things with Luc in a huge fight. The only reason Brent had ever agreed to go out with Sue was because of Luc and Nancy. Now that those two were apart, the flaws in the current relationship were making themselves known. Among other things, Brent was damn sick and tired of hearing about how he wasn't Luc. It wasn't anything new, of course, but it was doubly irritating when it came from his so-called girlfriend.

"You quit baseball; you never want to go out." That pout was really getting on his nerves. "All you want to do is sit here playing that guitar. And not even very well."

He grimaced, finally looking up at her. She was cute enough, with lots of rich chestnut hair and big brown eyes, but cute didn't make up for the attitude. "Go away and stay away."

She glared. "Are you breaking up with me?"

"Is there anything to break up? You don't like me anymore."

She stood. "I *never* liked you."

He rolled his eyes. "Fine." He bent his head over the guitar and didn't watch her flounce out. It was a relief to have her gone.

Two hours later, the front door opened seconds before Luc's "Hey!" sounded.

"Hey!" Brent called back from the living room.

Luc stopped at the foot of the stairs and turned, headed in the direction of Brent's voice. Brent was relieved to see the guitar case in his hand and no girlfriend in tow. Luc grinned, shoving a hand through the long auburn curls at the top of his head. The sides were shorn close to his head, exposing the new gold hoops he wore in both ears, thanks to Rosanne's suggestion. "I saw Sue at the mall," he said as he came to sit on the coffee table. The guitar case was dropped on the floor by his booted foot. "She says you broke up with her."

"Yeah."

"You okay."

"Heck yeah. I was sick of her."

Luc grinned, bending over to open the case and retrieve his bass. "Awesome. I've got a girl for you to meet."

Brent sat up straight. "No more girls."

Luc cradled the secondhand bass guitar in his lap. "Huh?"

Brent scowled, tossing his head to get his curly black bangs out of his eyes. "No more girls. I don't want you to set me up."

"But who you going to hang with when we go out?"

"I'm not going out with you."

Luc snorted, busying himself with the frets, sublimely uninterested in Brent's protest. "Sure you are." His grin was wolfish. "We've got to get you laid."

"No."

"Are you crazy?" He laid his hand on the strings and stared at Brent. "This girl's a *sure* thing."

"Maybe for you."

"For you, too, man."

"No."

"Yes."

"Luc."

"Brent."

They glared at each other for a moment before Brent sighed. He gestured at the guitars. "Do you want to do this or not?"

Now...

He wasn't even bitter, replaying the memory in his head as he finished his shower and got dressed. Sue was the first to drive home to him that girls only wanted him because he was connected to Luc. Like if they couldn't have the real deal, then the best friend was just as good. Except he never was just as good. On his own, he didn't have what it took to keep a girl's interest. He simply ran out of things to say to girls, which just pissed them off.

Luc had eventually gotten him laid shortly after they'd gotten into their first band at age sixteen. Dorine was the lead singer and very sexy. She would also, by her own admission, sleep with almost any guy. The occasion had been severely anti-climatic. Much to Luc's dismay, Brent had made do with his own right hand until right after they'd finally hooked up with Johnnie and Darien and formed Heaven Sent. That next time, the sex was more of a celebration than any reflection of either party, and he'd actually had a good time with Amber. He'd even slept with her a few more times before she'd moved on to a drummer from another band.

And that was the story of his life. At least his love life. He was either one night's entertainment, a stand-in for someone else, or he was more Heaven Sent's guitarist than a real person. Of the three, he preferred to be the latter and even played that up from time to time, but it did get old pretty quickly.

"And it's the same deal with Hell," he told his reflection as he checked himself out in the mirror after he was finished dressing. "Nothing new."

Mind made up, he decided he looked okay. Crisp white slacks, black belt, loose black tank top, and new white Nikes to concede to the black-and-white theme of tonight's show as well as the venue.

Humming one of the new tunes, he draped his white button-down shirt over one of his bare arms, saving it to put on until after Jen, the makeup queen, was done with him. Because although he was capable of dressing himself, he knew he was not capable of applying the makeup that was required.

Theo was waiting for him in the suite's main room, watching television. "Ready?" he asked, looking up.

"Yep."

Theo used the remote to switch of the television as he stood. "You have your glasses?"

"Yes."

"Good. Try not to lose them tonight, huh?"

Brent glared over the top edge of the frames of said glasses just after he put them on. "Smart ass." He was thankful that Theo was used to him and didn't make a big deal about what had happened that afternoon. When he'd gotten back, he'd shown concern, then dropped it, just as Brent preferred.

"I'm just saying…" Theo continued with a smirk as they left the suite.

They made their way downstairs and through a labyrinth of back hallways. Brent was okay, casual and relaxed, until Hell's melodic laugh filled his ears, distinctive even though he wasn't the only one laughing. Brent froze in the middle of the largely deserted hallway deep in the bowels of the Weiss, amazed by the immediate tingle in his balls at the very sound of the cherub. Well, wasn't that absurd?

Theo stopped mid-sentence a few steps ahead and turned. "You okay?"

He blinked at the man, then smiled. "Uh, yeah." He nodded at the open doorway ahead. "That the dressing room?"

Theo glanced over his shoulder, then back at Brent, frowning slightly. "Yeah."

Brent nodded. "Right."

Hell laughed again, and Brent fought not to shiver at the gorgeous sound. What was *up* with that? He so wished he'd had a chance to talk to Luc before seeing Hell again, but it hadn't been in the cards. As part owner of the club as well as part of the starring act, Luc was pretty busy.

Theo was watching him with a weird look, so he must be acting strangely. Fuck it. This was stupid. It's not like Hell was going to attack him or anything.

Maybe.

Shit.

Determined, Brent smiled at Theo, then breezed past him into the brightly lit little room.

"Gotta hand it to Johnnie, though," Darien was saying somewhere to Brent's right. "Not a hell of a lot of people could have pulled off the rest of the show holding his fly closed."

Hell laughed. He stood at a huge, six-foot-wide counter to Brent's left, leaning toward the big mirror that stood at least four feet high on top of the ledge. His hair was curled and shiny about that sweet round face, and the dark purple braid down his back was secured with a different rhinestone band. The black pants he wore were snug and laced. Laced. Up the sides. The pale skin of his legs, from his low-cut, pointed boots to his waist, was bared by a two-inch-wide strip, held together by crisscross lacing. The waistband of the pants rode low with more lacing instead of a fly, and his cropped, shimmery white top rode high, exposing a toned, hairless belly. The sleeves of the top billowed over his arms in poet sleeves, gathered in frilly lace at his wrists, but the V-neck was wide and low to expose a good amount of his chest. He turned, mascara wand still held up, as Brent entered. The huge violet eyes were lined with black, making them look even larger. Expertly applied makeup gave some definition to those round cheeks and gave the smiling cupid lips an inviting shine.

"Did that really happen?" Jen, the makeup lady, stood a few feet away from Hell, arms crossed and butt propped on the edge of the ledge.

"God's honest truth," Darien crowed. "Brent, tell them."

Brent tore his gaze from Hell to smirk at the drummer. Darien wore almost the opposite of Brent's outfit, black slacks and a white tank top. The tank showed off his muscular arms rather nicely. His straight blond hair shone, and makeup had made his dark eyes lustrous. He sat on the arm of a solid new couch, his socked feet on the seat cushions. Drumsticks were already in his fidgety hands, and he probably wasn't even aware of the beat he tapped out on his knee.

"Are you telling that story again?" Brent asked, affecting a nonchalance he really wanted to feel. He avoided looking at Hell as he made for the chair beside Jen.

"Ha!" Jen barked, pointing at Darien as Brent sat down. "That didn't happen."

"Brent!"

Brent laughed as he reached up to pull off his shades. "Actually, it did. Johnnie's tried his best to figure out how to do it again on purpose, but he hasn't quite managed it."

"See?!" Darien laughed while Jen scowled at him.

Brent set his shades on the counter. Looking up in the mirror, he couldn't help but see the cherub's gaze fastened on him, warm appreciation in those impossibly colored eyes. His heart flipped at seeing the small, approving smile that curved Hell's lips.

"Nice outfit," Hell purred.

Self-conscious, Brent ducked his head, draping his shirt over the arm of the chair. "Thanks," he murmured.

"You okay?"

Brent blinked at him as Jen took a brush to his hair. "Huh?"

"This afternoon."

"Oh. That. Yeah, I'm good. Just needed some time to chill."

"Oh, yeah, man!" Darien piped up behind them. "I heard about what happened. That bites. Was it bad?"

Brent met Darien's eyes in the mirror. Like Luc and Johnnie, Darien didn't have a problem with the press or the fans. The reason he wasn't in as many interviews was because he talked too *much* instead of too little.

He smiled at his friend. "It wasn't fun, but it's over."

Darien's brown-eyed gaze kept hold of his for an assessing moment; then the drummer grinned that wide grin. "Well, they didn't tear you apart, at least."

Brent rolled his head. "Yeah. At least."

He couldn't avoid meeting Hell's gaze in the mirror again, noticing how the cherub watched him carefully. When Hell knew he had Brent's attention, he smiled, then very casually went back to applying dark purple mascara to his long lashes.

Darien was saying something behind them about one of the interviews he'd done that afternoon, his patter filling the air more solidly than the alternative rock that was playing low over the speakers mounted in two of the room's four upper corners. Brent latched onto what he was saying to avoid thinking about Hell.

When Hell finished his makeup and went back to sit with Darien, Brent was amazed to see the change in his expression. The dark, secretive assessment melted away into burning, wide-eyed curiosity. Come to think of it, the same thing had happened at the press conference and in a number of little ways since Brent had known Hell. One minute he was the innocent, wide-eyed cherub; then the next he was more a calculating imp. He seemed to wear both masks with equal comfort and looked like he could switch between them with alacrity. So the question was, which one was he? Brent was guessing the imp.

Gretchen breezed in through the open doorway, dressed in a simple thigh-length white sheathe that made her red hair all the more vivid. Behind her, Ellen, one of her top aides, complemented her in a shimmering black velvet pantsuit. Gretchen stopped mid-sentence, sharp green eyes scanning the room. She scowled. "All right. I just talked to Luc, but where's Johnnie?"

Brent looked at her in the mirror. Darien and Hell shrugged. Jen kept brushing whatever she was brushing onto Brent's cheekbones.

Gretchen growled, heavily made-up eyes narrowed. "Damn it! I knew it was a mistake to take my eyes off any of you after the sound check." She checked her watch. "It's getting late, and the biggest prima donna is missing!"

Brent grinned. "Have you tried calling Tyler?"

Gretchen blinked at him. Then smiled. "Why, no. No, I haven't." She turned back into the hallway, already flipping her cell phone open.

Darien smiled, twirling a drumstick with nimble fingers. "Gretchen is obviously not familiar with the honey-and-bee concept."

"'Honey and bee'?" Hell asked. He now mirrored Darien on the couch, perched on the other arm with his boots on the seat.

"Tyler's the honey; Johnnie's the bee," Darien explained, switching to drumming a beat on his knee as he bounced the leg. "Where you find one, the other's not far behind."

Hell cocked his head. "Shouldn't it be flower and bee? Bees make honey; they're not attracted to it."

Brent cracked up at the look of surprise on Darien's face.

Hell's exaggerated blinking of his big eyes told them he'd known exactly what Darien meant.

Darien grimaced, pointing a warning drumstick at Hell. "Watch it, you."

Hell chuckled, well pleased with himself.

Luc rushed through the doorway, looking splendid in white slacks and an oversized black and white tiger-striped button-down. The shirt was open almost to his navel, all the better to display his cut, nearly hairless chest as well as the silver tiger pendant he wore. The cuffs of the shirt were rolled up to his elbows, and numerous bangles of varying materials clattered and jangled about his wrists. He made for the seat beside Brent, arms raised to take the band off his red ponytail.

Brent narrowed his eyes at his friend. "Where've you been?"

Luc glanced at him as he sat, shaking his shoulder-length hair out. "I was helping Reese out with something."

"Mmm." Judging from the muss of that auburn hair, the glitter in his eye, and the slightly swollen, reddish cast to his lips, Brent could guess what Luc had been "helping" Reese with.

Luc caught his smirk in the mirror and returned it with a waggle of his arched eyebrows, confirming Brent's guess.

"Hey." The smirk melted into a look of concern as Luc turned to face him. "I heard about what happened this afternoon. You okay?"

Brent sighed. It was nice that they were all concerned, but he really wished that there was no reason for any of them to be. "Yeah, I'm fine."

"Sorry I wasn't there."

Brent shrugged, then muttered a "sorry" to Jen, who was working on his eyes. "No biggie. Hell was there. He got a great introduction into the fucked-up psyche of Brent Rose. The rockstar who can't stand his fans."

"Fuck you," Luc growled. "Not every rockstar can do the whole fan thing. Not your fault that crowds of 'em freak you out."

"Exactly," Hell chimed in. "At least you can perform. There are some musicians who can't stand to be in front of a crowd."

Jen backed up, and Brent lowered his gaze to the mirror to see Luc and Hell sharing a look. A look Brent couldn't decipher.

Luc nodded, turning back to the dressing table to grab a brush. "Yeah. See? Hell gets it."

"Good. Then he can join the ranks of the rest of you who cover for me."

Luc rolled his eyes, and Darien snorted. In the mirror, Brent saw Hell just staring at him.

"Jesus fucking Christ!" Luc cried, switching his attention to the speaker up above them. "Who put on this shit? Can't we get some Zeppelin?"

Darien laughed. "It's your club, dumbass; you can get them to play whatever you want."

Luc's eyes lit up, along with a bright smile. "My God, I do believe you're right." He pulled out his cell.

Chapter Six

All in all, Brent thought the night went well. Troubles of the afternoon aside, the show had rocked. The fans were jazzed. The press was abuzz.

And the sexual possibilities were virtually endless.

It was often like this, especially when he hadn't played before an audience for months. He got on stage with the guitar in his hands, and his body came alive. The sheer carnal joy of their music and the fans was blatantly sexual. Even the relatively small crowd of fifteen hundred for which they'd played that night had set a fire in Brent's belly that demanded he quench it with the aid of a willing body.

Or two.

So there he sat on a stool at the bar, his sixth or seventh drink by his elbow, a cigarette between two fingers, and an arm around a beautiful woman. Two more beautiful women stood beside him, and he was enjoying their not-so-subtle battle, the winner of which would presumably spend the night with him.

Still amazed him. He barely spoke, too tongue-tied in public to manage many words strung together. Unless he was *really* drunk, and what he said during those times hardly ever bore repeating. But it didn't matter. Tonight he was back in the swing of being the guitarist of Heaven Sent. He didn't mind that they wanted to sleep with a Brent Rose that bore little resemblance to the real man. Heaven Sent's Brent Rose was cocky yet taciturn. Quiet and mysterious. He hid deep thoughts behind opaque shades. That Brent Rose attracted lovers like...flowers attracted bees.

Buzz.

He glanced over the mostly bare shoulder of the woman standing in front of him and saw the cherub. He perched on a table not too far away, with a gathering of heavily made-up men *and* women around him. He had a tall, colorful drink with an umbrella, held in both graceful hands, the base of the glass propped on the knee of his black laced pants. My, didn't he look tasty?

Buzz.

A pretty boy with buzzed black hair leaned in close to Hell's ear, clearly suggestive. Brent blinked at the sudden surge that filled his breast when Hell smiled and reached up to slide his fingertips along the boy's chin.

Buzz. Buzz. Buzz. Buzz Buzz.

Laughing, Hell turned his head. The light purple hair that seemed white in the ever-changing lights fell over his eyes. He reached up a ringed hand to brush it aside, and his eyes locked on Brent's. He smiled wide and raised his glass in salute.

Brent raised his in return.

Female fingers stroked his cheek, and he obediently turned toward the pretty face that went with the soft touch. She smiled, red lips curving invitingly. Long nails scraped lightly down his chest. Her fingers toyed with the first button of his white shirt that was actually fastened, halfway to his navel. He'd abandoned the sweaty tank top after the show, so her sharp nails grazed bare skin. She brushed soft breasts against his arm. But he'd lost interest. She was pretty. He could take her back to his room. But that's not what he wanted. Wasn't her fault that she was female. *Damn.*

He smiled, not letting on his thoughts. Not that anyone expected to read his thoughts behind the glasses. He grabbed her hand before it could trail any lower and raised her palm to his lips, kissed it, then leaned back to release it. "I need a break for a while, ladies," he proclaimed, downing the last of his drink.

"But Brent..."

"Brent, honey..."

"I'll go with you!"

He brushed a hand over one soft shoulder. *What are you doing, man?* But his hand fell back to his side. "Sorry."

He stood and one of them -- Gina? -- grabbed his hand, forcing him to look at her. "How about if we *both*" -- she tilted her head at...Veronica? -- "go with you?"

Are you stupid? he asked himself, watching his hand slide down her sweet neck as he shook his head. "Maybe later" Of course, it was already well after one in the morning. The bar itself would be closing soon to all but the VIP members, which none of these three lovelies were..

She smiled. "We'll be here."

He matched her smile and even leaned in to graze the corner of her mouth with his lips. *Damn it.* He placed the cigarette between his lips, shoved his hands in the pockets of his white slacks, then sauntered off.

You have got to get a grip, he told himself as he casually wound through the crowd, waving to anyone who tried to catch his eye, but not stopping. The shades helped. No one was ever quite sure if he was looking at them or not. He was good at it after many years of practice. Look like he was headed somewhere important, and people tended to leave him alone.

Three women aching to take you to bed, and you're obsessing over the cherub. He really should stop thinking of Hell as "the cherub." He was going to slip one day and call him that, and he wasn't sure the sentiment would sound right outside of his head.

He stubbed out his cigarette in an ashcan by the dark little passage that was his destination. Tyler had shown them the exit earlier. It led to a small, enclosed courtyard he'd promised to keep private, as well as an express elevator up to the luxury-suite floors. Brent would just take a brief cigarette break to get his head on straight; then he'd go back to the party and find a willing male body. That's all there was for it.

The guy manning the velvet rope across the way recognized him and lifted the rope before Brent even had to stop. He waved a hand in thanks and walked past. The beat of the music dulled just as one of Heaven Sent's songs came on. He smiled, lazily fingering an air guitar to his own riffs He still enjoyed their music. Had to be a good sign, yeah?

Brent made his way around a few turns. The lighting was subdued, the floor carpeted. Tyler's hotel was one class act. Heaven Sent was treated well at most hotels, but they got extra special treatment at this one.

He fished out his pack of Camels and was just popping one out of the box when he reached the entrance to the courtyard.

And froze.

Across the diamond tiles and beyond a few sturdy iron table and chair sets, an iron bench sat in a relatively dark corner. A couple he knew well sat on it, the white of their clothing standing out in the shadows. Luc had one arm wrapped around Reese's slim waist as the younger man with royal-blue-tipped black hair straddled his hips, their lips locked in a hot and heavy kiss that made Brent's mouth water. Luc's other hand was trying to burrow between them toward Reese's groin, but Reese had a grip on his wrist, obviously fighting.

Reese finally pulled back, tilting his head toward the glass ceiling that revealed the stars overhead. Luc's lips trailed down the pale column of Reese's throat toward the chest that was exposed through the V of his collar.

Reese hissed. "Quit it! We should get back to the party."

"No." Luc's voice was almost lost since he refused to take his lips from Reese's skin. His next words were muffled, but Brent was pretty sure he heard a "need you" in there.

Reese dug his free hand into Luc's fiery auburn hair and pulled the man's head back. "Then let's go upstairs." They spoke in whispers, but the acoustics of the area carried the words to Brent.

Luc sucked in air, hooded eyes drinking in the sight of his lover. "In a minute. God, you feel good!"

Reese bent his head, nipping at Luc's chin. "You, too. Let's go upstairs."

"Yeah. Okay."

But when Reese tried to pull back to get to his feet, Luc's free hand shot up into his hair, yanking his mouth down for another soul-searing kiss.

Brent blinked, mesmerized. As intense as he and Luc had ever gotten, Luc had *never* kissed him like that. Even when he was pretending Brent was Reese. The reality seemed to be far preferable to the fantasy. But Brent had known that from the start.

Movement at his side made him jump, and he spun. His mouth fell open to see none other than the cherub stepping up to his side, eyes on the oblivious couple. Hell cocked his head, studying them. Those precious lips, still glossy with makeup even after hours in the club, pursed. A long-fingered hand decked in gold rings propped on one cocked hip. Before Brent could think of anything to say, Hell darted a glance at him. Kohl-lined eyes went back to Luc and Reese, then back to Brent. He grinned, complete with teeth that Brent wouldn't have been surprised to see were pointed. He turned his head to the couple and stepped from the carpet of the passageway onto the tile of the courtyard. Brent reached for his arm, but he was too late. The two-inch block heels of his boots clacked on the tile.

Reese flinched.

Luc froze, eyes opening.

Hell stopped a few feet into the courtyard, hands now folded behind his back. "How pretty."

Reese turned a guilty look toward him, eyes going wider to see Brent standing there as well.

Brent popped his nearly forgotten cigarette between his lips and dug in his pocket for his lighter. It gave him something to do. "Really, guys," he said, hoping his voice sounded vaguely indifferent. "You've got a huge suite upstairs."

Reese turned back to glare at Luc. "That's what *I* said," he hissed through his teeth. To Brent's delight, he actually punched Luc. Hard. In the gut.

Luc grunted, his hold on Reese loosed.

Reese took the opportunity to push to his feet. Hastily, he untucked his long shirt, hiding what would probably be a bulge in his tight pants.

Luc sank back on the bench, blatantly pouting as he rubbed his stomach His tiger-striped shirt was completely unbuttoned and open, draping his broad shoulders. He obviously didn't care who saw the boner tenting his slacks. "We were doing fine until *company* showed." He glared at Hell and Brent.

Brent feigned indifference, flipping open his Zippo and lighting his smoke. "Not our fault the party's boring."

Hell glanced over his shoulder at Brent, one questioning purple brow raised.

Okay, it was actually a pretty rocking party, but he had to say *something*. He busied himself with putting away the cigarette pack and lighter.

When he looked up, Reese was at the elevator, staring across the courtyard.

Brent turned to look in the same direction.

Luc still sat on the bench, arms spread across the back. His head was tilted to the side, and his dark, speculative gaze was on Hell. Then it flicked to Brent. And back.

"Hey," Reese called, "aren't you coming?"

Grinning broadly, Luc stood and started across the courtyard. "Yep."

Brent felt his eyes go wide and belatedly realized Luc couldn't see them. He shook his head behind Hell's back.

Luc caught the motion and laughed softly. A minute nod, then his attention was fully back on Reese.

Reese held the elevator door for him, smacking Luc's hand away when the redhead reached for him. Reese looked at Hell and Brent. "You guys coming?"

"We'll take the next one," Hell proclaimed happily.

Brent almost groaned at the huge smile that comment produced on Luc's face, just before the elevator doors closed. Shaking his head, he stepped over to sit in one of the iron chairs. It wasn't until the elevator closed that he realized his error. He was now alone with Hell and the lingering effects of sexual tension between Luc and Reese. Not to mention his own needs. Brent was hard. *Oh, yeah*, now *you wake up*, he chided his dick, hoping the loose fit of his slacks hid his state.

Hell's tight pants, however, did no such thing. This was made evident to Brent when the cherub stepped up in front of him. *Nice!* was his first thought as he helplessly eyed the curve of Hell's cock in the tight confines of the shiny black pants. Then he realized what he was looking at and hastily sat back, trembling fingers bringing the cigarette to his lips. The angle might have been right for Hell to see his eyes checking out Hell's package!

Calmly, Hell sat down in the chair in front of Brent. He leaned an elbow on the table and propped his chin in his palm, watching Brent with a speculative look.

Shit! "What?"

"It was Luc."

"What was Luc?"

"You slept with Luc."

"Huh?"

"I thought it might be Johnnie, but no, I think it's Luc."

Brent avoided watching the cherub by looking around for an ashtray. None were in sight. "What are you talking about?"

"You and he are very comfortable together."

He flicked ash on the tiles beside his feet. "We've been best friends since grade school."

Hell cocked his head to the side. "When did you start fucking?"

Brent frowned. "We're not fucking."

"Not *now*. Of course not now. He's very much in love with Reese. That is obvious. Although, you do look like Reese. Was that the attraction?"

Brent's nostrils flared. He did *not* want to have this conversation. He glanced at the elevator, wondering if he could get in without Hell coming with him. The thought of being in a tiny enclosed space with the cherub made his dick throb. "You don't know what you're talking about."

"I've been watching you."

He patted his pocket for his pack of smokes. "Yeah." He'd just have another one, and hopefully Hell would head on up to his room alone.

"I want you."

Brent froze, anger draining as he was speared by an intense violet gaze.

Hell turned his arm so his fingers curled up in front of his chin. The frothy lace of his cuffs spilled down his forearm, displaying the gold bracelet, ring, and the chains that linked them over the back of his hand. "Mmm." He straightened his index finger slightly to trace the top curve of his upper lip with a manicured fingernail.

Brent swallowed. "We can't."

"Why not?"

"The band…" The finger was distracting. Or was it the lips?

"You slept with Luc."

"That was different."

The tip of Hell's pink tongue nudged out to lick one side of his upper lip. "I'd die to know what it's like to have those talented fingers on me." Oh, the accent just made that sentence so very amazing.

Said fingers went lifeless and dropped the cigarette.

Hell's gaze dropped.

Brent realized a hole was burning in his slacks.

"Fuck!" He jumped up, sending the chair clattering to the tiles behind him. He brushed off the burning ash. No flames, but there was a definite burn mark.

Brent froze again when Hell's boots and legs appeared in his downcast vision. He started to back away on instinct, but Hell's hands reached up to cup his face, tilting it so Brent had to straighten and look at him. With the heels on the boots, Hell's height reached Brent's chin. He gazed into the cherub's face. He'd never seen that hunger in those eyes. It made them a deep, beguiling indigo.

Hell grimaced slightly; then Brent felt thumbs and fingers at the arms of his sunglasses, pressing them up.

"Hey," he reached up to grab at Hell's hands.

He didn't get a grip on the slim wrists before Hell yanked his face down and took his lips in a kiss.

Oh, God! Brent heard the moan ooze from his throat as liquid heat shot through his veins. Just the touch of those soft lips with the remnants of gloss was enough to chase away thoughts and bring forward pure feeling. Fingers dug into his hair, pushing his sunglasses up farther, as the lips parted and the point of a warm, wet tongue teased the seam of Brent's lips. He opened without hesitation, sucking in the questing tongue, pulling hard. Hell let out a grunt of surprise that turned into a ragged groan. He stepped closer to Brent, his belly brushing Brent's erection through layers of fabric. Unthinking, Brent dropped his arms around Hell's waist, pulling the smaller man closer to increase the pressure. They both sighed. Hell's arms slid up to wind around Brent's neck, and Brent's hands spanned out, one over the middle of Hell's back and one dropping down to squeeze a firm ass cheek.

Fingers again tangled in his hair, this time at the back of his skull, and pulled until he was forced to break the kiss. Both he and Hell sucked in breath without breaking their embrace.

Hell recovered first. "Elevator."

Reason tried to wiggle its way to the surface of Brent's brain. "Wait."

"No. No waiting." Sharp teeth nipped at Brent's chin. "Need to fuck you."

He groaned. "But…"

Hell unwound the arm with the free hand from around Brent's neck and wormed it down between them. Brent hissed when firm fingers melded to his cock. "Want you." Need put more of the German accent into his voice so that it came out sounding like "Vant you." "Want to know how you taste."

Brent was only a flesh-and-blood human being, and at the moment, all of his flesh and blood was at the mercy of the cherub's hot little hand and seductive, commanding voice.

He closed his eyes and swallowed, walking backwards at Hell's nudge. He had to trust that Hell knew where they were going because the man had a solid grip on his cock and didn't seem to be anywhere close to letting go. Brent's back came up against a wall. Hell tilted his head down into another tongue-sucking kiss, only freeing his hand to lower it to press the elevator button once Brent was fully engaged in the lip lock.

When the doors opened, Hell pushed. Brent stumbled free of the cherub's hold and leaned against the low railing circling the three walls of the elevator. Hell stepped inside and reached to press the button with the hand that held Brent's sunglasses.

Brent stared at the glasses. They looked so odd, so ordinary in someone else's hands. Especially those hands. Long and elegant, somewhat hidden beneath the lacy flounce of his shirt cuffs. Rings shone from most of the fingers as he raised the sunglasses. Brent watched in fascination as Hell used the tip of one earpiece to trace the full curve of his bottom lip.

"Your kiss is divine, *Süsser*." The last word sounded like an endearment, kind of "si-ssur" with a hard *i* and a drawn out *s* in the middle. Hell stepped toward Brent, sucking the earpiece between his lips. "How does the rest of you taste?"

Brent swallowed, trying once more to regain some sanity. "Hell, we shouldn't do this."

"Oh, yes. We should."

Brent shook his head. "The band."

Hell stepped into his body, pressing Brent against the back wall. "You already slept with one other member of the band." He pressed his other palm over Brent's heart, the earpiece of the sunglasses still between his lips. Dark amethyst eyes met his. "What's one more?"

Brent couldn't take his eyes off that part of his sunglasses, disappearing in and out of Hell's lips. That pink tongue came out to caress the plastic, and Brent had to wet his own lips at the sight.

Hell leaned in, tilting up toward his mouth. "I want you so much." Lips hovered beneath Brent's, the plastic of the glasses an odd hardness at the corner of their mouths "Please don't say I can't have you."

The elevator doors hissed open.

Hell stepped back.

Brent stumbled forward, leaning into the kiss that Hell now backed away from.

Hell grabbed the front of Brent's shirt and led the way out of the elevator. "Come."

Mistake! Brent's brain screamed. Yet here he was, following the cherub like a stunned puppy.

Hell perched Brent's glasses up on top of his own head to free his hand to dig in the waistband of his pants. Brent wasn't sure where he'd tucked it, but Hell produced his key card just as they reached the door to his suite.

Brent cast a glance toward his own door, not twenty feet away. He should go there. He should yank away, grab his glasses, and lock himself safely away until these aching tremors passed.

Too late. Hell's door clicked open, and the hand in his shirt yanked. Brent stumbled forward into Hell's room.

Chapter Seven

Hell didn't release Brent's shirt, forcing the taller man to spin around to face him as they cleared the doorway. The door shut as Hell reached over to the touchpad that activated soft lighting around the suite.

Brent's eyes widened when Hell's gaze met his, and he couldn't look away as Hell again walked him backward. The cherub kept hold of his shirt, leading him around furniture.

"Hell, this isn't..."

"Isn't what?"

He shook his head, stumbled a bit, but Hell's hold kept him balanced. "We shouldn't..."

"Mmm, Brent, you should try and finish your sentences."

Words failed him. There were reasons he shouldn't do this. Sound reasons. But they melted away in the heat of Hell's stare. Brent could see the lust in that stare and quailed at the realization that it was all focused on him. His heart thrummed so loudly he was sure Hell could hear it.

They reached the entrance to the bedroom. Hell pushed, releasing his shirt.

Brent stumbled backward and fell onto the rough cream silk of the duvet on the neatly turned-down bed.

Hell chuckled, climbing on top of him, ended up straddling his waist. "Don't be afraid, *Süsser*," he crooned, fingers trailing down Brent's chest to his buttons. "I won't hurt you." Brent had never found German to be a particularly sexy-sounding language, but his opinion had taken an abrupt one-eighty.

"It's not that..."

Hell made short work of the buttons and pushed open Brent's shirt, exposing his chest and belly. Hell's happy little purr closed Brent's eyes in pleasure. "Don't you like me?" Lips, now devoid of gloss, brushed Brent's collarbone.

Brent swallowed. "Well, yeah."

Warm chuckle. Palms and fingers spread out over his chest, pressing the aching points of his nipples. "Don't worry, *Süsser*. I understand this is just sex. No harm, no foul." The cliché sounded weird with the accent, but Brent couldn't dwell on that. Hell paused, poised over him. The shades he'd nabbed from Brent perched on top of his head, holding back most of the errant bangs that usually dropped forward over his eyes. Hell smiled. "I will not hold it against you in the morning." He bent his head and uncovered one nipple so he could circle it with his tongue. "I only wish to taste you tonight."

One night can't hurt. Brent tried to decide if he sounded convincing in his head. It was hard to wonder anything, though, when Hell's talented teeth and tongue were tormenting his nipple. The keyboardist's hand plucked the other nipple, and his groin pressed down on Brent's. The lace of his cuffs tickled Brent's skin.

Brent brought his hand up to slide his fingers down the soft, silky lavender hair at the back of Hell's skull. For whatever reason he didn't care to name, he left the sunglasses, kind of enjoying the look of them there. He slid his hand down the back of Hell's head, finding the braid that started at the nape of his neck. He lifted it, watching with half-focused eyes as it slithered like a snake through his loose hold to coil on Hell's back, some of it draping over his side He held on to the flashy band at the end and idly brushed the fluffy tail of the braid against the exposed skin of Hell's back between the hem of his shirt and the waistband of his pants.

Hell purred, squirming deliciously as he kissed his way across Brent's chest to the other nipple.

Brent slid his hand down Hell's back as far as he could reach, curving around at the waist. He trailed his fingers down the laced sides of Hell's legs, fascinated by the feel of warm, smooth skin underneath tight bindings.

"Hell."

"Mmm?"

"Clothes."

"Mmm."

"Off."

Hell paused, and Brent felt a smile against his skin. Then the cherub surged up so that the tip of his pert, upturned nose hovered over Brent's. "Mine or yours?"

Brent purposely lost himself in violet depths. He was committed now. No turning back. He glanced down and brought up a finger to hook in the V opening of Hell's shirt. "Both."

"There's a button at the top," Hell told him, remaining poised over Brent.

Brent smiled. He found the button, freed it, then took hold of the zipper and pulled it down. A slight tug at the end opened the two sides of the filmy white material, exposing the creamy, toned expanse of Hell's chest.

Hell pushed up to his knees. He kept his eyes on Brent's face as he rolled his shoulders, letting his sleeves slip down his arms to his elbows. *So sexy!* Brent thought, reaching up to slide a hand over the completely hairless skin. Hell was far more toned than it seemed he should be, nowhere near bulky but certainly not as waifish as he could appear when fully clothed. Brent paused at one small pink nipple and pinched. Hell's eyes fluttered closed, an appreciative smirk on those perfect lips. Brent did it again, then drifted his fingers down the middle of Hell's chest, belly, down over his navel, until his fingers reached the leather of Hell's pants. He fingered the bulge beneath, wondering what could possibly have Hell's cock confined beneath the pants. It didn't seem like he could have on anything underneath, but something was straining that erection.

"How the heck are you going to get out of those?" he mused.

Hell's eyes opened. He grinned. "Watch." He practically jumped backward off the bed, landing catlike on his feet.

Amused, Brent pushed up onto his elbows to watch.

Hell let the filmy white of his shirt slide the rest of the way down his arms, turning to face away from Brent. It afforded a very nice view of Hell's sleek back, the muscles rolling smoothly and the dark purple braid swaying as he tossed the shirt aside. Casually, he placed a hand on the dresser for balance and raised one booted foot behind him. One-handed, he opened the short zipper on the side and pulled off the boot. He did the same with the other, and then the socks came off. He turned profile, gazing at Brent from under lowered lashes. Long fingers went to the lacing at the top of his left hip, and he deftly untied it. Fingers then flipped under a band of stiff fabric beneath the tie and unfastened it. The leather immediately snapped open, tugging at the ties that still bound it. Smiling, Hell loosened the laces to just below his hip, then turned to repeat the performance at the other side. He then faced away from Brent again and, hands at the waistband, proceeded to shimmy out of the clinging garment with a lot of flexing and rolling for his appreciative audience. Hell bent over, and Brent could see the thin white straps of a thong across the top of his ass and down through the crack. He did a slow bump and grind as he turned to face Brent once more. The thong had to be leather, the pouch sturdy enough to contain the erection that challenged it.

Brent smiled, letting his appreciation show. "God, you're beautiful."

Heavily made-up eyes fluttered. "Thank you."

"You gonna take the thong off?"

Hell hooked two thumbs in the straps, just next to the pouch. Bright hope sparkled in his huge eyes. "Do you want me to?"

Brent couldn't help but smile. How Hell managed to mix cute and sexy he didn't know. "Yeah."

"Then yes." He carefully pulled the thin bands of the thong out to clear his dick, then bent to slide them down his long, bare legs.

Brent's mouth went dry at his first eyeful of Hell's gorgeous, uncut cock. It was -- oh, God! -- flushed almost purple and bigger than Brent had expected for Hell's size.

Hell straightened and shot a hip out, posing for him. Brent was now achingly aware that the only thing Hell wore besides jewelry was the shades still perched on his head. Long fingers wrapped around the shaft of his cock and pulled, pinching his foreskin over the tip and rolling it.

"Come here," Brent heard his own voice rasp.

Hell's grin was worthy of his name, but he held up one slim finger and headed for a luggage rack beside the nightstand.

"Hey, where are you going?" Brent protested.

"Patience, *Süsser*." He took Brent's sunglasses off and set them on the nightstand before he bent to rummage through his suitcase.

Brent was kind of sorry to see the glasses leave his head, but wasn't going to say anything for fear of sounding silly. "What's it mean, '*Süsser*'?" he asked as he scooted higher onto the bed.

"It's an endearment." Hell rummaged in the bottom of the case, grinning. "It is like calling someone 'sweetie' or 'honey.'"

"Oh." He set his head back in the soft pillows, waiting. Unable to resist, he reached down to cup himself through his slacks, teasing himself while he waited for Hell's warm body to return.

It really wasn't that long before Hell produced a bottle of lube and two condoms from the bag. Brent brightened at seeing two. The night was looking up..

"As far as I know, I am clean," Hell told him, tossing the condoms and bottle onto the bed beside Brent. "I am always careful, and I have been tested."

Brent nodded, watching Hell as he crawled up over the foot of the bed. "Me, too."

Hell smiled, bracing his slim, pale body over Brent's, pressing a brief kiss on his mouth. "Good."

They kissed again, languid and slow, learning the taste of each other. Brent slid his hands up and down the smooth skin of Hell's sides, enjoying the near complete lack of hair. He finally gave in to temptation and brought his hand around to grip Hell's cock. The keyboardist groaned around his tongue. Brent pulled it hard and played the tip with his thumb, loving the way the foreskin felt. He was circumcised himself, so an uncut cock always fascinated him.

"Hey." He slapped one side of Hell's butt lightly. "Bring that up here." He smiled at those violet eyes. "I want to taste."

Hell grinned, bit Brent's lip, then crawled higher on the bed as Brent eased further down on his back. With Hell's knees tucked up under his armpits, Brent adjusted his hold on the silken heat of the imp's cock and urged the smooth head to his lips.

The headboard clattered against the wall as Hell grabbed hold of it, moaning.

Brent spared him a brief glance, but returned his full attention to the thing of beauty in his mouth. Warm, fragrant, and tasty. And shaved!

He slid his hand to the base, and his fist brushed the bare, slightly stubbly skin of Hell's groin. Brent laved the head of Hell's cock with his tongue, tickling the spot just underneath the head. Keeping his mouth wet, he slid his lips and tongue down the shaft, urging Hell's hips closer to his mouth by squeezing a firm butt cheek with his other hand.

"Ah," Hell moaned, his hips rolling easily under Brent's guidance.

Brent loved this. It was his second favorite part about sex with a guy He'd learned and perfected the fine art of sucking cock and put his skills to use, fully intending to drive the cherub out of his freaking purple mind. He lapped at his palm, then closed it and his fingers over the head of Hell's cock, holding it up so he could nuzzle the hairless balls beneath. He ran his wet tongue over the wrinkled skin, sucking one then the other sac into his mouth.

He nearly lost it when he realized that underneath the dark, musky smell of the man was the unmistakable trace of lavender. He even smelled like lavender *here?*

Brent moaned and urged Hell up higher with another squeeze to his ass. They shifted so Brent could get his arm under Hell's leg and Hell could bend his knee, allowing Brent to duck his head and lap at the sensitive skin behind Hell's balls.

"Brent," Hell moaned, shaking the headboard again.

Yeah. He lapped and pressed at the sensitive spot, briefly tonguing Hell's back entrance before roughly dragging his tongue all the way back over perineum, balls, and shaft before he sank the head of Hell's cock into his mouth all the way to his throat.

A string of words spilled from Hell's mouth, none of them English. The tone, however, sounded like cursing. So Brent figured by that, and by the way Hell's hips kept rolling for him, that he was doing all right. A glance up showed the cherub's eyes screwed shut and that pretty mouth twisted in a promising snarl.

Brent hummed and wetly sucked his way back to the tip. He decided to stop teasing. He himself was hard as a rock and could probably come from just sucking Hell off. He'd save his special, drawn-out blowjob for later. So he set to sucking, up and down, slurping, letting Hell hear it, letting his tongue rasp the sensitive skin. He cupped his free hand around those hairless balls and rolled them, pulled them, experimenting gently to see just how much Hell liked. Hell seemed to like it all. The German cursing continued, and his hips started to snap, groin pressing against the hand Brent had clasped around the base of his cock.

"*Oh, Gott, Süsser*, going to…"

Brent growled, loving the low rasp in Hell's normally lyrical voice. He spat on his hand and jerked Hell's throbbing cock, ducking his face under to lap again at Hell's anus. That was it. Hell cried out, hips twitching violently. Everything squeezed, and warm cum spilled over Brent's hand, oozing onto the pillow beside his head. Brent bitterly lamented that he couldn't taste it, but no matter what had been said, one didn't swallow on the first date.

Hell hissed, and Brent released him, letting his wet hand rest on the pillow for the moment as he grinned up at the cherub. Hmm, no, not cherub. He was having trouble making that moniker fit anymore. Imp. Yeah, that was more like it.

Hell lowered himself to lie on Brent's chest, sinking fingers into Brent's hair to pull his head up for a long, lazy kiss. He pulled his head up and smiled down at Brent. "That was wonderful."

"My pleasure."

Hell brushed his lips over Brent's again, then backed down. He stopped when his hands got to Brent's waist. "Are these still on?" he asked playfully, tugging the waistband of Brent's pants.

"How'd that happen?"

"I don't know." Clever fingers made quick work of the belt, button, and zipper. "But that will never do." Those same fingers wrapped over the waistband of Brent's pants and underwear and drew them down his thighs He stopped when Brent's cock was fully exposed, humming happily. "You are beautiful," he assured Brent, dropping a quick kiss to the shaft before backing off the bed with Brent's pants. He muttered. He scowled adorably as he had to switch to Brent's feet to get his Nikes off, but soon enough he had Brent naked from the waist down. The shirt that was open but still on Brent's shoulders he ignored.

It dawned on Brent: he'd probably have to be the top. Not that he minded so much. He'd topped before. But he actually preferred being the bottom. Sucking cock was his second favorite part of sex with a man. Getting fucked was his first. *Oh, well*, he mused as Hell knelt on the bed beside him. The idea of sinking into Hell's sweet little ass wasn't unappealing. Maybe he'd get lucky and Hell would want to ride him. He seemed to like calling the shots anyway.

Hell sped away to the bathroom and returned with a washcloth. He tossed and Brent caught it, using it to wipe up his hand.

Brent glanced at the pillow beside his head. "I think the pillow's toast." He grinned.

Hell matched the grin, kneeling on the foot of the bed. "There are plenty in the closet."

Brent tossed the cloth to the floor, pitching the pillow after it. He pulled one of the remaining pillows to fill the gap and lay back, folding his hands behind his head.

The little devil was poised over Brent's twitching, aching cock, looking at it like a kid would look at a plate of cookies. He even licked his lips. "I have neglected you," Hell murmured, easing down onto his elbows between Brent's bent knees. "Allow me to make it up to you." Brent's cock jumped at the proximity of that adorable mouth.

"You're doing grand," Brent groaned as Hell lowered his head and nuzzled the bend between thigh and groin. "But don't let that stop you."

"Mmm." Hell slid his hands up the backs of Brent's thighs to his knees, then back down and around until both palms spread across Brent's belly, his arms wrapped around Brent's thighs. He nipped at the hair that guarded Brent's balls, not quite touching, but his breath was tangible, a warm caress across sensitive skin.

"God," Brent moaned, watching his cock jump and drip pre-cum. Thoughts and concerns that didn't involve sinking his dick into some orifice of Hell's body flew from his brain.

Violet eyes met his over his cock. He saw Hell's mouth open wide and groaned loudly when he felt that tongue lapping at his balls.

"Shit, Hell…"

"Yes?"

"You're killing me here."

"Am I?"

"Stop teasing."

Hell shifted, watching his hands as they rubbed Brent's flat belly, spreading the pre-cum over his skin "Am I teasing?"

"Yes."

"Do you want me to suck your cock?"

"God, yes."

"Ah. I would be happy to."

Hell dragged himself up more, letting his tongue lick a dripping line from the base of Brent's cock to the head. Brent cried out when those pouty lips closed over the tip of him, then sank down the shaft. Hell hummed approval, letting gemstone eyes flutter closed as he raised up and again sucked down Brent's cock.

Oh, this isn't going to last long, Brent thought to himself, unable to voice his thoughts over the moans and grunts that had taken over his throat.

Hell's fingers bit into Brent's hips as the imp managed to take most of Brent into his mouth. He didn't even gag when the head hit the back of his throat. Good God, the little devil didn't have a gag reflex!

Brent was in heaven. There was a joke in there about Hell, but his mind couldn't function properly to find it. He let it go and clutched the duvet beneath him, happy to let Hell have his way.

Hell's hands massaged his hips, his thighs, as that marvelous mouth worked wicked magic on Brent's cock. Brent did everything he could to keep from coming, to keep this going.

Hell stopped briefly, grinning at Brent's protest. "One moment, *Süsser*," he crooned, grabbing the lube.

Brent watched as Hell poured clear liquid on the fingers of one hand, then capped the bottle again. *Is he...?*

Hell took Brent's cock back into his mouth and brought the wet hand down and between Brent's thighs. Slippery fingers caressed the skin behind his balls.

Oh, fuck yeah, he is! Brent shook, moaning. It had been so long.

Hell's right hand grabbed the base of Brent's cock, gold chain and bracelet jingling quietly as he released Brent from his mouth with a pop. A squeeze quelled the impending orgasm. "Not yet." He ducked his head to suck lightly on Brent's balls as his fingers continued to caress and explore around Brent's hole.

"Please," Brent heard himself beg.

"Soon, *Süsser*."

"Hell...agh!" He cried out, back arching as Hell's finger sank in.

"You like that." It was a pleased observation.

"Yes," Brent gasped, gripping the pillow on either side of his head. "More. Please."

A second finger joined the first. "You're tight, but you're already ready."

Brent couldn't answer, too caught up in the feel of fingers. God, but he loved that! The stretch, the burn, it was wonderful, and Hell had blessedly long fingers that would soon find -- He cried out again, writhing as Hell found his spot. Two fingers, maybe three, sank in and pulled out and sank in again, and Brent ground down to meet them.

"Brent, *Süsser*, may I fuck you?"

"Please, God, yes!"

Hell's mouth swiped around the head of his cock again, making Brent groan, but then it was gone, along with the hand that had held him. The bed moved, and Brent managed to look to see Hell kneeling between his bent legs, condom in hand and cock back to readiness. *Thank God!* Brent thought. Followed by wordless excitement that he really *was* going to get fucked!

Brent reached for the lube and popped the top as Hell smoothed the condom over his cock. Brent poured the lube into Hell's hand, then closed and tossed aside the bottle as Hell got into position. Hell's hands pushed up one of his knees, and Brent held up the other.

"*Gott*, you want this, don't you?"

Brent nodded, nearly reduced to begging.

"You are a dream come true," Hell assured him as he set the head of his dick at Brent's opening and pushed.

"Oh, *fuck* yeah!" Brent groaned, eyes dropping closed as that delicious, dark pleasure soared through his veins. He even liked the little twinge of pain right before his body opened up to draw Hell in. He shuddered and panicked to realize that this was it. He was coming. He couldn't hold it back. "Ah, shit!" His body shook, and cum spurted over his belly and chest.

Hell froze, watching with wide eyes until Brent subsided.

Brent bit his lip, wincing at he looked down at his belly. "Sorry."

Hell met his eyes, an amazed smile on his lips. "Should I stop?"

Brent shook his head. "Please don't."

Carnal heat suffused the imp's face, his mouth spreading into a demon's grin. Without warning, he shoved forward with his hips, sheathing himself fully in one hard thrust.

Brent almost screamed. As it was, it came out as a prolonged, shaking whimper.

"Are you all right?" Hell asked.

"Fine. Great. Do that again."

Hell did, and Brent just about died.

"Fuck me," he heard himself beg. "Hard."

Guttural German words poured from Hell's mouth as he took hold of both of Brent's knees, holding them up and apart. The blessed, awful imp leaned in and started to pound into Brent, giving it to him just the way he liked it. He took Brent's grunts and cries as the permission they were, and Brent happily lost all reason and thought, riding the brutal heat of the man fucking him. His cock tried to rise but wasn't up to it so soon. But the tingle still took his groin. He wasn't sure if he came or not, and didn't really care. The burn, the heat, the ruthless pleasure that ripped at his gut was a wonderful thing as far as he was concerned.

Hell lasted longer than Brent thought he could. He manhandled one of Brent's thighs across, forcing Brent onto his side. Brent didn't know or care how he managed it, but Hell kept fucking him, kept cursing or praising him in German. His hair was damp with sweat, turning the lavender to a shining amethyst. Some mascara smudged down the sheen that covered his high cheeks. Brent's hazy mind decided he'd never seen anything lovelier.

On a harsh shout of something Brent didn't understand, Hell jerked. His body convulsed as he came. And came. And came. Underneath him, Brent shuddered in echoed pleasure.

Hell fell forward over him, braced on his arms. He stayed there for a moment, breathing. Finally, eyes gone deep ultraviolet turned up to shine at Brent.

Brent's conscious revived just enough to tell him one thing: *You are in so much trouble.*

Chapter Eight

Brent woke with hair the color of an Easter egg tickling his neck and chin. Hell's small, lithe body was draped over his right side Brent blinked at the ceiling, sleepily judging by the hazy gray illumination in the air that it must be morning.

He let his head fall to the side and forced his eyes to focus on the clock on the nightstand. Six a.m.

He sighed and rolled his head back upright, closing his eyes. He wasn't getting back to sleep. No matter how late Brent stayed awake at night, he usually woke at about this time. His inner clock simply would not allow him to sleep past six or seven unless he was sick or profoundly hungover. But even that didn't work all the time.

Besides, he had to pee.

He pulled in a deep breath, careful to be quiet. He didn't want to wake the imp. For a moment he just let himself enjoy the feel of the warm body pressed to his, the nearly hairless leg twined around one of his. Brent's arm lay over Hell's smooth back, that long purple braid threaded loosely through his fingers. The clasp for the braid had come loose during the night, so the last half of the plait of hair was undone, dark streaks sifting over Hell's lower back. Brent gazed hungrily over the pert curve of the man's ass, plainly visible since they never had made it under the covers.

Brent caught himself looking and shut his eyes. What was he looking at? He'd had his fun. Now it was over.

Listening to his silent, chiding voice, Brent started to extricate himself from Hell's embrace.

He found two things out pretty quickly. First, the imp was compact and strong but relatively light, even in sleep. Second, he slept like the dead Brent managed to untangle himself and slip out from underneath the imp without so much as the man's breathing changing. Brent chuckled as Hell's loose limbs fell back to the mattress and stayed there.

Brent chose to move softly as he went about finding his clothes. He still wore his shirt. He located his pants and underwear in a tangle at the foot of the bed. After pulling them right side out, he put them on but just picked up his shoes and socks. He wasn't going far, after all.

He paused at the doorway to the bedroom. The imp still hadn't moved, his lovely pale skin practically glowing in the early morning light. Brent had a fleeting thought of covering him up but discarded the idea. The temperature in the room was just fine, and doing so only chanced that Hell would wake up.

Brent turned and left the room, then the suite. The hallway was, thankfully, empty, but then he was the only early riser in the band. Unless there was a damn good reason, they'd all be abed until breakfast was delivered somewhere around ten or eleven.

Brent found his keycard in his pants and let himself into his own suite. He was still sleepy but knew that lying down wouldn't help. He'd just toss and turn and think, and thinking right now wasn't a good idea. He might think of what he'd done, of how good Hell had felt. He might wonder what would have happened if he'd stayed in Hell's suite until the imp woke. Nah, best not to think of that. That could only lead to disappointment.

Yawning, he made use of the bathroom, discarded his clothes from the previous night, and changed into a pair of swim trunks. He pulled on a soft robe and stuck his feet into some battered tennis shoes. Per instruction, he called the courtesy desk and asked them if the pool was free. Tyler had already instructed the staff that Brent was to be allowed into the enclosed pool area even though it was outside normal hours.

Grabbing a towel, he went to catch the elevator to the proper floor.

A few hours later, Theo woke him from a nap when he arrived with breakfast. After his swim, Brent had returned to the room pleasantly tired from his exertions and had promptly fallen asleep in front of the television.

Theo rolled the cart closer to the couch. "So, did you get lucky last night?"

Brent froze mid-yawn, eyes on his aide. "Huh?"

Theo grinned. "Kick ass performance and all. I was wondering if I'd be walking in on something."

He's just guessing. Besides, if Brent had been with company, he would have put the sign on the door, and Theo knew it. Brent yawned again, sitting up. The robe he still wore fell off one shoulder, and he pulled it back. "Nosy. What about you?"

"Hey, I'm not the rockstar."

"Yeah, but you get the residuals."

Theo laughed. "That I do."

Brent smiled, edging forward as Theo put a covered plate on the table before him. The scents of omelet and bacon assaulted him as the cover was lifted. "So? You get lucky?"

"I did."

"Tell me."

"Ha! If you're not telling, neither am I."

Brent unrolled the silverware from the napkin, wondering. He *could* tell Theo. The man was one of the few who'd known about him and Luc, and as far as Brent knew, he'd never breathed a word. But Brent hadn't decided who he wanted to let know about what happened. He was trying not to panic wondering if Hell had told anyone. Of course, it was only ten o'clock. The imp probably wasn't even up yet.

Theo set the last of the plates and baskets on the table. He picked up the carafe of coffee and poured a cup. "Okay, I'll leave you to eat. You're due at a photo shoot at three. Sound check's at seven."

Brent nodded, continuing to eat. Five hours before he'd have to see the imp. Maybe he could manage to talk to Luc before then. That is, if his friend wasn't wrapped around Reese. *Oh, yeah, that's likely.*

Theo reached into the second tray of the cart and pulled out a newspaper and a pack of cigarettes. He set them both on the end of the table, within arm's reach. "You need anything else?" he asked, turning to fetch the ashtray from a side table.

"No."

Theo set the ashtray down, then disappeared for a moment into the next room. He reappeared with a frown. "Where are your glasses?"

"Huh?"

He set Brent's Zippo in the empty ashtray. "Your glasses. I found your lighter in your pants, but your glasses weren't there."

Brent tipped his face to look into Theo's curious blue eyes. His own widened, and his mouth fell open slightly.

Theo grinned slowly. "You left them in someone's bedroom."

Brent shut his eyes and his mouth. "Shit."

"Geez, Brent, that's two pair in one day." Theo laughed. "Want me to go get them?"

"No. Just... Shit. Just get me another pair."

Theo stood there, his grin fading a bit. "Seriously, Brent, you know you can trust me. I'll go get them and won't say a word."

Brent swallowed and avoided Theo's gaze. "I know that. But .. just get me a new pair."

Theo snickered. "Okay, man. I'll get another five, just in case."

"Fucker."

The snicker turned back into a laugh. "*I* didn't leave my glasses in someone else's bedroom last night." He turned and headed for the door. "Try not to go blind before I get back."

"You'll have them for the photo shoot, right?"

"Of *course* I will. Later, man." The door clicked shut.

Brent sank back on the couch, hand over his eyes. He'd left his sunglasses in Hell's room. How had he forgotten? He *never* forgot his glasses!

More importantly, how was he going to get them back? He hadn't quite worked out what he was going to say to Hell yet. Knocking on the imp's door to ask for his glasses, then beating a hasty retreat probably wouldn't go over well. Maybe he'd just let the imp keep them.

Maybe he was a coward.

Maybe he was just at a loss.

He sighed. Maybe he should just eat his breakfast and worry about it when it happened.

It was noon, and he still hadn't figured anything out. Twice he'd almost gotten up to go down the hall to Hell's room, but had stopped himself. He was pretty sure the imp was due for an interview earlier today. He might already be gone.

He sat on the couch, still watching television. The robe was gone, and he now wore jeans and a worn and faded David Bowie t-shirt. Bare feet were propped on the coffee table, and his acoustic guitar was cradled in his lap, his fingers idly trailing over the strings. He thought better when he had a guitar in his hands, but this time it wasn't helping.

When a knock sounded at the door, he put aside the guitar and got up to answer it. He figured it was Gretchen or one of her people checking up on him. Or housekeeping seeing if he needed something. Theo couldn't possibly be back yet, and he had a keycard to let himself in. Didn't housekeeping usually announce themselves?

Brent didn't expect to see the imp on the other side of the door.

Hell looked delicious. Today he wore a huge, ice-blue button-down shirt, the hem of which almost hit the faded knees of his dark jeans. His hair was glossy and curling around his round face. Shocked, Brent realized that for the first time he was seeing Hell completely sans makeup. The eyebrows were still purple, of course, but the lashes were nearly white, and no dark liner outlined Hell's eyes. He looked so very young and shining.

The glint in his eyes, however, was pure evil.

He grinned up into Brent's shocked face and lifted a hand. Brent's sunglasses dangled from his fingers.

Brent glanced down the hall to verify that it was empty. It was.

But his distraction gave Hell a chance to plant his hand on Brent's chest and shove him backward.

"Hey!" Brent almost caught himself, but Hell leaned into him, shoving him farther into the room and up against a wall as the door slowly shut itself. "What are you --?"

Words cut off when Hell grabbed his shoulders and yanked him forward, sealing their mouths.

Brent knew he should pull away. This wa a perfect opportunity to get a few things straight. But, oh, God! Hell felt good. All warm and soft and hungry and smelling wonderfully fresh. Brent's hands splayed out over his sides, then slid down to his hips when Hell groaned and pushed closer.

Brent was stunned when Hell pulled his lips away. The keyboardist's long fingers braced on Brent's chin, halting him from resealing their lips.

Hell smiled, lips shiny from their kiss instead of lip gloss. "I missed you this morning."

Brent swallowed, remembering where he was. He couldn't quite make himself part from Hell's embrace, but they needed to talk. "Yeah, uh, about that…"

Hell shook his head. "*Nein*.. There is no 'about.'" He brought both hands up and, grinning, propped Brent's glasses up on top of his head. "I will say nothing to anyone, if that is what you want, but I *did* enjoy last night. I hope that you did, too?"

Brent nodded.

Hell twirled a lock of Brent's black hair around one finger, staring deep into his eyes. Those gemstones glittered. "Let's do it again."

"Wait, no --"

Long fingers shoved into Brent's hair, then hauled him down into another searing kiss.

Brent moaned as he pitched forward, his hands gripping Hell's waist in an effort to keep them both upright.

Unconcerned, Hell held his face and ate at his mouth, sucking trembling moans from Brent's chest. Then one hand dropped down to the buttons of Brent's relaxed jeans, popped open the fly, and reached in to cup the urgent flesh within.

"God, Hell," Brent groaned, pushing his hips into that beautiful massage. His head fell forward, bracing on Hell's shoulder. "Don't you -- ah! -- have an interview or something?"

"No. I have nothing to do but you," Hell murmured into his ear, the fingers of his other hand massaging Brent's neck. "So good. So sexy. I want you so much."

Brent squeezed his eyes shut as Hell's hand shifted to delve into his briefs. Rumbling pleasure overrode any protest that might have been in his head.

Hell's thumb passed over the slit of his cock, gently probing.

Brent turned his face into Hell's neck, latching onto the skin. Sucking. Biting.

Hell groaned, the fingers in Brent's hair tightening on his scalp. "Ah, come. Come with me."

Brent followed the solid heat of Hell's delectable little body farther into the room. He didn't protest when Hell pushed him down onto the couch. Lost in the moment, he eagerly helped Hell with getting him out of his jeans and briefs, then nearly came out of his skin when the imp pounced and gulped down his cock.

He groaned, sinking his fingers into the silk of Hell's hair as that hot, wet mouth drove him crazy. No teasing this time. Hell was intent on bringing him off, and Brent couldn't find fault with that. Or, at least, he seemed intent on that. But when that gorgeous tingle started in Brent's balls, making his body shake, Hell gripped the base of his shaft hard. Brent came, but there was no release.

"What the hell?" he complained breathlessly.

Hell's wet, swollen mouth grinned as he reared up, revealing that his shirt and jeans were now opened and the resourceful little minx had already sheathed his cock with a condom and slathered it with lube. "I like when you come with me inside you."

Brent licked his lips, eyes caught on the hard-on Hell displayed for him. "Oh, yeah."

Hell laughed when Brent caught up one of his own legs and bent it back "Are you a slut, *Süsser?*" He inched up into place between Brent's thighs.

Brent snorted, grabbing Hell's hips with his free hand to urge him closer. "Hardly."

Hell shook his head, that dark purple braid sliding down over his shoulder as he leaned forward. The soft end trailed over Brent's belly. "But you do like this, don't you?" he murmured, pushing the slicked head of his cock into Brent's body. "God," he groaned, pushing forward slowly into Brent.

Brent didn't answer. Didn't care to try and keep up with the conversation. Words were meaningless when the imp's cock was filling him up so wonderfully. He tried to keep his eyes open, captivated by the gorgeous look on Hell's face, a combination of agonizing pleasure and sublime relief. The imp's eyes fairly glittered as they locked on his under slumberous lids, Hell's smile one of triumph. But the dark, burning heat of that brand sinking into his body forced Brent to close his eyes, the better to feel every thick inch as it dragged through his inner walls.

Hell ground in once he was fully seated, his balls slightly slapping Brent's ass. His hands sank down on the couch under Brent's arms, and his belly gently pushed underneath Brent's balls.

So deep. Brent reached above his head to clutch the arm of the couch, needing to claw at something while a storm built inside. "God, Hell, move," he demanded. "Fuck me. Fuck me hard."

Hell groaned and obeyed, pulling out and shoving back with more force.

They grunted and moaned. Brent wrapped his legs around the imp's slim hips, pulling him as deep as he could. It lasted forever, glorious, beautiful friction.

Brent reached down to pump his own cock while Hell shoved inside him again and again. He didn't last long. It was too damn good. With a cry, he came, spattering both belly and Bowie shirt. He clamped down hard on Hell as he came and wrung Hell's orgasm out of him.

Hell stayed braced over Brent, breathing hard, the open lapels of his shirt shrouding their bodies. He stared at Brent as they caught their breath. "Don't say we have to stop, *Süsser*," he said finally. "This" -- he nudged his hips forward, pushing his softening cock farther into Brent -- "is too good."

Brent swallowed. "It's just sex." He groaned as Hell slowly pulled out. "We can't let this affect the band."

Hell nodded, pushing back to his knees. "Agreed."

Brent adjusted back to sit against the arm of the couch while Hell removed the condom and tied it off. He licked his lips as Hell leaned back to deposit it into the wastebasket between the couch and the wall.

Should they really do this? He still didn't think it was a very good idea.

But when Hell crawled forward to place those delectable lips on his again, he had trouble recalling why exactly.

Chapter Nine

"It simply isn't fair."

Brent switched his attention from the hi-def television mounted on the wall showing the video game Johnnie and Hell were playing to Ellen, Darien, and Theo, who stood right behind the couch on which he sat.

"What's that?" Darien asked.

Ellen pouted, looking over the gathering of roughly thirty people. "Look at this. The men outnumber the women here at least three to one, but over half of them are looking at the other *men!*"

Theo and Darien laughed, along with a few others who were within earshot, Brent included.

Darien put an arm around her shoulders, pulling her into a consolatory embrace. She was a tiny thing and just fit just underneath his chin. "Aww, sorry, sweetheart If it's any consolation, I'm not."

Smiling through her pout, Ellen cuddled in close to him, winding her arms around his waist. "You're a sweetie, Darien. I knew that."

Theo caught Brent watching and rolled his eyes, smiling.

Brent matched the smile and turned away. Her statement was funny, but it was also true. Somewhere in the last year or so, the band's hangers-on had taken a distinct trend toward the masculine. Brent blamed Johnnie, for not only getting the other members of the band curious, but also for so spectacularly hooking up with Tyler.

Not that Brent could fault him. Brent turned his attention to the blond, who stood with a few others in the corner, talking. Tyler was, without doubt, a gorgeous man. Also, without Johnnie's influence, Brent doubted he or Luc would have so easily accepted their own homosexual tendencies.

Speaking of which...

Brent turned around on the couch, settling back into a deep slouch with a bottle of beer propped with both hands on his belly as he watched Hell and Johnnie battle in some futuristic, fantasy fighting game. He couldn't have told you the name of it if he tried, but Johnnie had been jazzed to find that Hell could play. He'd claimed to have not found his match yet, which had made Tyler snort in offense. So Johnnie and Hell sat on the floor between the couch and the wall where the huge television was mounted.

Hell looked like a child, so small next to Johnnie. He even had his tongue peeking out between those full lips, biting it as he concentrated. *How cute is that?* Those long, talented fingers were wrapped around the game controller, and Brent let his mind happily wander to vivid recollections of those fingers wrapped around his cock, pulling pleasure out of him as surely as had that wet mouth and the tongue that was currently being bit.

Brent wrapped his own hand around the neck of his beer bottle and brought it to his lips, visions of sinking his fingers into the imp's soft curls while the imp sank balls deep into his ass dancing through his head.

Around him, the casual, impromptu pizza party continued. Luc and Reese had graciously accepted having guests for this last night of the week that the band would spend in the Weiss Strande East. The next day, they would hop on a plane to Los Angeles to film the second part of the video.

Deciding he'd watched enough of Johnnie and Hell duke it out, Brent got up to head toward the table to see if there was pizza left. He wondered how much longer he'd have to stay. Then he wondered if he could lure Hell back to his room afterward. Or duck into Hell's room. So far, they'd spent every night since the first together. Brent's ass was quite happily sore, and his cock had never been more ready nor more sated, a strange juxtaposition, but he was enjoying it.

He'd just snagged a piece of pepperoni pizza when someone grabbed his arm. He shoved a bite into his mouth as he turned to see Reese, who was pulling him into the deserted bedroom. He chewed and swallowed thoughtfully when they got there, watching Reese drop his wrist and turn to face him. His blue-tinged black hair made for odd shadows in the half-lit room.

"Okay, Luc and I have a bet going. He *says* he doesn't know for sure." Reese glanced over Brent's shoulder.

Brent glanced back to see Luc coming through the door, fingers tucked in the front pockets of his jeans. Casually, he flipped on the overhead light, meeting Brent's curious look with a smirk.

"Are you sleeping with Hell?"

Reese's words got Brent to turn back to face him, eyes open wide. He also stopped chewing in shock.

Luc laughed.

Reese scowled. "Well?"

Brent swallowed and twisted his neck to look at Luc, who now leaned against the heavy wooden armoire at the foot of the bed. "How did you find out?"

Reese hissed, slapping his hands on his thighs, which only made Luc laugh again.

"You knew," Reese accused, pointing at his lover.

Luc shook his head. "I didn't." He smirked at Brent. "I guessed."

Brent flushed, shoving another bite of pizza into his mouth. "When'd you guess?" he asked around the mouthful.

"At Sunday night's performance. You two were acting strange, and you" -- he grinned and cocked his head -- "were walking funny." He laughed, and Brent felt the blush on his face that prompted it. "If I had to take a guess, I'd say something happened after the performance Saturday night." When Brent winced, he chuckled. "And it looks like my guess is right."

"Damn it," Reese grumbled, dropping to sit on the edge of the neatly made bed.

Luc cast a fond look on his lover. "I told you, tiger, don't test me where Brent's concerned. I know him too well."

"Yeah, yeah." Reese pointed a mildly accusing look at Brent. "I just didn't think you'd sleep with another member of the band."

Brent blinked and turned quickly away from Reese, keeping his face averted from both of them. "Yeah, well." He took another bite of pizza.

"Oh, hey, I'm sorry, Brent. It's not that you *can't*, of course." Reese grinned at him, leaning forward eagerly. "I think it's great that you and Hell are together."

Brent glanced anxiously toward the door, flapping his free hand at Reese. "Hey, keep it down." The music from the other room wasn't up all that loud, so he wasn't sure if anyone just outside the door could hear.

Reese frowned. "Is it a secret?"

"He hasn't told anyone, tiger," Luc reminded Reese gently.

"Uh, yeah. Right." Big blue eyes tossed the question at Brent. "Why not?"

Brent shrugged, then glanced toward the door again. "It's just sex. There's nothing to tell." He looked up, pizza poised at his lips, just in time to see them exchange a look. "What?"

Luc returned his look calmly. "Nothing."

He tore a bite of pizza. "Well, it is." To drive home his point, Brent put on a wolfish smile. "It's awfully good sex."

Luc grinned at him, but it seemed a bit placating. "About damn time you got laid."

Brent sneered and flipped Luc off. "Anyway, it's no one else's business but ours."

"As long as you two are happy with it," Luc said.

Brent met his gaze. He was happy. For now. Until Hell was done with him. But he didn't have to think about that right now. "Yeah."

"So?!" Reese actually bounced on the edge of the bed. "Tell! How'd it happen?"

Brent gaped at him. "Jesus, are you a twelve-year-old girl, too?"

Reese's mouth fell open in shock, and Luc doubled over in laughter.

Brent was about to take pity on Reese and explain when a commotion in the other room lured all three of them to the doorway. Just about everyone was ringed around the couch, watching Hell dancing like a football player who'd just made a touchdown. Which was a funny sight considering he wore a big indigo jacket that fit kind of like a dress and snug white pants that fit like tights. His hair flailed around like one of the Muppets. Johnnie was on his butt on the floor, back against the couch, staring in disbelief at the television screen.

Tyler rushed up, looked at his spouse, looked at the television, then at Hell, then broke into a belly laugh. "Oh, my God! Did he beat you?"

Johnnie glared up at Tyler. "Shut it, Blondie."

Which only made Tyler laugh harder.

Hell hooted, dropping the controller and skipping away when Johnnie made a grab for his legs.

"You get back here!" Johnnie ordered, getting up on his hands and knees.

"Oh, no. I will enjoy my victory."

"Once! You beat me once!"

"Once is enough."

He danced over to Tyler's side, and the blond readily held up his hand for a high-five. Johnnie was not amused.

Hell spun and spied Brent at the bedroom door with Luc and Reese. Beaming, he trotted over. All three of them obediently high-fived him and congratulated him, and if Hell held Brent's hand just a touch longer than the others, probably only Luc and Reese would notice.

"We're going to have a rematch, Hellion!" Johnnie called after him. Brent had seen the consolatory kiss Tyler gave him, so Johnnie sounded a lot angrier than he surely was. And anyway, Johnnie just didn't stay angry. Not about things like this, even if he did take his video games seriously.

Hell chuckled, turning back to Johnnie. "Indeed. That is why I will enjoy this night. In fact" -- he struck a dramatic pose, one hand splayed over his chest and the other raised like a Shakespearean actor's -- "I believe I will call it a night."

"Oh, please," Johnnie grumped, pushing to his feet and heading for the food table.

Everyone laughed; some bid Hell a good night and more congratulations, then generally turned back to their own conversations.

Laughing, Hell bowed, then straightened, turning to face the three in the doorway. He smiled big at Luc and Reese. "Good night."

Brent heard them both murmur replies, but he lost interest in anything they had to say when those purple eyes landed on him. Hell's smile twisted just that little bit into the demon grin. Promise was in those eyes Nothing anyone who didn't know could decipher, but it was there. "Good night."

Brent nodded, glancing over Hell's shoulder. No one but Luc and Reese were paying any attention. "I think I'll turn in, too." He very carefully didn't look at Luc, knowing there was a smirk there. He didn't care. Hell was leaving, so there were far better reasons to leave than to stay.

No one batted an eye as Hell and Brent walked out together. Why should they? Just two guys who left the party at the same time. Both of their rooms were just down the hall, after all, and the band was leaving at around noon the next morning.

He followed Hell through the door into the deserted hallway. He watched the sway of that purple braid as Hell headed for his own doorway without looking back. He knew what he needed to do. He'd learned the key. After one night where he'd been afraid Hell didn't want him, he'd tried something and it had worked. Beautifully.

Hell still didn't look back. He dug in the pocket of his jacket/dress and brought out his key card. Brent waited until he was at the door before reaching out to nab that braid. Hell's head fell back at the slight tug, but he didn't turn around..

Brent crowded in, pressing against his back while wrapping the braid around his hand twice. He leaned in over Hell's shoulder, putting his lips close to the imp's ear. "Please."

The imp's head turned partway, enough that Brent could see the eyes shadowed by long bangs and the tilt of the smile. "Come in."

The door snicked open, but Brent didn't see it. His face was buried in the sweet curve of Hell's neck, his lips open and his tongue out to taste that gorgeous, pale skin. He followed Hell blindly into the room, one hand still wrapped in Hell's braid and the other sneaking around his chest. He spread his fingers out on Hell's belly and brought the imp up short when they were fully inside the room, plastering the man's back against his groin so Hell could feel his growing erection.

Hell hummed happily, reaching back to insinuate a hand between them and cup Brent's crotch. He also tilted his head to give Brent more access to his neck. "All for me?"

"All for you," Brent assured him, nipping at his neck.

"Don't mark me there, *Süsser*," Hell purred. "We have filming the day after next."

Brent did some humming of his own, raising his fingers to start unbuttoning Hell's jacket. "How about marks in places no one will see?"

"But we'll be nearly naked in the video."

Brent groaned, taken partially out of his sensual haze by the thought of what they were going to do for the video. "Don't remind me."

Laughing, Hell turned in his arms. The hand Brent had in his braid stayed at his back, wrapping the arm around Hell's side. "But I'm looking forward to it," Hell purred, tilting his head up for a short, warm kiss. Both of their hands worked at the buttons of Hell's jacket now. "I want to see you naked and wet."

Brent chuckled, sliding his hand inside the now open jacket and up the warm, hairless skin of Hell's chest. "You've seen me naked and wet."

Hell's hands eagerly untucked Brent's t-shirt. "Yes. But this way I'll have it on film for all time."

"You make it sound kinky."

Hell just laughed low in his throat and pulled Brent in for an involved kiss.

Brent pressed in, hovering over his diminutive lover. The man seemed so delicate, but there was nothing fragile about the hands that yanked open Brent's pants nor the fingers that delved in to find his cock. He groaned, sucking in Hell's tongue as the imp tugged on him, making him crazy.

"Hell," he moaned, wetly releasing the imp's tongue.

"Mmm?"

"Fuck me."

"I thought you'd never ask."

Hell grabbed a handful of Brent's t-shirt and turned, hauling the taller man into the bedroom. Brent went willingly, skin alive with anticipation. The imp let him go once they were in the room, stepping forward so he could slip out of the deep indigo jacket/dress. He glanced over his shoulder at Brent. "Strip."

Grinning, Brent hastened to obey. So far in the times they'd been together, he'd always managed to get his clothes off faster than his lover. Of course, he cared far less about his clothes. Hell's outfits were all very carefully thought out, and much of the clothing was custom made. This was due both to his size as well as his tastes, no doubt Brent, on the other hand, was a jeans and t-shirt man. The only times he dressed up were when someone dressed him up. So, Brent crawled naked onto the ivory sheets of the bed before Hell even had his pants off. He watched Hell practically roll the tight clothing off his slim legs.

"Wait. Please," he said, when Hell's fingers went to the thong.

Hell grinned, eyes at half-mast. "Yes."

Brent crawled to the foot of the bed and dropped to his belly, reaching out with greedy hands. "Let me."

Chuckling, Hell sauntered over until he stood before Brent. The bed was one of those high ones, the top fully three feet off the ground, so their positions were just right to put Brent's mouth in line with Hell's crotch.

Brent slid his hands up the soft, nearly invisible down on Hell's thighs, then back to cup his silky buttocks. He pulled the imp closer until the hot pouch of the thong pressed into his face.

Hell sighed, fingers settling lightly on Brent's head.

Brent mouthed Hell's cock through the thick satin, wetting it with his tongue and breathing heavily through it so the heat would further stir Hell's excitement. A tensing of the fingers in his hair was his reward. He lapped at the satin until it was quite wet, even tasting a small bit of pre-cum, then used his teeth to squeeze the shaft just so.

Hell groaned.

Happy with himself, Brent threaded his fingers in the straps of the thong and very carefully pulled it down, releasing his prize. He deliberately didn't touch until he'd gotten the thong down to Hell's knees, then brought his hands back up to brace on Hell's hips.

He looked up.

Hell's eyes were deep indigo pools under the pastel mop of hair, focused on him. Smiling, he wound his fingers in Brent's hair and nudged him close.

Matching the smile, Brent opened wide and let Hell pull his head up the shaft to the tip, then let the imp push deep into his mouth.

They both groaned. *So good.* Hell tasted so good. Brent clutched those slim hips, helping to guide that gorgeous shaft farther into his mouth. He swallowed around the head, using his tongue to caress the velvety skin on the underside. Hell pulled away, and Brent just let his tasty treat slide over his tongue, making sure to suck hard so that its owner knew he wanted it back. His message was received, because Hell did push back in. A glance up at the imp showed those eyes now mostly closed and his mouth slack with pleasure. Brent hummed, happy to be the cause of that look.

Hell fucked his face for a few glorious moments, but Brent could tell that he was going to pull out. After their second night together, they had decided to trust that they were each clean, and Brent had gotten to swallow Hell down. He loved it and was happy to do it again, but Brent knew now that if Hell was intent on coming in his mouth, he'd let himself go. He was holding back this time. Which meant he intended to have Brent's ass.

Brent was not complaining.

Sure enough, after a few ragged hip snaps, Hell hauled Brent's head up and away. Brent opened his mouth for the kiss that the imp bent forward to slam onto his lips.

"Stay there," Hell ordered when he tore from the kiss.

Brent wouldn't have moved for the world. He let his hands dangle over the foot of the bed as he watched Hell head for the bag that sat on the nightstand. In a moment, the lube was out and Hell was climbing up on the bed behind him.

"Do you want me, *Süsser?*"

Stupid question, but he now knew that Hell liked to hear the answer. "Yes."

He knew because it made Hell purr, and it prompted exciting, gorgeous caresses like the one Hell bestowed on his back. "So beautiful," he heard Hell murmur as the imp leaned in to kiss the small of Brent's back. Brent didn't bother to correct him as those sweet lips trailed down to kiss and nip each globe of his ass.

The lube top popped. Brent sighed happily, resting his forehead on his forearms. He lifted his hips with Hell's guidance and spread his legs.

Hell, blessed little angel that he was, didn't bother with fingers and didn't have to bother with condoms anymore. He pressed the slick head of his cock at Brent's opening and pushed slowly.

Brent groaned, loving this. This was sex. This was what it was about. This was penetration with a bite of pain that blossomed into the most wonderful, dark sensation one could share with another person. Brutal little tingles shot up his spine, making him twitch, making him moan. "Oh, yeah." His stomach flipped and his cock jumped as Hell pushed into his body. He let his thighs slide even wider until his hips met the bed.

Hell sank forward, draping that hot, hard body over Brent's back.

Brent was torn. Part of him didn't want to move. This was perfect. This right here. He could stop time right here, right now, when he was happy and Hell wanted him. But he couldn't stop. He had to move. Had to feel that delicious friction in his ass. Had to make Hell swell and push. Had to make the imp crazy so that he'd throw every bit of strength in that little body into fucking Brent into the mattress. He could do it, too. Brent knew it, and wanted it again.

"Fuck me," he moaned, clutching the edge of the bed. "Do it, Hell."

Long-fingered hands braced on the back of Brent's shoulders. The imp positioned himself and pulled out. Then slammed back home, enough to make Brent want to arch his back. He tried, but Hell's weight kept him prone.

Hell did it again. And again. Slowly. Precisely. Driving Brent nuts as he found an angle that hit Brent's gland. Brent released the garbled scream he hoped Hell was waiting for.

"Oh, fuck, yeah, more," Brent begged as Hell picked up speed. "Ah, God, yes, fuck. Shit. Damn it! Fuck!" He had no idea what he was saying and was quite sure neither of them cared. The sound was important. Hell wanted to know Brent loved it, and Brent was more than willing to voice it if it meant that Hell wouldn't stop. "More, yes!"

He shut up when Hell fell forward, one hand sliding up the light sheen of sweat on Brent's back to sink three fingers into his mouth. Eagerly, Brent sucked them in.

The guttural German muttered into his spine set Brent to bucking underneath Hell, slamming himself up when Hell drove forward. Hell was close. So close. *Fuck yeah!*

He lost it. Crying out around Hell's fingers, he felt his balls clutch and he spurted onto the duvet beneath him.

Hell gasped. Cursed. Hips snapping as he pushed his own orgasm deep into Brent's body.

Hell collapsed on his back, heavy breathing cooling the sweat on Brent's skin.

Smiling, Brent brought his forearms up to cushion his own head, happy to play mattress for Hell for a while. Knowing there was probably a round two coming.

Yeah. This he could get used to.

For as long as it lasted.

Chapter Ten

"Is it good? The sex?" Luc asked.

Brent's eyes instinctively shuttered as sense memory filled his flesh with phantom caresses. "Yeah."

Luc leaned on the dusty railing and stared out over the studio parking lot. In the distance, the hills were barely visible through the oppressive smog. "Did you say anything like 'I love you'?"

"No."

"Then what's the problem?"

Brent took a drag on his cigarette, thinking. "What does he want with me?"

"Maybe a good fuck or twelve?"

"Yeah, but --"

Luc sighed, a frustrated sound. "Jesus, Brent, I've known you most of my life, and I still don't get how you can think you're not worth anyone's attention." He flicked the butt of his cigarette to the pavement below.

Brent scowled. "It's not that."

"It *is* that. You're going to think a possibly good thing out of existence, you know."

"I don't get it. He's gorgeous. He can get anyone."

"And he wants you. You're not such a bad catch, y'know."

Brent made no comment, watching a couple of finches investigate a scrap of paper.

Luc sighed and stood up, adjusting the robe that he wore over his bare torso. There was a flash of his tiny blue swim trunks before he retied the belt that had fallen loose while they were leaning on the balcony rail. "As long as you don't go making any promises and the both of you know what's what, I don't see the harm in the two of you fucking. But if you think it's going to be a problem, then you should stop it."

Brent flicked his spent Camel onto the pavement below the railing and stood, readjusting his own robe. He stared up at the waning sunlight, knowing it seemed even darker to him thanks to the shades. Say what you like about California smog, it did make for colorful sunsets sometimes. "I'm not sure he'll let me stop it."

That got Luc's attention. He stopped mid-turn and spun to face Brent again, frowning. "What?"

Brent cast a glance toward the thick, closed door that led back into the studio. "I don't get the feeling that he'd accept it."

Luc raised a brow. "Have you tried?"

Brent scowled, shoving his hands deep into the pockets of the deep-blue robe. "Sorta."

"'Sorta'?"

Brent pushed a burst of air past his lips. "Okay, not really. But what am I supposed to say? I like being with him. I just don't think we should be together so much."

"You're overthinking."

"And what else is new?"

Luc leaned back against the railing, arms crossed. "How about you say just that? That you think you two shouldn't be together so much?"

Brent stared at an abandoned plastic bag fluttering on the ground near the wall. "And then it stops."

"What if it doesn't?"

"It always does."

"And you don't want it to stop."

"Did I mention that the sex is *really* good?"

Luc chuckled. "It's only been two weeks. If the sex is as good as you say, then no wonder he wouldn't let you go."

Brent nodded. It had actually been a little over two weeks, but he wasn't going to quibble.

Luc reached over to squeeze his shoulder. "You think it's dangerous?"

"Huh?"

"You think he's a psycho killer or something?"

"No. Nothing like that."

"You sure?"

"About that, yeah." Brent shrugged. "He's just...intense."

"Then just go with the flow. As long as you both know the score, who does it hurt?"

Me, when he decides he's done with me. He sighed, combing a hand through his hair. "Yeah, who am I kidding? For sex that amazing, I should just go with it."

"That's the spirit." Luc pulled a pack of Camels from his pocket, then shook his head and put them back. "I'm going inside"

Brent moved to follow him. "Yeah."

Keeping his hands in his pockets while they headed for the door, he cocked his head at Brent. "I thought you didn't like topping."

Brent flushed. "I'm not."

Luc stopped. "Whoa! You're kidding? The cherub is a top?"

"God, don't call him cherub." He squeezed his eyes shut and shook his head.

Luc chuckled, throwing an arm around Brent's shoulders. "I wouldn't worry about it, man. Maybe he really does like you." He snorted as he walked them both toward the studio. "Or he's amazed to find anyone taller than him that'll let him top."

Brent elbowed Luc in the gut as they walked through the door, but that only made Luc laugh harder.

They entered the huge studio. Two-thirds of the wide-open space was crammed with technical equipment, including at least five cameras and countless lights and monitors as well as things that Brent never had figured out a use for. The other third was the set.

It was a miniature waterfall. There wasn't even a top to it. The faux stone and moss of the background went up about fifteen feet and stopped, and right about there was a huge, ugly contraption that would pour or dribble water on cue. Catching the water was a twelve-foot-wide basin made up to look like a deep, gorgeous pond.

Brent had soundly disagreed with this part of the video concept, but he'd been overruled thanks to something that Johnnie and Todd, the director, kept calling "fan service." At some point during the day, all five members of the band would get their turn standing beneath the water, looking as naked as possible. Johnnie and Darien had already had their first of what was supposed to be three turns each in the pool. They had been sent on their way to dry up for their second turns while Hell, Luc, and Brent had their first.

He hated this crap.

Although, at this particular moment, the concept had a perk. Hell was currently taking his turn in the pool. Or, rather, was standing up to his waist in water, waiting to be drenched. All around him, the camera crew crawled like bugs around the set, getting everything ready.

Hell had his long hand shading his eyes from the ultrabright lights, staring toward the main camera and Todd. The gold that normally adorned Hell's hand -- a slave bracelet, Brent had finally found out the name -- was there, together with another inch of gold bangles about his wrist. Two gold necklaces gleamed around the pale column of his throat, and one of the makeup crew was standing in the water beside him, arranging his purple braid so it draped over his shoulder and bisected his chest.

"He's beyond cute," Luc murmured in Brent's ear, his arm still companionably around Brent's shoulders.

Captivated by the sight of his lover, Brent could only nod.

Hell turned his head, and there was no doubt that his shaded eyes caught sight of Brent and Luc. His pink lips fell open slightly, then pressed together in a small grimace. But it was brief. Just as Brent noted it, Todd called the imp's attention.

Self-consciously, Brent shrugged out from under Luc's arm and wandered to the sidelines to watch. Technically, neither he nor Luc needed to be here. Well, not in the studio itself. There was a very nice waiting room just on the other side of one of the doors, where Darien was drying off and Johnnie was playing video games. There was another television, and they'd even been given the password for the building's wireless network. But Brent wanted to be here to see.

It didn't mean anything, or so he told himself. Well, anything more than that he happened to think Hell was one of the most gorgeous sights a body could watch and it would be a shame to miss him getting all wet.

"I'm going back inside," Luc said from somewhere behind his left shoulder.

Brent nodded, not bothering to look.

It was still a good ten minutes before anything happened on the set. Hell stood very patiently, speaking in low tones with the girl in the water with him. Then she got out, and two guys busied themselves with checking the lighting. Finally, all seemed done and Todd crouched on the bank of the small pond before Hell. Brent was too far away to hear everything they said, so he just watched Hell's big eyes as they fastened on Todd and he nodded at what was said. Todd stood and turned away, spouting directions at those around him.

Hell turned his head and caught sight of Brent. He smiled that smile that made Brent want to devour him, or let Hell devour him, he didn't care which.

"All right, Hell," Todd called from his director's chair. "You ready?"

Still smiling, Hell faced the camera. "Yes."

The music cranked up, nothing that would be put into the video itself, but the ambience seemed necessary. Hell's smile changed to that one of sweet, angelic innocence, and he reached up to cross his arms over his chest, each hand loosely gripping the opposite shoulder. It showed off both jewelry and slim limbs to great advantage just before the water carefully poured onto him. Enough to get him wet pretty quickly, but not so much that the onlooker couldn't get their fill of the liquid turning soft lavender hair to a deeper amethyst, sluicing through the hair and over his cherubic face before pouring onto his naked torso. Brent licked his lips, wanting to be that water, wrapping around that slim little body, caressing every curve and crevice. Not that he hadn't already done that with hands and tongue in a more private setting, but he craved to do it again and again.

And that, he could be honest with himself at least, was what scared him the most. As much as Hell insisted on being with him, he couldn't find it in his heart to truly disagree. He wanted the imp with him at all times, sleeping or waking, and didn't think the attachment was at all healthy.

Chapter Eleven

That night, the band, Gretchen, and her top assistants took over a private room at their hotel and started seriously discussing plans for touring.

As usual, Brent mostly sat on the sidelines. He listened dutifully and chimed in when asked, but he rarely put forth an opinion. What did he care where they played, as long as they played? Truthfully, he kind of liked playing in the little dive bars that they used to get booked in during their earlier days, and he really missed their ongoing run at Purgatory, but he wouldn't part with the ten-thousand-seat arenas, either. He'd given up participating in these discussions with the last tour, leaving the decisions ultimately to Johnnie, Luc, and Gretchen. They let him lead when it came to the music itself; he let them have their way -- mostly -- when it came to the band's persona.

Not surprisingly, Hell dove right in there with Luc and Johnnie. He didn't know the venues in the States very well and asked a ton of questions, but when they started discussing abroad, he knew the European and Asian markets better, despite the fact that Heaven Sent had toured there twice. Johnnie and Luc were impressed, and Gretchen positively devoured any and all information Hell gave her about venues or important people.

So Brent ate quietly, nodding when he was supposed to. Gretchen, Johnnie, Luc, and Hell did most of the talking. Ellen and another assistant took notes. Darien spoke up now and again, but usually just with a comment. Like Brent, he left these things to the others.

Brent and Hell left together. They hadn't even made the pretense of getting separate rooms this time. Not since hardly any of the media or fans knew they were in town. Gretchen had grilled them earlier about what she needed to know about their relationship. Brent had been relieved when Hell readily agreed that they should keep it low-key in the public eye for now.

Brent dropped onto the suite's couch to start taking off his boots. He had them off before he realized Hell was perched on the arm of the chair not three feet away from him, arms folded over his chest, legs crossed.

"What?"

Hell frowned, obviously not pleased with his own thoughts. Violet eyes snapped.

"What?"

"Why do you let him make all your decisions?"

Brent blinked. "What?"

"Luc. All through dinner, any decision that was yours to make, he made it; then you just agreed."

"He did?"

"You know it's true."

Uh-oh. When the German accent got thicker during sex, it was a good thing. But he had a bad feeling that outside of sex it wasn't so much. But he couldn't quite figure out what the problem was. He shrugged. "I leave all that stuff to Luc, Johnnie, and Gretchen. They're better at it."

Hell's foot started to bounce. He was still frowning.

Brent scooted down to the end of the couch, close enough so he could reach over and put his hand on Hell's bouncing knee. He felt the joint working underneath the thin, worn denim of Hell's faded jeans.

Gemstone eyes glanced down at his hand, then back up at his face.

"Seriously, Hell, that's how it's always worked. You've seen me with the press. You know I'm hopeless."

The imp's nostrils flared as he took a deep breath. "That's true."

Brent tried a smile. "You know it." He slid his hand farther up Hell's thigh, kneeling on the couch so he could lean closer.

Hell shook his head. His arms uncrossed, and he grabbed the trailing end of his braid, fiddling with it. "I just... You're always with Luc."

Brent snorted, leaning in even closer to nuzzle aside the loose collar of Hell's oversized button-down so he could get at the warm skin of his neck. "I think, lately, I'm always with you."

Hell tipped his head down, actually pouting. "When you're not with me, you're with him."

"He's my best friend. We've always been close."

"Especially when you were sleeping together."

Brent tensed. "I told you. That's over."

Hell slanted him a nasty glance. "Is it?"

What? The virtual wool over his eyes got swept away, and he stared in shock at Hell. Was he jealous? Were things at the point now where Hell was being proprietary? And over *Luc?* Miffed and not a little concerned, Brent sat back on his heels. "When do you think I had the time or energy to fuck Luc in the last two weeks?"

Hell's jaw worked. "I meant before."

"Yeah. It happened before, like a year ago, and now it's over. You didn't come into this a virgin either, y'know."

"Does Reese know?"

"No." Brent pushed to his feet. "And don't you tell him." He stalked across the room to the bedroom door.

"Why not?"

He slammed on the light and reached for his bag, throwing it on the bed. "Because Luc hasn't told him, and it's Luc's place to do it. Not yours and not mine."

"What are you doing?" Hell was in the doorway, clutching the frame with one hand.

"I'm outta here."

"What? Why?"

Good question But he was working on gut instinct here. Something was telling him to get out now, or things were going to get deep and harder to get out of later. "This has gotten out of hand." He headed for the bathroom for the toiletry bag he kept there.

"What?"

"You heard me."

"One little difference of opinion, and you're just going to leave?"

It wasn't just that. Hell was getting attached, and that just wouldn't do. If Brent let himself get similarly attached, he'd be a rotten mess when Hell finally came to his senses. He emerged from the bathroom and tossed a glare at Hell. "Fuck it. I'm not staying here with you when you think that I'm fucking someone else's boyfriend."

Hell glared back. "It's not a huge leap. You were fucking him."

"What part of 'in the past' is so hard for you to understand?" He threw the small bag into the big bag. He had to reach in to rearrange barely folded clothing to make it fit.

"Where will you stay?"

"I don't know. There's got to be other rooms in the hotel." He stood straight, hands on hips as he glared at Hell. "Or, hey! I know. I'll just go shack up with Luc. After all, Reese is still in New York, right?"

Hell snarled. "All right, all right. I was wrong. I'm sorry. It's just…"

"Forget it." Brent shook his head and bent back over his luggage.

Hell appeared at his side. He grabbed Brent's bag and shoved it to the other side of the bed, out of reach.

Brent glared down at the imp who scowled up at him. He turned.

Hell's hand whipped out to grab his arm, preventing him from stepping away. "Don't go. I said I was sorry." His cheeks were flushed. "I just...it's hard to watch you let him lead you like that."

"He wasn't leading me."

"He *was.*"

He slapped at Hell's hand to get him to let go, then turned toward the closet. "Fuck this."

"Brent --"

"No." He shoved open the closet to grab the three things he'd hung up. When he turned back around, Hell was kneeling on the bed, straddling his bag. "What the hell are you doing?"

"Stopping you from going."

"Get off of my bag."

"No."

"Hell..."

Hell knelt up when Brent reached the side of the bed. He snatched handfuls of Brent's shirt and held fast. Violet eyes glanced at him briefly, but couldn't hold his gaze. "I don't want you to go. I'm sorry. I'm jealous of the way you feel for Luc."

Clothing draped over his elbow, Brent reached up to clasp Hell's wrists. "You think?"

Hell held on. "Can you blame me? You and he are so close."

"We fucking grew up together, Hell. He's closer than family. You know that."

"I do know that. I do. I just..." He let his head fall forward, forehead thumping Brent's collarbone. Wisps of soft hair caressed Brent's chin. Warm lips brushed the skin exposed by the deep V of his t-shirt collar. "I want you so much. I go crazy thinking of anyone else who might have you."

Brent froze. Yeah, this was bad. Yes, Hell liked to play games during sex, and Brent was happy enough to play along, but the words hit him. Hard. Was this another game? Was this a child being possessive of his toy? A toy he'd discard once he found a shiny new one?

Those lips trailed little wet kisses up Brent's chest to the sensitive skin of his neck, just under his jaw. "Don't leave."

"You think I'm fucking Luc."

"No. I don't. I overreacted." The words drifted on warm breath over the wet trail Hell's tongue left on his neck. His little body edged closer, pressing as best he could against Brent. "I don't think you're fucking Luc. I know that's over."

"*Now* you know?"

"I knew before. I was angry. I was hurt. I want you all to myself."

"Hell --"

Sharp teeth bit gently on his earlobe. "I'm sorry, *Liebling*. I'm so sorry. Let me make it up to you."

Bad idea, he told himself. *Go with your first instinct. Leave.* Yeah. That's what he should do. Leave because this didn't feel right. This was a stronger attachment than just a sexual attraction. This was something Brent had never felt before. It felt *big*, and that equaled *scary* because he was going to get burned in the end. He always did. He should go.

But his body had other ideas. For the first time in…ever, he was getting fucked regularly. And well. For the first time, he was with someone who wanted him for him and wasn't sleeping with "the rockstar" or using him as a substitute or as available meat. Even if it wasn't going to last. Even if Hell was sure to find something better. Hell's body fit with his. Hell's hands knew him. Hell's mouth belonged on his skin. On his mouth. At least for a little while longer.

Like now. Hell's lips slanted over his, and those strong fingers slid up his neck and into his hair, holding him in place. His own hands had fallen from Hell's wrists and now rested on the waistband of his jeans. His fingers slid inside to tease the soft, warm flesh at the top of Hell's buttocks.

Hell caught him unaware and pulled. Squeaking into Hell's mouth, Brent fell forward, falling on Hell, who landed on his back on the mattress. The pants and shirt draped over Brent's arm crumbled into a pile at their sides.

Still holding his head, Hell let their faces part just enough so that he could suck and nip at Brent's lower lip. Brent kissed while trying to readjust his position so he wouldn't crush Hell.

"Perhaps you should fuck me, *Geliebter,*" Hell murmured. He bit Brent's lip. "Show me my place."

Brent's eyes opened wide. He couldn't help the shudder of delight that made his body tremble.

Hell smiled. "I was wrong. I need to be taught a lesson."

"But…" Yes, Brent liked bottoming, but he had nothing against topping every once in awhile. Hell's murmured suggestion poured like molten lava into his gut, enough to fill his cock inside his slacks.

"Yes. I want it. I want you. Inside me." Another kiss, enough to sear Brent's brain. "I want you. Please."

Please. The word that usually set Hell off turned out to have the same effect on Brent. At least when uttered by those supremely kissable lips.

He groaned and bent his head to properly take Hell's mouth in a kiss. The imp let him in, opening his mouth to Brent's tongue. Brent disentangled his arm from the loose clothing at their sides and scrambled to his knees, giving himself room to reach between their bodies and start on Hell's jeans.

Hell's hands came out of his hair to pull up Brent's t-shirt to his armpits, those strong fingers gliding down his chest and belly before they found and made quick work of the fastening of his slacks. Hell found Brent's cock at just about the same time that Brent finally managed to find Hell's, and they shared a breathless few moments of shuddering, mutual masturbation.

Then Hell splayed his free hand on Brent's chest and shoved him up. "Now. You need to fuck me now."

Brent grinned, a comment about pushy bottoms on his lips, but he didn't release it. Instead, he jumped back off the bed, the better to shuck his pants.

Hell wiggled out of his shirt, jeans, and shoes as Brent dropped his slacks and removed his t-shirt. He knelt naked on the bed as Hell arranged himself on his back in the middle of the mattress. A quick reach into the top drawer of the nightstand put lube in his hand.

Hell put his hand out, palm up, and Brent obediently poured a generous amount of liquid in it. He thought Hell meant to lube up his cock, but instead the imp's long fingers dropped down as his legs raised. With his dry hand, he cupped his balls out of the way for the wet fingers to dip down and push into his own hole.

Brent held his breath, entranced by one of the most erotic things he'd ever seen.

"Brent," Hell moaned, sliding another finger inside himself.

The sound helped Brent to move. Well, that and an insistent urge in his cock that it had to be touched. Had to be squeezed. Had to be wet down so that it could replace those fingers in that tiny little opening.

Hell had a third finger playing with the first two by the time Brent got in place. Obviously, bottoming was not new to him. Given his size and looks, that wasn't at all surprising.

Brent grabbed one knee and pulled the leg up against his chest.

Hell's fingers pulled from his anus and grabbed hold of Brent's cock.

With the imp doing the aiming, all Brent had to do was hold on to both slim legs and lean forward, letting gravity take him into the imp's greedy little hole.

"Ah, fuck! You're tight."

Hell's face was screwed up in a grimace. Whether pleasure or pain, Brent wasn't sure. "*Ja. Gott!*" Okay, that sounded like pleasure. "Tight. For you." Deep, German-accented pleasure. When Brent got deep enough that Hell had to let go his cock, his hands reached out and clutched Brent's hips, continuing to pull. "More."

Brent paused, panting, hilt-deep in the imp's body. "There isn't any more."

The fucking minx actually purred! He rolled that sexy little body, making Brent's eyes cross as the angle and the squeeze changed. His eyes snapped open, and the dim lighting made the violet eyes far darker and more seductive. His grin really should have shown fangs. "Fuck me."

He didn't have to say it. Brent couldn't have denied the rock of his hips if he'd tried. Deep, primal urges were upon him, and he could only hang on and ride the wave. He slid in and out of the heat of Hell's body, aware from the start that he just couldn't last too long. He met the imp's eyes, hoping it showed in his face. "Hell."

Hell just kept grinning. He released Brent's hips, grabbed his own cock with one hand, and rolled his balls with the other.

Brent groaned, and rocked, and fucked and...*oh, shit!* He cried out, arching back as heat poured from him into that hot little opening.

Spent, he kept upright just by leaning on Hell's legs. The imp bucked and writhed under him, chasing his own orgasm. Not knowing where he found the energy to move, Brent pulled out and dropped to his belly between Hell's thighs. The imp started to protest, but it cut off in a cry when Brent took the top of Hell's cock into his mouth. Brent wrapped his hand around the one Hell had on his dick, and they both pumped as Brent sucked. It didn't take long anyway. A few pumps, and Hell shattered, moaning Brent's name as he shot into Brent's mouth.

The imp sagged into a panting heap on the mattress. Brent had enough energy to crawl forward to lay his cheek on Hell's chest.

This was good. Earlier was weird, and he still didn't like what Hell had thought, but this right here? This was good.

Chapter Twelve

Music and heavy, wet sea air filled the resort room, carried along on the breeze that drifted through the open balcony doors. Brent let the susurrus of the waves outside underline the melody that followed his fingertips as they danced over the keys of Hell's Casio. He wished for the live beat of Darien's drums but made do with the electronic throb of the instrument's drum machine. The song was almost done, started in his head a few weeks ago and now actually heard for the first time by someone else.

Brent turned his head and watched the imp as he let go of the last few notes. Hell lay on his side on the bed, naked, his cheek resting on one arm. His gemstone eyes were mostly closed, matching the dreamy smile on his face. "That is beautiful, *Liebling*."

"Thanks." Brent let his own smile blossom as he reached out to hit the button that stopped the recording and saved it. Seemed fitting that the new song was saved on Hell's machine. He was the inspiration for it, after all. All the bright, laughing notes mixed into the slower melody were homage to Hell's laughter.

Not that he'd tell the imp that.

After two long months of smaller gigs in key cities across the country, Heaven Sent had split up for a month's hiatus. The hiatus was due to end next week when the band would meet up in New York again to start another round of smaller shows, working up to the real start of the world tour.

When Hell had suggested that the two of them spend the time alone, Brent had hedged. They'd been spending a lot of time together, and it was only a matter of time before Hell either got tired of him or started to think that they had more than just sex. Which they didn't. But Hell was a persistent little imp and had eventually convinced him. Unwilling to let go of the fun he was having with Hell, he'd pushed aside his worries and come with Hell to a posh Florida resort. Neither one of them had been there before, and it was known for catering to celebrities, so Brent didn't have to worry about the fan thing. If the press found out about it, well, that didn't much matter. There were already rumors going around about him and Hell, and it only seemed to be lending another layer to the band's popularity.

Switching off the Casio, Brent went to drop down on the bed beside Hell. He spread out on his belly, cheek cushioned on the backs of his hands. He closed his eyes and just listened to the sound of the ocean. He hadn't been this relaxed in years.

Hell's hand trailed down his naked back, sliding briefly over his buttocks. The bed jostled, and a moment later Hell's weight settled on top of him, chest to back, cheek between shoulder blades. For a long time, they just lay like that, with

Hell's hands gently drifting up and down Brent's sides and arms.

"Three months," Hell sighed.

Brent dragged his eyes opened and cast them sideways, but he couldn't see Hell from this vantage unless he actually shifted his cheek from atop his hands. "What?"

"Three months we have been together."

Brent swallowed and shut his eyes. "Hmm."

Hell's fingertips lightly scratched down his spine. "Even so, that is a long time."

Brent kept his eyes closed and avoided squirming. Some of that beautiful lassitude was draining from his limbs as Hell talked. Why was he bringing this up? They'd been so good about not talking about it. If they didn't talk about it, then things were okay.

He felt the jab of Hell's sharp little chin as the imp rolled his head, then the warm satin of his lips as he pressed a kiss to the back of one of Brent's shoulders. "Is that not a long time, *Liebling?* Haven't we been good together?"

Brent stared at the back of his own wrist. Had to nip this conversation in the bud. "Long time. Hey" -- he pushed up, lifting Hell and unseating him in the move -- "do we have any more of that cake?" He rolled aside and got off the bed.

There was no answer behind him, but he didn't dare look back. He left the suite's bedroom for the main room and went to the cart with the leftovers from their dinner. He knew very well it didn't have any more of the pound cake he referred to.

"Damn," he muttered, loud enough for Hell -- who he knew was behind him -- to hear. "Hey, how about I order some cake and ice cream?"

"Why do you do that?"

Brent picked up the phone and punched the room service button. "Do what?"

Hell glared at him from the bedroom doorway, refusing to speak while Brent was on the phone.

Brent missed talking for a moment, caught by the amazing beauty of the naked man in the suite with him. Small and compact, pale and gorgeous as a cream-and-purple rose, he looked so sweet and innocent, and he was really anything but.

"Sir?" came the voice over the phone.

"Oh, hey." He turned around to take the distracting sight of the imp away. "Can you send up some of that pound cake and ice cream? Vanilla." He finished his order, then turned back around, smiling. "They'll bring it right up."

Hell was still scowling, arms crossed as he leaned one shoulder against the doorjamb. "Why do you do that?"

"What? Order ice cream? Haven't you realized that I like ice cream yet?" Boldly, he stepped up to Hell and put his hands to either side of that gorgeous little face. "I like creamy things."

He pressed a soft kiss to those scowling lips, hoping against hope that Hell would let himself be distracted.

Hell allowed the kiss, but frowned up at him when Brent pulled back. "That's not what I mean."

"But I *do* like creamy things," Brent purred, sliding one hand down Hell's neck.

Amethyst eyes narrowed even as Brent's hand continued to drift downward. "Do you like me?"

Brent smiled and let his eyes heat. He'd come to the conclusion that he couldn't very well deny it, so why bother. "Yeah." He bent his head to press his lips to Hell's shoulder. His hand found Hell's cock.

The soft organ twitched as he fondled it, starting to harden. "Then why won't you say it?"

Brent nipped at Hell's shoulder. "I've got better things to do with my mouth." He dropped to his knees, quickly taking most of Hell's dick into said mouth.

The imp hissed, both strong hands coming to rest on and squeeze Brent's shoulders. "Brent," he moaned.

No talking, Brent willed, suckling the velvety-soft skin, loving how it grew in his mouth. *Think about this. Just this.*

Brent nuzzled and sucked until he had Hell fully hard.

A knock sounded.

Grinning, he popped Hell's dick from his mouth. He tipped his head to meet Hell's eyes. "Oops."

Hell growled.

Brent laughed as he pushed past Hell into the bedroom to grab his sweatpants.

"You did that on purpose," Hell accused, retreating to the bed as Brent stepped into his pants.

"Did not."

Hell snorted and flopped back on the bed. His hand went immediately to his cock.

The knock sounded on the door again.

"You should get that," Hell told him airily, waving his free hand in the air.

Brent narrowed his eyes and grunted, sure that he'd just gotten the rotten end of this deal. He turned and went to retrieve the tray of ice cream and cake from the guy, but only after making sure the bedroom door was mostly closed. He brought the tray back into the bedroom with him.

Hell lay spread in the middle of the navy-blue duvet, one pale, slim arm thrown above his head while the other languidly massaged his erection. Lavender bangs fell over his eyes, but Brent was pretty sure they were closed.

Watching avidly as Hell's fist forced his foreskin over and back from the dripping tip of his cock, Brent set the tray down on the long table that stood beside the bed. "Cake and ice cream's here."

Hell hummed absently, not deigning to open his eyes.

Brent licked his lips. Hurriedly, he dropped his sweatpants to free his own throbbing erection. He pulled on his cock a few times before deciding that he really did need to taste what Hell had in his hand. He practically jumped on the bed, crawling over until his head was above Hell's cock.

"I thought you wanted ice cream?"

Brent tilted his head to see amethyst eyes fastened on him from beneath a heavy fall of shiny purple hair. He smiled and stuck out his tongue, letting it skim across the pre-cum dripping from the tip of Hell's cock. "I found some better cream."

Hell's eyes narrowed, and he jerked his cock flat against his belly, away from Brent's mouth. "I should make you talk to me first."

Brent scowled, averting his eyes from Hell's. "What for, when I'm offering myself up for your pleasure?"

Hell was silent long enough for Brent to find the courage to look back up at his face. The smile there warmed his blood. A smile that Brent had grown to crave. The wicked tilt and the fire in his eyes exposed the demon that lived inside the cherubic body.

"Are you?"

Movement caught Brent's attention, and he looked down to see Hell again massaging his own cock. When Brent bent his head toward it, however, Hell's other hand shot down to grab his hair, preventing him.

He obediently froze, eyes closing and heart sinking. Again he willed Hell to drop the subject.

Hell released his hair with a sharp push. "Sit back on your heels."

Brent did.

Hell scooted up farther on the bed until he had his back against the headboard. He considered Brent, then reached over to pick up the tray of ice cream.

Brent's eyes widened in curiosity.

Hell picked up the spoon, slowly scooped up some of the cold treat, and brought it to his mouth. Brent licked his own lips as the lucky spoon disappeared between Hell's soft lips.

"Come here. Hands and knees," Hell said, pointing with the spoon to a spot between his spread legs.

Brent complied, happy to find a spoonful of vanilla ice cream waiting for him when he arrived. Eyes locked on Hell's, he took the spoon and cream into his mouth.

Hell fed him three silent spoonfuls, alternating with spoonfuls for himself.

"Don't swallow," Hell ordered after the third spoonful.

Brent watched him, keeping ice cream in his mouth.

Hell grinned and pointed to his dick with the spoon. "Suck me."

Humming happily, Brent lowered himself to Hell's upright dick. He parted his lips and let some of the melted ice cream dribble onto the tip. Hell hissed, but didn't tell him to stop. He placed his lips at the tip and smoothed his mouth down over Hell's cock without losing too much more of the cream.

Hell cried out, arching his back and very nearly toppling the rest of the mostly frozen ice cream onto the duvet. Brent disregarded the bowl, intent on trying to cover Hell's cock with cream without losing too much. It was a losing battle, but one he enjoyed thoroughly.

"Mmm, *ja*," Hell murmured. The spoon clanked loudly in the bowl as he set the dish aside.

Brent lowered to his belly on the bed, freeing his hands to dig fingers into Hell's sharp hipbones. He finally swallowed what cream remained in his mouth so that he could properly work Hell's cock. Brent laved the tip, teasing the hole and the sensitive ridge, before sliding his lips and tongue down over the head and the shaft, cleaning up the sticky cream with his tongue. He let his mouth slide wetly up to the tip, then back down, repeating that move in a slow, languid pace that soon had Hell bucking up into his mouth on the downward slide. Once all the ice cream was gone, Brent settled down to serious sucking that soon enough had Hell crying out and spurting down his throat.

He sat up, licking his lips. Hell lay beneath him, staring, catching his breath. Before Brent could read his intent, Hell lunged up at him, tackling him to his back. His head dropped over the foot of the bed as Hell descended his body and swallowed down his cock. It was his turn to cry out, his turn to writhe, and his turn to spurt as Hell used lips, teeth, tongue, and fingers to bring him off.

Then he was floating again, happily panting as the tingles in his body subsided.

Hell pulled him further onto the bed so that his head wasn't hanging off, then climbed his body. Hell's hands circled Brent's wrists, pinning them to the bed as Hell braced over him. Amethyst eyes held black. "Tell me that you love me."

Brent's eyes went wide.

Hell scowled. "Tell me that you love me. Because I love you."

Brent's mouth fell open, but no sound escaped.

"Tell me!"

"I --"

Hell waited.

"I --" He swallowed. Instinct told him to jump up, push away, but Hell's steady gaze held him pinned more surely than the hands at his wrists. "Love is a big thing. I don't know --"

Hell snarled, shoving up to sit across Brent's lap. Brent tensed, not knowing if something painful was coming. But Hell just sat, fingernails digging into his own thighs. "You don't know? You've spent the last three months with me, and you don't know?"

"Three months isn't that long."

"It's long enough."

"I've never been in love before. How the hell should I know?"

Hell's nostrils flared. His eyes narrowed. "Maybe because you've been in love so long and you never knew it."

Brent pushed up to his elbows. "What?"

With an angry grunt, Hell tumbled from the bed. "I knew it," Brent heard him grumble. "All along. There was no fighting it."

"What are you talking about?"

"You. You and your damned feelings. You won't let yourself fall in love with me."

"What?"

"You won't. Because you're in love with Luc."

Brent gaped. "Where did that come from?"

"It's true, isn't it?"

"I haven't seen Luc for weeks."

"Yet you talk of him nearly every day. You're in love with him."

Brent pushed up onto his elbows, glaring at the man who paced across the room. "God damn it, Hell, I've told you that --"

"That's over, I know. That you're not sleeping with him, yes. That you're best friends, and he's closer than family, and you grew up together, and you've been through hard times together. Yes, yes, yes, I've heard it all. But I still think you're in love with him."

"I'm not in love with Luc!"

"No? You won't make a decision without him."

"That's not --"

"You talk to him at least once a day, if not more."

"That's just because --"

"You are full of 'Luc this' and 'when Luc and I that.' I am *sick* of it."

"Damn it, Hell, Luc is with Reese. When will you get that through your head?"

The German accent was as thick as it had ever been. "I did not say that Luc was in love with you. *That* I know. He has love and a lover. I said that *you* are in love with him, and it's pathetic to watch when I offer you everything that I am."

Brent got up, sitting cross-legged in the middle of the mattress. "Hell, we agreed that this was just sex."

"Yes. I agreed. I thought it would be. But it's so much more I want to be with you always"

"You're with me now."

"I want to know that you will stay with me."

"How do I know you'll stay with me? We're going to be on tour. You're going to meet a lot of guys --"

"I don't want a lot of guys. I want you."

Now, maybe. He shook his head. "This is a bad idea."

Hell stopped pacing at the edge of the bed, leaning toward Brent. "No, this is a *good* idea. You and me. We're good together."

Brent wasn't aware of shaking his head until Hell spoke. "Why no? Because you are in love with Luc."

Brent spoke through panic. "I don't love you, so I have to be in love with him?"

The imp froze, head snapping back as though he'd been slapped, gemstone eyes blazing. Then he turned and, without another word, stalked to the closet and yanked clothing from the hangers.

Brent watched him for a few silent moments until it was obvious that Hell was packing. To leave. Part of him wanted to stop Hell. But how? Brent would admit that he liked him, yes. How could he not? Hell was bright and lively and funny and too damn hot for words. Just touching him was nearly an orgasmic experience. But that was it.

Wasn't it?

Hell disappeared into the bathroom, slamming the door. A moment later, the shower sounded.

Brent fell back on the bed. What the fuck? He couldn't just say he loved Hell. He didn't. Did he? What he felt was just sex. Wasn't it? It had to be. Because if he felt more and let himself fall and then Hell left him, that would break him. And the accusations about Luc were just plain fucking absurd.

Weren't they?

Great! Now the imp had him questioning things he knew were true.

Angrily, Brent rolled off the bed and grabbed up his sweatpants. He stepped into them and took his cigarettes and lighter out to the balcony. He stayed there, intent on chain-smoking the entire pack, when he heard Hell come out of the shower. The imp could see him through the screen door, but didn't come out. There were a few more moments filled with the sounds of packing, followed by angry footsteps.

The door opened. "I'll send someone for my other luggage."

Hell was gone.

Chapter Thirteen

Brent waited the next day, but other than a porter arriving to take Hell's suitcases and garment bags, there was no contact from him.

Brent continued to resist the urge to call Luc and tell him what had happened, still smarting from Hell's accusations. He was pretty sure that Hell was wrong about him being in love with Luc, but he did recognize that he didn't have to tell his friend *everything*.

Brent stayed that day in the beautiful beach hotel that he and Hell had come to on a whim, but the quiet serenity of it lost its appeal without the imp. Late that afternoon, he called the airline and booked a flight to New York. Heaven Sent was due to meet up at the end of the week for a charity performance in Connecticut anyway. He'd just be a little early.

Tyler met him in the lobby of the Weiss and took him up to his room personally.

"The suite we had booked for you for this weekend isn't ready yet," Tyler apologized, leading the way into a perfectly respectable room.

Brent shrugged, entering and stepping aside for the porter to bring in his luggage. He tipped the guy while Tyler pushed open the curtains and cracked the window to let in the afternoon air.

Tyler turned as the porter left. He looked sharp in his gray suit, his blond hair waving artfully around his face. He frowned slightly. "Will you tell me what's wrong?"

Brent tried for casual. "Wrong? Nothing's wrong." *Except this ache in my chest.*

"Where's Hell?"

Brent shrugged, dropping onto the couch. "Haven't a clue."

"Did you two break up?"

"Wasn't anything to break up."

"But...?" He trailed off, and Brent didn't see the need to clarify. "Okay. If you don't want to tell me."

Brent sighed. "There's nothing to tell."

He could tell by the look on Tyler's face that the blond didn't believe him, but Tyler left it at that. He nodded. "Okay. Do you want me to have some food sent up?"

"Nah. I'm beat. I'm just gonna crash."

"Okay. Breakfast?"

"Yeah, That'd be great."

"And the normal arrangements for the pool?"

He smiled and stood, stretching. "I love staying at your hotels, man. You take good care of me."

Tyler came forward, reached out to squeeze his shoulder. "That's what friends are for."

Brent almost broke. It'd be easy to talk to Tyler. He knew the blond cared, and Tyler was far enough removed from the situation that it might actually do some good. He really should talk to *someone*. He knew that. He hadn't even called Luc since Hell left. He hadn't talked to anyone.

But Brent kept his mouth shut. If he talked, that would make it real, and he was kind of okay with the empty feeling even if the ache went with it. If the empty went away, the pain would start. He just wasn't ready to acknowledge what that meant. So, instead, he smiled and nodded, hoping Tyler saw the sincere gratitude in his eyes. "Thanks."

Tyler waited, but when Brent said nothing else, he nodded and dropped his hand. "I'll see to everything. You get some rest."

It was inevitable, really. He'd known Tyler couldn't stay silent. He was surprised that a call from Johnnie hadn't been waiting for him when he'd arrived at the Weiss East. It took until the next morning for any of his band mates to contact him. Of course, he'd put a hold on the hotel phone's calls and had turned off his cell.

When he turned on his cell, there were messages waiting from Johnnie, Darien, and Gretchen. Two from Luc. The last was quite simple: "Damn it, you'd better call me."

He waited until he'd had his breakfast and his morning swim before returning the last call.

"What the hell happened?" Luc demanded, not even bothering with a hello. As usual, caller ID told him it was Brent.

He closed his eyes as an invisible fist gripped his heart. This was it If he said it here, it was real. "Nothing."

"Don't give me that, asshole. Tell me what happened with you and Hell. Why are you at the Weiss?"

He tried for flippant, easing toward what he didn't want to face. "What's the big deal?"

"You two have been joined at the hip for three months now, and you suddenly show up without him and won't tell Tyler why. That's the big deal. Something's wrong. I can smell it."

"From Seattle? Whoa, that's a feat."

"Fuck you. What happened?"

Brent sighed. He closed burning eyes and felt the tears start to fall down his cheeks. "He said he loved me."

"And?"

"And I didn't say it back."

"Why not?"

"Why not?"

"Yeah, why not? You do love him, don't you?"

"Why would you say that?"

Luc snorted. "Christ, is that what this is about?"

"What?"

"How can you say that you're not in love with Hell?"

"Because I'm not in love with Hell." *See? Not hard to say at all. It's true, isn't it?*

"Delusional much?"

"Fuck you."

"No, fuck you. God, you're such a fucking moron sometimes."

"Hey!"

"No, I mean it. You've been happier with Hell than you've been with anyone else I've *ever* seen you with, and you go and mess it up by overthinking it."

"It's better this way."

"Why?"

"He was going to get tired of me sooner or later."

"Oh, for… Have you talked to him?"

"Not since he left."

"You should call him. Brent?"

A lump in Brent's throat kept him silent. He swallowed repeatedly, but the effort to keep the crying quiet so Luc didn't hear was all he could handle.

"Gretchen called me last night after she couldn't get you. She said Hell called her and made some noises about leaving the band."

Brent winced. He'd wondered when and if that might happen. He *knew* he shouldn't have started anything with Hell. Look where the relationship had brought them!

"She said he didn't give any real reasons why, just that we might not want him anymore. She called you and didn't get an answer."

Brent took a deep breath, managing to clear his throat. "I had my phone off."

"Hiding?"

"Fuck you." His voice cracked.

Luc sighed. "Okay. So what do we do? Can you and Hell work this out?"

"I don't know. I haven't talked to him."

"When are you going to?"

"I don't know."

"If it was just your love life, I'd stay out of it --"

Brent snorted.

"Okay, maybe not. But this concerns the band. I don't think any of us wants to lose what Hell's added."

"No."

"So you and Hell have to work this out."

"I know."

"You'll call him?"

"Yeah."

"What'll you say?"

"I don't know."

"You should tell him that you're a bonehead and that you love him and hope he'll take your sorry ass back."

"Gee, thanks, buddy."

"I'm the only one who'd tell you straight, and you know it."

"I'm not in love with him."

"You are."

I am. "I'll get over it."

"Christ! What for?"

There wasn't much of a conversation after that. Brent clammed up, shocked and scared by his own internal admission. Luc gave up and, after another order to call Hell, hung up on him.

He loved the imp. He tried the thought on, poked at it from a few different angles, and kept coming to the same conclusion. Somewhere, although he'd tried to avoid it and just remain casual, he'd fallen for the imp. It made sense if he let himself think about it. Except for Hell's insistence that he was hung up on Luc, there wasn't much Brent didn't like about him. But love was impossible. Even if Brent came out with it and admitted it, it was doomed to failure. All of his few serious relationships had ended badly, and he just couldn't chance that with Hell.

Of course, with how he'd handled things so far, he was about to get the same result.

Damn!

He called Hell.

"Hello."

Brent hesitated, surprised both to hear the imp's voice and to feel the surge of warmth that spread throughout his chest at the sound. "Hey."

Silence. Hell waited.

"I, uh…" He sighed, scratching his head. *Think about the band.* "You're not leaving Heaven Sent, are you?"

Pause. "I'd rather not."

"Well, you shouldn't. You're one of us now, and we, uh, that is the band… God. Hell, we shouldn't let what's between us spoil what goes on with the band."

"Or what isn't between us." Ouch. "I agree."

"It'd be unprofessional."

Did he hear a snort? "Quite."

"Good. Good. So will I... Are you coming to New York this weekend?"

"We have two performances. Of course I'll be there."

"Good. And, uh, Hell, the other guys. I mean, they...they've got nothing to do with this."

There was a long pause before Hell sighed. "We'll see if they feel the same."

"They do. You'll see."

"All right."

Another long pause. Brent didn't know what to say. Luc's prodding and his own revelation aside, he really didn't know how to express this or if Hell still felt the same. He'd probably ruined any chance he had with Hell by now.

"Okay, then. See you Friday." *Lame.*

"Yes." Hell's answer was clipped and followed by his cutting the connection.

Brent stared at his cell phone through watery eyes. He had to put his feelings aside. He'd obviously severed any romantic ties between himself and Hell, but it looked like the band wouldn't suffer. That's all that mattered.

Chapter Fourteen

"Hey."

Brent briefly turned from his contemplation of the trees in the backyard of the house where the party was being held. Reese stood beside him, his newly dyed, brilliant blue hair stirring in the early November breeze and his big blue eyes full of...something.

Brent turned back to stare at the trees, kicking the lip of a little brick planter with the toe of his boot. "Hey."

"You've been quiet."

Brent shrugged. This wasn't a newsflash. Other than backing vocals during the performance, he'd barely said ten words all night. Not since seeing Hell earlier that day at the sound check. Not since he'd realized that everyone could and did talk to the imp but him.

"Want to talk?"

"No."

"We're worried about you."

"'We'?"

"Me. Luc. Johnnie. Tyler. Darien. Y'know, your friends."

Not Hell. Brent nodded but remained silent.

"What gives?"

Brent sighed. "Look. They've all already tried talking to me Just let it rest."

Johnnie, Luc, and even Darien had all grilled him when they'd shown up at the Weiss during the previous two days. Luc had damn near throttled him. Reese, in fact, had intervened.

"I can't let it rest. You're hurting."

"No. I'm not. I'm fine."

"You're not fine."

"Why can't everyone just let it go?" *Hell has.*

To prove his point, Brent heard Hell's laugh drifting out into the night through the open balcony doors. Funny how he could pick out that laugh so easily.

"Because you haven't let it go. This thing between you and Hell is gnawing at you, and it shows."

"There's nothing between me and Hell."

Reese sighed. "Have you tried talking to him?"

"There's nothing to say."

"But --"

"Just stop. Does it even matter? I was onstage tonight, and I made music. The band sounded great. The fans got what they wanted."

"Yeah. You come alive on stage. But as soon as you're off it, it's like you're dead."

"So?"

"So?"

"Yeah, so? What does it matter?"

"It matters."

"Why? Who cares?"

Reese pushed an exasperated breath through his lips and took a drink from the glass in his hand. "Look, Brent, it may help if you --"

"God damn it, Reese, would you leave me the fuck alone?"

He didn't see Reese's reaction because he didn't look. He kept staring at the damn trees, hoping Reese couldn't see the tears welling in his eyes behind his sunglasses. After a moment, Reese walked away.

Brent ducked his head and swiped at the moisture in his eyes. How long before he could escape this damn party? He didn't want to be here in the first place. Behind him was a small cocktail party being thrown by a local business CEO. Brent forgot the business, but the company was going to be a major contributor to the tour, so the band was expected to show their pretty faces. For color. Like trophies Gretchen had made him come. So he'd come. He'd smiled for the pictures. He'd shaken hands. He'd done his duty. Now he was standing alone in the backyard, waiting to be excused, while Hell joked and flirted and acted like nothing was wrong.

But maybe for him, nothing *was* wrong.

Didn't that prove Brent was right and there wasn't any love between them?

Brent groaned softly, grinding his teeth. He was so very sick of thinking about this. One moment he had himself convinced that he was in love with Hell and he should throw himself at the imp's feet. The next, all signs pointed toward the fact that Hell was over it and that he should get over it, too. He'd been lectured, berated, and nearly strangled over the subject in the past few days, and he dearly wished it'd all stop.

A rough hand took hold of Brent's elbow and yanked.

Brent's head shot up. "Hey!"

Luc scowled at him with coolly angry eyes. "Come on. We're going back to the hotel."

"What?"

Luc hauled Brent toward the terrace door. "You want to leave, right?"

Bristling, Brent tried to snatch his arm away, but Luc held strong. They stopped just outside the doorway, glaring at each other. "You don't have to baby-sit me."

Unmoved, Luc stared at him. "We're going to the same place. I'm leaving. You coming?"

Brent wanted to refuse, but the urge to leave was stronger, and he knew no one would let him leave alone. "Fine."

Luc hauled him toward the door again.

"Hey!" he protested, but Luc just continued to drag him. He stared at the floor rather than looking around to see if anyone was watching them. Probably not. Most of the party was in the sunken living room, which did not lie between the terrace and the front door. "Is Reese coming?"

"He's talking to an art dealer over there." Luc waved toward the living room, never taking his eyes from the front entrance.

Brent seethed silently until they got to the door and out of it. He wondered why they didn't have to let Gretchen or their host know they were leaving, but since he *was* leaving, he decided not to question it. However... "Why are you leaving without him?"

Luc finally let go of his arm as they were descending the winding walkway of wide, shallow brick stairs that led from the house down a steep incline to the waiting cars below. Each turn of the path was practically hidden from the next by thick shrubbery. "We're not attached at the hip."

"No. Only at ass, mouth, and dick."

"Gee, that's a pretty statement."

Brent scowled, shoving his hands deep into the pockets of his slacks. "Not any less true."

"What the fuck is your problem?"

"My problem is that everyone thinks I have a problem."

"You do."

"I don't."

"Christ, Brent, why won't you admit that you're in love with Hell?"

Brent froze at the curve of one turn halfway down the hill. Tall, crisply trimmed shrubbery and overhanging flowering trees hid the way they had come. "Not this again."

"Yes, this again. Everyone else knows it's true except for you. And maybe Hell, since you keep denying it."

Brent shoved past Luc down the path. "You have no idea what you're talking about."

He heard the clack of Luc's dress shoes as his friend followed. "Don't I? Let's see, a month ago, when the two of you are humping like bunnies, you're happier than I've seen you. *Ever.*. But the minute the sex stops, you sink into the worst depression I've ever seen you in."

"I'm not depressed!"

"Bullshit. You're an antisocial freak, but even you've never been this bad before."

Unfortunately, Luc would be the one to know this. But that knowledge only made Brent seethe.

He held up his hand in a one-finger salute for Luc. "Mind your own business."

Luc caught him by the arm and spun him to slam his back against another tree, hard enough that loose leaves rained down on them. Luc ripped off Brent's sunglasses and stuck his nose into Brent's face, matching Brent's snarl. "*You're* my business. You're one of the people I care about most in this world, and I can't *stand* to see you like this."

"I'm fine."

"You're anything but fine, Brent."

"Just let it go!" Brent hissed, trying to twist out of Luc's grasp. Unfortunately, Luc had always been the stronger of the two of them.. Horrified, he felt tears burning in his eyes, matching the roil of angry heat that burbled in his chest. "Fucking leave me alone."

Luc ground his teeth, shaking Brent. "I've let it go long enough. We're going to hash this out tonight."

Brent shut his eyes, letting his head fall back to thump against the bark of the tree. Tears rolled down his cheeks. "Damn it, just leave me alone." But the anger didn't sound in his voice.

Luc's hands switched from his shoulders to cup his face. Gently but firmly, he righted Brent's neck. "Talk to me, man. Let me help you. You've at least got to vent."

He opened his eyes to stare wide-eyed into Luc's concerned face His friend. The person who knew him best. If he talked to Luc, he'd have to acknowledge the pain, and that was not something he was willing to do.

Luc brushed a brief kiss on Brent's temple. "I love you, man," Luc told him. "It kills me to see you hurting like this."

Brent opened his mouth, feeling the floodgates open.

Another icy voice froze them. "I thought so."

Brent blinked, flinching at the sound of the voice. A familiar voice. A voice that haunted his mind, waking and sleeping.

Luc's hands fell from Brent's face, and he turned as he stepped aside.

Hell stood behind them on the path. The incline and the distance made him seem taller and far more imposing than he was. Hands on hips, hair and loose gray silk shirt stirring in the breeze, he glared at Brent. "Are the two of you off to fuck in a dark corner?"

"Hell, man..." Luc started.

"I thought better of you, Luc. I know he's still in love with you, but I thought you'd keep your hands off."

"What?!" Luc cried, his anger finding a different target.

Brent groaned, hand over his eyes since Luc still held his glasses. "Hell, damn it, this is not what you think."

"Isn't it?"

"No."

Luc growled. "You've got some nerve."

Hell scowled. "I have nerve? At least I'm not fucking my best friend behind my boyfriend's back.."

"What?!" A fourth voice stopped them.

It was like movie slow motion. Brent dropped his hand and saw Hell flinch and turn as Reese rounded the corner behind him.

Reese glared at Hell. "What are you talking about?"

"Tiger." Luc moaned softly, stepping toward the other two.

Reese kept talking, focused on Hell. "You've got a lot of gall accusing them of such a thing."

Hell sneered, rounding on Reese. "Didn't you know that they were fucking each other before you?"

"Shit, Hell!" Brent cried, pushing away from the tree. He wasn't sure how, but he had to keep Hell from talking.

Luc got to them before Brent did, roaring. He saw Luc's hand on Hell's shoulder. Saw him spin the smaller man around.

Instinct had him catching Luc's right arm as he cocked it back for a swing at Hell's face. "Luc, stop!"

Hell crashed head over heels over a low bush that lined the pathway.

Reese stumbled back in the other direction.

Brent had his hands full trying to stop Luc from diving after Hell. Like a wildcat, Luc twisted and yanked until he finally rounded on Brent in frustration. Brent had to fall back and let go for his own safety, ducking a half-hearted swing Luc made at his head. Growling, Luc turned back toward Hell.

"Luc!"

Reese's voice stopped Luc before he got to Hell, who was just scrambling to his feet on the small patch of grass on the other side of the bush.

Luc turned toward his lover.

Reese's face said it all. "Is it true?"

Luc didn't answer immediately. His mouth opened, but nothing came out.

If possible, Reese's eyes went even bigger. "Oh, my God, it *is!*" His huge blue eyes flicked to Brent. "You're *sleeping* together?"

"Not anymore," Brent heard himself say, belatedly realizing he should just shut up.

"Anymore?"

Luc stepped toward Reese. "Tiger --"

"Don't you fucking come near me, you asshole," Reese cried, backing up with a fist raised toward Luc.

"What's going on here?" Brent looked up to see an unfamiliar man round the pathway behind Reese.

But right behind him was Gretchen, then Johnnie.

Great.

Luc took another step toward Reese, which set the smaller man off. He started to launch himself, fist first, toward Luc, but the unknown man caught him from behind.

"Reese, tiger, it's not what you think…" Brent couldn't see Luc's face, but he clearly saw the tension in his shoulders and the bunching of his hands into fists.

"Oh, really?" Reese cried, struggling with the man who was proving stronger than he. "You're fucking your best friend, and I'm supposed to just *accept* that?"

"Whoa!" Johnnie barreled the rest of the way toward them to help hold on to Reese, who writhed and spat like a blue-haired cat.

"No, Reese! We're not --"

"*O*-kay!" Gretchen yelled over any further words from either Reese or Luc.

A little bit of a crowd had formed behind her, including Darien. Darien, after a quick look, hurried down the path toward Hell, who was brushing dirt from his clothes.

Gretchen stopped between Reese and Luc, looking at Reese. Her sharp look halted his writhing and words, but the anger he glared at Luc spoke volumes.

Brent sagged back against the tree and slowly sank to a crouch, trying his best to just disappear.

Chapter Fifteen

"Brent!" A heavy hand pounded on the door. "Open this door! You owe me an explanation."

Brent kind of thought that he should feel surprise, but the events of the night had drained his emotions. At least for the moment. His eyes were still puffy and red from crying, but for the moment they were dry. He crossed the darkened main room of the suite and opened the door.

The blue-haired man stormed inside and spun, facing him. He still wore the same outfit he'd had on at the party, but the carefully applied makeup he'd been wearing had been washed clean. His eyes were puffy and red, too. "I promised myself that I'd find out what this is all about before I fly off the handle again. So. Is it true?"

Brent closed the door and braced against it, his hands splayed flat on the door at the middle of his back. "It's not true that we're sleeping together now, but we have slept together."

"God!"

"Before you," he hastened to add. "I swear to God, Reese, it was before you. We haven't done anything since."

Blue eyes a few shades lighter than Reese's hair bore into Brent's face. Reese took a deep breath and stood straight. "I believe you. I just can't believe either of you would do that to me."

Brent shook his head. "God, no. We wouldn't."

"So why didn't he tell me?"

"He was afraid of how you'd react."

Reese's hands flexed open and closed as he continued to stare at Brent. "Okay. I can buy that." He wet his lips with his tongue. "Do you love him?"

"Not like that. Not like Hell thinks."

"*Were* you in love with him?"

Brent shook his head again. "No. Not ever like that. God, Reese, the entire time we were together, he used me as a substitute for you."

That brought Reese up short. "What?"

Brent nodded. "Cried out your name and everything."

"When-when was this?"

"Before he came back for you. Before we got the invite for Reegan's wedding."

"Before...?"

Brent sighed. "He's been in love with you for years, Reese. It just took him a while to work up the nerve to see you again."

Reese snorted, turning toward the couch in the center of the suite's main room. "That man is *all* nerve."

Brent couldn't argue that and decided to stop talking since things seemed to be going well. Reese was calmer now. He watched the man drop onto the couch, but stayed where he was at the door. "Have you talked to him?"

Reese shook his head. "I can't. Not yet. I know the things he'd say. I wanted to hear it from you first." He wiped a hand across his face. "He knows where I am."

Brent was profoundly grateful that Reese was listening. He didn't think he could handle breaking up their relationship on top of his own misery. "Reese, I'm sorry about this. I really am."

Reese nodded. "Thanks. I believe you."

Brent sagged in relief. "You should go talk to him. He's got to be going nuts wondering what you're thinking."

Reese nodded again. "I will." Those blue eyes turned up to focus on him again. "But first I want you to tell me why Hell would think you're in love with Luc."

Brent swallowed, tilting his head down, letting a fall of black bangs hide his eyes. Where were his shades? Oh, yeah, he'd never gotten them back from Luc, and he hadn't bothered to get a spare pair when he'd returned to his rooms.

"Brent?"

"He thought that I was in love with Luc because I wasn't in love with him."

"Is that what you told him?"

"No."

"Why would he think it?"

"Because I talk to Luc, like, every day."

"True." Reese laughed a little. "I guess I hadn't really noticed. You guys have always been like that."

Brent shrugged.

"Brent, are you really not in love with Hell?"

Shit! There were the tears again, along with that awful pull in his chest. What was up with him tonight? Too much happening. His fingertips hurt from clutching at the solid wood at his back.

Footsteps padded toward him, and Brent averted his head, keeping it down, trying to keep the tears hidden.

"Brent?"

"I don't know." He took a breath, trying to squelch the wail that threatened to escape his throat.

"God, Brent, come here." Reese took hold of his shoulders and led him to the couch, pushing him to sit, then sitting beside him. He squeezed Brent's shoulder. "Talk to me."

Brent shook his head. "Doesn't matter. Doesn't matter anyway."

"What doesn't matter?"

"If I did love Hell. I fucked it up."

"You could talk to him."

"After what happened tonight? No."

"You're going to have to do something. You guys can't work together like this."

Brent crumpled forward, elbows on his knees, face in his hands. A dry sob escaped.

An arm slid around his shoulders. "Talk to me, man."

Without any other options, Brent did. He took the sympathetic shoulder Reese offered and spilled on it. How it started with Hell, how he felt about the imp, and what had happened that afternoon when it had all gone to shit. Everything. Even some of the things he hadn't told Luc, all the stuff about Hell being jealous of Luc. To his horror, he was even telling Reese how he'd always been used as a substitute or as a false version of himself and never the real him.

Reese listened attentively and said little. He waited briefly after Brent's words finally trailed off. "Is there beer in your mini bar?"

Caught off guard by the comment, Brent frowned and nodded.

Reese got up and fetched two cold bottles, returning with them. He handed Brent a beer and a napkin, then sat on one end of the couch. Brent sat on the other, wiping his nose and eyes as he faced Reese.

"Luc had to convince me that I loved him, you know."

Brent had to smile. He was pretty sure Luc had filled him in on most of what had happened between him and Reese. "I know."

Reese just nodded. "I didn't believe him. I mean, sure I wanted him. Who wouldn't?" He glanced sharply at Brent, realizing what he'd said and to whom, but then let it go with a shrug. "But *love* was an entirely different thing. I couldn't possibly love him, because he deserved someone…better."

Brent saw where this was going, but stayed silent, nursing his beer.

"My sister was the one who pointed out that I wasn't being fair to him. By seeing him as something more, I wasn't seeing him as the asshole that he really is."

Caught off guard by the humor, Brent nearly spit up a mouthful of beer. He frowned up at Reese's bright grin.

"He's just a guy, Brent, despite the fact that he looks like a Kewpie doll. And I'll tell you, from everything I've seen, it looks to me like the two of you are in love. You said that your lovers in the past never saw the real you, but it sounds like Hell's been focused on you from the start."

Brent sighed. This was his cue to brush off the conversation. Throughout his life, people had been telling him that he didn't give himself enough credit. He barely heard it anymore. But for some reason Reese's words sank in. Maybe it was the horrible past few days. Maybe he was emotionally drained. Or maybe, just maybe, he was starting to believe that he was in love with the cherub. And maybe that the cherub was -- or had been -- in love with him.

Scary thought.

"Could be," was all he said.

Reese shrugged. "You deserve to give it a chance."

"Don't know that Hell will give me a chance."

"All you can do is try."

Chapter Sixteen

Brent left the moist, heated air of the bathroom to answer his cell phone, hoping Hell had finally deigned to return one of his calls.

It was Gretchen. "Brent, honey, you have *got* to let me know what's going on with you and Hell."

He frowned, dropping down into a straight-backed chair. He let the towel with which he'd been drying his hair drop to the carpet at his feet. "I'm not really sure what *is* going on," he admitted on a sigh. "I've been trying to call Hell all morning, but he's not answering my calls."

"You know he left the hotel last night?"

"I know he cleared his stuff out of our suite last night before I got back. Didn't know he'd left the Weiss."

"He did. And he's been a busy little beaver this morning."

Brent started to get a sick feeling. On top of the nausea in his empty stomach, it was not a good thing. "Oh?"

"Yes. I got a call from a Christopher Faith this morning. He claims to be Hell's new manager."

"What?"

"Yes. Want to tell me what the heck is going on? What happened between you two?"

"We had a fight."

"Oh, yeah? I couldn't tell."

"Ha ha."

"Mmm. I don't like being kept in the dark about these things, Brent. Your sex life is your business until and unless it interferes in *my* business, and Heaven Sent is my business."

"I know."

"Are you and Hell breaking up? Is he leaving the band? Should I start making arrangements with this Faith person?"

"No!" The word was out of his mouth before conscious thought. "Do not start making arrangements. I have to talk to Hell first."

"Okay. Well, you'd better make it quick. Hell's going to talk to the press at two."

"What?"

"It's not surprising. I've been fending off calls for you all morning. There was press there last night, you recall. This guy's probably advised him to talk to them all in one group."

A look at his watch showed him it was now almost noon. "Shit. Where?"

"At the Marriott."

"You think he's going to say he's leaving the band?"

"I can't think of much else he could say, do you?"

"Shit! Fuck!" This had gone beyond what he'd expected. He'd intended to get hold of Hell first thing this morning so they could talk, but Hell was already making arrangements to leave the *band?*

"What do you want to do here, honey?"

"I don't... Gah!" He tore into his hair, trying to think.

"Calm down. You want me to come to your suite so we can make arrangements?"

"Yeah. Hurry."

"I'm on my way."

Brent pressed the button to end the call and stared at the readout on his cell phone. Without much further thought, he pressed the quick dial for Luc's cell.

"Yeah?"

"Man, I need your help."

Brent stared at the tinted glass façade of the hotel while Luc and the driver discussed where to meet up. This wasn't going to take long, probably. Either Brent would succeed or he'd fail. Either Hell would agree or he wouldn't.

This sucks.

"Let's go," Luc prodded him.

Nodding, Brent got out of the car. He adjusted his long overcoat and glasses while Luc got out and stood beside him. They exchanged a glance, nodded, and headed toward the hotel's revolving front door.

"Could you tell me where's the Embassy room?" he asked the nice lady at the information stand.

She smiled that hotel clerk smile and pointed. "It's down that hall and to your left. Your press passes will be checked at the door."

Brent just nodded and led the way.

Luc chuckled at his side. "Guess she's not a fan."

"Guess not," Brent said, hardly listening. His heart was pounding.

They turned the corner and saw about a dozen reporters milling in the hallway.

Brent froze in the middle of the walkway.

Luc put a hand on his shoulder. "Maybe we should come back."

"Too late," Brent murmured.

A few of the reporters noticed them. Recognized them. At once, all the people in the hallway were hurrying in their direction, microphones and tape recorders out, cameras rising up to shoulders and flashbulbs going off.

A familiar surge of panic seared Brent's chest, stopping his breath. He shook and knew Luc could feel it. But he resisted his friend's tug and started walking toward the flood.

"Brent! Luc!" They were on him, like rabid dogs on a side of beef. "What are you doing here? Is Hell really leaving the band? Are you part of the press conference? We weren't told you'd be here."

Sticking to his plan, Brent ignored them and waded through the crowd. Hands gripped at his arms, trying to make him stop, but he kept on. Up ahead, he saw more reporters streaming out through the double doors.

The guards at the door exchanged a puzzled glance but didn't do anything to stop it. But they did stop Brent when he reached the door. "Sorry, press only," the man told him.

Brent stared at the guy, taken aback. He hadn't counted on anyone preventing him from getting into the press conference.

But a pretty little brunette reporter came to his rescue. "Are you crazy? Don't you know who these guys *are?*"

Obviously, the one guard did not.

The other, however, did. He brushed his companion's hand from Brent's shoulder, then nodded to Brent. "Sorry, Mr. Rose. I'm sure it'll be okay if you and Mr. Sloane are admitted."

Brent returned the guard's nod. He tried to smile, but he was still too nervous. So he just went inside the doors, leaving Luc to smile and do his thing behind him. Luc was here for backup, after all, because during the hour they'd discussed this improvised plan with Gretchen, Johnnie, and Darien -- and then even Reese and Tyler -- everyone had known there was no way Brent could have gone through with it alone.

He felt and saw the reporters follow him into the room and heard Luc's murmured answers to some of their questions. It turned out that their appearance had cleared the room, because every metal folding chair in front of Brent was empty.

Empty until Hell appeared through a partially open door toward the back. *Oh, God!* Brent halted halfway down the makeshift aisle, filling his gaze with the vision. Lavender hair curled sweetly around Hell's face, his features angelic despite his scowl. Gemstone eyes narrowed, and his glossed mouth twisted down at both sides. He wore one of his dresslike jackets, this one a deep burgundy in a vaguely Asian design, complete with a gold embroidered dragon over his left breast. Dozens of bangles clattered on each wrist, and he had on a pair of heeled boots that added at least two inches to his height. *Beautiful.*

Someone grabbed Brent's arm from behind, but he yanked away, focused on the dais and the surprised little pixie who stood on it.

Brent had to wind around to the side of the platform and the three steps that led up to it. Hell's heels clacked as he walked toward the center podium, the sound loud to Brent's ears despite the tidal wave of flashes that went off when the two of them got close enough to be photographed together. A man in a suit followed Hell into the room, but Brent dismissed him, his entire focus on Hell.

Hell stopped an arm's length away, hands on hips, glaring. "What are you doing here?"

"I want you back." His voice cracked, and he cleared it with a cough.

A hush fell, so complete that Brent could actually hear the hum of the various cameras. Or was that the buzzing in his head? God, he was dizzy!

Hell's gaze flicked behind Brent, presumably registering Luc's presence. At least, Brent was pretty sure his friend stood behind him. Hell's frown deepened as he glanced at their audience, making sure Brent was aware of them. "You want me back for what?"

"For the band. For me."

Hell's chin twisted aside, his skepticism plain in his face. "For you?"

Brent forced a deep breath into lungs that felt full of water. He raised one shaking hand to his face and took off his sunglasses so the cherub could see his face.

Hell's eyes went wide.

More flashbulbs went off.

"For me. I love you. Please don't leave me because I was too stupid to say it."

A few shrieks -- feminine, by the sound of them -- erupted from the crowd of reporters, followed by a wave of hisses hushing them. Quiet settled again.

Through it all, Hell's eyes didn't leave his face, nor did his skeptical look fade. "What?"

Brent hadn't expected it to be easy. But he knew that this was his best chance. Hell knew he hated this, knew he didn't want an audience. By doing it this way, Hell had to see that he was desperate.

"I love you."

"How do I believe you?"

Brent swallowed. "How's this for a start?" He closed the distance between them, carefully making that step on watery knees. He reached up with both shaking hands to cup Hell's face. He let Hell see the worry and the torment, kept nothing from his gaze, as he lowered his lips toward Hell's.

Hell could pull away. He could refuse. This was an excellent opportunity for him to shun Brent.

But the soft skin of Hell's cheeks stayed within Brent's hands. Shining pink lips parted, and violet eyes closed just before Brent's mouth touched his.

Any sound and any sensory awareness outside of the feel of the man he was kissing didn't exist for Brent. The icy shards of panic and fear in his chest started to melt when he felt Hell's arms snake around his waist, pulling him closer. The cherub sighed, mouth opening and head tilting to invite a deeper kiss, and Brent was helpless to deny him.

He was too keyed up to stay in the kiss for long. He pulled up and opened his eyes, hands still trembling where they held Hell's jaw. He looked into those black-lined eyes as they opened. "I love you," he murmured, far to low for their audience to hear. "Please talk to me."

Hell smiled. He reached up, cupped Brent's chin, used a thumb to swipe away some of the lip gloss that had smeared on Brent's lips. "All right. Let's talk."

Brent's eyes went wide. He glanced toward their rapt audience. "Can we go somewhere else?"

He took heart when Hell burst into joyful laughter.

Chapter Seventeen

Hell took Brent's hand and turned toward their audience. "My apologies to you all, but my announcement has changed. I fear I must cancel this press conference."

Brent shuffled next to him, far too aware of the flashbulbs and roar of questions. He concentrated on the shine of Hell's hair rather than the eager crowd watching them. Of course they wanted to know what had happened, how long this had been going on. Most of the questions, in fact, were directed at him.

But Hell just smiled and waved and led the way toward the back door. Luc and the man in the suit followed.

Shutting the door between them and the press helped Brent's nerves only a little. He held fast to Hell's hand, unwilling to let it go now that he had it.

Hell turned to face him, heedless of the other two in the room. "Do you mean it?"

Brent nodded. "Yes."

"This isn't just a trick to get me to stay with the band?"

"No. That wouldn't work anyway."

"No. It wouldn't." Violet eyes strayed from Brent's face and past his shoulder. "And you are all right with this?"

Brent glanced over his shoulder at Luc. His friend shrugged. "I am if he is." He gave Brent a small smile. "And I don't think I've ever seen him so sure of something."

"I am sorry." Brent looked down at Hell to see the sincerity in his face as he continued to look at Luc. "What happened last night... I was angry, and I spoke out of turn."

Luc nodded. "Thank you for that. It was a bad secret to be keeping anyway. I should have told Reese already."

"Are you and he...?"

Luc's grin was huge. "We're fine. I got lucky and Reese decided to believe me." The grin faded a bit, his look a bit more serious. "You should believe Brent."

Brent again filled his eyes with a vision of Hell, who glanced back up at him, squeezing his hand. "I agree."

He knew the grin that took his lips was goofy, but Brent couldn't help it. Besides, it made Hell chuckle, which wasn't a bad thing.

Hell looked at the man in the suit. "Christopher, thank you for coming to my rescue, but..."

The brunet waved a hand, dismissing the apology. "What are friends for?" he asked in a crisp, British-accented voice, pushing classy wire-frame glasses up on his nose. "I'll admit I'm glad we didn't have to go through with it."

Hell squeezed Brent's hand again, regaining his attention. "Yes, well, if you'll excuse us, I have an empty room upstairs."

Luc laughed. "I'll head out, then. See you guys back at the Weiss later."

Brent waved as Hell dragged him from the room. There was a hallway on the other side of a door opposite the one they'd entered. Hell headed for the elevator at the end of it.

"Who was the guy with you?" Brent asked, glancing back to be sure no one followed them.

"Christopher? He is a friend of mine from school. A lawyer."

They stopped, waiting for the elevator.

Brent scowled. "Were you really going to leave the band?"

Hell stared at their clasped hands. "I didn't want to, but I couldn't stay knowing I couldn't have you."

"Why me?" Brent asked before he could help it.

Hell growled, but the elevator doors shushed open before he could answer. He pulled Brent into the elevator, forcing them face to face. "I love you."

Unwilling to push it, Brent nodded, sliding his hands up to rest on Hell's shoulders. "Okay."

Hell grabbed his wrists, backing away from the kiss Brent leaned forward to give. "You don't sound as though you believe me."

Brent's fingers dug into the rough burgundy silk of Hell's jacket. "I…do."

Hell frowned. Again the doors opened and again Hell led the way out. He didn't say another word until they were in his suite. Just two rooms and not nearly as nice as what they had back at the Weiss.

Brent hovered, uncertain. He wanted very badly to just kiss Hell and lose himself in sex with the man, but Hell obviously had other ideas.

The imp led him into the bedroom and pointed at the bed. "Sit."

He did.

Hell stepped between his knees and held Brent's face in his hands, tipped up to look at him. "I love you."

Brent wet his lips. "I love you."

It wasn't enough. Hell's eyes bore into Brent's skull, his fingers tense at Brent's temples. "I loved you before I met you. You may ask Christopher, if you like."

Brent frowned a bit at that, not sure he liked Hell being so close to this Christopher guy, but he couldn't very well complain when his relationship with Luc had been at the center of their problems.

Hell's thumbs smoothed over Brent's cheeks. "I fell for your music. I knew that I wanted to work with whomever was responsible for those glorious sounds. Imagine my delight when I found not only was a single man responsible for them, but also that he was the beautiful man of my dreams."

Brent's eyes narrowed. How was he supposed to believe that Hell found him more attractive than Luc or Johnnie? The idea was preposterous. And he wasn't the *only* one responsible for the music.

But now was not the time to quibble. Now was not the time to think. Thinking got him into trouble.

Hell leaned in and kissed him, only allowing a soft brush of lips. "I love you."

Brent clutched Hell's hips, opening his mouth to that kiss. "I love you," he said when those lips released his.

The look of pleasure on Hell's face when he pulled back was worth the fear of saying it. So he said it again. "I love you, Hell." He pulled those hips closer. "Please."

The word had the desired effect. Hell pulled his face up into a crushing kiss, all lips and teeth and tongue and even a slight trace of blood when delicate tissues broke from the pressure.

Brent moaned, scrabbling at the cloth buttons of Hell's jacket to get it open and reveal the skin underneath. Hell released his face to work on Brent's clothes. They might have managed better if either one of them had given up the kiss, but neither would, so getting naked was an exercise in fumbling But they did manage it. Brent fell on his back, Hell covering him. It was Brent's turn to sink fingers into hair while Hell's hands explored.

"Ah, *Liebling*," Hell murmured into his mouth. "We'll go slow next time, but I need to be inside you"

"Oh, yeah."

Brent scooted higher onto the bed while Hell dashed to his bag to find lube. The bottle was open and clear liquid was pouring into his hand as he came back across the room. He closed the bottle and tossed it onto the mattress beside Brent as he knelt between Brent's thighs. Helpfully, Brent held his legs up.

"Ah, God, yes, please!" Brent groaned as the blunt invasion burned its way into his body.

Hell leaned in, kissing Brent's chest as he set to pounding Brent's ass.

Brent grabbed handfuls of hair. "Hell, please."

"Love you," Hell grunted, fingers clutching the bend of Brent's knees.

"God, love you, too." Brent moaned.

"Yes!"

"Fuck!"

"*Gott!*"

They came together in an explosion of white light that nearly made Brent pass out.

Afterward, they lay on their sides, facing one another, kissing and cuddling and not speaking with words at all. Brent let himself relax, let himself feel it. Hell loved him. He loved Hell. That's all that mattered for now.

Epilogue

Brent's hand descended, pick dragging across the strings of his guitar. He closed his eyes, starting his solo for "Saving Paradise." The crowd of thousands almost hushed, and little lights flickered in the darkness in homage to the slow love song. It was a Heaven Sent favorite, and the guitar solo was the climax. For years he'd played this part without any sound from his band mates.

But now it was different. Halfway through, a trickling sound like water surrounded him, laughing its way over the audience before Hell's harmony picked up underneath the guitar's main line. For a moment, the two of them held everyone's attention, connected by music even though Hell stood on a platform ten feet behind Brent. It was the music that did it. The music that started it and the music that ended it.

The connection.

The others joined in. Darien's drumbeat edged in slowly, followed by the throbbing heart of Luc's bass. Last, but not least, Johnnie's voice sang out, seducing the crowd with words of love.

Love.

Brent smiled, opening his eyes. His spotlight wasn't on anymore, so he was bathed in blue. Hands moving on the strings without conscious thought, Brent turned and put his back to the crowd. His gaze landed on the head he sought, curls bright even bathed in blue light. Initially, the imp's concentration was on the racks of keyboards before him, but Brent fancied that Hell could feel his attention. Because the imp looked up, saw him, and smiled. Maybe he winked.

Brent blew him a kiss, hoping he saw it.

Then it was time to work. He turned around and bent his head over his guitar, turning his concentration back to the music and the performance for now.

Sweat dripped from his face as he stood with Johnnie, Luc, Darien, and Hell at the front of the stage, waving at the audience, accepting the ovation that would have deafened them if not for the plugs in their ears. This was what it was all about. This was worth having to live in the public eye. The pure joy. The waves of love.

Love.

On impulse, he turned, hand out to wrap around Hell's neck. The imp looked up at him, gorgeous with wet, sweaty hair and smeared mascara. They smiled at each other and kissed.

The crowd went wild.

Oh, yeah. This was good.

HEAVEN SENT: FAITH

Dedication

This one is for all of the readers who've written in expressing love for the boys. As their creator, I can safely say that they love you all back and are very happy to have entertained you! Bless you all.

Chapter One

"Damn straight," Darien crowed.

No one heard him. The roar of the crowd was deafening after the final beat of "Careless Surprise," bringing the concert to a resounding close. Heart racing and blood pumping, Darien stood. The front half of the stadium crowd was brightly lit in blinding white and gold, allowing a sea of screaming faces to become one giant, roiling mass. Screaming in adoration, just for Heaven Sent. He fucking *loved* that! Grinning like an idiot, he bounded around the drum kit and followed the long burgundy skirt of Hell's jacket as the little keyboardist descended from their shared platform to the lower main stage. He caught up with Hell just at the bottom step and slung an arm around his shoulders.

Hell grinned up at him, hooking an arm around Darien's waist. His lavender hair was wet and clinging to flushed, rounded cheeks. The two of them went toward the front of the stage to meet their bandmates, neither terribly worried about the fact that they were sweating like dogs since they were *both* sweating like dogs. They reached Johnnie, who stood in his tight, shiny green T-shirt and ripped white jeans with his waist-length brown hair draping his shoulders and back like a cloak as he waved toward the crowd at the rear of the arena. Dark sunglasses shielding his eyes, Brent returned from stage right without his guitar, his sleeveless black button-down hanging open as he chucked a guitar pick into the screaming mass, then lifted his hand to wave. Luc approached from the other side of the stage, shirtless, torso gleaming with sweat, and loose hair hanging in deep crimson tendrils to his shoulders.

Darien lifted his arm from around Hell. He took the drumsticks he still carried and tossed them into the crowd, hoping, as always, that he didn't bonk someone's head with them or put an eye out. Standing straight, he waved with both hands to the crowd at large, loving the tidal wave of admiration and excitement evident in the crowd's roar.

Man, he loved this! It never got old. Lots of crap about being a rockstar really bit the big one, but being up on stage made up for all of it. That's where it all came together -- in front of an audience who were *into* you, who knew your music and loved it, who stood and sang and danced for two hours straight because your music kept them so pumped they didn't mind that their feet hurt and their throats went hoarse.

After a few minutes of waving, Luc led the way off stage, followed by Johnnie, then Darien, with Hell and Brent bringing up the rear. They passed from garish, overbearing light into the relative darkness. A girl named Stacey waited just offstage with towels for each of them. Darien took one and used it to mop at the back of his neck. His loose tank top had absorbed all the moisture it could somewhere in the first hour, so it was now soaked. The relaxed jeans that he preferred to wear while performing hadn't fared much better, and he could practically feel his socks squishing in his boots.

Ellen, their manager's main assistant, met them in the hall and directed the band to a side area not far off the stage, where a few excited teenagers awaited them. The kids were flushed and sweaty and looked exhausted. One of the girls was seated in a folding chair, her arm around her middle, clearly in pain.

Johnnie walked right up and dropped to kneel before her. "Hey there, sweetheart. You okay?"

Her big brown eyes got even bigger as the singer took her hands into his and smiled at her. Johnnie was very good at this. Even though he wasn't feeling particularly well that night, he always had an eye out for the fans. This small girl had been in one of the front row seats and had been crushed toward the beginning of the show. Johnnie had watched her being carted off and had asked about her during the encore.

The girl -- who couldn't be more than sixteen, if that -- nodded, a delighted smile erasing the pain from her face.

Assured that she was okay, Darien turned to one of the boys standing beside her and stuck out his hand. "Heya. Darien Hughes."

The boy took his hand with a smile to match the girl's. "Oh, man, do I ever know that!"

Darien laughed and set about doing his job. He chatted as he signed first a T-shirt, then a program, then a ticket stub. He stood for a bunch of pictures. This part of being a rockstar was pretty cool, too. Just the knowledge that meeting him and carrying away a souvenir of the occasion could make these kids happy was a tremendous rush.

All this for rock and roll!

After maybe ten minutes, Ellen led the band away and farther into the backstage area. A few members of the press were lurking in the hallways, but security kept them at bay as the band entered the private room. If Heaven Sent had learned one thing in the years they'd been touring, it was that you didn't do interviews at certain times. Right after a show was one of them. When the adrenaline was up, they tended to say stupid things. Darien didn't have a clue if it was true for all bands, but it was certainly true for them. So, this time right after coming off stage was limited to band, immediate assistants, and personal company for the night.

He pulled off his tank as he passed into the quiet room, tossing it and the towel on an empty chair. A guy named Ron offered another towel and a bottle of water. Darien shook his head at the former but took the latter, eagerly twisting off the cap.

With a loud sigh, Johnnie flopped face first onto an overstuffed couch. Loose, long brown hair fell in wet hanks, obscuring his face and half the back of his shimmering shirt. Moaning, he folded his arms underneath his head, letting one leg drop over the side of the couch. "I feel like shit." Johnnie had been complaining of a sore throat for the past two days and had been dosed to the gills on cough suppressants and throat medications for the last two performances. Wasn't the first time where it'd happened and wouldn't be the last.

His husband, Tyler, knelt on the floor beside his head, blond hair gleaming in the room's soft white lighting. "How's your throat?" Loving hands came up to brush hair away from the singer's face. Heedless of the sweat and Johnnie's grumbling, Tyler leaned in to kiss Johnnie's forehead and offered up the cup of tea that he held in his other hand.

Darien frowned, turning from the loving scene.

Just in time to hear Hell shriek, then spin with the clear intention of slugging Brent in the gut. Water flew from his drenched hair, wetter than before. For all that he looked like a cherub, Hell was a spitting cat if you got his dander up, and his current target -- frequent target -- was his lover. Laughing, Brent scuttled back out of reach, cradling the half-empty bottle of ice water in one hand and holding out the other to fend off the angry imp. He caught Hell's next punch and somehow managed to twist things around so Hell fell against him. The skirt of Hell's burgundy jacket swirled around his lover's long legs, and the open sides of Brent's black shirt half embraced Hell as Brent wrapped his arms around him. The imp snarled. Brent leaned into an open-mouthed kiss. Predictably, Hell melted. Geez, they'd been together officially nearly a year and they still acted like it was brand new.

Upending water into his mouth, Darien crossed the room to an empty chair.

Luc sat in the chair beside it, cell phone propped between ear and shoulder as he leaned down to unlace his boots. "Where are you now?" he asked.

Darien sighed, sitting back to nurse his water. No doubt in his mind that Luc was talking to Reese.

Darien wondered where he was, then heard Luc's: "So I'll meet you at the hotel then. We're leaving in a few minutes. Shouldn't be more than a half-hour. Did you bring the painting?"

Darien sank deeper into the chair, looking around, determinedly *not* listening to Luc anymore. Reese was his friend, yes. A good friend. So was Tyler. And Hell had become as much of a brother to him as Johnnie, Luc, and Brent. But it rankled sometimes. More often, as time wore on. They were *all* in relationships. All of his best friends happily shacked up with other men. With each other! What the fuck was it with his life that *all* of his friends were gay? Okay, not really all of them. He had friends outside of the band, but his really *good* friends were these guys, and they were all gay. Because Johnnie and Luc could claim bisexuality all they wanted -- and it once had been true -- but they were true-blue monogamous rump rangers now. "True blue?" Wasn't that a reference to bluebloods or something? Were there gay bluebloods?

"Hey."

He looked up, distracted from his mind's ramblings as Nicole sat on the arm of his chair. *There* was his date! "Hey." He grinned, switching the bottle from one hand to the other so he could slip an arm around her waist. Curvy, soft, and plush. A *girl!* "You made it."

"I said I'd be here. Thanks for the ticket. The show was great!" She brushed hair from his face. "You okay?"

Caught by the sweet gesture, unavoidably comparing it to Tyler's caress of Johnnie, Darien's heart swelled. He tilted his head into her caress. "Yeah, I'm good."

"You looked a bit lost."

Out of the corner of his eye, he saw Tyler haul Johnnie to his feet. The tall singer stood, grumbling, and immediately slung an arm around the blond's shoulders as they headed toward the door. There were no sounds from the corner behind Darien where Hell and Brent were, which meant they were probably still kissing. Luc stood, now in bare feet, and crossed to the other side of the room. Still on the phone, his voice was just a low murmur, words indistinguishable, but the loving intent behind them made obvious by the devilish grin on his face.

Darien sighed, pulling Nicole closer so he could nuzzle her side. She smelled good. At least her sweater did. Some light, flowery perfume. Or was that her laundry detergent? Didn't matter. Guys didn't smell like that. "Just feeling a little down."

"What? You? How could you possibly feel down? You're Darien Hughes, remember?" Her tone was obviously teasing as she continued to play with his hair.

He tilted his head up to get a good look at her oval face and light caramel skin. Her eyes were somewhere between brown and green, closer to the former, and rimmed with full, black lashes. Her soft black hair was currently pulled back into a tail, but he'd seen it in soft waves that fell to her shoulders. They'd met at the Grammy's ceremony where Heaven Sent had won for Best Short Form Music Video. She'd been there with a friend who was up for Best Female Pop Vocal Performance. He'd started talking to Nicole at the after party, found out about her friend, found out Nicole was an actress with an occasionally recurring role on one of the new nighttime dramas. They'd talked a lot that night, which was a feat, since not many people could keep up with Darien in talking, and he'd made a habit of calling her when he was in town. Like tonight.

He let his eyes close partway, hoping interest showed in them. "I'm lonely."

She laughed, a sweet sound. "Well, we can't have that, can we?" Her eyes twinkled in clear invitation. Sweet girl rarely had trouble reading his intentions.

He stood, drawing her up to her feet. "No. We really can't." Keeping hold of her hand, he pulled her off to the side. "Come back to my hotel with me tonight?"

"You don't have a party to go to?" She stopped at his side, willingly weaving her fingers with his.

"No." There was a party, but he wasn't going. Neither were any of the others. Well, maybe Hell and Brent, but that was their business. This late in the tour, their manager chose carefully on the events that she requested the guys attend. There was nothing he *had* to go to tonight.

He brushed his lips over her forehead, sliding his hands down the curves of her sides. Curves. Something else guys didn't have.

"In that case..." she said, smiling as she slid her arms around him. She didn't seem to mind the drying sweat on his bare torso. "I'd love to."

Chapter Two

One month later...

You could have heard a pin drop. Darien expected surprise, but he wasn't entirely comfortable with the amount of shock that showed on their faces. Johnnie fell back in the stuffed chair, staring with wide eyes. From where they sat at a nearby table, both Luc and Brent held lit cigarettes aloft, forgotten. Hell froze halfway across the room, photos he was toting from the table to a box close to the main door of the suite nearly dropping from his hands. Gretchen and her assistant, Ellen, openly gaped from their seats on the couch.

Darien had arrived late to the suite where the others were signing yet more promo material. The scent of coffee, cigarettes, and Chinese food permeated the air-conditioned room, and the harsh Nevada sunlight was cut by off-white sheers.

Darien scanned the tired faces. The perpetual weariness of being on tour for over a year now was etched into their expressions. The shock only abated that a little. "What?"

Johnnie was the first to recover, holding a stack of forgotten CDs on his knee as he stared up at Darien. "You *what?*"

Darien beamed, holding up his left hand to show of the shiny new gold band on his third finger. "I got married last night."

Luc exhaled a cloud of smoke and set his cigarette on the lip of a nearby ashtray. "To who?"

Darien scowled. "Nicole, of course."

"Of course?" Johnnie again.

Darien stuck his hands on his hips, glaring around the room. He was tired, it was hot outside, and they had a gig in a few hours. He hadn't gotten much sleep the prior night thanks to a "honeymoon night" for him and Nicole, thus the reason he was late this morning. He'd hoped to get a better reaction to his news. "Okay, I knew you'd be surprised, but what gives?"

Gretchen laughed. Her red hair was pulled back into a no-nonsense bun and she wore jeans. She, too, looked worn. Her eyes darted to the others as though seeking their help. "Forgive us, Darien, but this is something of a shock."

"Well, yeah, I know." He felt his cheeks flush and dropped his gaze to the weird gold-and-green pattern on the carpet. "We kind of just *did* it. But I've been dating Nicole."

This time it was Brent. "You *have?*"

He looked up to see the genuine surprise on the guitarist's face. "Well, yeah."

"For how long?"

"About a month."

"When?" Johnnie asked.

"Come on, man, she was around during the whole New England stretch." Yes, things got crazy during a tour, but hadn't they even *noticed?*

"She's here in Vegas?"

"Of course she is. I thought I should probably tell you alone." He crossed his arms over his chest. "Humph. I'm glad I did."

Luc sighed, shaking his head as he turned sideways in his chair and leaned against the back. "Leave it to you, man, to let Las Vegas go to your head."

"What's that supposed to mean?"

Luc hooked a long arm over the back of the chair. "What the fuck did you get married for?"

"I love her."

"How the hell do you know that?" Johnnie demanded.

Darien stomped across to the room to the mini bar, ignoring the whispers between Gretchen and Ellen as he passed them. "I don't want to hear it from you. You say you fell in love with Tyler on sight." He ripped open the little refrigerator and took out a Coke. "I do love her." When he turned around, they were all exchanging glances again. "Fuck you all. What?"

Johnnie and Luc were having a whole discussion just with their eyes, scowls, and small head gestures. Finally,

Johnnie sighed and turned back to Darien. "Are you sure this was the right thing to do, man?"

"Yes. What? You don't like Nicole?"

"I don't really *know* Nicole."

Darien sighed, relieved. "Is *that* all? She's great, man." He smiled, perching on the back of a big green chair, sandaled feet on the seat. "We should do something so you guys can get to know her better." He set the Coke on the table beside him and reached for the stack of photos Ellen was handing to him. "Maybe we can all do dinner tonight?"

"Do *you* really know Nicole?"

Darien's relief faded at hearing Johnnie's careful question. He took the stack of photos, eyeing his friend. "What do you mean?"

"You just got married to the woman, dimwit," Luc snarled. "Do you really *know* her at all?"

Darien slammed the photos on the table and shoved to his feet, starting for Luc. "You asshole --"

CDs scattered as Johnnie shot up between them, hands catching hold of Darien's shoulders to stop him. "Okay, hold on." He threw a glare over his shoulder at Luc, then turned back to Darien. "Luc asked it badly, but it's a good question, Darien. Do you really know this woman?"

He met Johnnie's concerned gaze rather than Luc's annoyed one. "Did you know Tyler?"

"By the time I married him, yes."

Okay, Johnnie had him there. Darien shrugged off Johnnie's hands and stepped back, trying without success to turn what he knew looked like a sulk into a scowl. "Fuck you guys. I thought you'd be happy for me."

"Darien..."

"You're supposed to be my *friends.*" How was it possible to feel lonely in a room full of people you loved? "You're all just pissed because she's not a guy."

Johnnie grabbed his arm. "What?"

He stared at the wall rather than look at anyone in the room. "It's obvious, isn't it? I'm the odd man out. The only one who chose not to be with another guy."

Johnnie tugged, hauling Darien around to face him. "Is that what you think?"

Darien briefly glanced at his friend's face, then let his gaze skitter away on seeing the anger. "Isn't it true?"

"It's absolutely *not* true." Johnnie shook him by the shoulders. "There's no one in this room who wants you to be with a guy if that's not what you want."

Darien heard the words. He just didn't believe them. Okay, maybe he was putting words in their mouths, but he just knew they'd all be tickled if he chose to be with a guy. "Yeah, well, it's *not* what I want. I married Nicole. If you're really my friends, deal with it." He shook out of Johnnie's hold and turned toward the door.

Johnnie caught him, arms surrounding his shoulders from behind. "Don't leave, man."

He refused to wipe at the tears none of them could see because he was facing away from them. "Let me go, ass wipe."

Hell appeared in front of him, ruining his chance at getting away without them knowing he was crying. "We *are* your friends, Darien," Hell said, violet eyes locked on his. The imp was so very cute. So small with all that glossy lavender hair. Almost feminine. No wonder Brent was in love with him.

"If you tell us this is what you want, we're happy for you, man," Johnnie said. Trouble was, it *sounded* like he was trying to convince himself. Or the others.

"It's what I want," was all he could think to say, staring helplessly into Hell's eyes.

The imp smiled, a sunny expression that did a lot to banish the empty feeling in Darien's chest. "Then this is a cause for celebration." Hell stepped aside. *"Liebling,* call room service."

Johnnie turned Darien around as Hell crossed the room toward Brent. Brent gave Darien a troubled look but smoothed it away as he reached for the phone.

Luc stood and came over just as Johnnie released Darien. "Sorry, man." He tossed his head, scattering loose auburn hair from his face. "You just shocked me, y'know?"

Darien dredged up a smile and punched Luc's flat belly playfully.

"And we know he doesn't handle shock well," Johnnie quipped as he walked away.

Luc rolled his eyes as he turned. "And fuck you, too, asshole."

"Bite me." Johnnie flopped back into his chair, bending over to gather scattered CDs.

Luc picked up a new stack of photos from the table before Gretchen and Ellen. "Whip it out."

"Oh, baby."

"Must I call Reese and Tyler to let them know you two are flirting again?" Hell asked, taking a seat at the table beside Brent. He uncapped a Sharpie. "Oh! I think the two of them should get together. They'd make a *lovely* couple, don't you think?"

Johnnie and Luc both gaped in astonished outrage.

Darien burst out laughing.

Chapter Three

Seven months later...

"This isn't working."

Darien sighed, picking up some finger-sized fruit tart thing from a pretty platter and sticking it in his mouth. Nicole's words continued to echo in his brain.

"It's not that I don't love you. I do. Just...not like that."

"Not like that." And what the hell was that supposed to mean, anyway? He picked up a pair of tongs to poke around in a fruit arrangement. She loved him, but not enough to be his wife. Not enough to share a life with him. Then how the hell did she love him?

Viciously, he popped a grape with the end of the tongs, then sighed, putting them down. Abusing innocent fruit didn't help. He actually wasn't mad. Not at her. It'd been three days now and he'd thought a lot about it, talked with friends, and he saw her point; they hadn't really been man and wife. For the first two months of their marriage, he'd been on the road and she'd been working in New York. After that, they'd taken three months to travel. Now *that* had been fun! But when they got back, the subject of where they were going to live hit home. Nicole had been kind of freaked to learn that he didn't really have a house. Not anymore. Not since he let the lease go on his condo in San Diego before the last tour. He didn't see much need in a place. Most of the stuff he kept for posterity was in storage. His drum kits were in the safe hands of the Heaven Sent road crew. His mail was all delivered care of Tyler at the Weiss Strande Hotel on the west coast. They'd looked for a house, and that's where the arguments started. That's when they began to realize that they weren't all that compatible. She wanted a showplace, and he wanted someplace he could relax. She wanted someplace to entertain, and he decided if he was going to do this, it'd be his retreat to get away. They clearly had different goals in mind. Well, according to Nicole, *she* had goals, he just *was,* and she wasn't sure she could deal with that until death do them part.

He wasn't quite sure what that meant either.

"We need to end this before we hurt each other." And that was the upshot of it all. Divorce. He was going to be alone again. A seven-month marriage. How very rockstar of him.

He picked up a bite-sized cake with mint-green icing and stuck it in his mouth. A glance up showed there was still no one in the food room with him except for two guys chatting at the other end of the table and the two waiters who waited to refill the platters as necessary. Not four steps away was a big open arch leading into the main area of the banquet hall. The murmur of the crowd was only slightly drowned out by the music playing through the speakers. For the moment, he was alone and therefore excused from talking about it. But the guys knew. Johnnie was the first he'd told, and it wasn't long before they all knew. Gretchen was working on the official press release but had agreed that it was okay to talk about it that night. There weren't that many members of the press in attendance, and those who were could be trusted not to break the news. He just hoped they'd all give him a break tonight. *That* was the last thing he wanted to talk about.

Which didn't stop him from thinking about it.

Sipping his champagne, he picked up another fruit tart. *Should mingle some, though.* Darien rounded the table and headed for the arch. He knew his job at these parties, and it wasn't sulking over the food that was almost too pretty to eat. He was Darien Hughes of Heaven Sent, damn it, and this promo party was for a charity show they'd be doing two weeks from now. What was the charity again? He wasn't sure, but it was named after a cow or something. He remembered that it was a good cause. Feeding children around the world or something. Whatever it was, he was glad to be talking about doing a gig. It'd been five months since the end of the tour, and he was already itching to go back into the studio, even more so after Nicole's request for divorce. Nothing better than music to help him get back on track.

Tossing aside the gray mood that threatened to settle on him, he paused at the top of the five steps that led down into the sparse gathering below. Johnnie held court over to the right, seated on the edge of a sofa with a group of admirers ringed around him. His long brown hair flowed like water over the shoulders of the vivid green shirt that made his similarly colored eyes sparkle. Light gold streaks in his hair and a dark tan were evidence of tropic vacationing during the Heaven Sent hiatus. Over at the bar, Luc and Reese stood among a gaily laughing group of which they were the center of attention. Luc, he knew, would be of special interest tonight since he was currently working on a movie. It wasn't a starring role, but it was a large enough part that it took several months of his time. He was on a break for a few weeks before heading back up to Canada to resume filming. Turning to the left, Darien spotted Hell close to an open balcony door. Hell had less of a crowd around him than Johnnie or Luc, and the balcony beyond looked to be practically empty. Ten to one, Brent was just outside that door, having a smoke. Hell and Brent had spent most of their time during the hiatus traveling and enjoying each other's company. Lots of time with each other's families, as Darien had heard it.

They'd all had lives with their loved ones while he was playacting at having one. They were still together and he was breaking up. "Yeah," he muttered under his breath, bringing his champagne up for another sip, "we *need* to get back into the studio."

Maybe he'd go talk to Brent. After all, Brent was a master at avoiding being social.

Decision made, he swallowed the last of his fruit tart and started down the short stairs, licking his fingers.

"Darien!"

He faced front, smile instantly in place for the woman who stepped up in front of him. "Hey, 'Chelle." Reaching the bottom of the steps, he transferred his champagne glass into the hand that was sticky from the fruit tart and raised the other arm to hug the heavily made-up blonde who approached him.

She brought up a hand to hold his cheek, angling his face up for brief but warm kiss. She was just a little taller than he was. "Johnnie told me," she murmured, thumbing lipstick from his mouth with one long-nailed thumb. "How are you, sweetie?"

He kept his smile and hugged her waist tighter for a second before letting his hand slide down to just above the swell of her ass. *Mmm, backless dress. Soft skin. Smells good. Very nice.* "I'm fine, thanks."

Michelle shook her head, keeping her arm about his neck. "She's crazy to let you go."

He laughed over the pull in his heart. "She said I was too crazy to be with."

"Oh, honey, we all know you're crazy." She laughed. "But there's nothing wrong with your kind of crazy." Her laugh melted into a sensuous purr as she traced his chin with the tip of the nail on her index finger. Her blue eyes were shadowed by the heavy mascara she wore, and she tilted her head so she looked at him through the lace of those lashes. "You know I'd be happy to console you, right?"

He searched her face, waiting. Waiting for the surge of lust that should rise. Waiting for that inner voice to goad him on, make him take her off to a secluded corner. After all, he was free now, wasn't he? Nicole had said so. And Michelle was safe enough. She was a former-model-turned-singer and something of an old friend. He'd slept with her before, no strings attached, just fun. But the spark wasn't there. There wasn't even much interest in his dick, which really pissed him off. No way his dick should be passing up on a fine woman like Michelle!

He reached up to smooth the backs of his fingers over her cheek. "Thanks. The offer's tempting, but I'll have to pass."

She studied him a moment, then nodded. She kissed him lightly. "You know how to find me if you change your mind."

"I do."

She trailed her fingers down his back as she stepped away. At the end, she grabbed his hand. "Come talk with me?" she asked, tilting her head to the side so that some of that loose blonde hair caressed her shoulder.

He smiled and shook his head, squeezing her hand. "Maybe later."

She let go of his hand. "Okay." And walked away.

Moron, he labeled himself, watching the sway of her hips. He should be all over that. Instead, he turned back toward the balcony doors.

He passed by Hell with a wave. The angel-faced keyboardist sat on the wide back of a leather couch, the skirt of his long dove-gray jacket fluttering onto the couch's seat behind him. His arms were braced to either side of him, and he even kicked his booted feet slightly, lending to the illusion that he was a kid rather than a full-grown man. Darien was sure he recognized a few of the men standing with Hell, but wasn't interested enough to try and recall names. He just smiled the smile he used as a mask and stepped into the cool night air.

As predicted, Brent stood outside at the railing, looking over the hillside below, and thankfully, he was alone.

Darien stepped up next to him, turning to brace his elbows and back on the railing so he could watch the partygoers. Gretchen or one of her assistants would likely descend on them soon, requesting that they talk to someone. "Hey."

Brent glanced at him. "Hey." Darien kind of missed the dark sunglasses that Brent used to always wear. Hell had mostly broken him of the habit. He still wore them around big crowds and usually onstage, but in smaller gatherings he left them behind.

A few quiet moments passed. Darien felt like he should say something, but he was at a loss as to what. At least Brent would understand his silence.

"You doing okay?" Brent asked finally.

Darien shrugged, eyeing Brent's jacket. It was nice. Faintly shiny navy. If he thought about it, he could probably come up with the designer, but he couldn't be bothered. "Yeah. Just…not into it tonight."

Brent nodded. "Welcome to my world."

Darien chuckled. Not quite. Brent preferred to drift off to the sidelines when they weren't performing onstage. People thought it was just his mystique. They didn't know that crowds scared him. But Brent handled it with class. Usually. Darien would never be able to pull it off. Of course, he *liked* talking to people. Usually. Tonight just kind of sucked.

His gaze drifted over the colorful clothing of the partygoers, eventually landing on Hell, who he could just see inside the doorway. Damn, he was cute. Almost like a girl. In fact, one could easily think he was a flat-chested girl. Brent got a kick out of assuring people that Hell was, in fact, all male.

I could do guys, Darien told himself, considering Hell seriously. Heck, everyone else in the band screwed guys; why *not* him? Maybe that was the trick to a relationship and he'd just let that pass him by all these years? Then an inward sigh. *Nah.* Yeah, Hell was cute, but Darien wasn't especially into the cute pixie look on girls. He could admire it, but didn't really want to take it to bed. So Hell wouldn't be his type.

He turned to his side, facing Brent. "So, what do you think of Luc's news?"

Brent cocked an eyebrow. "The second movie deal?"

"Yeah. Ha, you knew, didn't you?"

"Yeah."

Figured. Luc and Brent told each other everything. They even used to be lovers, back before Hell and Reese. *Maybe someone like Luc...?* Nah. He put up with Luc because the man was like a brother, but a romantic relationship with someone who bulled through life like that would drive him nuts. He wasn't Reese. *Someone like Reese?* Nah. They got along well enough as friends, but he and Reese were too much alike in many ways. "You think it'll hurt the band?"

"How?"

"Luc might decide to be a big-time actor."

"Not a chance." Brent put out his cigarette in a standing ashtray on his other side. He stood straight, brushing a hand down the front of his black silk shirt. "He'll do fine, but the band means too much to him."

Darien wondered. The band meant everything to Brent, always had. Darien felt the same way. They were rockstars, sure, but they were musicians first. But Luc and Johnnie were different. Oh, they were totally into the band, but they were also a lot more into the "rockstar" part of it than Brent and Darien were. Both Luc and Johnnie liked to be seen, liked to be admired. They took great pains to look the way they did and act a certain way. They read the trades and knew how Heaven Sent was perceived across the globe. Darien wasn't so sure that, if either were given the chance at a solo gig, they wouldn't take it. He'd gotten the impression that Hell was very similar.

Okay, that's depressing. "If you say so."

Brent patted his shoulder. "Don't worry about it. Luc made a deal to do the next one sometime next year. Meantime, we'll go back into the studio and make some music."

"Yeah." Darien grinned. Boy, did that sound good. "Hey, I was thinking, you know…"

For a little while, he lost himself in talking music with Brent.

Engrossed in their conversation, he almost missed Hell approaching from the doorway. "Darien."

Darien looked around to see Hell standing beside them with a much taller man at his side. It took a second for Darien to recognize who it was, due to the shadows from the lights behind the man. It was a radical effect, actually, putting pretty much his entire face in shadow except for the gleam of moonlight on the small square lenses of his glasses. The soft lighting from behind him gave a golden cast to his hair, while the moonlight made silvery shadows of his face. It was like a comic book for a moment. *Awesome!*

Gold glittered on Hell's elegant hands as he indicated the taller man. "Darien, you remember my friend Christopher Faith?"

The man turned as he extended his hand; the light finally caught his face, illuminating the smiling curve of his wide mouth. "Darien."

Darien nodded, taking the hand, still a bit dazzled by the initial visual. "Sure, sure. I remember. How are you, man?" Sure he remembered Chris. An old friend of Hell's.

Chris retrieved his hand, and those hazel eyes remained fixed on Darien's face. Studying him? "I'm well, thank you." That accent was so cool. Darien wanted an accent!

Now here was a man who was good-looking in an entirely different way than most of the men Darien knew. Darien was used to flashy looks, like Johnnie or Hell or any number of the other musicians and actors that he counted among his friends, but he could also appreciate the sedate look. Even though it was a trick of the light, that initial shadowed face intrigued Darien, made him wonder what was behind that crisp, cultured voice. Chris wore a thin charcoal sweater with a high neck. His straight, light brown hair was clipped short on the sides and only slightly longer at the top, the fringe halting maybe an inch or so above the classy glasses with thin wire frames that did nothing to hide the hazel eyes. Dark, arched brows slanted into the bridge of a straight, patrician nose that pointed to a wide mouth. He was classically good-looking without an in-your-face-ness about it.

Hell glanced toward the doorway, then back at Darien, violet eyes nearly black in the dim lighting. "I know you didn't want to talk about your situation here, but since we'd discussed your need to find a lawyer for your divorce?" Hell held his hand out, palm up, toward Chris. "Chris is a lawyer. He's handled divorce cases before."

"I assisted on two," Chris clarified, frowning slightly down at Hell. Then those eyes turned back to regard Darien. "One was somewhat high profile, however."

Hell rolled his eyes, flapping his hand. "Chris enjoys downplaying his abilities. He's a fine lawyer, and you can trust him."

The "D" word poked at Darien's heart. He ignored it as best he could, seeing the sincere concern in Hell's eyes. He turned to regard the tall man again. Wow, he had broad shoulders, didn't he? "Aren't you English?"

Chris smiled, pursing out his lips a little, making them look fuller. Hey, that was a nice smile! "I was born in England, yes. But I studied law here. My practice is in New York."

Darien's eyebrows lifted with surprise. "You go to court and all?" With that voice? Oh, man, the juries didn't have a chance.

Chris laughed. A nice laugh, too. Low and soft. "I don't tend to do so, no. I'm more of a contracts lawyer."

"But he *has* handled divorces," Hell clarified.

Chris shrugged, sipping his wine.

Darien studied him. He wouldn't bring it up now, but he knew Hell had intended for Chris to be his manager when he'd threatened to leave the band when he and Brent were having troubles right before the last Heaven Sent tour. Brent was a tad sensitive about it, although he didn't hold it against Chris. But Hell trusted him. Darien had no reason not to do so as well.

"I don't think my...divorce" -- he was proud for only barely tripping over the word -- "will be that flashy. Nicole just wants to get it over with."

Hell's I-told-you-so look up at Chris told Darien that they'd discussed this already.

Chris, however, stayed focused on Darien. He slowly brought his glass to his lips and sipped. "She doesn't want anything from you?"

"We weren't married all that long."

"Regardless, given that you are a celebrity, you should have some legal authority review the agreement."

"I was just going to let Gretchen have one of the Heaven Sent lawyers look it over."

Chris tilted his head. A few strands of straight hair fell toward his eyes, brushing the top rim of his glasses. "It wouldn't hurt to have someone look it over for you personally."

Oddly, a shiver of delight crept up the back of Darien's neck at the sound of the last word. What the fuck?

Ignoring the shiver, he gave the offer serious thought. Chris looked like an upstanding guy. If he was Hell's good friend, he had to be worth it. He nodded. "Okay." He held out his hand toward Chris. "I'm game if you are."

Chris took his hand in a warm grasp. "I'll do my best to look after your interests."

Chapter Four

"How the hell do you work this thing?" Darien demanded, glaring at the jumbled mess of metal pieces and wires.

"It's a brain teaser. If I told you, it would defeat the purpose."

Darien transferred his glare from the "executive puzzle" -- or so Chris had called it -- sitting on the desk before him to the calm lawyer seated across from him, laying out an arrangement of papers.

Chris wasn't even looking at him, his attention solely focused on the laptop screen to his left and the neatly spread papers on the blotter. Waning afternoon sunlight streamed through the blinds on the windows behind him, setting off the gold highlights in his hair. He twiddled a fountain pen between two fingers as he turned to read one of the legal-sized sheets before him. A lefty, which Darien thought was too fascinating, even though it wasn't anything Chris could help. A gold band surrounded the base of the little finger on that hand. Darien sat up a little straighter to see if he could make out the design.

"Before I forget" -- Chris reached for a small note-sized slip of paper off to the side of his desk and held it out to Darien -- "here's a few websites that cover what we were discussing the other night."

Darien blinked, taking the paper. "The other night?"

Chris tilted his head slightly to one side. "The copyrights?"

"Oh! At the party." He scanned the list of eight web addresses. "Hey, cool, thanks."

"Quite all right. So..." Chris sat forward, elbows on the desk as he picked up a short stack of papers in front of him. With his sleeves rolled up, the dusting of light brown hair on his arms gleamed in the sunlight that shone over his shoulder. Geez, did all of his hair shine like that? "You've listed your place of residence as the Weiss Strande Hotel?"

Distracted, Darien had to shake his head a little to get his thoughts back on track. "As much as anyplace, yeah."

"You don't own a home?"

Realizing he was staring at Chris's arm for no good reason, Darien resumed his attention on the brain teaser. "Not anymore."

"Not even an apartment?"

"Nope."

"You did at one time?"

Darien nodded, letting go of one of the oddly shaped metal pieces and picking up another. "For a while, before the last tour, I had a condo in San Diego. I let the lease go."

"Why?"

"Seemed a waste to pay for it when I wasn't using it."

Chris's pause made Darien look up. The man was scowling, confused. "You could have purchased it outright. Or rented it out in your absence."

"Yeah."

"Why didn't you?"

"I didn't really like it."

"Why'd you rent it?"

Darien shoved the puzzle away and folded his arms on the edge of the desk. "Well, I liked it fine when I started the lease." He pulled a pen out of the cup beside him and uncapped it, trying to figure out if the color was black or a really dark blue. "A friend of mine, Alec Taylor, mentioned the complex on the beach and that some others of our friends were renting there. So I got one. Seemed like a good idea at the time. I never really moved in."

"Alec Taylor from Urban Dogs?"

"Yeah."

Chris shoved a little notepad his way. "You never moved in?"

Darien smiled a thanks at Chris, then started to doodle on the notepad. "Nah. Once I started needing to get furniture and stuff, I lost interest." Blue ink and a very fancy design on the grip of the pen.

"You could have hired someone to shop for you."

Darien glanced up to see Chris's amusement. "Yeah, I know. Luc's done that, and Johnnie did it for one of his places." He shrugged, doodling out lopsided, interconnected squares. "Didn't seem worth it. I don't have that much stuff really."

"Do you have items in storage?"

"Items," not "stuff." Darien smiled, loving the primness of Chris's vocabulary. "I've got stuff at my parents' place and some stuff in storage, yeah."

Chris made a note on the yellow legal sheet to his far left. "I'm going to give you the name of a real estate agent I know. He may have some ideas for you."

Darien paused, watching Chris write. "Thanks." *I think.* "Uh, could you just email it to me? That's easier."

Without looking up, Chris nodded. "I'll need your address."

"Here." Darien turned to a clean sheet of the little notepad and started writing.

Chris tapped his pen on the papers before him. "Why have you listed the Weiss as your place of residence?"

"Tyler offered to keep track of my mail and let me know if anything important comes." Tyler, like just about everyone else, had been concerned when he found out that Darien was, essentially, homeless. Ha! Last he checked, he was at least a millionaire and he was homeless. No one thought that was as amusing as he did.

Chris shook his head, accepting the slip of paper with Darien's personal email address and setting it aside. "All right." He made another note on the notepad beside him and flipped over a paper. "You are aware that Nicole has asked for a settlement?"

Darien nodded, resuming his drawing with triangles now. "Yeah. I agreed to help her out for a while."

"She needs the money?"

"Sorta. She lost her job because she went off with me. I said I'd help her out until she got settled on another show."

"That could take quite a while. She's an actress?"

"Yeah."

"This is open-ended."

Pen poised over the triangles, Darien looked up, clued in by Chris's tone that this was more important than he'd thought. "So?"

"Phrased as it is, you could end up supporting her for the rest of her life."

He blinked, staring at Chris. "Well...I hadn't thought about it."

Chris raised an eyebrow. "Do you think your future wife would approve of your supporting your former?"

"Hmmm. Good point." He let the "future wife" part go.

Chris sighed softly and made another note. "Let's put a finite date on this. If the split is as amicable as you claim -- and I've no reason now to believe that it's not -- she should be amenable to, say, three years?"

"Five."

Chris gave him a look.

"What? I'm generous."

"To a fault."

Darien shrugged. "The marriage thing was my idea, and I kind of talked her into bailing out of her job when she probably shouldn't have. Now she's got a bad rep. I feel guilty."

"Hmmm. All right, five."

Darien grinned. "Good thing I've got you to look out for me."

Chris paused, pen hovering over the notepad. He tilted his head only enough to roll his eyes up to look at Darien. Chris studied him for a moment before carefully setting the pen down. Calmly, he folded his hands and looked at Darien. "If you don't mind my asking, why did you get married?"

Darien opened his mouth to give all the reasons he'd given before, but stopped. "It seemed like a good idea at the time."

Chris didn't laugh it off with him. "Why?"

Darien started filling in some of the triangles. "All my friends were paired up. Seemed like it was time to settle down."

Darien glanced up to see Chris with his head tilted and his eyebrow up to nearly his hairline.

"I know, I know. Bonehead reason. Sue me. Wait, you're a lawyer. I take that back." He grinned.

Chris opened his mouth to say something, but something over Darien's shoulder distracted him.

Darien turned in his chair just as the man in the open doorway knocked on the frame. He was a good-looking blond, probably in his early twenties. He smiled. "Am I interrupting?"

Darien glanced at Chris just in time to see a scowl wipe from his features, replaced by a patient smile as he stood. "Not if it's quick."

Darien stood as the blond entered. He was about Darien's height, a little shorter, and his hair was actually a few different shades of yellow. Some of it looked fake, but not in a bad way. He was all flirty blue eyes, with a big smile, wearing a tight blue T-shirt and equally tight white jeans. He and Chris met at the side of Chris's desk and exchanged a brief kiss.

Kiss? Darien blinked. Did he know Chris was gay? That was a lover's kiss, right? Had to be. Wasn't just a friend thing. Well, no, guys don't do that sort of thing. Well, guys who weren't into guys. *Dayum.*

"Darien," Chris said, holding out a hand, "this is Nathan Thomas."

The blond extended a hand in Darien's direction, beaming. "His boyfriend."

Oh? Darien took the hand, pretty sure he kept his surprise under wraps. "Nice to meet you."

At least Nathan didn't seem to notice. "It is an *extreme* pleasure to meet you." He gave a good squeeze to Darien's hand, bringing the other hand to grip his wrist. "I am a big fan."

Darien put on the smile he used when meeting press and fans. "Really? Hey, thanks." Images started swirling in his head of Chris and this guy kissing, touching, fucking. He couldn't have said why he was so taken with this new piece of information about Hell's friend, but he was.

"My apologies, Darien," said Chris, standing beside his desk with a frown for the blond. "I'm quite sure Nathan's timely arrival has something to do with your presence."

Nathan grimaced up at him.

Darien laughed. "Hey, that's okay. I don't mind."

Nathan stuck his tongue out at Chris, and Darien nearly choked at the immediate pictures that put into his mind of just what portions of Chris's body that tongue had touched.

What the hell?

Nathan turned back to face Darien, swinging a backpack off his shoulder onto the seat Darien had just occupied. "I'm sorry. Chris told me I couldn't come. But when he said that he'd be meeting with you, I simply *had* to see if I could meet you."

Darien frowned, glancing at Chris. "Haven't you met Hell yet?"

"No. Not yet."

"We haven't been together long," Chris explained, crossing his arms and leaning his hip against the edge of the desk. "So, Nathan, do what you've come to do, and let us get back to work."

"Spoilsport."

Darien laughed. Inspiration hit him. "Hey, why don't we go to dinner?"

He couldn't have made Nathan happier, judging by the bounce and clap together of hands.

Chris, however, frowned. "It's only five o'clock."

"That's okay. We're done here, aren't we?"

"No."

Darien pouted. "Then can't we do that tomorrow?"

"We don't have an appointment set for tomorrow."

"We could. I'm free; are you?"

Chris's jaw dropped a little, his eyes none too happy. *Oops, may have gone too far.* He knew his attitude came off as flip, especially when he didn't want to do something, and reading legal papers and answering questions about the divorce was something he didn't want to do. Even if being with Chris made it a bit tolerable.

"Or any time this week...?"

Chris narrowed his eyes.

Nathan sidled up to Chris, sliding a hand up his chest. *"Please,* Chris."

Darien wondered at the frown that threatened his own face as he battled it. *Weird.*

Chris reached up to take hold of Nathan's hand, grimacing slightly at the smaller man. He looked up at Darien. "You don't mind?"

"Heck no."

Chris sighed. "All right." He turned back to the desk. "Let's set up a time for tomorrow."

Nathan beamed. "Wonderful! Thank you."

They settled for a little steakhouse in the lobby of the building where Chris's office was located. It was the kind of restaurant that Darien loved to find in New York City. Kind of hidden and off the wall, but the food promised to be delicious.

Nathan held his menu but didn't read it. He barely waited for the host to leave with their drink order before leaning toward Darien. "I have to ask. It must be so exciting being a rockstar! You've been all *over* the world."

Darien smiled, skimming over the entrée list. *Steak, yeah. Hmm, which kind?* "Yeah, I guess so."

"You guess so? You guys have even toured Russia."

"Well, yeah." He smiled, dividing his time between glancing at Nathan and the menu. "We did shows in Moscow, Leningrad, and Samara, but we didn't get to see much of the cities."

They paused while the waiter came with the wine Chris had ordered when they sat down. Chris did the classy thing, smelling the cork and tasting before nodding his acceptance. Darien had never mastered that. Luc had tried to teach him once, claiming the chicks loved it, but Darien preferred other methods to impress the ladies. After the waiter left, Nathan folded his menu, unread, and laid it on the table.

"You didn't get to see any of Russia? Why not?"

"That's kind of the way it is." Oh, yeah, prime rib sounds good. Darien set his menu down and picked up his glass. "When we're on tour, there's so much to do and so much security that usually we see the venue and our hotel. Sometimes they'll take us somewhere on a press thing or for a photo shoot, but that's it. Oh, hey, this is good!"

Chris nodded his agreement as they both sipped the dark red -- Darien turned the bottle toward him -- cabernet.

Nathan glanced between them, then picked up his own glass. "Still, you've *been* there. I've never been out of the country."

Darien smiled at Chris. The gold rims of his glasses shone in the dim light from the small candle lamp set in the middle of the table. "You've probably really seen more of the world than I have." Did Chris realize he was stroking the lip of his wineglass with two fingers? Well, if he didn't, Darien did.

Chris glanced up from where he was staring into the light, fingers halting. "I'm not so sure of that."

"Hey, born in England, live in the States. I know you've been to Germany. You probably get to *do* more than I get to do when I go anywhere." Darien sat back as a waiter brought a bread basket. "Where else have you been?"

Chris shrugged, setting down his glass to reach for a slice of the hot bread. "Italy, France, Greece..."

"Oh, man." Darien sat forward. "I did get to see some of Athens when we were there. That place rocks! All the old together with the new. And the people were so cool."

Chris smiled, just a small curling of the corners of his mouth, but it was a beautiful thing. "Did you visit the Parthenon?"

"Pile of old rocks." Nathan sniffed. "But the nightlife is incredible, I hear."

Darien watched, but Chris didn't react to Nathan's snipe. "I don't know, I thought the Parthenon was pretty awesome. We wanted to play in this theater attached to it that's actually one of the ancient theaters, but they ended up not letting us do it." Darien shrugged.

The waiter returned to take their order. Darien was bemused when Chris ordered for both himself and Nathan. *What's the deal with them?* Was Nathan just a boy toy? He certainly looked it. He was in his early twenties at most, while Chris had to be, what, mid-thirties? Chris didn't seem the type to want a just a pretty face, but what other explanation was there? Darien didn't get the sense that they were head-over-heels. He'd been around too many lovey-dovey couples -- male ones at that -- in the past two years not to recognize the emotions, and that's exactly what was lacking between these two. *I could be wrong.* Inwardly, he shrugged.

Once the waiter left, Nathan leaned into him again. "So can you tell me what's in store for Heaven Sent? Or is that hush-hush?"

"No hush-hush. I'm due at the Weiss West in May, actually. We're all meeting up after Luc finishes his movie thing, and we're going to start putting together ideas for the next album."

Nathan's eyes went big. "Really? How does that work?"

Darien glanced at Chris, who seemed interested as well. Seeing no objection, Darien went ahead and explained the process, answering any and all of Nathan's continual questions.

Darien liked to believe that he was honest with himself. He tried to be, at least. It helped to take things in stride when he just took his own thoughts at face value and dealt with them. So that night, long after leaving Chris and Nathan's company, he wasn't all that freaked to figure out that he was attracted to one Christopher Faith. Surprised, yes, but not freaked.

He laughed about it as he flipped through the late-night shows. It wasn't odd for him to think that a man was attractive. He thought a lot of guys were attractive. It helped with the Heaven Sent bisexual rumor thing that he didn't mind flirting. Flirting was harmless and fun, even with guys. But he was drawn to Chris, a new experience. He loved to look at him, certainly, but there was more to it than that. That afternoon in Chris's office and later at dinner had been fun because Chris was there, because he liked talking to Chris. Had liked talking to him at the party the previous week, as well. If Chris were a woman, Darien would have already started coming on hard. Heck, if it weren't for the fact that Chris already had a boyfriend, Darien might make a move anyway.

Wasn't *that* amazing?!

Next afternoon, Darien showed up at Chris's office, as scheduled. He waved and said hello to the nice receptionist and walked on past her. He walked down the darkened hall, past a few other offices with busily working people, until he got to Chris's open door.

Chris looked up at his knock.

Oh, yeah, you've got it bad, he chided himself as his heart skipped a beat. The man sat there in one of those crisp pin-striped dress shirts. No tie, a few buttons undone at his collar, but the cuffs were fastened. His fancy watch gleamed just a tad more gold than the highlights of his hair.

"Darien," he greeted, standing.

"Hey." Darien sauntered in. Was it wishful thinking that Chris was checking him out? Appreciating the care he'd taken to make his blond hair shine, maybe admiring the fit of his tight blue T-shirt? Had he dressed to impress this morning? Well, maybe a little. Chris may have been taken, but it didn't mean he couldn't look, right?

"Before we begin," Chris said, sitting again. He paused, considering Darien closely. "I want to thank you."

Darien sat and purposefully shoved aside the infernal puzzle that had distracted him the day before. "For what?"

Chris removed his glasses. Darien watched his face, fascinated by his first glimpse of it without the glasses, as Chris used a small rag to clean the lenses. He looked less...imposing without them. "For humoring Nathan last night."

"Oh. That? That wasn't a problem at all. I had fun."

Chris studied him for a moment. How cool. His eyes were usually hazel, but in the right lighting -- like now -- they looked brown. Then he smiled that small little smile and put his glasses back on. "Good. I'm glad. Nathan can be a little...much at times."

Darien chuckled. "So can I. I'm sure you've noticed."

Chris's smile took on the look of a smirk.

"Go ahead. I know. I'm a chatterbox."

Chris laughed, making Darien's heart swell. He vowed to do anything he could to cause that laugh often.

Chris slid a neat stack of papers from the corner of the desk to the spot before him. "Yes, well, thank you just the same."

"How long have you two been dating?"

Chris looked up, startled. "Nearly five months."

"Exclusively?"

A blink and a pause, but the answer that came was: "Yes."

Not sure, huh? Perhaps Nathan wasn't so much.

Darien wanted to ask. All night, both at dinner and through to this morning, curiosity had burned in him. He wanted to know how serious they were. He wanted to know if they were as close to breaking up as he thought from last night. But how sad was that? He wanted them to break up because he was attracted to Chris? No, he wanted them to break up because Nathan really didn't treat Chris right. He'd been dismissive and inattentive all night. Every conversation that had actually involved Chris has been started by Darien, not Nathan. That had to mean they were on the outs, right?

"What?"

Darien startled, blinking up at Chris. "What?"

"You're staring at me."

Smooth move, Ex-Lax. "Am I?"

"Yes. What is it?"

Darien felt his eyes get big. He bit his lips together. What the hell could he say? Certainly not what he was thinking. But he so wanted to *know!* "I was just wondering..."

"Yes?"

"Are you...I mean, are you guys...?"

Chris sat back in his plush chair, folding his hands across his belly. "Yes?"

Darien sat forward, gripping the edge of the desk. "You're the top, right?"

The look of incredulity didn't belong on Chris's face, but there it was. Eyes wide, mouth agape. He even flushed a little.

"I m-mean..." Darien stammered, afraid he'd gone too far. Him and his big mouth. Was that really better than what he'd been thinking? Yeah, he'd wondered, but even he knew that was pushing the bounds of politeness. "I mean, Brent and Hell have my way of thinking on this one all messed up, and it's just... I mean, I'm pretty *sure* you're the top, but you never know, right? I just --" He broke off, feeling his face heat as he looked down at his lap. *Oh, great, Einstein. He's gonna throw you out of here.*

Laughter filled the office. Deep, joyous, surprised laughter. Darien looked up to see Chris's head thrown back against his seat, his hands spread over his flat belly as though to hold it in. His eyes were closed and his mouth wide open as he laughed. After a moment, his head came forward, teary eyes opening behind his glasses, but one look at Darien and he cracked up again.

Darien grinned, loving this. "It's not *that* funny."

Which only made Chris laugh louder. He fell forward over his desk, forearms braced on the top, head hung between his shoulders.

"Chris?" came a voice from the doorway.

Darien looked over his shoulder to see Chris's assistant, Max, who usually sat in the next office.

Max glanced at Darien with a curious smile.

Darien shrugged.

"You okay, Chris?" Max asked.

"I'm fine," Chris panted, waving a hand at the man. "I'm fine."

Darien screwed his lips to the side, waiting for the laughter to die down.

Chris took off his glasses and wiped at the tears streaming down his cheeks. A beautiful flush marked his face and neck, and when he looked up, his eyes shone like Darien had never seen them before.

Darien nudged the box of tissues from the edge of the desk closer to Chris.

Chris took a few and dabbed at his eyes. Peeks at Darien threatened to start him laughing again, but he held it in. He sighed, still chuckling.

Darien waited to speak until Chris was mostly calm. "Well, are you going to answer my question?"

One look and Chris was off laughing again.

Chapter Five

When Darien was playing his drums, nothing else existed. The world and all its problems got pounded into the background by the beat of the bass drum at his feet, and the crunch of the snares kept it at bay. He was barely aware of his own body. Even when he was just practicing, really just keeping in shape, he lost himself so wholly that he rarely acknowledged the presence of another.

Which was why he didn't know Chris was there until he passed a final drum roll over the toms and happened to glance up to see the man in the doorway.

He didn't stumble over his moves often, but the sight of Chris leaning in the doorway separating the practice room from the smaller sitting room threw him off. Glasses perched on that long, straight nose, short hair gleaming in the diffused overhead light, a slight smile on wide, generous lips. No button-down today. He wore a pale yellow polo shirt that fit snugly over broad shoulders and chest, looser over the waist that tapered into faded jeans. Jeans. Chris was wearing jeans. And black lace-up boots. For nearly two months Darien had seen Chris at least once a week, often more, and he'd yet to see Chris in anything more casual than Dockers, and that only once. He liked it.

"Hey, Chris," he greeted, sitting back on his stool.

"Hello." Chris nodded his head, smile widening. "That was wonderful."

Darien blinked, reaching up to scrape a lock of hair from his eyes. It wasn't dripping or anything, but it was definitely wet. Now that he'd stopped playing, he was aware of the sweat that beaded his brow and plastered his loose tank top to his chest and shoulders. He probably looked awful. "What?"

"What you were just playing."

Darien looked down at the snare drum before him, then back up at Chris. He laughed. "That? Oh, that was nothing." He twirled one of the sticks in his fingers. "Just keeping in shape."

"Well, it sounded good to me."

Darien chuckled. "Cool. That's what they pay me for, right?"

"Right."

He kept twirling the stick, checking Chris out while trying not to be too obvious about it. *Does he work out?* He had to do something to keep his arms looking like that. Who'd've thought he had such nice muscles underneath those prim button-downs? "Uh, what're you doing here?" This practice studio at the Weiss East was on the second floor, near a staircase that led down to the wings right beside the main stage of the White Tiger, the hotel's nightclub. You needed security clearance to get anywhere near it, and Darien was aware that he was the only musician currently in residence, so he hadn't expected to see another soul while he was practicing.

Chris smiled and pushed from the doorway, then bent to pick up the briefcase sitting by his feet. "I have something for you."

Darien's mind reeled at the sensual possibilities of that. Surely Chris didn't mean...?

Chris straightened and patted the briefcase. "I have your divorce papers."

Darien blinked, tamping down the lust that had surged along with his rabid imagination. "Oh."

"I stopped by the front desk when you didn't answer your room phone. When they eventually believed I was your lawyer, they gave me a passcard to get into the studio." He lowered the briefcase to his side, reaching up with his free hand to push his glasses up further on his nose. "I hope you don't mind."

"Oh, no, I don't mind." Darien carefully set his sticks on the snare, glancing down at his torn jeans and tank top. Yeah, he looked like shit. Oh, well, no help for it. He stood, glancing up.

And caught Chris staring. It was fleeting and Chris turned away almost immediately, but he couldn't have imagined the heat in that stare, could he? Yeah, he probably could. Since he'd discovered this attraction for Chris, he'd convinced himself that he'd caught the man checking him out a lot. If he was right, was that so wrong or so bad? Darien knew he wasn't a bad-looking guy. There were thousands of screaming fans who thought he was the living end. It wasn't out of the question for one gay lawyer to find him attractive, even if said lawyer was currently in a relationship. Right?

"You didn't have to bring them here." Darien rounded the drum kit and jumped off the riser. If the rest of the guys had been in town, their equipment would fill it, but since he was the only one around at the moment, all the rest of the practice gear was tucked safely away in one of the storage rooms.

"I don't mind. I was in town." Chris looked around the empty room, but there was nowhere to sit except the stool behind the drums and a few folding chairs leaning against the wall in one corner.

Darien pointed to the room behind Chris as he approached. "Let's go in there."

Chris nodded, turned, and bumped into Darien. Since Darien was shorter, he had an excellent view of the surprise that came over Chris's face at their touch. Not a bad sort of surprise. A sharp inhalation and a momentary freeze, followed by a brief fluttering of those green-brown eyes behind those thin lenses of glass.

"Sorry," Darien muttered with a smile, bending his head to lead the way into the main studio. Okay, that was a *definite* sign of attraction there. Too bad he was all skanky and sweaty. Maybe Chris liked that.

Self-conscious despite the favorable reaction from Chris, he walked into the sitting room. It was painted a calming blue, with big windows in one wall overlooking the street below and the buildings opposite.

He led Chris to a couch and chairs set around a small coffee table. "Sorry if I stink," he said, figuring he'd just acknowledge it.

"Oh, no, you're fine." Was Chris's voice lower? Was that a flush across the back of that long, fine neck? Chris watched his hands as he set the briefcase on the table and opened it. Yeah, he was a little flushed.

"I'm gonna go towel down." Darien indicated the door to a small bathroom. "I'll be back in a minute."

"Oh. All right."

Darien closed himself in the little washroom that contained a narrow shower at the far end, a toilet, and a counter with two sinks. He grabbed one of the fluffy white towels Tyler's staff kept handy and turned to the big mirror over the sinks.

Shit! Yeah, he looked awful. Well, no. He didn't look any worse than he usually did after playing solid for an hour and a half in a room with the air-conditioning turned on low, but he was all sweaty and his hair was lank and sticking to his skull and neck. He glanced at the shower, but figured that would take too long. Even if it was quick, he didn't want to make Chris wait forever. So instead he tore off his tank top and used one of the white washcloths to wipe his chest, neck, and armpits. He wet his hands and combed them through his hair, figuring the wet look was better than the sweat look. Almost done, he grabbed up the tank top and paused before putting it on. He studied himself in the mirror. He actually had a pretty nice chest. He was shorter and a little stockier than, say, Luc or Johnnie, but he had more muscle than either of them. It came from playing drums and the fact that he liked lifting weights on occasion. He wasn't bulky, but he was toned. He had a nice summer tan, which made the sparse mat of gold hair across his chest almost glitter. He'd always thought was a great effect. *Would Chris?*

Grinning, knowing he was flirting where he probably shouldn't, he left the tank on the counter and returned to the next room.

The reaction was gratifying. His shirtlessness obviously caught Chris off guard because when he looked up he froze. And stared. Hazel eyes locked on Darien's pecs and didn't look like they could be dragged away.

Yeah, he likes. "Sorry," Darien said, not meaning it at all. "The tank's soaked."

Chris shook his head. Eyes darted away but returned to check Darien out. "No, no, I don't mind." Yeah, his voice had definitely gone down an octave. He cleared his throat and bent over the papers laid out on the coffee table. "Everything seems to be in order."

"Cool." Darien went right past the couch to a mini-fridge in the corner. "Want something to drink? There's beer, water, Coke, and juice."

"No, thank you."

Darien snagged a Corona and brought it back to the couch with him, opening it as he went. He paused before sitting to take that first drink. He was, of course, posing. Making sure Chris got a good look. Wicked of him, yes, but he was enjoying this.

Besides, Chris seemed to like the view. At least if that furtive look as Darien sat was any indication.

Careful, you're gonna get hard. He could feel it stirring in his pants. 'Course, would that be a bad thing? *Yes! He's got a boyfriend, asshole. Cool it.* He set the Corona down on the table and slid the stack of papers in front of him. "So, what have we got here?"

Chris explained the papers to him, and Darien tried not to let his focus wane. This was important. Chris had convinced him that he needed to pay attention to the particulars of his divorce. Even though he trusted Nicole and still considered her a friend, legal matters were not something to be taken lightly. Certainly not as lightly as he'd taken the marriage ceremony in the first place. It wasn't easy, though. The legal mumbo-jumbo was a drone in his head even when delivered with Chris's sexy accented voice, and Chris's cologne was distracting. As was his warm body. Their knees and arms kept brushing as Chris reached in front of him to turn papers over. Darien was more than capable of doing that himself, but if Chris wanted to snuggle up, Darien wasn't going to stop him. It was a struggle to keep focused on the papers and not turn to look his fill at the gorgeousness beside him. Look, ha! He wanted to throw down his pen and find out if Chris was hard inside those jeans.

He still thought that was just plain weird -- for him to want a guy -- but he'd come to terms with it in the past few weeks. Besides, it was new and exciting. Sure, he'd thought about feeling up another guy before. He couldn't have spent years with Johnnie as his best friend and not at least have thought about it. But he'd never wanted to *do* it. Not really. Not to the point where it was a near compulsion, like now.

But the weight of what was in the papers before him slowly sank in as Chris talked. He was about to be divorced. His marriage was over. But then, had he ever really been married? His friends didn't seem to think so. His parents were of the same opinion. At first, his mother had been tickled pink to hear the news. Put out that she hadn't been at the ceremony itself, of course, but she'd been delighted to have a daughter-in-law. She and Nicole even got along really well. Still did, as far as he knew. But his mom had not been surprised when he'd told her about the divorce. She'd cried, but not so much because he and Nicole were splitting as because he hadn't, in her words, "found what he needed."

"I want my baby to be happy," she'd said.

"I'm happy, Mom."

"No, honey. Not completely. Not really. You need someone to take care of you."

He'd laughed. "Mom, I've got tons of people taking care of me."

"Not the way I mean, honey. No one's taking care of your heart."

That conversation haunted him. He tried to write it off as his mom's romantic streak. She had one a mile wide, always had. But something about what she'd said beat in his heart, and he couldn't shake it. *No one's taking care of your heart.* It was enough to put a damper on the intriguing new interest in the lawyer seated beside him.

Finally Chris pointed to the last signature line, and Darien signed. He stared down at the illegible scratch that was his autograph. "So that's it? I'm divorced?"

Chris gathered the papers before him and stacked them neatly. "Almost. I'll need to file them with the state of Nevada, of course, but this is, effectively, it."

So I'm alone again. Actually, he'd been alone since Nicole had asked for the divorce. No, really he'd been alone longer than that. God, how depressing.

With a sigh, he set down the fountain pen, then held up his left hand to stare at the gold band on his third finger. Without a word, he took it off, then held it in his right palm for a moment.

"You've been wearing that all this time." It was a statement, not a question, telling him Chris had noticed.

"Yeah."

"May I ask why?"

Why. Darien chewed the inside of his lower lip, wondering what to tell Chris.

"You don't have to answer that."

"No, it's okay. I just..." He shrugged, turning over his hand to roll the ring across the backs of his knuckles. "We were married. You're supposed to wear the ring, right?"

"The ring is not as important as what it symbolizes."

Darien sighed again, leaning back on the couch, the better to slip the ring into his front pocket. "Yeah. That's the kicker, isn't it? It's a symbol of love, and I didn't really love her." He rubbed at his eyes with one hand, then left the palm over his eyes. "Not like I should."

"It's more than love. Marriage is not just love."

Darien peeked through his fingers at Chris, watching the man's profile as he slowly arranged the papers into a neat stack. His expression told Darien that he took what he was saying very seriously.

"Many, many couples get married thinking that if they love each other, it'll just all work out. That's not the case. Love is important, yes, but making a marriage last takes work and commitment."

"Were you ever married?"

Chris blinked, startled. He glanced at Darien. "No. But I've been in a serious relationship where love wasn't enough."

Darien frowned over the pull at his heart. "Nathan?"

Chris laughed, but there wasn't much mirth in it. "Oh, no, not Nathan. Long before Nathan." He bent to pick up the briefcase he'd set beside the table.

Darien was torn, wanting to ask two questions at once. He wanted to know who this other love was, but the more immediate question came out: "But you love Nathan, right?"

Chris turned his head. Darien couldn't tell if he was smiling or not, and if he was, it wasn't exactly happy. "No."

"No?"

"Nathan and I broke up."

It felt like a boulder bounced on Darien's chest, taking the breath out of his lungs. "What? When?"

"Tuesday."

The day before yesterday. "I didn't know."

Chris chuckled, securing the papers in his briefcase. "No. I didn't think it important to tell you."

Darien sat forward, laying a hand on Chris's shoulder. "Are you okay?"

Chris glanced at the hand but didn't shrug it off. "Me? I'm quite all right. Thank you."

"Yeah, but you guys have been together…what, seven months now?"

"Yes. But we were never in love."

"You weren't?"

"No. We enjoyed each other for a time, but that was all."

So Darien's instincts hadn't been that far off after all. He was rarely wrong about other people's relationships. It was his own that he had troubles with. "I'm still sorry."

Chris gave him a genuine smile and reached up to pat the hand on his shoulder. "Thank you." He stood, briefcase in hand. "I should be going."

Mild panic drew Darien to his feet. "What? Why? Stick around." He hadn't quite processed the implications of what Chris had just told him or what was going on in his head. But he couldn't help thinking: *Chris is free.* "Or, better yet, go out with me."

Chris blinked, clearly caught off guard by the choice of words. "Pardon?"

"Yeah, let's go out. I'll take you to dinner."

Chris frowned. "Why?

"Why? Because I'm a newly divorced man and I don't want to be alone tonight. Because you just broke up with your boyfriend and you shouldn't be alone." Seeing Chris start to shake his head, Darien hastened on with: "Because I want to thank you for helping me when divorce isn't your area of expertise."

"You don't have to thank me."

"Then because I want to." He gripped Chris's arm and put on his very best smile, with teeth and everything. That smile got him a lot in this world, and he gave it his best effort at that moment. "C'mon, Chris, let me take you out to dinner."

Chris stared at him, frowning slightly as he studied Darien's face. "I don't know…" But the tone wavered. The smile was having its effect.

Knowing he wasn't playing fair, Darien put on the plead. "Please? I don't want to be alone tonight, and no one else is in town."

Chris looked torn between scowling and laughing. The laugh won. "All right, then."

Chapter Six

Johnnie would be so happy when Darien finally got around to telling him that he was attracted to a guy. He'd get razzed mercilessly, but he was used to that.

So now that he knew Chris was free, what was he going to do about it? Before today, it was just a thing that couldn't go anywhere because Chris was in a relationship. Well, now that relationship was a thing of the past. Did Darien want to go through with more? Was he ready for all that came with it? Was he seriously contemplating sex with a guy?

Darien was still mulling it over when he got out of the shower. Chris waited in the main room of Darien's suite at the Weiss while Darien made himself presentable. A glance in the mirror showed him that he needed a shave, so he gave himself a little extra time to pass a razor over his face to get rid of a day's worth of stubble.

Did he really want to fuck a guy? Usually the answer came out to "no," but tonight was different. Chris was different. He had a feeling he might not mind with Chris.

He stared at himself in the mirror as he ran a hand over his now smooth chin. He'd put on his best jeans, the ones he knew hugged his ass to emphasize its shape. He had on a dark orange button-down that someone had told him made his brown eyes look deeper and his hair look brighter. For whatever reason, his eyes looked bigger tonight, and he counted that as a bonus. His hair was doing its thing, drying about his head and neck, and he decided not to be annoyed that it was straight as a board with no curl to it whatsoever. Shrugging, he undid two more buttons of the shirt, leaving it open halfway down his chest, and left the bathroom.

He looked good, if he did say so himself. Would Chris think so? Would Chris even think about fucking him?

Just take it as it comes, he told himself, grabbing his keycard from the dresser and stashing it in his back pocket as he entered the main room.

Chris was seated forward on the couch, elbows on knees and head bent over the day's *New York Times,* which was spread on the low table before him. He glanced up as Darien entered, and kind of froze.

Darien sauntered toward Chris, *aware* he was sauntering. Aware he put an extra sway in his hips. What the hell was that? He didn't do that with girls. But like the bare chest earlier that day, the move had a very cool effect. As Chris sat up, his eyes started at Darien's face, but they fell almost immediately to his groin. They paused for a brief heartbeat on their way back up to take in Darien's chest before those eyes, green at the moment, came back to his face.

Darien smiled. Oh, yeah, that was promising. "Sorry to make you wait. You ready?"

"Yes." Chris's voice was a touch raspy, and he cleared his throat as he reached for the briefcase at the corner of the table.

"You can leave that here if you want." Because that'd mean Chris would have to come back up to the room with him after dinner.

Chris raised an eyebrow at him, hand hovering over the handle of the briefcase. Then he shut his hand and stood, nodding. "All right."

Darien headed toward the door. "There's a great Italian place here in the hotel. Okay to go there?"

A glance over his shoulder, and he caught Chris checking out his ass again. This time, he wasn't so quick to look away, even when he had to know Darien saw. "Sounds good."

"Great!" His heart gave that little jump it did when he knew he was on the right track with a potential lover. "They serve you *tons* of food. 'Course, it's not really like the food we had when we were in Italy." He held the door for Chris to pass by, then let it fall shut. "Oh, man, you said you'd been to Italy, right?! The food there is terrific! When we were staying…"

Darien picked up the wine bottle to refill Chris's glass. "So, what happened between you and Nathan?"

Chris caught Darien's hand to stop him when the glass was half full, giving him a look. Darien just grinned. He'd made sure that Chris's glass was full during salads and entrees, not sure until now if Chris really noticed. He couldn't even be sure how many glasses Chris had drunk, technically, but they were on their second bottle. It seemed like a good idea to keep Chris mellow. Besides, he liked the heavy-lidded look that had come over the lawyer. Very sexy, especially since the mood lighting of the dim lamp on the wall beside them made interesting shadows of Chris's sharply angular face.

Chris picked up the glass, his pinkie ring flashing in the light. "We wanted different things, I suppose."

"Not ready to settle down?"

"Not with Nathan."

"That because of that relationship in the past?"

"Pardon?"

"When you were talking about marriage earlier, you mentioned you'd been in a serious relationship before."

"Ah. Yes. Yes, I did." Chris sipped again, thinking. "Yes, I suppose Simon is much of the reason."

Simon. Darien filed that information away. Sounded English. Someone Chris knew before he moved to the U.S.?

He was about to ask when Chris set down his glass, right on the handle of his fork. Darien reached for it, knowing he wouldn't make it, but Chris caught the glass before more than a few drops could slosh over the rim. He frowned at his error.

Darien grinned. "You okay?"

"Mmmm." Still frowning, Chris brought his hand to his mouth. Darien's mouth fell open slightly when Chris's tongue darted out to lick at the fleshy part between thumb and forefinger. Hazel eyes -- brown in this light -- darted up accusingly. "I think you're trying to get me drunk."

Darien snapped his mouth shut and cocked his head. He let his eyes go half-lidded, still grinning. *Am I really doing this?* "Are you drunk?"

Chris couldn't miss the look. Couldn't misunderstand what it meant. But he said nothing, plucking his napkin from his lap and using it on his hand in lieu of his tongue. "No." He replaced his napkin in his lap, then brought his hands back up to prop his elbows to either side of his empty plate. He smiled, and Darien's heart thumped at the sight. "I'm just relaxed."

Darien laughed, shoving his empty plate aside. "Yeah, I'll say." He folded his arms on the tablecloth before him. "This is the most relaxed I've ever seen you. You're usually so..."

"Uptight?"

Darien chuckled. "Put together."

"Mmm, nice distinction." Chris laughed, casting his gaze out across the restaurant. There wasn't much to see. They sat in a secluded booth toward the back. Only a few other tables were visible to them, and just one of those had a couple sitting at it. "It's all right. I know the face that I present to the world. It's habit. Breeding."

"Oh? You come from an upper-crust British family?"

Chris arched a brow at Darien's awful attempt to copy his accent. "Somewhat, yes."

"You one of them English lords or something? Got a family history that goes back to King Arthur?"

"Hardly. My mother would prefer that we had a finer pedigree, but, alas, we do not." Chris picked up his fork and poked at the linguine before him. "My father, however, is a rather prominent barrister, so we were well off. My older brother is an MP."

"How'd you end up being a lawyer in the States?"

"My choice. When time came to go to university, I chose to come abroad."

"Your choice?"

A small quirk of a grin. "Heavily influenced by the fact that I am, and always have been, openly gay."

Darien nodded. "Ah."

"Yes, 'ah.'"

"How long have you lived in the States?"

"For the better part of thirteen years."

"I thought you went to school with Hell?"

Chris nodded. "I spent two semesters in Germany. While I was there, I took some classes in music."

"How old was he?"

"Nineteen, I think."

"That's right, he went to school young."

"A prodigy. And a brat."

Darien smiled at the fond tone in Chris's voice. "How old were you?"

"Twenty-six."

"How old are you now?"

"Thirty-two."

A sudden thought occurred, and Darien leaned forward eagerly. "Was his hair purple back then?"

Chris laughed. He set his fork on his plate and sat back in his seat, taking the wineglass with him. "Oh, no. It was his natural white-blond."

"So *that's* what color his hair is!"

"Don't tell him I told you that."

"Do you know why he colors it?"

Chris shrugged, smiling. "He likes it. I'm not sure if you've noticed, but he's rather outlandish."

Darien hooted. "Oh, yeah, I noticed. Hey, can I tell Brent about his hair?"

Smile turned to smirk. "I imagine that Brent would know by now."

"Oh." Darien blinked, then grinned. "Yeah, he probably does, huh?" He took a sip of his wine, deciding which of many questions to ask next. "Did you ever sleep with Hell?"

Chris was relaxed enough to not be surprised. "Very early on, yes."

"Hot young thing? Nice."

Chris cleared his throat.

"Didn't work out between you?"

"It was very clear we were better friends."

Darien nodded, squelching a twinge of jealousy. It was stupid anyway. Hell and Chris had been friends for years, and Hell quite definitely had Brent now. But Darien couldn't help the sudden images that popped into his head. Of tiny

Hell in Chris's arms. Of them kissing. Of them…"What's it like?"

Eyes blinked at him from behind thin-rimmed glasses. "Pardon?"

"What's it like, sleeping with a guy?"

Chris stared at him blankly. There was that look that Darien liked to inspire, torn between incredulity, shock, and laughter.

Darien twirled his mostly empty glass on the table. He was concentrating so hard on not blurting out *"I want you"* that he was having more trouble than usual filtering the rest of what he was saying. Not that he was really good at it anyway. He watched the dark wine tumble in the glass. "You don't have to answer."

"It's not that. I don't know *how* to answer."

He stole a glance up and was mesmerized by the golden sheen the candlelight gave to Chris's smooth, high cheekbones. "Why not?"

"I've only ever slept with men. I'm not sure how to compare it to anything else."

"Oh."

"You should ask Johnnie or Luc. Or Brent."

Darien nodded, averting his gaze to finger the sugar packets in a little ceramic box near the edge of the table. "I've heard their answers." And a lot of what they'd said was starting to make perfect sense. His cock, he realized, had started to fill with blood, lazily pulsing at him, reminding him it was there. Yeah, like he could forget it.

"I take it you've never slept with a man?"

His hand froze. "I thought you knew that?"

"I suspected."

Darien shrugged, chewing. "It's never been my thing, y'know? Well, except for one blowjob, and I don't really remember it."

"Drunk?"

"Yeah. Plus there was this girl with us, and I was more interested in her." He glanced at Chris, curious to see if the fact that he'd been in a ménage a trois bothered the other man.

Didn't seem to. Chris only shrugged, a small smile tugging at the corners of his mouth as he stared at the dregs of his wine. "I'm sure you haven't lacked for offers to experience it again."

Mmmm, now if the guy had been Chris…Those sharply defined, dusky-pink lips wrapped around his dick could definitely keep his attention. Darien chuckled at himself, resisting the urge to reach down to adjust his cock. "Nah. That's kind of the nature of the band, isn't it? The word is, I swing both ways. I get all sorts of offers."

"That doesn't seem to bother you."

He grinned. "No way. It's fun. 'Course, it's all kind of changed now, what with Tyler, Reese, and Hell being in the picture." He sighed, picked up the wine bottle, and upended the last of it into his glass. Did they need another bottle? "Everyone assumes we're all just gay now."

"Except you. You were married to a woman."

Darien snorted, looking up for their waiter. "And now I'm divorced. The rumors started weeks ago."

"No more wine for me, thank you."

"No?"

"No. Rumors?"

"Huh? Oh, yeah. Rumors I'm really gay and was trying to hide it." He grimaced. "'Course, that's what Luc's been saying all along. He thinks my marriage was a desperate attempt to prove I'm not gay. I'm pretty sure the other guys feel the same way, but Luc's the only one who's said it to my face."

Chris set his glass carefully on the table, still sitting back in an almost-slump in his seat. Well, as much of a slump as Darien had yet to see him in. "I'm sure that's not true. You should know whether you're gay or not."

"I wonder sometimes."

Sleepy gaze sharpened. "Pardon?"

Darien shrugged, breaking direct eye contact. This was it, right? He was making his pitch here. For some reason, he was afraid to look Chris in the eye, so he spoke to the candle between them instead. "There must be something to it, right? My best friends have slept with both men and women, and they all settled on guys."

Chris snorted. "Because your friends are gay certainly doesn't mean you are."

"Oh, I know. But there's gotta be something to it."

"Are you attracted to men?"

Darien folded his arms on the table again, leaning on them. "Not usually."

"Not usually?"

Darien paused as the waiter returned to clear their plates. He forced himself to breathe normally while they both refused dessert and their table was cleared. He cradled his wineglass in his fingers, studying Chris over the rim. "What about you? You've only ever wanted to sleep with guys?"

"Yes." Confusion marred the relaxed look on Chris's face, and Darien was anxious at the sight of it. He wanted to tell Chris what he wanted, but what if Chris didn't want him? Maybe he only liked Darien's looks and nothing else.

"When did you figure out you were gay?"

Chris took a moment to compose himself back to that familiar calm expression. But Darien had seen what was behind it now and really wanted to try a few things to heat it up. "When I was fourteen. I had an unnatural fascination with the local rugby team."

Darien laughed. "Did you play?"

"Only for a year when I was sixteen. I broke my leg, and my mother wouldn't allow me to play after it healed. She'd prefer I played golf."

"I thought all lawyers liked golf."

Chris grimaced, his generous lips turning down at the corners and his patrician nose wrinkling some. "I play, but it's not my preference. I prefer the rough and tumble."

Whoa. Darien's cock twitched. "You ready to go?" Warmth suffused the skin of his neck, creeping through his chest. He needed to do this. Now.

Chris glanced the way the waiter had last gone. "What about the bill?"

"They'll charge my room."

"Ah." Chris stood. "Sometime you must allow me to take you to dinner."

Darien grinned, happy to hear that Chris wanted to see him again. "Sure thing. Next one's on you."

He stood. With both excitement and panic, he watched out of the corner of his eye as Chris's gaze drew down his body. There was no way the other man missed the bulge. Not if the little widening of the eyes was any indication. Still amused that he wanted this, that he was absurdly pleased that Chris noticed him, Darien turned to lead the way out of the restaurant.

So. How was he supposed to do this? Jump Chris in the elevator? Wait until they got back to the suite? With a girl, he'd have already been obvious about what he wanted, probably done a lot more flirting over dinner. This was different. Was he really ready for what he was thinking? Did it really matter all that much? Sex was sex. At least, that's what Johnnie had tried to convince him of for years. Darien was finally curious. *Really* curious. There was some chemistry between them. Chris didn't seem to be looking for anything long term at the moment. Wasn't that perfect?

His brain chewed as they walked the short hallway to the elevators. He had to use his keycard to get the button for his floor to light up. They stood, backs against opposite sides of the confined space as they started to rise.

"Are you all right?"

Darien startled out of his thoughts, meeting Chris's eyes. The lawyer looked perfectly calm and relaxed, leaning against the elevator wall, hands deep in the pockets of his jeans. He smiled. "You're thinking again.

"Huh?"

"You get this look on your face when you're thinking hard."

Darien laughed. "I do? Huh, I must not get it often."

They laughed.

The elevator door opened, and again Darien led the way, flicking his keycard with his thumbnail as he thought.

"Hey, Chris?"

"Yes?"

They stopped at his door, and he inserted the keycard. "The divorce is final, right?"

"I have to file the papers with the state of Nevada, but it's just a formality since Nicole has already signed. For all intents and purposes, it's final."

The door opened and they walked inside. "Does that mean I can have sex again?"

"Pardon?"

"Can I have sex again?"

"What do you mean?"

Darien stepped down into the sunken sitting room and turned to find Chris frozen just a few steps into the suite. Again there was that incredulous-amused look. The door clicked quietly shut behind him. "I haven't had sex in, like, five months. Well, with another person."

Chris stepped up to the edge of marble step down to the sitting room. "You've been separated for two months."

"Yeah, and Nicole and I stopped having sex before that."

"But...you were separated."

"I was still married."

Chris stared down at him. "You were faithful the entire time?"

Darien frowned. "Well, yeah. Marriage is marriage. You don't fool around with something like that."

Chris smiled, shaking his head as he took the step down onto the carpet, headed toward the table and his briefcase. "You are truly a wonder."

"Yeah, people tell me that sometimes." He took a step closer and caught Chris's hand, stopping the other man. His heart was racing, but his voice was amazingly calm. "So, can I have sex now?" Okay, maybe his voice was a little breathy.

Chris swallowed, the only sign that he wasn't completely calm. "Yes. I would say you are now allowed to have sex."

Darien took that last step, stopping mere inches from Chris. He looked up into those sharp hazel eyes and brought his other hand up to splay it over Chris's heart. Rapid beat to match his. A widening of the eyes and a sharp inhalation of breath. All good signs. He let his eyes go heavy and licked his lips. "Wanna have sex with me?"

Wide lips parted in shock. "Pardon?"

He released Chris's wrist and used that hand to hook the side of Chris's waist, holding him as Darien stepped closer. "Wanna have sex with me?"

Chris scowled, standing tall, which put Darien's eye level just below his chin. His hands found Darien's shoulders, holding him at bay. "You're not gay."

Darien balled his fist in Chris's polo shirt, using it to try and pull Chris's mouth within reach. "Can we forget that for tonight?" He licked his lips and watched Chris quickly mirror the move. Unconscious? Didn't matter. Now that Darien had made the request, he wanted very badly to taste. He pulled again, and Chris's face got closer to his.

"No!" Chris stiffened his arms on Darien's shoulders. "Why this, all of a sudden?"

"I want you."

"Why?"

"I get a boner whenever I'm around you. I'm sick of fighting it."

Chris gaped. "What?"

"It's true. Let me show you." He tried to pull Chris's waist flush with his, but Chris was just strong enough to hold him back. He glanced down and saw the evidence of Chris's interest in the front of those jeans. *Okay, that's a definite advantage to doing this with a guy,* he thought, amused. *Visual evidence.* He grinned up at Chris. "You're gorgeous, you know that?"

"Me?"

"Yeah. I want to lick you all over. Let me?"

Chris shuddered, his eyes closing for a brief moment.

Darien used his moment to slide both hands up and around the back of Chris's head. Before Chris could protest, Darien pulled and their lips met. Chris froze. Darien froze. *Whoa.* He tilted his head, letting his lips slide against Chris's. That was nice. Softer than he'd expected and so very warm. No lipstick or lip gloss, either -- another plus. Not that different from kissing a girl, really, except Chris was taller and smelled different. Darien parted his lips and traced his tongue along the edge of Chris's lower lip. Chris's fingers dug into Darien's shoulders, but he didn't push away. Darien kept hold of Chris's head and opened beneath him, tongue pressing the seam of his lips. They parted, and he gently pushed inside, pausing for a slow swipe over Chris's top teeth before delving inside to invite Chris's tongue out to play. Tasted different. Tasted wonderful. There was the wine and tomato sauce mostly, but under that was a spice that was different than what he was used to.

Maybe it was the moan that came unbidden out of Darien's throat that kicked Chris's brain back into thinking. Damn it.

Chris pushed away, forcing their lips apart. Darien tried to pull him back, but Chris speared his hands in Darien's hair and did some pulling of his own. Pulling his hair happened to be one of Darien's hot points. He loved it but never actually told any lovers that, because you didn't go around telling people to pull your hair. That was just --

"What are you doing?"

Darien blinked his eyes open, sucking in a breath. "Kissing you."

"Why?"

"I want to fuck you."

Chris narrowed his eyes, lenses of his glasses shining in the lamplight. "What are you trying to prove?"

"I'm not trying to prove anything."

"Liar."

Darien snarled softly. He loosened his firm grip on the back of Chris's skull. The fingers, however, stayed, sifting gently through Chris's short hair. Soft but kinda thick. Probably why it always stayed just so. "Okay. I want to know what it's like."

"'What it's like'?"

"Sleeping with a guy." *Sleeping with you.*

"Why?"

"Maybe I do want to prove something. I don't know." He tried to push closer, got his groin to brush Chris's thigh before the other man pulled back. He sighed. "All I know is that when I'm with you, I want to fuck you. It's been like that for over a month now. So why not go with it?"

"Do I have a say in the matter?"

That stopped him. Darien blinked, eyes widening. "I thought you wanted me."

"Why would you think that?"

"Oh, come on. I've caught you looking plenty."

"Looking is one thing. Touching is entirely different."

"And fucking's even more," Darien added with an eyebrow waggle. "Come on, Chris. You want me."

Nostrils flared. Oh, that was new. "Perhaps..."

"Good, then. You want me. I want you." Darien settled his arms around Chris's neck. Weird, he'd never hugged a guy like this before, not with his arms up. Since he was usually shorter, his arms went around the waist. *Who cares? Focus!* "What's the harm? Neither of us is looking for anything serious right now."

Darien's move closer forced Chris's hands to readjust. Hands let up on his hair and slid down his back. "So that's what all the questions were about at dinner?" Darien took heart that the hands settled at his waist.

Darien winced. "Not all of them." He studied Chris's Adam's apple. "I did want to have dinner with you." He peeked back up at Chris's face. "It was nice, wasn't it?"

Fingers toyed with the top of his waistband, a hopeful sign. As was the way Chris's shock was melting into warm speculation. "Yes, it was nice."

Darien licked his lips, drawing Chris's attention to his mouth. "Kissing was nice, too. Can we do it again?"

Chris groaned. "Darien, this is probably not a good idea."

"Sure it is." Darien twisted one leg just enough so that a nudge forward pressed his cock into the meat of Chris's thigh. "More would be nice, too."

Sighing, Chris tilted his head up, taking his mouth out of range. *Damn.* Darien leaned in and brushed his lips against the thin skin beating over Chris's pulse, right under his jaw.

A slight tremor shook the body pressed to his.

Darien licked a line over that pulse. He liked that; Chris should like it. "Come on, Chris. Fuck me."

Chris groaned, swallowing. "Then what?" he asked the ceiling.

Darien kissed his clavicle. "Then we do it again?"

Chris laughed. "What if you don't like it?"

Darien rocked his hips again. "I kind of doubt that."

"You might not."

"Fair enough. If I don't, I won't hold it against you."

Chris laughed again, sliding his arms fully around Darien's waist to hold him close. *Yes!* His head came down and he nuzzled Darien's temple. "So if you do like it, what are we then? Lovers? Fuck buddies?"

That's nice. "Yeah. Sure."

"I need a better answer."

"Such a lawyer." Darien sighed, tucking his forehead in against Chris's neck. "I just want something different for a change. I haven't actually *wanted* anyone like this for a long time. It feels good. It's been a while since I felt good." He heard the wistful pain in his own voice and wondered at it.

A hand slid up to span between his shoulder blades, fingertips just teasing the nape of his neck. "If we do this, I'm going to fuck you. Do you hear me?"

A hot sizzle shot up Darien's spine, forcing him to shiver. "I hear you."

"You know what that means?"

"You want to fuck my ass."

The hand at his back slid up into his hair, grabbing a fistful. Chris used the hold to make him tilt his head back so they could look at each other eye-to-eye. "Yes."

"So you *are* a top," Darien joked, just a little nervous. *Whoa, that's heat,* he thought, watching Chris's eyes burn dark brown. He really needed to get those glasses off.

"Yes."

Darien swallowed, then nodded. "Okay."

"You're all right with that?"

"You'll make it good." It was not a question, rather a statement. He'd never particularly wanted his ass reamed, but the thought of Chris doing it didn't seem so bad.

Chris's eyes roamed his face for a brief moment. Then he smiled. The hand at Darien's waist slipped down to cup his ass. Squeezed. "Oh, yes."

There went that sizzle again. Geez, his cock was rock hard. "Then, yeah."

The growl deep in the prim lawyer's chest was just about the most sexy fucking thing ever. "That doesn't bother you?"

Darien would have shaken his head, but Chris still had a firm hold on a good chunk of his hair. "I told you, I want to know what it's like."

The hand in his hair and the hand on his ass both moved. Then Chris was cradling his face. The heat behind those glasses mesmerized Darien. "By the time I'm finished with you, you'll know."

"Excellent!"

Chapter Seven

The press of Chris's mouth back onto his muffled Darien's laugh of triumph. *Oh, yeah!* Chris's real kiss was awesome! All lips and tongue and so fucking take-charge that Darien couldn't even think to take the lead. All he had to do was receive and suck in that tongue and Chris growled again. Oh, yeah, the growl was great. He had to make that happen lots.

Chris's hands slid down his neck to his chest and pushed. "Get in there," came the order, along with a point toward the bedroom door behind Darien.

Grinning, Darien walked backward. He knew the suite well enough to avoid the furniture.

Chris stalked him. Enjoying it, Darien backed away at the same pace, just out of reach. He loved the wicked smile on Chris's lips. It promised great things to come. He'd used a version of that smile on many a woman. How cool to be on the receiving end.

He passed through the bedroom door, managing to just bump it a little. He didn't want to turn around, some irrational part of his brain telling him that if he didn't keep his eyes on Chris, the man would disappear.

"Stop."

Darien froze, halfway across the room to the bed. It wasn't a conscious decision. Chris said stop, and that tone just stopped him. A thrill of pleasure crawled over his skin.

Chris paused for a brief moment just inside the doorway to take off his glasses and set them on the dresser. So calm, so collected. Like Clark Kent taking off his glasses just before he became Superman. And oh, man, did *that* comparison heat Darien's blood! Chris turned on the light. Blue shadows fled from the recessed lighting along the ceiling. Those gold sparkles shone in Chris's hair. "Do you mind the light?" Chris asked, closing the distance between them.

And damned if Darien hadn't moved an inch! He shook his head. "No."

"Good." Chris reached up to tuck Darien's hair behind his ear, those eyes, brown in this light, roaming his face. "Because I want to see every bit of this."

Darien felt like a dog: told to stay, but itching to launch himself at the man before him. He wanted to lick all over. If he had a tail, he'd be wagging it hard.

Chris's hand dropped to span across the flesh bared by the opening of Darien's collar. *"This,"* he said, watching the hand slide slowly down the center of Darien's chest, "has been driving me crazy."

Darien swallowed. Damn, he was going to start drooling any second! "What?"

"Watching your chest all night. Wanting to touch." The hand reached the bottom of the V opening, then slid back up, slipping underneath the shirt on the right side. "You did it on purpose, didn't you?"

Darien's eyes fluttered when Chris's fingers found his nipple. "Yeah," he sighed.

"You took your shirt off this afternoon to taunt me."

Darien grinned. "A little."

Chris snorted and pinched, making Darien jump. "When did you decide to seduce me?"

Darien had to grin, even as he winced when Chris rolled the pebbled nub. "I didn't really decide it." He shivered as Chris's fingertips played through the hair surrounding his nipple. "But tonight seemed like a good night."

"Because your divorce is over?"

"And you told me about Nathan."

"Ah, yes. That." Chris pulled his hand out and started to unbutton Darien's shirt the rest of the way. "How long have you wanted this?"

"A few weeks."

Chris smiled, watching his hands. "Do you know how long I've wanted you?"

"No."

"But you knew I wanted you."

Darien nodded, even though it didn't sound like a question.

Chris yanked the shirt to open the final buttons. "How?"

Darien shuddered as Chris's palms returned to his chest, sliding outward to open the shirt. "I caught you watching me."

Chris smiled. "Did you like it?"

"Yeah."

Chris leaned in to brush his lips across a shoulder he exposed. Darien's head fell back and the shirt slid away, snagging halfway down his arms. "You're beautiful," Chris murmured, pulling back and slowly mapping Darien's shoulders and chest with his hands.

Darien itched to touch, but Chris seemed to be enjoying himself, and who was Darien to deny him? Besides, the touch of those hands was awesome. They slid over his shoulders and down his arms, squeezing slightly when they found muscle. They pushed the shirt from his arms, then explored their way back up, across his shoulders again, then up his neck. Fingers speared in his hair, tilting his head back.

Chris kissed him, and that was the trigger that released Darien's limbs. Or at least his arms. Eagerly, he reached up between them and found the buttons of Chris's shirt. As Chris played with his mouth, Darien got rid of the shirt and did some exploring of his own. Okay, maybe not with as much finesse, but who could blame a guy? So much smooth, satiny skin! There was some hair covering his chest, but not a lot. Probably about as much as Darien had himself. Enough to cushion the fingertips and make you dig a bit for skin. He found a nipple and tweaked it, loving the groan that caused.

Chris's hands closed on his shoulders and pushed. Again Darien was walking backward. After a few steps, he bumped into the bed and Chris let him fall onto it. He landed on the soft blue sheets, missing the spread, which had been turned down by housekeeping.

Propped back on his elbows, he watched as Chris put a foot up on the chair by the window to unlace his boots. When Darien moved to get his own boots, Chris stopped him with a snap of his fingers and a look. Grinning, Darien sat back and waited as Chris removed his footwear and socks and set them aside. Coming to the side of the bed, Chris reached toward Darien's left foot, wiggling his fingers. Obediently, Darien lifted and watched Chris untie his boot. Okay, probably not the best choice of footwear when he'd been planning on taking the man to bed, but it was too late to gripe about that now. Chris dropped the boot, then peeled off the sock. Then, to Darien's amazement, he ran his hand over Darien's foot, exploring, pressing on the pad beneath his toes. Darien groaned. Chris smiled. He dropped Darien's foot and reached for the other. The whole process was repeated, and Darien fell back to enjoy.

Oh, man, *was this a good idea!* He'd thought it'd be hot and heavy, fast and furious. He hadn't expected slow and seductive. He wasn't complaining. It was a new experience on top of a new experience. With women, he was usually the one doing the exploring.

Chris dropped his foot and leaned over, reaching for his waistband. Those eyes fastened on his face. "Not going to stop me, are you?"

"Hell no!"

Fingers made quick work of his button-fly, then flipped it open. He grinned to see Chris's surprise at the lack of underwear. Hey, he liked to go commando, and tonight he'd even had reason. Darien felt the air on his cock as it nudged out of the opening.

Chris's eyes locked on it, closing halfway in lambent appreciation. Leaving the jeans open and just barely off Darien's hips, Chris braced on the bed, leaning in to press a kiss just under the head of Darien's cock.

"Shit." Darien hissed, gripping the smooth sheets beneath him. His head dropped back.

Hot breath ghosted over his cock. "Been a while?"

"I told you."

Lips nipped at his crown. "Are you going to last long?"

Darien gulped. He wished he could say yes, but..."No."

The bed jostled, and Darien looked down to see Chris staring at him.

"Please say you have condoms."

Darien grinned. "Yeah. With the lube in the drawer to your left."

"Ah, good." Chris bent his head to lick as much of the length of Darien's cock as he could. "I'll assume that you're clean."

Darien swallowed, hardly able to concentrate while Chris treated him like a lollipop. "I am."

"Good."

"You don't have to trust me. You can -- Ah, shit!"

Darien curled forward on the curse, driving his fingers into the longer hair atop Chris's head as the man swallowed him down in one gulp. The moan that tore out of Darien's throat came from somewhere deep in his gut, loosing warm liquid through his veins.

"Oh, shit, Chris," he groaned, clutching the man's hair. "I can't...It's been too long. I'm gonna..."

Fingers curled in his jeans to pull them down some, exposing more of him as Chris devoured him. Oh, damn! Chris had one fucking *talented* mouth!

Darien tried. He really did. He fell back on the bed and clutched at the sheets, trying to hold on. Thinking about something else just wasn't an option. It felt way too good. "Chris, I'm gonna come."

The man didn't let up. If anything, he swallowed harder.

Well, Darien had warned him. Fire ignited at the base of his spine and shot through his groin. Darien heard the little whimpers that erupted from his throat, but couldn't do anything about them.

Chris drank, suckling until every drop was gone. As Darien's body went limp, Chris grabbed his jeans, taking them with him as he backed off the bed. He kissed down Darien's thighs, nipped at his knees, and lapped at his calves. Sliding back up on the bed, he pushed Darien's knees apart and bent to lick the crease between thigh and crotch. Darien shuddered, not expecting the, well, *zeal* with which the man touched him. Hands, lips, and tongue mapped his body.

"Oh, shit," he groaned, enduring the electric sparks stirring just below his belly. "Chris, you're killing me, man."

Chris chuckled. He planted his palms underneath Darien's thighs and pushed them up high. Darien's ass came off the bed, his knees nearly touching his shoulders.

"Hey, what -- Oh, God! What are you doing?"

Is he tonguing my asshole? Oh, man, he was! Darien's first reaction was to jerk away, but Chris had him bent double, and he was still humming from a pretty rocking orgasm, so he wasn't in full control of his body. Darien spread his arms out, grabbing the sheet, trying to decide if he liked the feeling or not. Oh, who was he kidding? That felt damn good! He closed his eyes and groaned as Chris's wet tongue played with his hole, tracing, tickling, then pushing in.

He was half hard again by the time Chris stopped. The tongue left his hole and dragged up the sensitive skin toward his balls. He glanced down to see Chris watching him as he took one testicle into his mouth.

"Oh, man, you're good at that." Darien sighed.

Chris chuckled, mouthing Darien's other testicle before he sat back, gradually allowing Darien to unfold so he lay prone on the bed. "You liked that," Chris proclaimed, licking his lips.

"Yeah."

Grinning a little cat grin, Chris turned to the drawer Darien had mentioned earlier. Darien kept his eyes on Chris's face as he rummaged around. This Chris was very different than the Chris he had known for the past few weeks. Just as he'd thought -- hoped -- there was fire under that cool exterior. *Excellent!*

Chris dropped lube and two condom packets on the bed beside Darien, then knelt up, hands at the fly of his jeans. Darien's eyes dropped to watch, his own hand lazily traveling down the center of his chest and belly to wrap around his cock.

Chris watched avidly as he stepped backwards off the mattress, opening his fly. A darker spot on his dark gray briefs spoke of leakage. He hooked his thumbs in the waistband of both jeans and briefs and shoved them down to his thighs. His cock sprang free, pointed full and accusing at Darien. After shedding the rest of his clothing, Chris stood and wrapped his left hand around his cock. "Are you sure about this?"

Darien licked his lips, squeezing his own cock tight. "Yeah." Okay, yeah, a part of him was screaming, *You're going to fit* that *in* where? But for the most part he was all for it. It'd been a great ride so far.

Chris smiled. "Turn over."

Darien complied readily enough, even got up on his knees, spreading them. He figured Chris was going to need room to work with that thing. Folding his arms beneath him and sticking his ass in the air, he turned his head to watch Chris pick up a condom packet and tear it open. *Shit, this is it.* He closed his eyes and waited. Chris seemed to be more than happy taking charge, and given the burble of unease in his belly, Darien was willing to let him.

Two hands took a good hold of the cheeks of his ass, squeezing, massaging. Darien had to groan. The hands parted his ass, and did he imagine feeling a breeze on his hole? Yeah, probably. He yelped when a tongue stabbed him. *Maybe not,* he thought, glaring over his shoulder at the man grinning down at him. "You like that?" He had to ask.

"Oh, yes." Chris reached for the lube.

Darien watched him pop the cap. "Do all guys do that?" He thought briefly of Johnnie and Luc and just couldn't quite imagine it.

Chris laughed, pouring a generous amount of liquid on his left palm. "No more than every man likes to go down on a woman."

"Yeah, okay. That makes sense." Darien tossed his head. "It's weird."

Chris grinned as he recapped the bottle. "You liked it.

"Yeah."

Chris swiped his wet fingers down Darien's crease, then back up. "I liked doing it to you. You taste fresh. I like it very much."

Good thing I took a shower, Darien thought, but just couldn't voice.

Chuckling softly, Chris teased his hole with the tip of one finger before slowly sinking it in to the first knuckle.

Darien winced, fingers gripping the rumpled blue sheets beneath him.

"Relax," Chris soothed, smoothing his other hand across Darien's lower back. "So hot and tight. Just as I knew you would be." Chris twisted his finger, pulling out a little before pushing farther back in.

Darien's eyes fell shut; his breathing hitched.

"Breathe, pet." Chris pulled out his finger and pushed it back in again. "Talk to me."

Pet? "Talk?"

Chris chuckled, finger pumping slowly. "You talk more than anyone I know. Talk to me. Tell me if you like this."

"I like it." He was only convincing himself a little. Actually, as he got used to it, there was kind of a cool thrill.

"Have you done this to yourself?"

"No."

Chris turned his wrist, pressing his finger against the sides of Darien's opening. "Have you fucked a woman's arse?"

The breath whooshed out of Darien's lips. His eyes bugged, staring unseeing at the far wall as Chris's finger hit something *very* nice! The finger wiggled over that spot again, and Darien's back arched all on its own. "Oh, fuck."

"Have you?" Chris asked, his voice calm despite what he was doing to Darien.

Was that another finger slipping in, stretching his hole? Darien pressed his cheek against the hands he had clutching the sheet beneath him. "Have I what?"

"Fucked a woman's arse."

"Oh. Yeah." Carefully, Darien rocked his hips, trying to get Chris to hit that spot again.

"Did they like it?"

"Ah!" There it was!

"Darien."

"What?"

"Did they like it?"

He was pretty sure he was breathing along with the slow in-and-out pull of Chris's fingers. "Did...did who like what?"

Soft chuckle. "The women whose arses you fucked."

Oh. "Some."

"They liked it a little? Or only some of them liked it?"

The sound Darien emitted was somewhere between a chuckle and a moan. "How do you expect me to talk when you've got your fingers up my ass?"

Chris's free hand smoothed over the expanse of his back. "You love to talk. I like your voice. Tell me that I'm making you feel hot."

"Oh, yeah, I'm hot."

Chris wiggled his fingers. A third pressed in, making Darien gasp. "Relax."

"Yeah, yeah, I know the drill. It's just...Jesus!"

"Does it hurt?"

Did it? Yes, but no. It burned; it was kind of uncomfortable. "Not...really." But it was kind of hot.

"You get used to it."

Darien laughed, breathy. "God, I hope so, if you're going to put that horse cock inside me."

Chris laughed, low and evil. He leaned in over Darien's back, scooting closer so his cock nudged Darien's balls. "Do you like my cock?"

"Oh, shit, the way you say that."

"Say what, pet?"

Darien rose up to his elbows, trying to get better leverage. His hips were rocking now. "Your fucking accent's gonna drive me out of my mind."

Chris laughed, worming in another finger. "You like my voice?"

"I love your voice."

"Then perhaps I should tell you what I'm going to do." He fingered what Darien could only assume was his prostate.

Shit! Johnnie had told him that it felt good, but he should have been a little more adamant about it. If he'd known, Darien would have tried this ages ago! Chris pushed him down with his free hand, lowering him until his chest was flush with the mattress. "I'm going to take my 'horse cock'" -- he enunciated with glee --"and I'm going to fuck this tight, gorgeous little round arse of yours."

"Chris, you...*damn!*...keep talking like that, and I'm -- ungh! -- gonna come again."

Warm breath preceded soft lips ghosting over the back of his shoulder. "Just from my saying I'm going to fuck you until you can't walk anymore?"

Darien groaned, burying his face in the mattress. "You're killing me."

Chris laughed and actually fucking *bit* the back of Darien's shoulder. Shocked, Darien arched up, only to have Chris's free hand slam him back down again.

The fingers kept pumping slowly in and out, scissoring over each other, stretching his backside. "I'm going to ride you, pet. Are you going to come just from that?"

Pet. He liked that. "Do it," Darien gasped, chancing a glance over his shoulder again. "Fucking fuck me already."

Darien would not have believed before tonight that Chris could look demonic, but there it was, staring down at him. His long face was shadowed from above, and those wicked eyes almost glowed. He should have had fucking horns, fangs, and a forked tail to go with that face.

"Fucking fuck you," Chris repeated, fingers sliding from Darien's ass. Calmly, he reached for the lube bottle and poured more on his hand. "Is that what you want?"

"Yes."

"My fingers felt that good?"

"Yeah."

His wet hand swiped over that sheathed cock, which looked even bigger than before. It was probably just Darien's perception, considering what was about to happen, but it seemed real.

Chris grabbed his hips. "Then this'll feel even better."

Blunt pressure on his hole made Darien squeeze his eyes shut.

"Breathe and relax. Push back."

Darien sucked in air and let it out with a shudder.

Chris pushed in.

Darien gasped at the burn. The fingers had prepared him, but those particular muscles had been virgin too many years to give too easily. It didn't really hurt, not really, but it was still something to get used to.

Chris's dry hand slid over his back. "So fucking tight," he growled, fingernails scratching the meat of Darien's shoulder.

Darien groaned, taking another deep breath. Chris flowed with it, pushing in another bit as Darien exhaled. "Shit."

"Hurt?"

"No."

"Are you all right?"

"Yeah."

"More?"

Another breath, another inch. "Yeah."

They worked together until Chris was in, fully seated *inside* Darien's body. The taller man draped himself over Darien's back, nuzzling the bend of his neck through his hair. "God, Darien!" Hands slid down his arms until fingers found his within the rumpled sheets. They both clutched the fabric and just breathed for an endless moment.

But Darien had never been very good at staying still for long. He squirmed and couldn't believe the whimper that squeezed from his throat. He also couldn't believe how it felt to be impaled. "Chris."

"Mmmm." The taller man drew back a little, rolling his head so that his lips could caress the back of Darien's shoulder. He slowly pulled his hips back, and Darien shuddered through an electric thrill that took his body.

Just before he was almost out, Chris switched direction and pushed back in. "Feel good?"

"Yeah."

"So hot," Chris murmured, reaching his limit again before pulling back slowly. "Your arse is gripping me so tight."

Darien buried his face in the sheets beneath him. "You can't talk."

Chris chuckled. "I have to talk. I have to let you know what a tight fuck you are."

Another shudder wracked Darien's body. "No fair, Chris," he whined.

Chris shifted, kneeling higher behind Darien. The new position had him gripping Darien's hips and allowed him more control as he picked up the speed a little. "Very fair. You teased me for weeks. It's my turn."

"I did -- ungh -- not!"

"You did." He slapped the side of Darien's ass, and Darien felt his own hole clutching Chris's cock. "Parading this beautiful fucking arse before me when I didn't think I could ever have it."

Darien arched back on a cry. Chris's cock was rubbing over that spot mercilessly, setting off bolts of electricity from somewhere in Darien's balls.

Chris pushed forward. "It's mine right now, though."

"Fuck yeah."

"Fuck yeah."

Fingers bit into Darien's hips as Chris thrust in earnest. Little atom bombs started detonating along Darien's spine, making him jump, making him writhe, causing him to cry out as Chris leaned in and pounded him. Chris kept talking, but Darien couldn't make sense of the words. Chris's cock was sliding easy now, and the burn of penetration had Darien's entire lower half aflame. There was too much sensation, too much to feel.

When Chris's hand reached forward to wrap around Darien's dick, it was too much, period. Two strokes, and Darien came.

Chris bit out a "Bloody hell!" pumping jerkily at Darien as he came as well.

When his muscles let loose, Darien fell forward in a heap. Chris, braced against him, fell on top of him.

Darien rediscovered his voice on a laugh. "Oh, yeah, that was *definitely* a good idea!"

Chapter Eight

The warm body draping half of his back moved. Mostly asleep, he shifted as Chris got up and out of bed. Darien grumbled as cool air hit the warmed skin, waking him further. He ground his face into the thick pillow wedged between his head and his arms, trying to regain sheets. *No use.* The sheets were down somewhere around his waist, baring his back to the air, and his morning wood was pressed into the sheets.

Hmmm, morning wood. He cracked an eye and twisted his head just enough and just in time to see Chris's wide back and bare ass walk through a swath of light that shone through the partially open drapes and disappear into the bathroom. *Nice view.*

With a sigh, he turned over on his back and stared blearily up at the ceiling. He'd fucked a guy last night. Correction: a guy had fucked him last night. Johnnie had been trying to convince him to do it for years, at first with him, then later with anyone. But back when he'd had a chance to experiment with Johnnie, he hadn't been able to get his head around sucking a guy's cock or getting fucked up the ass. Fucking up the ass he'd done to girls, of course, but that was different, wasn't it? Well, not that he knew now even, since he'd been on the receiving end. And it really hadn't been that bad. Had been great, in fact. He wiggled his hips experimentally. A little sore, but in a good way. He wondered if this was what girls felt like the morning after.

He laughed aloud, finding his hand around his cock, stroking languidly. What the hell was he doing lying there jacking off *thinking* about it when there was a warm body in the other room? A warm, *wet* body, judging from the sound of the shower starting.

He rolled out of bed and padded across the room. Chris had left the bathroom door cracked, so it only took a push to get it open.

The long counter to the right with the double sinks sat under a wide mirror surrounded with vanity lights. Across the green-and-white-tiled floor from the counter sat an extra-long bathtub. Directly across from the door was the wide shower. It was big enough to fit two, maybe three people, and had showerheads mounted on the walls to the left and right. A bench sat on the far wall, underneath a small, high window. The wide door was clear glass. Johnnie had once indicated that there was a "damn fine" reason all the luxury suites at both hotels had glass shower doors rather than curtains. Darien was pretty sure it was a sex thing between him and Tyler but had never asked for specifics. Right now, however, he had reason to appreciate the concept.

Mmmm, very nice. Darien leaned against one side of the door and just took it all in. Chris stood under one of the showerheads, his back to it, head thrown back as the water flattened his hair to his head. It was a crying shame that Chris usually wore so many clothes, because he had a really nice body. Toned with muscles, although not overdone. Clearly the muscles were from the gym, but that was okay. Long, strong legs to match long arms, a broad chest, a flat belly, and a nice, fat cock.

Chris turned, reaching for the soap, and saw him there. He froze, water dripping from his pointed chin.

Darien grinned, letting his gaze rake Chris's body again. "Mornin'."

There was the start of a smile. "Good morning."

"Mind if I join you?"

Surprise flitted over Chris's face, but then his smile grew. "Not at all."

Darien crossed the floor and opened the shower door. Disregarding Chris's hesitation, he stepped straight into the man's chest, sliding his arms up and around his neck to bring those tasty lips down to where he could reach them. The kiss they shared was gentle and soft, mostly lips. Darien knew he had morning breath and didn't want to gross Chris out. He let his kiss slide to the side of Chris's mouth, then drew a trail across the stubble on that sharp jawbone with his tongue until he could nibble at the prickly skin where jaw met neck.

Chris hummed, hands sliding over Darien's back and shoulders to help spread the water that streamed over them. "You should be careful. Someone might think that you're queer."

Darien ducked his head to nip at Chris's collarbone, letting his hands do some roaming of their own across Chris's lower back and the top of his ass. "Yeah, huh? That's okay."

"Is it?"

He took two proper handfuls of ass and squeezed, liking the spasm in the cock against his belly that resulted. "A little late to be worried about it now."

Chris's hands halted. "No. It's not. I don't have to tell anyone about this."

Darien tilted his head up to see the serious look Chris gave him. He smiled. "Thanks, but it's not necessary."

"Are you sure?" The hands started again, sliding over his shoulders. "I promise I won't tell anyone."

"I believe you, but I don't care." He leaned back, locking his hands at the small of Chris's back. It pressed them together in a really nice way, with Chris's growing erection against Darien's lower belly and Darien's wood pressed against Chris's thigh.

"Yes, well…"

Hearing the hesitation in that smoothly accented voice, Darien cocked his head to the side. Water streamed off a lock of his hair into his eyes, so he shook his head to dislodge it. "What?"

Chris reached up to smooth the offending lock back from Darien's forehead. Chris looked so different without the glasses. Well, not really -- he looked like him, but he looked more…approachable? Real? "I gather you would like to do this again?"

Darien laughed. "Oh, yeah. How about now?"

Chris chuckled. "That's a distinct possibility."

"Only a possibility?"

There was that Satan grin Darien liked. "A certainty."

Darien matched the grin, watching the green shine in those changeable eyes. "But?"

Chris thought about it. Darien could almost see the wheels churning in his head. "I'd rather not have a paparazzi following."

Darien blinked. "Oh. Oh, right on. I get you. That's cool."

"It is?"

"Totally. Just 'cause they hound me doesn't mean you have to suffer." He grinned. "'Sides, I'm not sure I'm ready to let the gay thing out yet."

Chris laughed. "And are you gay now?"

Darien dropped his gaze and pulled back a little, looking pointedly at the two erections pressed between them. He looked back up at Chris and laughed. "Well, I haven't wanted to be with a woman since it happened."

"Well, well. And that has been all of, what, six, seven hours?"

"Yeah, something like that."

Chris dropped his hand down to wrap it around Darien's boner. "Then allow me to take full advantage while I can."

Oh, yeah! Darien thought, but couldn't say since Chris's hand felt too good. He rested his forehead against the bend between the other man's neck and shoulder and wrapped his own fingers around Chris's prick. He hadn't gotten to do that last night. Chris had fucked him twice, and both times had been from the back, so he hadn't gotten to do a lot of exploring of his own. It was weird holding a cock that wasn't his own. Not bad. He stroked up, gathering wet, loose skin over the purple tip. Chris was uncut. Darien wished he was. He'd heard that the sensations were out of this world.

"Damn," he murmured, squeezing and matching the rhythm Chris set on his cock. "I had this in my ass?"

A warm chuckle caressed his ear. "You did. It felt wonderful. So alive and tight, squeezing me." Chris matched his words with the motions of his hand.

Darien groaned, watching his hand, watching Chris's hand. He wished he were a little taller so they could put them together. He promised himself that they'd do that. Later. For now, the mutual jacking was good.

Too good. Chris nibbled at his ear, tongue darting out to tease the entrance. His hand picked up speed and pressure, probably goaded by the fact that Darien's hips started to rock. This was great. Maybe it was a little selfish, but Darien was digging the not-being-in-charge part. When he'd been with women, he'd always had to take charge. At least, for the most part. It was so cool to be on the receiving end, to let someone else direct and to follow someone else's lead.

He let his thoughts drift, losing himself in the feel of warm, wet skin pressed against him, a strong arm surrounding his shoulders, a hot mouth eating at his ear, and a knowing hand wrapped around his dick, squeezing just right.

"Fuck!" he muttered, clutching the meat of Chris's back as he picked up speed on Chris's dick, pumping it like he needed his to be pumped.

God bless him, Chris got the hint. The tongue left his ear and the breathing in the vicinity grew ragged. Chris's thigh rubbed Darien's as they ground together, both so close...so close...

"Fuck yeah!" Darien cried, throwing his head back, exposing it to the sheet of water careening down on them as he shot his load up against Chris's belly.

He managed to remember that his hand wasn't on his own cock and kept jerking for another few seconds before Chris let go and something warmer and thicker than the water from the showerhead splattered Darien's chest.

Chris pulled him close, and their arms slid around each other. They held on for a moment to catch their breath.

Chris nuzzled Darien's ear, groaning softly. "I have to go to work."

"Oh, man, really?"

"Mmmm." Chris's tongue batted the simple hoop Darien wore in that ear. "I have to file your divorce papers, if nothing else."

Sighing, Darien pulled away. "Yeah. Okay." He paused, hands on Chris's hips as he looked up into those ever-changing eyes. He couldn't quite read the facial expression. A little serious, maybe a little confused, but overall Chris seemed pleased. "Come back tonight?"

A smile teased the corners of Chris's mouth. "Haven't gotten enough of me yet?"

"Hell no. You haven't let me suck your cock yet."

Chris stumbled. Okay, he wasn't walking, so that wasn't exactly right, but his knees kind of gave out or something, because Darien had to grip his hips to steady him. That terrific laugh started in his chest, bursting from his mouth. Grinning, he reached up to caress Darien's jaw. "How can I possibly refuse that?"

Darien grinned, teeth and everything. "Excellent." He stepped away toward the shower door. "You go ahead and finish. I've got to brush my teeth. Hey" -- he stepped onto the bath mat and reached for a towel -- "I'll call down and get them to send up another brush."

"No need. I have to go home before I go into the office."

Darien glanced over his shoulder, distracted for a second by the sight of Chris's long hand sliding down his flat belly, wiping away any traces of their cum. "You'll be even later."

Chris dipped his head backward into the spray, exposing his lean neck. "I don't have a suit with me."

Oh, yeah. The jeans. *Mmmm.* "Right." He watched for a few more seconds, jealous of the water. "Should I be sorry about that?"

Chris lowered his head and opened his eyes with a wry grin. "No. I'm not."

He made it until four o'clock before he called. Chris had given him his personal cell number a few weeks ago, and Darien was real glad of it now because he didn't want to hear anyone's voice but one man's.

"Hello, Darien." And there it was. Caller ID was a marvelous thing, in Darien's opinion.

"Hey." He flipped through the comic book in his lap, but only saw a blur of color. Didn't matter. He'd already read it. "What time will you be here?"

"Tonight?"

"Yeah, tonight. I was thinking of ordering food and didn't want it to get cold before you got here." He patted himself on the back for a reasonable excuse for the call. "What do you feel like?" *Mmmm, actually I know you feel good.*

He didn't like the pause. "Chris? You're not backing out on me, are you?"

"Backing out?" He knew stalling when he heard it. *Oh, shit, you're not backing out!*

"C'mon, Chris. You've got to teach me how to give a blowjob, remember?"

Chris groaned softly.

"I figure there's a lot of tongue and sucking that I gotta master, right? I mean, I tried to pay attention when you were sucking me last night, but I kinda got lost." No, Darien did not play fair when potential deprivation of good sex was before him. Nope. Not gonna happen.

Another moan, a little lower.

Darien chuckled. "Sorry. Are you alone?"

"Yes." Chris cleared his throat. "Yes, I'm alone."

"You're coming over tonight, aren't you?"

"Yes. I'll be there. I'll leave my office around six."

Excellent! "You're going by your place first?"

"Yes."

"Good. Hey, I was thinking…" He paused for effect.

"Yes?"

Hmm, didn't take the "thinking" opening. Oh, well. "Why don't you stay the weekend?"

"The weekend?"

"Yeah. I'm headed out on Tuesday for the west coast. Why don't you stay with me until then? Or at least until Sunday?"

"You're leaving town?"

"Remember? I told you. We're going back in the studio. Luc's finished up his movie, and we're rarin' to go." The prospect of making music with the band again had him all excited, but the thought of being without Chris when he'd just discovered this great new sex wasn't all that pleasant.

"What about the paparazzi?"

"No worries. They know how to keep it under wraps here at the Weiss. Tyler sees to it, for obvious reasons. We'll stay in." *Come on, that's got to appeal.*

When he heard the dark little chuckle, he knew he'd won. "All right." *Yes!* "I was going to pack an overnight bag anyway, but I'll pack enough for the weekend."

"Sweet! So, what do you want for dinner? There's a great Greek restaurant that I've had deliver before…"

Chapter Nine

Darien twirled the stick around the back of his right hand and back into his grip, then resumed the simple 4/5 beat he rattled out on the coffee table. The smell of lamb and chicken souvlaki and pastitsio tempted him from the cart set beside the couch, and MTV blared at him from the television, but most of his attention was on the cell phone sitting before him.

He should call Johnnie. He needed to know. Well, no, he didn't *need* to know. Darien had long ago given up trying to keep up with Johnnie's conquests. Although, in the past two years, Darien had certainly had more since Johnnie became monogamous. *Have I caught up? Probably not.* But Johnnie would want to know this. He'd tease Darien mercilessly, of course, but that was part of being friends, wasn't it? Damn, Luc was going to read him the riot act for this, and Brent was going to shake his head and laugh.

He couldn't wait!

Yeah, he could. Better to tell them in person. Let them get their digs in. He'd see them Tuesday anyway, and they'd be together for months.

Yeah, he'd wait.

He glanced up at the television, realizing he'd missed the whole show. But that was okay. He knew enough about what was going on. He just liked to know what others were up to. Helped to stay in the know.

But the only thing he knew right now was that his dick was hard, his skin tingled, and how the hell long did it *take* to get from Chris's place to Manhattan?! Where did Chris live, anyway? Surely he was in the city. Geez, he didn't live in, like, Long Island or anything? Because that would suck --

The sound of the room phone had him dropping his sticks in the general vicinity of the coffee table and lunging toward the side of the couch. He told the desk clerk that, yes, it was okay to let up a Mr. Christopher Faith.

Hanging up the phone, he sat forward and took a swig of some of the Greek beer he'd ordered with the food. Chris was here. For the weekend. Chris was going to fuck him into the mattress a dozen times over.

How cool was that?!

He laughed at himself. A few months ago, he was adamant about nothing going up his ass, and now he was all for it. Guess it needed to go with the fingers and the mouth and the...oh, yeah, the *mouth!* Not only did Chris have that sexy accent, but he had a mouth to suck you right into heaven!

A knock sounded at the door. Darien stood and palmed his cock through his shorts before hastening to the door.

Hot damn, jeans! Faded jeans, even, clearly old favorites. The T-shirt was a David Bowie tour shirt from the '80s, faded from many washings.

"Damn, man," Darien exclaimed, backing into the suite and holding open the door. "You keep dressing like that, I'll forget you're a stuck-up English boy."

There went the eyebrow, hiking up toward his hairline. Chris snorted as he walked over the threshold, an oversized laptop case in his hand. He set it down at the edge of the carpet and turned as Darien released the door to let it slip closed. And there was that demon grin again. The one that made Darien's cock sit up and take notice. Well, sit up *more* and take *more* notice, since it'd been up before the man had arrived. "'Stuck-up English boy'?"

"Well, yeah," Darien teased, taking the two steps to close most of the distance between them. "Normally you're in a suit or something. But you look *damn* sexy in jeans."

Chris reached out a hand to hook around Darien's neck, yanking them flush up against each other. "For a man who's supposedly straight, you talk an awfully good game."

Darien grinned, sliding his arms around Chris's waist. "Hey, I'm *supposedly* bi."

Chris chuckled, shaking his head, then pulled Darien in for a kiss that made his bare toes curl on the chilly marble. Oh, *man!* Darien sucked in Chris's tongue, letting his hands splay flat over the long, hard muscles of Chris's back. He really did *like* how Chris kissed. No holds barred, no hesitation. Once he decided to kiss, he fucking *took,* and it was fucking awesome to be taken.

When Chris pulled back, it took Darien a few seconds to open his eyes and close his mouth. Fingers curling in his hair made him groan.

"This stuck-up English boy wants your lips wrapped around his cock as soon as possible."

Darien's fingers clutched Chris's back. He felt the huge grin that took his mouth. "You want me to drop to my knees here? You already got 'em all weak and shit."

Chris laughed, his embrace loosening. He glanced over Darien's shoulder. "Not here. That couch will do."

Darien nodded, turning out of Chris's arms. He twisted the dimmer on the wall beside him to bring up the lights as Chris stepped down into the big room.

"You sure you don't want to eat first?" Darien asked, grinning as he followed.

Chris's hands were at his jeans, and he had his fly open and his cock out almost as soon as his butt hit the soft upholstery of the couch. "It smells divine, but it has to wait." He spread his arms out across the back of the couch, wearing that devil grin again. "First, you need to take care of the stiffy you've made me carry all day."

Darien hadn't thought his grin could get bigger, but it did. This Chris was *so* different than the everyday Chris. "*I* made you carry?" he asked as he moved the coffee table back to give himself room.

"Yes," Chris said, calm as you please, as though his cock wasn't sticking up straight out of his fly, red and swollen and stiff as a plank. He reached over and plucked a pillow from the couch, throwing it on the carpet between his legs. "You and your mention of wanting to learn how to give a blowjob."

Darien chuckled, dropping to his knees on the pillow, touched by Chris's thoughtfulness. "You liked that, huh?"

Chris snorted. "Rather." As Darien leaned forward, Chris reached out a hand and stopped the motion by gripping Darien's shoulder. "Take your shirt off."

Darien gave him a skeptical look. "You need your shirt off to give a blowjob?"

"No. But you've got an amazing back and all this beautiful skin that I want to touch while you're doing it."

Sweet! "Oh. In that case." Quickly, Darien ripped off his T-shirt and tossed it aside.

"Very nice," Chris purred, putting his hand back on Darien's shoulder. "Now" -- with his other hand, he gripped his cock -- "do you really need instruction?"

Darien leaned in, reaching out to wrap his hand around the top of Chris's shaft. Yeah, thick and hard. Felt a lot like his own, but not. And all that loose skin! "Maybe. I've never done anything with an uncut cock before."

Chris purred. He pushed up with the hand at the base of his cock, forcing Darien's hand higher. Darien watched, fascinated, as the skin bunched up over the head, just leaving the deep-pink, leaking tip peeking out. Chris's other hand came down and he plucked at the foreskin, pulling it up and entirely over the head.

"Whoa!" Darien cried softly, impressed.

"Lick it."

"The skin?"

"Oh, yes."

Darien glanced up quickly and saw the dark look of pleasure on Chris's face. Trusting the man to know what he wanted, Darien bent his head, stuck out his tongue, and licked at the skin Chris still held.

"Run your tongue inside."

Really? Darien thought, but didn't ask. He was far too intrigued by the salty-spice taste of Chris's cock and the liquid drops that leaked from the tip. Chris held part of the skin for him and Darien stuck his tongue inside, searching out the silky head of Chris's cock.

A sigh of contentment sounded above Darien's head, so he guessed he was doing it right. Chris's hand slid back to the base of his cock, and Darien let his go with it. The fingers holding the foreskin released it, and suddenly Darien was sucking at the bare head of Chris's cock.

"Just like that." Chris sighed. Darien saw him grip the hem of his T-shirt and pull it up high, exposing his belly. The hand at the base of his cock released and fell away, clearly a sign for Darien to take over. "Suck me. Do to me what you like done. The foreskin just adds to it."

Darien whimpered. An honest-to-God whimper. This was so cool! He let his lips slide wetly down Chris's shaft as far as he could go, going slow so he could adjust to the width. He had a guy's cock in his mouth! He really did. And it was good! He pulled back up and let his tongue play at the place just underneath the head of Chris's cock, knowing that the spot drove Darien himself crazy. Seemed Chris liked it, too, if the husky groan was any indication, so Darien did that for a while.

Fingers speared in his hair, gently pushing his head down. He went with it, letting that awesome cock fill his mouth again. He gagged when the head went too far in the back of his throat.

"Easy," Chris crooned, tugging gently on his hair to bring his head back up. "Just do what's comfortable."

Darien brought his head back up, pumping the shaft with his hand while his tongue played around the tip. This was fun! Especially when Chris made those moaning sounds and his hips started to rock. Darien sank down and took as much of Chris as he could into his mouth, covering the rest with his fist. He took a firm grip and started to bob up and down, sucking as hard as he could.

"Oh, shit!" Chris's hands double-fisted in Darien's hair. "You should…I'm going…You'll have to stop…soon…or…"

Darien understood well enough but kept on pumping. Knowing he was making Chris crazy, hearing the abandon darken that crisp accent, drove him on.

He gasped when Chris's fists ripped at his hair, forcing his mouth off that delicious cock with a pop.

"What --?"

Chris shoved him back, then quickly pumped at his glistening wet cock. Within seconds, cum shot from his cock and over his bare belly.

Darien licked his lips. "I would have swallowed."

Chris settled down deep into the couch, clearly enjoying the afterglow. "You shouldn't."

"You swallowed me last night."

"And I shouldn't have done that."

"We're clean, aren't we?"

"As far as I know, but why should you trust me?"

Darien jerked back. "Why shouldn't I? You planning to screw me? Well, other than the physical, that is?"

Chris just smiled at him, shaking his head slightly. "You have no reason to trust me."

Darien grimaced. "I have every reason." His cock ached for attention, but he ignored it, wanting this discussion done and gone. "You've been Hell's friend for, like, ever. You stood by me through the divorce --"

"You paid me well to do that."

"You went above and beyond the call of duty, and we both know it. You didn't have to take my calls like you did."

Chris took a deep breath and let it out, his eyes glittering green behind the lenses of his glasses.

Darien leaned in, bracing his thighs against the front of the couch between Chris's splayed legs and taking hold of the back of the couch to either side of Chris's shoulders. He brought his face to within inches of Chris's. "Can I trust you, Chris?"

Chris's eyebrows hiked up. Startled, he searched Darien's eyes intently for a moment before his smile resumed. "Yes."

"I'm clean. I got tested before we got married, and I *know* I can trust Nicole. Are you clean?"

"As far as I know, but I can't be positive about Nathan."

Damn. Picturing the little twink, Darien had to agree with the caution. He sat back on his heels. "You think he cheated on you?"

"No, but I can't be sure."

Darien frowned. "Oh. Damn."

"Yes."

Darien reached up to smear his fingers through the cum splattered across Chris's belly. He was amazed at how much he wanted to taste it. "You need to get yourself tested."

When Chris didn't answer immediately, he glanced up. Chris was watching him curiously, eyes first on the hand and the cum, then on Darien's face. "Even if I were to be tested today, it wouldn't matter."

"Well, of course not. But later --"

"You do realize, to be absolutely safe, another test is required in six months?"

"Yeah, I know." He realized what Chris was getting at. "What? You think this is just a weekend thing?"

"To be honest? Yes."

Why did that sting? It was the natural assumption, given who Darien was. He flattened his palm over Chris's navel, feeling the spunk spread between them. "Listen, you're a friend. Hopefully a good friend." He grinned. "A friend with benefits? I hope we're still gonna be friends after this weekend?"

A hand settled over his. "I would like that."

"I mean, I'm not asking you to stop dating or anything." He didn't want Chris to think he was asking for *too* much. "I know you've got a life and all, but if we're both still free..."

Chris's other hand cupped his chin, making him look up. He was smiling. "If we're both free, we can still fuck."

Darien overexaggerated a shiver. "Fucking hell, I *love* how you say 'fuck.'"

"Do you?" Chris leaned forward until their faces were mere inches apart. The hand stayed on his chin, rubbing gently. "How about 'suck'?"

"Yeah, that's good, too."

"Brilliant." The finger and thumb on his jaw applied pressure. Darien got the hint and knelt up. Chris's eyes, deep green in this light, never left his. "Then what say you come up here so I can *suck* you dry; then I'll bend you over the arm of the couch and *fuck* you hard?"

"Oh, man."

Before he could leap to obey, Chris's mouth closed over his, tongue immediately sliding in between Darien's open lips. Lips and tongue toyed with him, pressing in, then pulling back, making him chase down the pressure and invasion that he so very much wanted. Darien brought his hands up to sink his fingers into the thick silk of Chris's hair, holding the other man so Darien could plunder his mouth.

Eventually, Chris managed to escape, pushing Darien back despite his whimpering protest. "Get up here so I can suck your cock." Chris grinned, glancing toward the food containers on the little warming plate. "Then we'll eat."

Sounded like a plan to Darien. He flung himself into the corner of the couch, eagerly unfastening his shorts and shoving them down. Chris caught them when they were halfway down Darien's thighs and pulled them the rest of the way off. He removed his glasses and set them on the table. Then he was kneeling between Darien's legs, swallowing down his cock.

"Oh, man!" Darien gripped Chris's shoulders, digging in.

Chris popped his mouth off the tip of Darien's cock and, with his eyes on Darien's, sucked on two of his own fingers. When they were good and wet, he lowered them between Darien's thighs, his dry hand pushing one of Darien's legs up so that his foot was braced on the edge of the couch.

"Shit!" Darien groaned, throwing his head back as the fingers wiggled their way into his ass.

Chris chuckled and gulped down Darien's cock again, swallowing around the head.

Darien cursed, pumping up into that hot mouth, then groaned as he pulled back, impaling himself further on those fingers. "Ah, shit, Chris, fuck!" He was too keyed up. He was too hard and wanted this too much. "Oh, man!" Too soon, fire sparked at the base of his spine, forcing him to pump, releasing the ache in his balls and clenching his muscles around Chris's fingers. He came with a cry, curling forward over Chris's head as the man swallowed him down.

Yeah, he could get used to this.

Chapter Ten

If Darien ever doubted that the guys in the band were like family to him, having dinner with all of them together reminded him. Dinners with just the four of them -- no, five, no, really seven -- had to include Tyler and Reese these days -- were every bit as loud and comforting as any dinner he'd shared with blood relatives when growing up.

The house they'd rented was terrific. A hotel guest had mentioned it to Tyler, who had passed on the information to Johnnie. Johnnie was even toying with the idea of buying it outright. It was set up on a cliff, overlooking the ocean. A winding, tree-lined trail led down to a private beach that was kind of rocky, but that was okay. There were some neat tidepools nearby, too, that Darien spent much of his first early afternoon exploring. The house itself had seven bedrooms, a living room, game room, formal dining room, and a wicked cool kitchen. But the selling point for the band was the third floor loft. It took up the entire length of the house, and the wall that faced the ocean was nearly all glass.

Currently all of their equipment had been set up in that space, along with assorted seating arrangements. It was all ready for the five of them to get their ideas together and make some music, an idea that made their record company very, very happy.

They all arrived at the beach house at varying times on Monday and Tuesday. Well, Johnnie was already there since he'd rented the house and it was only a few miles away from the Weiss West. Darien flew into Los Angeles and drove up to the central coast with Luc and Reese. Brent and Hell had already arrived when they got there, having flown into San Francisco from Germany, then driven down. So, except for Johnnie and Tyler, they were all exhausted, but they sat at the big twelve-seater dining table in the sunny, formal dining room and had a loud reunion over pizza, calzones, and beer.

It took a while to get caught up, and for once, Darien kept his own news under wraps. He listened and helped to grill Luc about his experience in making the movie. That was actually fascinating enough to take up half of the meal. Then Brent and Hell told about their extended trip through Europe. Everyone toasted Reese's new gallery opening, then listened as he and Tyler explained the new murals he was going to paint for various parts of the Weiss West.

They adjourned with beers to the living room with the French doors that stood open to the ocean vista and breeze. Darien followed his friends, chewing on the realization that he wanted Chris to be there. He would have fit in nicely, Darien thought.

He was taken off guard when Johnnie threw an arm around him and hauled him down to sit on one of the deep, plush pale yellow couches.

"All right, you." He released Darien and leaned back against the arm of the couch, crossing his arms over his chest. "Out with it."

Darien blinked, trying for innocent. He was awful at keeping stuff from his friends, and he knew it. "What?"

He glanced around the room as they all took seats, each naturally keeping close to the man he loved. Tyler came to sit on the arm of the couch behind Johnnie, gathering Johnnie's long braid in his lap and toying with it. Reese sat in an overstuffed chair that matched the couch, and Luc sat on the plush carpet at his feet. Hell and Brent sat in the other overstuffed chair and a loveseat, respectively, but they were close enough to whisper if they wanted.

I want that, Darien acknowledged to himself. *I want what they have.* What he'd never had with Nicole. Was he jumping the gun to think he could have it with Chris? Probably.

"Don't give me 'what?'" Johnnie grimaced, watching him carefully. "You've been way too quiet, and you haven't even mentioned the divorce once. Something happened. Spill."

Aha! Diversion! "I haven't? Oh. Well. I signed the final papers on Thursday."

"So it's done?" Reese asked, big blue eyes sympathetic under the long hang of royal-blue bangs. Darien had confirmed with Reese on the drive from Los Angeles that the hair was bluer than the last time Darien had seen him.

"Yeah, it's done. Chris got me through it with very little muss or fuss." He smiled at Hell, who smiled back.

Tyler reached over to pat his arm. "Congratulations."

"Thanks." He grinned at the concerned looks around him. "I'm fine, really."

"Sure he's fine. Because something happened," Luc pronounced, sipping his beer.

Johnnie nudged Darien with his bare foot, a sudden grin on his face. "You met someone."

Darien beamed. "Yep."

"So give. Who is she? Why didn't you bring her? You know we have to approve of your dates now, don't you?"

Darien squirmed, too excited to take the bait of Johnnie's teasing. "I didn't bring him, because he's working." *Yeah, good delivery.*

Silence thick enough to cut with a knife. Darien glanced around at the blank, shocked faces. At almost the same time, similar grins drew up the corners of each of their mouths. He laughed.

Johnnie hooted, throwing back his head to land in Tyler's lap. "Oh, man! You finally fucked a guy?"

Happily, Darien nodded.

Tyler slapped his palm over his face, laughing. Reese fell back in his chair, curled into himself with his own laughter. Luc grinned, shaking his head, matching Brent's reaction. Hell was torn between laughter and shock.

Johnnie reached over and punched his arm. "What the fuck, man? What made you do it? Who is he?"

Darien shrugged, picking at a tear in the knee of his jeans. "I dunno. You guys seemed to like it a lot, so I was just thinking about it. And, thanks to the divorce, I didn't really want to *think* about women."

"Hey," Brent spoke up, "you can't rule out all women because of what happened between you and Nicole."

"Yeah," Johnnie agreed, mirth sliding into concern. "Just because it didn't work between you guys doesn't mean you have to change your whole life."

Darien blinked at Johnnie. "You've been telling me I should fuck guys the entire time I've known you."

Johnnie flushed. Guilt from Johnnie? Whoa, call the international press! "Well, yeah, but not just because you got divorced and were depressed or anything."

Darien cocked his head to the side. "Me? Depressed?"

"It *has* happened." Johnnie scowled.

"Yeah, okay." Darien laughed. "Well, whatever. That's not why I did it. I mean, yeah, I didn't really want to sleep with any women, but..." He shrugged again, "I was really curious, y'know? Seemed like a good time and all. And the guy's really hot."

Luc's grin was wolfish. "So, you pick up some hot piece of action from a club?"

"Nope. It's Chris."

"Chris?"

Again he looked to Hell, who was frowning slightly. "Chris Faith."

"*Chris?*" Reese asked. "Your lawyer? Hell's friend?"

"Yep."

Hell gaped. "Why him?"

"Hel-*lo?* Have you seen him? He's hot."

"Is he?" Johnnie asked. But it wasn't so much a question for his own benefit. Sounded more like he was confirming that Darien thought Chris was hot.

"You don't think so?"

Johnnie sat back. "Doesn't matter what I think."

Darien grinned at Tyler. "You've got him well trained."

Tyler rolled his eyes and snorted. "Yeah, right."

See, that was the thing. Maybe before now, Darien just hadn't met his type. Now, Tyler was one hot piece of ass. He knew that. The blond man's looks had been a topic of discussion between the members of Heaven Sent before and after Johnnie had hooked up with him. Those shining blond curls and huge blue eyes over that wide, generous mouth brought to mind a delicious butterscotch sundae. At least they did to Darien, although he'd never told anyone about that particular imagery. But Tyler wasn't what Darien wanted. Darien didn't even have a twinge of lust for the man, just admiration, like for the sunset behind him. He turned back to Johnnie. He knew his friend was stunning. Had known it since he'd joined the band way back before they were famous. Johnnie was good-looking and knew it well. *Used* it well, both for himself and for the band. Darien wondered sometimes if the band would have been half or even a quarter as successful without their flamboyant, excessive lead singer. But, again, Darien only felt admiration for him. Hell, he'd had a chance to sleep with Johnnie -- many chances, in fact -- and he wasn't sorry to have turned him down. Nope, seemed Darien was into tall, stuffy-looking Brits with a wicked streak.

He smiled at that and met Johnnie's gaze. "Yeah, Chris is hot."

"Wow."

Johnnie watched him for a long, measuring moment, then slowly smiled. "You like him."

"Yeah."

"You like him a lot."

"Yeah."

One dark brow arched over a snarky grin. He glanced Luc's way, then back at Darien. "You liked fucking him?"

Darien heard Luc's chuckle and smiled. "Oh, yeah."

"You go the whole nine yards?" Luc asked.

Quite happily, he turned to the redhead and nodded. "Yeah."

"I had no idea I was matchmaking when I suggested you ask him to be your lawyer for the divorce," Hell said with a self-satisfied smile. "How wonderful."

Darien shrugged. "He didn't expect it either."

That made Brent laugh. "Well, yeah, since you kept on telling everyone that you were straight."

Darien met Brent's teasing condemnation with a grin. "Yeah, well, I *was* until recently. Why didn't you *tell* me butt sex was that good?"

Caught off guard, Brent snorted, then coughed. Hell broke into a fit of laughter.

Brent raised a skeptical eyebrow. "You fuck or get fucked? Or both?"

Calmly, Darien sipped his beer before answering. "Actually, I got fucked."

Johnnie whistled. "So the ass is no longer virginal, is it?"

"Nope."

Johnnie chuckled. "I'm hurt that you didn't let me pop your cherry years ago."

Darien heard Tyler's shocked gasp and laughed, seeing the teasing twinkle in Johnnie's eyes. Tyler yanked hard on Johnnie's braid, which just made the singer laugh. He laid his head back in his lover's lap, making big eyes up at Tyler. "That was years before you, blond-of-my-heart."

Tyler snorted and shoved Johnnie's head off his lap. He stood and pointedly went to sit next to Brent on the loveseat. "See if *you* get any tonight."

Which made it Johnnie's turn to gasp in outrage.

The rest of them laughed.

Chapter Eleven

He'd made fun of Johnnie during the tour that had separated him and Tyler when they first got together. They all had. Johnnie, their brash lead singer, had been celibate and almost a damn hermit while they toured Europe and Asia, more concerned with getting things for Tyler or emailing Tyler than he was with finding a bed partner for the night. At the time, it'd been laughable.

Now... Darien stared at his laptop screen, wondering if he should send the email to Chris.

The first few weeks working with the band had taken most of his attention. He'd managed to forget that he wasn't getting laid, by diving into the music. It worked, for the most part. Since Reese and Tyler weren't staying at the beach house, it really was just the band and they could concentrate on work. Brent and Hell got so focused in music that Darien sometimes wondered if they even had sex during that time. Not that it was any of his business. There were times that they all went out, either together or separately. Mainly they hung out at the White Room, the nightclub at the hotel. But when Darien went, he spent more time watching the bands performing and analyzing the music than talking to people. It wasn't exactly odd for him. When Heaven Sent were writing or recording, he did tend to get preoccupied. They all did. This was what they *did,* after all. The music was why they were millionaires and known the world over.

But it finally got to him. He realized that he was *missing* Chris. And wasn't that just absurd? A few months in Chris's company to handle the divorce and one absolutely stellar weekend of sex, and he couldn't get the man off his mind. The week before last, Chris had emailed to let him know that the divorce was officially final. Darien had written back to ask a stupid law question. He couldn't even remember what he'd asked. Chris had been nice enough about it and sent a reply. Even made a joke at the end. Which was heartening. Darien sent a follow-up the next day. A few days later, he'd sent a link to a blog with an entry that was just too funny. Chris had sent a laughing reply back. After which came another email from Chris, remarking on a news article that just couldn't be believed. In the last week, they'd emailed daily. Never anything of real importance, but it was a constant stream of conversation. And sex wasn't even the main topic, although it did come up. Namely in innuendo and sly remarks.

But now Darien wrote something real. *I miss you. Take a vacation and come out and see me.* Yeah, it'd be stupid to send that.

He stood and walked to his room's window. His beach house bedroom overlooked the ocean since he didn't mind the constant pounding. What did it matter to him? He had drumbeats constantly going in his head; the surf just acted as another one. It was still early and the day was bright. His bandmates had yet to rise, or that'd been the case when he'd gone down to the kitchen a little while ago to get breakfast. He was an earlier riser than most of them anyway. He'd expected to see Brent, the only other one likely to be up, but the guitarist must have decided to sleep in.

Spur of the moment, he decided to go swimming. He spun and dug through the dresser for the trunks he knew he'd packed somewhere. Ah, yes! Quickly, he shed his sweats and changed into the shorts, stuck his feet into some sandals. He grabbed his cell phone and sunglasses on the way to the linen closet at the end of the hall that contained all the towels and stuff.

An hour later, he sat on the sand, letting the sun bake into his skin, drying the ocean water from his swim into a thin layer of salt. He stared at the waves crashing over a line of rocks and watched the seagulls circle overhead.

He picked up his cell phone and dialed.

Chris answered on the second ring. "Hello, Darien." *Man, that voice.*

He leaned forward, bracing elbows on his bent knees. "Heya, Chris. I'm calling you from the beach." He scooped some sand and watched it slip away through his fingers.

"That would explain the sound of waves in the background."

Darien smiled. Chris was in a good mood. "Yeah. You should see it. It's gorgeous."

"I imagine it is."

"Do you like the beach?"

"Pardon?"

"Do you like the beach?"

"Occasionally. I prefer boats."

"Oh?"

"I go scuba diving once a year. Usually in Hawaii."

"Really? How cool! I've always wanted to do that. When do you go?"

"I'll be in Kona the last week in August."

"Oh, man, I wanna go."

Chuckle. "You'll still be with the band, won't you?"

He tossed sand onto the pile in front of him. "Yeah. Probably. But I could take a week off, I'll bet. We'll be sick of each other by then." Not entirely true, but not entirely false. They'd probably need a break before then, but Chris didn't need to know that. "So, do you have any more vacation time?"

"Vacation?"

"Yeah. Say, a long weekend? I was hoping I could talk you into coming out here."

"Why?"

I miss you. But Chris might not want to hear that. Darien picked up a small rock and smoothed it through his fingers. The wind played with his hair, blinding him temporarily. "I'm lonely. I need company."

Chris snorted. "You can't possibly be lonely."

Darien speared a hand through his hair, grunting when his fingers caught on a snarl. "I am."

"You're with your friends. I'm sure you've visited every nightclub on the central coast and then some. Where are the fawning teenage fans?"

"All right, I'm horny. I can't have sex with teenage fans." He worked at the snarl with his fingers.

"You have plenty of fans who are of age."

"Yeah, so what? I'd rather have you."

Pause. Damn, he hated it when Chris paused like that. Meant he was thinking. What good did that do? "I'm sure you could find a willing man."

"With a stuffy English accent and a horse cock, who's gay? Come on."

Luckily, that made Chris laugh. That was it. Just compliment his cock and it cracked that shell.

Darien warmed to his cause. "C'mon, man. You got me hooked on getting pounded in the ass. Least you can do is come here and help a guy out."

"The least I can do?"

"Yeah."

"I do have a job to do."

"That's why I mentioned vacation."

"I don't know that it's a good idea…"

Darien snorted. "C'mon, if you won't do vacation, bring a laptop. There's excellent broadband access. I'll even promise to let you work some during the day."

"'Some'?"

"Well, yeah. When we're working."

"Big of you."

"Did I mention your tasty horse cock?"

"You failed to mention 'tasty' before."

"Silly me." Darien tossed his hair from his eyes, gazing at the horizon. "Well? What do you say? If you come for the weekend, I'll even get you backstage for our anniversary show at the Weiss. It's sold out, y'know. Pretty big deal around here. But I've got an in with the band."

Chris laughed. "How can I possibly pass on that?"

"That's what I'm thinking."

"I asked Chris to come out for the show this weekend."

Hell paused, knife hovering over the tomato he was slicing for his sandwich.

They were alone in the kitchen at the beach house. The others were upstairs. Brent and Johnnie were hashing out lyrics. Luc was kind of his in own space, working out a passage in one of the new songs. Darien and Hell had figured it was as good a time as any to come down to get eats. Well, Hell had decided to come get some eats, and Darien had followed, seeing an opportunity to talk to Hell alone.

"Oh?" Hell said casually, knife again descending through the tomato.

"Yeah. I called him this morning." Darien bit into a pickle before resuming mixing the tuna salad in the bowl before him. "He's bitching about where to stay, but I think he'll come."

"It'll be nice to see him."

"That's it?"

"What's it?"

Darien studied Hell's profile. The little guy looked cute and innocent, but Darien knew him far too well now not to know there was something going on underneath that lavender hair. "No comment about my asking Chris to come for the weekend?"

"No. Should I comment?"

"You haven't said much about me and Chris being together."

At that, Hell turned, regarding him steadily. *"Are* you together?"

"Well, there's the sex thing."

"That doesn't mean you're together."

"True. I dunno, but it definitely wasn't just a weekend thing like he thinks."

Hell dropped the tomato in a plastic container, then started spreading mayonnaise on three pieces of bread. "That's what he thinks?"

"Yeah. I told him it wasn't, but I don't think he believed me."

Hell nodded. "Has he told you anything about his past?"

"He told me about you and him."

Hell glanced at him, the nodded. "Yes. We had a brief sexual relationship."

"But you were better friends."

"We are. Did he tell you about Simon?"

"He mentioned that he was in a serious relationship in the past that kind of messed him up. Well, no, he mentioned the relationship. I'm guessing that it messed him up."

Hell smiled sadly. "Yes. Simon wasn't good for him."

"Tell me about him."

"Simon?"

"Yeah."

"Why do you want to know?"

Darien met Hell's curious gaze steadily. "It's important to him."

"Why not ask him?"

"I will. But you're here now."

Hell smiled and started stacking lunch meat on the three sandwiches. Then he frowned. "Luc said ham, didn't he?"

"Heck if I know."

Hell scrunched up his lips in a grimace, then shrugged and went with the ham. "You've heard of Simon Ritter?"

Darien started dumping tuna on the two sandwiches he was making, frowning. "Sounds familiar."

"Have you seen the Volton movies?"

"Oh, yeah! He was that sidekick guy."

"Yes."

Connection made, Darien could picture the young man he'd seen in the movies. Slim, toned blond with blue eyes and wicked smile. He was all the rage for a while a few years back. Nothing new that Darien could think of. "Whoa. He's cute."

"Yes, he is."

"Chris was dating him?"

"Yes."

"Y'know, for a lawyer type, he meets all sorts of famous people."

Hell chuckled. "When Chris was young, he went to acting school. He's Shakespearean trained, in fact. When he first came to the United States, he worked part-time at a law firm while he was looking for work in the theater."

"No shit, really?"

"Yes. So you can see why he's always enjoyed being with actors and musicians far more than he enjoyed being with his fellow law students."

Darien finished spooning tuna and stood to dump the bowl into the sink. "So why not do it professionally?"

"He hates to audition. He doesn't believe he's good enough and manages to sabotage himself. At least, that's what he's said. I've never seen him perform."

That's a shame. Darien could imagine that Chris was a pretty good actor. "But he knows enough people now to get past that, doesn't he?"

"Most likely. But I think he enjoys what he does now. Most of his clients are in the entertainment business. He is able to spend time with the type of people he enjoys. I believe that is enough for him." Sandwiches built, Hell started to clean up.

Darien nodded. That fit the man he knew. Still would be cool to see him perform. "So what happened with Simon?" He opened the cupboard where there were all kinds of chips and stuff.

Hell sobered a little. "He and Simon were together long before Volton. When Chris moved to the US, Simon came with him. Simon was a struggling actor and lived with Chris while Chris was a student. I do believe they were in love. I don't know firsthand, as I didn't see much of Chris during that time."

"Let me guess, Simon dumped Chris when the movie happened?"

"More or less. It wasn't that clean of a break. Eventually, Chris found out that Simon cheated on him during the filming of the movie. With a woman."

"Hey, yeah, didn't he just get married like a year or so ago?"

"Yes, he did. And he now proclaims that he never was gay."

Well that made a lot of Chris's reservations more clear, didn't it? "Damn."

"Yes."

"Hmmm." He poured some chips onto both plates, knowing Johnnie would want some. "Was Chris set on marrying Simon?"

"I don't know if they talked of marriage, but he certainly had decided to spend the rest of his life with Simon. He practically supported Simon in the early days."

"Ouch."

"Yes."

They worked in silence for a few moments, putting various items away. When they were ready to head back upstairs, Hell stopped him by grabbing his arm. They stood face-to-face in the middle of the sunny kitchen. "Darien?"

"Yeah?"

"How serious are you about Chris?"

"Honest?"

Nod. "Please."

Darien glanced out of the window over the sink, watching a fluffy white cloud race by. "I think I'm pretty serious. I can't stop thinking about him."

"Him specifically?"

He looked back to Hell. "What do you mean?"

Hell shrugged. "He's the first man you've slept with."

"Oh, I get it. Yeah. I thought about if it was just the guy thing." He crossed his arms and leaned back against the counter beside the sink "I've thought about doing other guys. Almost picked up one when we went out the other night. The model. You met him."

Hell nodded.

Darien shrugged. "But it's just…not that appealing."

"Really?"

"Really."

"Do you know how he feels about you?"

"Not really." He sighed. "Not at all. I think he likes me. We had a lot of fun together."

Hell shared his chuckle.

"But if I talk about anything remotely serious between the two of us, he shuts off. I mean, I didn't push that much because, yeah, it was just one weekend, right? But even when we've been emailing each other, he's been…distant."

Hell stepped up to put a comforting hand on his arm. "Chris has learned to protect himself from his feelings.

Perhaps too much. He hasn't allowed himself to have a relationship since Simon."

Darien nodded. "I hear you. Take it easy."

"That might be best."

"Yeah. Okay. I can do that. At least until I figure it out myself, right?"

Chapter Twelve

Darien sat in the VIP bar just off the lobby of the Weiss, sipping a Coke and half watching the baseball game on the high-def television mounted to the side of the bar. Normally he could sit in the regular bar in the restaurant with the picture window that looked out over the town, but this weekend, with the show and all, it got to be kind of crazy for any member of Heaven Sent to be seen in the public areas. Most of the time, fans were cool about it as long as you smiled, signed something, and let them snap a picture. But on weekends like this, they tended to mob.

He thought, of course, about Chris. It had taken some negotiation, but Chris was finally on his way. Darien had wanted him to stay at the beach house for the weekend, but when Chris asked if Reese or Tyler were staying, that idea got nixed. Darien saw his point of not wanting to be the only non-band member staying at the house. Kind of screamed "I'm here for sex." Not that Darien minded, but Chris wasn't him. So they had to arrange for him to stay at the hotel.

Chris got all weird about Tyler having to pull strings since the Weiss was technically sold out for the weekend, but it ended up being no big deal. Not that Chris would believe that or anything.

The guys were surprisingly quiet about Chris's arrival. Darien had expected Johnnie and Luc, at least, to give him no end of shit about bringing his *male* lover all the way across the country. Especially when it would be absurdly easy to find one close by.

But that was the thing, wasn't it? Darien didn't want anyone else. Male or female. When he'd gone out in the last few weeks, he'd looked, sure, but he'd politely declined all offers. Of which there were plenty. After all, he was the only unattached band member. Again. So although the opportunities were there, he didn't take advantage. What he wanted was to experience more of the heat that existed underneath Chris's composed exterior.

Could he be in love? Now wouldn't that just beat all? Kind of weird for *all* of Heaven Sent to end up with men. But then, why not? They were all alike in some way or another, which was why they were such close friends. Brothers almost. Why not all have the same leaning? After all, he'd tried it with a woman, right? Well, the marriage thing. He'd tried a *lot* of other things with women. He enjoyed it, but it wasn't a long-time thing. Never had been. He wasn't the slut that Johnnie used to be, but he'd had more than his fair share. He could try other men, but why? It didn't interest him. If he hadn't taken Johnnie up on his offer years ago, it wasn't likely that other men would surpass that offer. After all, Johnnie was...well, Johnnie. In comparison, if Chris had more appeal to Darien, then there was something special about Chris, right? Right.

"Mr. Hughes?"

He looked up at the bearded bartender in his crisp white shirt and snazzy little bow tie.

"The front desk just called. Your visitor has arrived."

"Sweet." He stood and pulled a tip out of his wallet. "Charge the rest to my room?"

"Of course. Thank you, sir."

He'd tried to get the man to not call him "sir," but knew why he didn't comply. Tyler wasn't an ogre of a boss, but he was very keen on how his employees should act, even with -- or maybe especially with -- his close friends.

Shoving his hands into the deep pockets of his khakis, Darien exited the bar into the deserted hallway beside the elevators. Neat place, actually. Big potted plants kept the area kind of secluded. So he saw Chris headed his way before Chris saw him. He stepped out just as Chris hit the elevator button.

"Hey."

Chris jumped, spinning around. Whoa, his eyes were all big. Well, maybe not really big, but big for Chris. "Darien! Where did you come from?"

Darien jabbed a thumb toward the secluded hallway. "There's a bar down there. I had them call me when you checked in."

"You were waiting for me?"

Ding. The elevator doors shushed open and they stepped inside.

He waited for the doors to shut before stepping into Chris. Chris stumbled a little, back hitting the side of the elevator. Right where Darien wanted him. His arms went up and around Chris's neck, hauling the other man's tasty lips down for a kiss. "Yeah."

Oh, yeah! That was nice. Chris was hesitant at first, receiving, not responding. That was okay because Darien liked the feel of his lips. Soft and warm, with a little stubble around the edges for added sensation. Then Chris sighed into it, dropping his bag beside them and letting his arms slide around Darien. His mouth opened and his tongue swiped Darien's teeth. Their tongues met in a lazy, swirly hello. *Very nice.*

The ding of the elevator reaching Chris's floor broke them up. Darien smiled up at Chris before stepping away. They both bent for Chris's bag. Darien backed off, chuckling.

"Shouldn't you be working?" Chris murmured, leading the way down the hall.

Jeans, yum! He did like what jeans, even relaxed ones, did for Chris's ass. He wondered if Chris would let him fuck it. "Nope. We gave ourselves a few days off. Well, except for tomorrow night's gig, of course."

Chris glanced at him as he stopped at his room's door and swiped his keycard. He smiled. "Must be nice to be your own bosses."

Darien snorted. "We're not our own bosses in most things. Usually, Gretchen or the record company people are telling us what to do. But since the gig is for the Weiss..." He stopped beside Chris, who'd frozen just inside the room. "What?"

"There must be some mistake."

"Why?"

"This room is huge."

Darien grinned. "Yeah. This is the room I usually get when I stay here."

Chris frowned at him.

"Oh, come on, don't be like that. It was the only thing Tyler had left. And he only had it left because I was technically still reserving it." He walked farther into the suite, completely at home in the spacious green-and-black-accented sitting room. "I figured I'd better keep the room open in case I wanted to come stay here for the weekend." He turned and let his grin go wicked for Chris. "Nice, huh?"

Well, shit. Now what? Chris didn't like it. His frown said as much. "What?"

"You didn't tell me I'd be staying in your suite."

"No, I didn't. Is it a problem?" He cocked his head to the side, striking a pose that he hoped Chris found appealing. "I was kind of hoping that we'd spend most of the weekend together anyway."

Chris blinked, then took a breath, and the frown eased from his face. "There is that."

Darien stepped into him, bumping groin to groin. He slid one arm around Chris's waist, then used the other to make him release his bag. They indulged in another long, drawn-out kiss that made the boner in Darien's pants ache. Chris's lips were just so...*ungh!* And his tongue. Darien sucked it in, relearning the subtle, dark taste that was Chris. He slid his hands down Chris's back, then took some handfuls of polo shirt to yank it out of his jeans. Underneath the shirt he found warm, satiny skin. Skin he'd missed touching. Skin he wanted to taste.

Chris pulled back from the kiss, hand toying lightly in Darien's hair. "Impatient?" he teased.

Darien slid his arms forward, spreading his palms over Chris's flat belly before he let one travel lower to cup the erection that pulsed behind the zipper of those jeans. "Yeah. You mind?"

"Oh, no, not in the least." Hands on his shoulders pushed and his thigh nudged; then they were walking -- Darien backwards -- toward the open bedroom door. "I'm here for your pleasure."

Darien chuckled, an evil tone to it. "Hey, I like the sound of that."

"Do you?"

Darien hooked his fingers in the waistband of Chris's jeans, right over the zipper, and used it to pull. "I hope it's your pleasure, too."

Chris smiled. "It is."

"Good." He let go, quickly popping the button of Chris's jeans before stepping back. He whipped his T-shirt over his head and tossed it aside. "What say we get naked?"

Chris took off his glasses. "Sounds like a plan."

Suppressing a giggle, Darien toed off his sandals and quickly dropped his briefs and khakis. He plopped on the bed and watched as Chris slowly peeled off his polo.

Wearing that demon grin that Darien had come to crave over the weekend they'd spent together, Chris approached. Without a word, he lifted one foot and set the sole of his boot down on Darien's thigh. "Do you mind?"

Grinning, Darien obediently lifted the cuff of Chris's jeans so he could untie the boot. With Chris leaning on his shoulder for balance, he also eased the boot off his foot and dropped it to the carpet, then got the sock as well. They repeated the same for the other foot.

Then Chris was standing between Darien's spread knees, hands on his fly. "So quiet," Chris murmured, long fingers toying with the zipper without opening it. "Nothing to say, magpie?"

Darien chanced a brief glare up before returning his attention to Chris's hands. "Don't call me magpie."

"But you usually chatter just like one." Chris chuckled, holding the waistband with one hand and exaggerating the hold of thumb and forefinger of the other on the zipper's tab. "What if I want to call you magpie?"

Darien licked his lips. "Take out the horse cock, and we'll negotiate."

Chris laughed, the full, rich sound that Darien could only recall hearing when it was the two of them. His laugh elsewhere seemed so...careful. Chris pulled the zipper down, exposing white briefs underneath. "You'll let me call you magpie for just the sight of my cock?"

"More than just sight." Darien reached up and hooked his fingers into the sides of Chris's waistband, helping the man to ease both jeans and briefs down over his hips. Once free, his hard cock sprang out, nearly slapping Darien in the face. Darien abandoned his hold on the clothing to reach up and wrap his fingers around that long, thick rod, mouth watering.

Chris hissed. "What else do you want with it?"

"This," Darien rasped, then opened his lips and let them slide down the shaft until they met his fist at the base.

"Bloody fucking hell," Chris cursed, hands sliding into Darien's hair.

Darien hardly heard him, eyes closed and tongue working as he rapturously relearned Chris's taste. He pulled back wetly and lapped up the precum at the tip, delving as much as he could into the hole before sliding back the loose foreskin so he could tease the rim of the head. He'd paid attention when they were together before and thought he'd clued in on what Chris liked. He glanced up at the tight expression on Chris's face and decided he was doing okay.

Chris's fingers in his hair tightened, and then all Darien had to do was keep his mouth open and watch the teeth as Chris's hips took over and slowly thrust in and out of his mouth, so very careful when the head got near the back of his throat. He wanted to tell Chris to stop being so careful, but he wasn't quite certain he could take it and, well, his mouth was a little busy at the moment.

Then Chris pulled away entirely, ignoring Darien's groan of disappointment. "Are there condoms handy, or do I need to get my bag?"

Darien licked at the saliva coating his lips. "In the drawer, right here." He pointed.

Chris nodded. "Good." His eyes locked on Darien's tongue, and with a little hungry groan, he swooped down and took Darien's mouth in a punishing, involved kiss. Then he stood, turning toward the nightstand. "I'm glad your mouth is good for something besides talking."

"Hey!" Darien protested, edging back to the middle of the bed. "That's not nice."

Chris found the condoms easily and tossed the bottle of lube onto the mattress beside Darien. "No, it's not." He paused at the side of the bed to stare at Darien, who had taken the moment to lie back, knees bent and spread. He stroked his cock for good measure, in case Chris had forgotten it was there. The heat in Chris's eyes at the sight was worth any amount of teasing. "Are you aware of how beautiful you are?"

Now, Darien had actually been told that on a number of occasions. He tried not to let it go to his head. He thought he was a reasonably good-looking guy, leaning more toward traditional cute than out-and-out gorgeous. But the look in Chris's eyes and the rasp in his voice told Darien that Chris really meant it. "I'm glad you think so," Darien replied, putting as much sincerity into the words as he could.

Chris inhaled sharply, eyes locking on Darien's for an endless moment. He opened his mouth as though to say something, but he evidently changed his mind. He turned his attention instead to opening the condom packet.

What were you going to say? Darien wanted to ask, but he was uncharacteristically tongue-tied. He picked up the lube and poured some on his palm, the better to jerk himself off.

Chris kneeled on the bed between Darien's legs, plucking the bottle from his hand. "I'll have to taste you later," he promised, squeezing some liquid onto his fingers, then rubbing it between them as he snapped the cap shut and tossed the bottle aside. "Right now" -- he pushed at one of Darien's knees, forcing the leg back against his chest -- "I need to fuck you."

"Oh, yeah," Darien moaned, jerking himself harder as Chris reached down to poke fingers into his hole. Why that felt good, he hadn't a clue. But it did. Especially when Chris rubbed around and found -- *"Shit!"* He arched -- *that!*

"You like that."

"Oh, God, yeah."

Fingers left and something bigger prodded at the opening. "You like this more."

Something like "um-n-ah" escaped Darien's lips. He hadn't a clue if it was a word. There was no thought process behind it. Not when Chris's cock was stretching him, pushing inside of his body.

"You want that," Chris murmured, bracing his hands on the mattress beside Darien's shoulders, edging his hips closer so that steely rod could slide in deeper. "You want my cock in your ass, don't you, magpie?"

"Oh, fuck, not that." Darien groaned, throwing his free arm over his eyes. It was too much to try and focus when his body was igniting from the inside out.

Chris chuckled, the rat! "Talk to me, magpie." He stopped moving, that entire cock now fully encased in Darien's body. "Tell me you love being filled with my cock."

"Chris, damn it!"

Teeth bit at the forearm covering his eyes. "Say it."

Snarling, Darien looped the arm up and around Chris's neck, hauling the man's face closer to his. He opened his eyes and locked gazes with Chris, immediately and totally serious. "I love being filled by your cock." If Chris wanted to play that game, he was up for it. "I wanted it every night since I left New York."

Chris blinked, and some of the heat faded from his eyes as he heard Darien's words.

"Fuck me, Chris," Darien demanded, not letting him look away. "Fuck me like I need it. Fuck me like only you can do." *That scared him.* Darien saw it. He couldn't exactly blame him. Darien heard what was in his own voice just as well as Chris did. But he wasn't sorry, and he wouldn't take it back. He rocked his hips, squeezing as best he knew how on Chris's cock, forcing a heated moan out of that gorgeous, cultured mouth. "Fuck me."

That did it. With a snarl, Chris switched positions, getting into a near crouch, gripping Darien's hips. All pretense at gentleness was gone as he grimaced and set to pounding. It actually hurt some. Nothing that Darien would complain about, of course. The physical assault was awesome. It took him out of his own mind, distracted him from wondering at his own heated words, and drowned him in a lava flow of friction and flood.

He came before he really knew it, spurting onto his hand and belly. But Chris wasn't done with him. Those hazel eyes were screwed shut, and that mouth was drawn into something between a snarl and a cry. Sweat dotted his forehead and chest, then gathered in rivulets that streamed down his neck and belly, some of it splattering on Darien's chest. Darien spread both arms out on the mattress, grabbing hold of the raw silk of the bedspread and hanging on for dear life, getting off on the punishing rhythm and the fact that Chris had completely lost control.

"Fuck," Chris snarled, his rhythm wavering. "Ah, fuck!" he cried, fingers bruising Darien's sides. "Bloody. Fucking.

Hell!" He thrust on each snapped word, hips lost in a feeling Darien knew from experience. Knowing Chris came that hard almost made Darien come again.

Chris faltered, falling forward over Darien, barely catching himself on his elbows. Darien brought his hands up to slide his palms over the sheen of sweat on Chris's back.

"Darien…"

Darien glanced down, only seeing the top of Chris's head. The gold sheen of Chris's hair twinkled at him. "Yeah?"

"I…I…"

What?

But Chris shook his head. He collapsed forward, falling on Darien's chest. The new angle of his hips slid his cock out of Darien. "I'm knackered."

Darien chuckled, but his heart sank. *That's not what you were going to say.* But he let it go, content for the moment to just hold the man struggling to regain his breath.

Chapter Thirteen

Crack! Billiard balls scattered over the green felt of the table, but not one of them dropped into a hole.

"Crap!" Darien cursed, setting the butt of his cue stick on the hardwood floor between his feet.

Luc chuckled, chalking up the tip of his cue stick as he eyed the balls. "You just aren't good at this."

Darien snorted. It was true. He wasn't very good at playing pool. He hadn't caught on to the knack of the angles and crap. No amount of practice here in the game room at the Weiss had improved his game. But he did love cracking the balls together.

Luc leaned over the table, legs spread and long arms working as he carefully slid the cue stick over the backs of his knuckles.

"Mmmm, nice view."

Reese's words as he passed through the entrance to the room didn't throw Luc off. The bastard just smiled as he pushed forward with the stick and made the balls crack again. He stood and kept watching the balls, even as Reese walked up to his side.

"Hey, tiger," Luc murmured, lifting an arm to encircle the shorter man's shoulders.

"Here." Reese handed a glass of Jack and Coke to his lover.

The sight of Chris entering the room with Tyler distracted Darien from the sight of Luc and Reese. Tyler laughed at something Chris said as they both approached the pool table. Tyler stopped beside Johnnie, who sat on a high stool to the side, awaiting his turn at the game.

Chris rounded the table to Darien's side, holding up a glass toward Darien. He smiled. "For you."

Darien couldn't help the goofy grin on his face. He felt...well, damn it, he felt special. Chris had gone to get him a drink. A small thing, sure. But he'd left the private room with Reese and Tyler, who had also gone to get their lovers' drinks. He was here with Darien, with Darien's best friends, sharing a quiet night playing a game. It was all so ordinary, but at the same time...

Sap. "Thanks." He took the black Russian from Chris and sipped it.

"Your turn," Luc announced.

Darien turned back to the game, realizing he hadn't even heard Luc take a shot. Several shots, actually, judging by the few striped balls that remained on the table.

He grimaced, setting his drink on the counter behind him. Dutifully, he studied the table before him, but none of the straight shots he could actually make lay on the table.

"Word of advice?" Chris asked softly.

"Yes!"

"No!" Luc snapped, frowning. "You're a ringer."

Chris grinned, a shadow of the demonic expression he wore during sex, but it was still effective. "I'm merely suggesting a shot."

Reese laughed, slapping Luc's arm. "Oh, shut up. Darien probably can't make the shot anyway."

Darien flipped Reese off, which only made the blue-haired ass smirk at him.

"Fine." Luc sighed, hitching up into one of the high stools as he sipped his drink.

Chris stepped up to the edge of the table and leaned over slightly. He briefly glanced over his shoulder at Darien, glasses shining in the harsh pool table light. "This one."

Darien scowled, eyes scanning the table. "How the hell am I supposed to get *that* one?"

Chris stood straight, then crossed behind Darien, placing a hand on his lower back. "Lean over, take aim, and I'll show you."

Darien felt them. Luc, Johnnie, Reese, and Tyler didn't make a sound, but they were watching. Their attention was palpable. Darien wondered if he was blushing as he bent over the table.

Chris bent over beside him, hand still on the small of his back as he pointed at the cue ball with the other. He calmly explained that hitting the ball at a certain angle would cause it to bounce and catch the ball he'd pointed out. Darien struggled to concentrate, distracted mightily by Chris's warmth and the subtle scent of his cologne.

Chris drew back after he finished his explanation, his hand slowly slipping from Darien's back as he stepped to the side. Darien remained bent over the table, eyes focused on the white ball with the tiny blue chalk smudges on it, far too aware of other, more intimate scenarios where Chris could have him bent over a table.

He took the shot before he collapsed on the table. With distracted amazement, he saw the cue almost hit the ball Chris had him aiming for.

A warm hand squeezed his shoulder. "Very good. You almost had it."

He grinned.

Johnnie groaned. "Oh, God damn. Would you please just kiss him?"

Darien's head snapped around, and his eyes bugged out at his friend.

Johnnie was looking at Chris, though. "Please? He's dying for it, and I'd really love to see the proof myself."

"You asshole!" Darien cried, hands gripping the cue stick. "What the fuck --?"

He barely heard Chris's chuckle underneath his own outburst. Chris's hand on his chin shut him up. Shocked, he let his head be turned.

Chris grinned at him. That wicked grin was back, but Darien didn't see it long, since Chris dipped down to seal their lips together.

Well, at least Darien managed not to let the whimper in his throat escape. Chris's thumb pressed his chin, and he opened up to Chris's tongue, sucking in the faint taste of Chris's martini before the taller man pulled out of the kiss.

Darien stared up at him, licking his lips, willing to forget that his friends were present if Chris would kiss him again.

Chris, however, aimed a smile up over Darien's shoulder. "Like that?"

Now Darien did blush. He could feel it heating his neck and cheeks. He ducked his head as Johnnie laughed.

"Oh, yeah. That was great."

"Well, damn," Luc murmured. Darien glanced up to see the tall redhead smirking, with arms crossed. "You were telling the truth."

Darien scowled. "I wouldn't lie."

Luc grinned. "Yeah, I know, but it's something to see the proof." He stood, grabbing his cue stick. He looked at Chris. "My condolences, man. This one's a handful."

Chris's hand closed gently over the back of Darien's neck. Gentle, but it made Darien shiver even so. "Of that, I am well aware, I assure you."

Later that night, his head pillowed on Chris's naked chest, Darien remembered to apologize.

"Sorry?" Chris asked.

Darien toyed with the fine layer of hair over Chris's left pec. "Johnnie and Luc can be real assholes sometimes."

"Oh, that." Chris chuckled. "Nothing to be sorry about. I quite enjoyed staking my claim." Amusement laced his voice.

Darien had thought the same thing, that the scene had been some kind of pissing match. Didn't make much sense, but then, they were his friends and probably just trying to look out for him. "Is that what you were doing? Staking your claim?"

Warm lips nuzzled Darien's forehead. "For the weekend, certainly."

Darien didn't like the phrasing, but he decided to let it go. It was enough, for the moment, that Chris had felt comfortable enough to kiss him in front of his friends. He wasn't going to push it.

Chapter Fourteen

Darien tossed aside the towel he'd been rubbing on his hair and glanced at himself in the mirror. *Freshly fucked.* He grinned at himself. *Best way to go to a show.* Of course, he'd never played a show sitting on his stool when his ass had been thoroughly pounded a few times in the last several hours. Should be interesting. Chuckling, he wrapped another towel around his waist and went to the bedroom.

Chris lay back against the headboard, propped up on most of the pillows, watching the evening news. One arm was bent over his head and the other was draped over his bare chest, the remote tucked under his hand. One leg was bent, the other lying flat on the mattress, which sort of kind of put him in an open position. He turned his head to watch Darien, a grin growing on his lips. Did Darien imagine that they were still slightly swollen from kissing? From sucking? From...

Darien pointed at him. "Don't you start. I've got to get dressed."

Chris raised that damned eyebrow. "Start?"

Darien licked his lips. "Laying there all naked and reeking of sex. You're not making it easy for me not to pounce, y'know that?"

Chris pulled the sheets up over his hips. "There."

Darien snorted. "Like I don't know what's underneath there." He dropped the towel as he turned to his bag, which was open on a luggage rack near the closet.

"Mmmm, nice."

Without looking back, Darien wiggled his ass. "Yeah, yeah, you can't have any until later tonight."

"Cruel."

"Hey, I gave you as much as I could."

"Mmm, that you did." The feline rumble in Chris's voice made Darien's skin tingle.

Down boy, he thought at his cock as it started to take notice. He turned his attention to dressing and tried to ignore the man in the bed. White briefs, white jeans, and a white button-down with the sleeves torn off were his outfit for the night.

"All white?" Chris mused, reminding Darien of his presence.

Darien turned, but bent his head over buttoning his shirt rather than look at Chris. "Yeah. The White Room, get it?"

"Ah, yes. I've heard of it."

That made Darien look up. "You have?"

Chris half-smiled. "I've had reason to do some research on Heaven Sent lately."

Darien grinned.

"The White Room isn't the one Luc owns, is it?"

"No." He sat on the edge of the bed with his socks, setting his white sneakers on the carpet at his feet. "He and Reese own the White Tiger at the Weiss East in New York. The White Room belongs to Tyler and his two friends. Well, I guess Johnnie owns part of it now. Do you know the story about it? Our first gig here?"

"Yes, it seems to be Heaven Sent legend. It was that performance where Johnnie and Tyler met?"

"'Legend.' I like that." He chuckled. "Tyler and his partner wrote our management, asking if we'd play there, and we thought 'why not?' It was as good a place as any to warm up for the tour, and it was different, y'know. Being the first band to play at a nightclub is kinda cool, yeah?" He tied his shoe. "Anyway, we get here and Tyler meets us and it's like -- pow! -- Johnnie's hooked. I mean, really hooked. He got one look at that curly blond hair and those big blue eyes, and he was a goner. He bored us with it *all* weekend. It was nauseating." He smiled as he said it.

"It was love at first sight?"

"If you ask Johnnie, yeah. If you ask Tyler, no. 'Course, Tyler thought he wasn't gay at that point, so Johnnie says his opinion doesn't count."

"Tyler wasn't gay?"

Darien heard the hesitation in Chris's voice even though he was sure he wasn't supposed to. He was getting rather good, he thought, at reading Chris's moods. Well, he was normally pretty good at it with anyone, but it meant more to him with Chris.

Which means...?

"Nope. He'd even been engaged a few months before he met Johnnie. Or was it a year? Well, something like that. But I've talked with Edward, his best friend, and according to him, it was always kind of hard to tell which way Tyler swung." He tied his second shoe and turned, bringing one leg up on the bed so he could face Chris. "But he's completely into Johnnie now. So that proves that straight guys can be turned, right?" He said it with a smile, but both he and Chris knew there was more to it than that.

Chris's eyes narrowed slightly. Without his glasses, he looked far less uptight. Or maybe it wasn't the glasses and more the fact that he sprawled naked in sheets that smelled of sweat and sex. "Some men, perhaps."

Darien crawled up the bed, careful not to touch as he positioned himself on hands and knees above Chris. All of a sudden, jeans felt really tight. "I like what we do," he said seriously, planting a soft kiss on Chris's lips. "I really do."

Chris's smile was forced, some deep conflicting thought behind it. "I'm glad."

Darien wanted to say more. He wanted to shake Chris and make him speak his thoughts, but that wasn't fair. Because he wasn't speaking all of his, was he? But right at that moment, he didn't have time. He needed to get downstairs and limber up for the gig.

He kissed Chris again, lingering a little this time, knowing this would have to last for hours. "I've got to go."

Chris reached up to cup Darien's jaw with both hands. "Yes." He pulled him in for a thorough kiss.

Darien pulled away reluctantly. "Go down to the front desk when you're ready. They know who you are. Someone will take you to the VIP section for the show."

Chris nodded, tongue darting out to quickly trace Darien's bottom lip. His hands slid down Darien's neck, over his shoulders, and rubbed lightly up and down his forearms, making the hair stand on end. All the while his eyes searched Darien's face. "All right."

Darien wanted to talk about that look, but he didn't have time. Not now. Maybe tonight. They kissed again, and then Darien sighed, slowly crawling backward off the bed. "I've got to do the mingling thing after the gig," He grinned as he stood. "Good news is, the dancing at the White Room is killer. Johnnie hired an awesome DJ. You dance?"

Chris slid a hand down his chest, coming to a stop low on his belly. Darien wasn't sure he was even aware of doing it. "Not in a long while."

"I'll bet you're good." Darien forced himself to step away.

"I've held my own in the past."

Darien laughed, forcing levity when what he really wanted to do was rip off his clothes and follow that hand's suggestion down underneath the sheet to what he knew lay beneath. "There you go again, sounding stuffy." He stopped at the doorway. "See you later."

Chris nodded. "Later, yes."

"Tyler! How has your life changed since you met Johnnie?"

Darien barely held in a giggle as he looked over at Tyler's wide-eyed gape.

"Where do I begin?" Tyler finally said, holding out his hands helplessly.

Standing beside his lover, arm slung possessively around his shoulders, Johnnie leaned in to kiss Tyler's cheek. "His life sure hasn't been the same."

Tyler snorted. "Now *that's* for sure."

Flashbulbs continually went off, but Darien took it in stride like his friends. This was part of what they did. He stood with Johnnie, Tyler, Luc, Reese, Brent, and Hell and smiled like he was supposed to. The performance had gone great. They'd cleaned up and changed into their second all-white outfits for the night, and now the press was getting their piece of Heaven Sent before everyone joined the invitation-only party in the main area of the White Room.

Where's Chris? Darien wondered, keeping his smile as his eyes darted through the room behind the dozen or so reporters that had the band cornered. He'd been there. Darien had talked to him briefly before he'd been dragged away for this mini-press conference. He'd complimented the performance, and he seemed to really *mean* it, which was very cool. Darien wouldn't have pegged Chris for someone who liked their music, but then, he wouldn't have pegged Chris for a Shakespearean-trained actor, either. And damn it, he'd forgotten to ask about that earlier!

But he wasn't there now. Darien was sure of it. *Where'd he go?*

Luc elbowed him in the gut to get his attention.

"What?"

Luc gestured with his chin, and Darien turned to face a female reporter who was eyeing him expectantly.

"Oh, sorry, what was the question?"

She giggled. "I asked if you've started dating again since your divorce?"

He sighed and put on the look that he and Gretchen had agreed on. "Not just yet."

The reporter showed sympathy, although who knew if it was real or not. "Are you and your ex-wife still on speaking terms?"

"Nicole and I are great; we just weren't great together." He smiled, *really* not liking this woman. But they'd expected the questions, and this was the first real time any press had access to him since the divorce.

"So there's hope for the women of the world?" she asked coyly.

He laughed. "Well, sure." When what he was really thinking was "Not likely."

Another reporter barged in and asked when the next album was going to be released, and Darien happily turned to Luc or Johnnie to answer. Soon after that, the questions stopped and there were a few minutes of pictures. Then he was free to mingle. The nasty woman reporter tried to catch him, but he managed to evade her with Gretchen's help. He ended up chatting with a reporter from a local magazine.

Still no Chris.

Luc was standing near the doorway, talking to tall, skinny guy with a small recorder. The bassist's arm was wrapped around Reese's shoulders, holding his shorter lover against his chest. Reese took it in stride, leaning back against Luc as he talked to a reporter on their other side. So easy. They touched each other like it was just natural.

Darien wanted that. He'd sort of had it with Nicole. They'd touched easily. But not like *that*. Not like it was necessary.

He parted ways with the first reporter and found Edward, Tyler's friend. He liked Edward, and they spent a few minutes catching up.

Then Tyler stepped up. "Sorry, Darien, but Edward has announcements to make in the main room."

Edward checked his watch. "Oh, shit, I do. See ya, Darien."

"Yeah, later." He smiled at Tyler. "Everything okay?"

"Crazed, hectic, and out of control. Yeah, everything's okay." They laughed. Tyler reached out to squeeze his arm. "Everything okay with you?"

"Yeah, sure."

"You sure?"

"Yeah. Why?"

Tyler glanced around. They were far enough away from everyone else so that when he leaned in, no one else could hear. "Where's Chris?"

Darien grimaced. "I don't know."

"He did show up?"

"Oh, yeah, he's here. He's just not *here* here. I don't know where he went off to."

"You need help finding him?"

Darien snorted. "Yeah, right. You're not using me as an excuse to get out of talking to more press."

Tyler opened his eyes wide, but the innocence was feigned. "What do you mean?"

Darien shook his head. "Don't even try it."

Tyler grimaced. "Gee. Thanks, buddy." He looked up. "Looks like it's time to join the crowd."

Darien laughed and slapped Tyler's shoulder. "Buck up, Tyler. It's not so bad."

"I've told you that you're insane, right? You and the rest of the members of your band."

"Quit with the small talk, ladies," Johnnie said, appearing behind Tyler. He nudged his lover forward, urging him to follow the people who were filing out of the door. "Let's go, blondie."

"Don't rush me."

Smiling, Darien left them to their playful bickering. He wanted that, too. Didn't he kind of have that with Chris? When they were alone?

And where the hell *was* Chris?!

Darien wanted to go look for him, but there were a few hundred people filling the main room, not to mention the balconies. So he settled for doing the mingling thing while keeping a watch to see if he saw Chris. Although, he wasn't sure what he'd do if he found him. He couldn't jump him, couldn't kiss him, couldn't hold him, and just that frustration alone was getting in the way of his ability to carry on a conversation.

So he didn't fight when three women dragged him onto the dance floor. At least there all he had to do was move. Besides, dancing would help blow off a little steam. He was surrounded. Not surprising. Normally, it's what he cultivated. He had about six of them around him, some he'd met before and some were new. None of them were especially close, and none of them had shared his bed before. Which was a relief, actually. Made it easer to keep them at bay, although he tried not to make it seem that way. Had to keep up appearances, right?

He spun one of his partners around so that her plump little ass fit into the curve of his groin. Laughing over her shoulder, he looked up.

And saw Chris. Dancing not twelve feet away from him. *Oh, yeah, he can dance!* Darien was kind of surprised to see Chris holding his own on the crowded floor. He moved easily with the music, just a little stiff around the edges. Nothing that made it awful, just made him look a little bit off. Darien thought it was endearing. Made him compare it to how smooth Chris moved during sex.

You've got it bad, he told himself, tearing his gaze away from Chris as he released the hot little number in his arms.

But she didn't go away. She turned and wound her arms around his waist as the pulsing beat of song around them morphed into a slower thump. Going with it, he slid an arm around her shoulders and drew her close. It was nice, but he wondered what it'd be like to dance with Chris. Different, surely, not the least of which because Chris was taller than him.

He let his gaze drift to the side.

And froze.

Chris was dancing. With a guy.

Well, of course he was dancing with a guy. He was gay. He wouldn't dance with a woman. Well, gay men danced with women, sure, but...No, hey, not the point! The point was that Chris was holding another *man* close when Darien wasn't even twenty feet away from him.

"Darien?"

He heard the plush female in his arms, but he couldn't take his eyes off Chris's hand, pinkie ring glinting where his hand was spread over the black-shirted back of the man in his arms.

No!

"Sorry, sweetheart," he murmured, brushing a kiss across the woman's brow. "I've got to talk to someone right now."

"But..." The rest of whatever she said was swallowed in the music as he stalked away.

He grabbed the wrist of the hand with the pinkie ring and yanked.

Chris faced him, completely unsurprised to find Darien there. Was that a challenge in his eyes. *Oh, no way!*

"I need to talk to you," Darien ground out.

"Right now?"

No way! He turned to the guy who'd been dancing with Chris. "Excuse us."

The guy stammered a reply, but again Darien didn't hear. Hand still clamped around Chris's wrist, he led the way off the dance floor and through the crowd to the guarded back entrance.

"Let go," Chris muttered, flanking him, shaking his imprisoned arm.

"No." It was exceedingly important that he didn't let go. That he didn't think too much about what he was doing. He just had to get Chris out of the crowd and in private.

They reached one of the dressing rooms, which was thankfully empty. Only then did Darien release Chris's arm as he turned to close the door.

"What was that all about?" Chris asked, insufferably calm. He looked way too good in a loose black button-down and charcoal slacks. His hair was arranged just so, and his glasses failed to hide the fire in his eyes. Good, he was pissed, too.

"You know what it was about."

"I'm afraid I don't."

"You were dancing with a guy."

There went the eyebrow. "You were dancing with a woman."

"That didn't mean anything."

"Oh?"

He'd hoped that Chris would come back with an answering "it didn't mean anything" about his dance. That he didn't just pissed Darien off. "Of course not."

"Where does 'of course' come from?" Heat was in Chris's eyes, but his body language and voice were as cool as ever. "You're straight. Why shouldn't I believe it could mean something?"

"*You* were the one who didn't want anyone to know about us!"

"Which doesn't mean I particularly want to watch you dance with a woman."

"It was just dancing!"

"For now, yes."

"What the fuck? Do you think I was going to take her up to the room and fuck her while you were down here?"

"Perhaps you wouldn't have taken her to the room." He glanced at their surroundings, pointedly at the couch. "I'm sure you know plenty of private places in this hotel."

"Fuck you! Is that what you think of me?"

"Quite honestly, I don't know what to think of you."

"Care to explain that?"

"Certainly. Only a few months ago, you were a married man. Before that, you were an acknowledged playboy, having slept with God knows how many women."

Darien took exception to the word "playboy," but he let it go for the moment.

Chris was in full lawyer mode. "Then you seduce me because you're curious about sleeping with a man. I will admit to being flattered and star-struck. You are both an amazingly attractive man as well as a famous one. I thought this would be a one-, maybe two-time, instance, after which you would go back to your merrily heterosexual life. But first you spend a weekend with me; then you invite me here, claiming to have missed me."

"I did miss you."

"Why? I'm nothing to you but an experiment."

"That's not true. I *told* you it wasn't like that!"

"You said we were friends. That we could do it again. Which makes me a convenient fuck buddy when you get the urge to have a cock up your ass. Which is fine, but you can't be jealous of a fuck buddy."

Darien shook his head. "You've got it all wrong."

"Do I? Then enlighten me. What are we doing?

Ah, crap, this is getting serious. Darien paced away from Chris, toward the battered couch up against one wall. "I wouldn't sleep with someone else when I'm with you. No matter what you think of me, I don't do that."

"Darien, you're not *with* me."

"You're here this weekend because of me."

"Yes. I know. And I still don't fully understand why."

"Fine." Darien balled his fists together, staring at the colorful splotches in the framed print mounted on the wall before him. "I like you," he told it, trying to sense the man behind him without turning. "I like you a lot."

No answer. No hint of movement.

He took a deep breath and turned. "I think I'm falling in love with you."

Chris's reaction was far from anything he could have hoped for. Hazel eyes went saucer-wide, and he took a step back, one hand coming up waist-high as though to ward Darien off. "No."

"Yeah. I think so."

"No." It was amazing Chris's glasses didn't fly off when he shook his head so hard. "No, you can't mean that."

"Why the hell not? I think about you all the time. I see things and I want you to see them. I laugh at a joke and I wonder if you think it's funny. I wasn't even tempted to sleep with anyone else when I was away from you. I just want to *touch* you when we're standing near each other." He reached out.

Chris stepped away, turning from him. "Stop."

"Why? Why's that so bad?"

"Why?!"

Darien flinched at the rage in Chris's voice when he turned back.

"Why?" Chris's hands clawed into fists, a visible indication of an anger out of control. "Why should I believe anything you say? You don't know anything about relationships."

"I --"

"No! You got married on a *whim.* I'd be willing to wager that your seven-month marriage is the longest romantic relationship you've experienced in your short lifetime. You have women -- *and* men -- falling at your feet, begging to share your bed. Why should I believe that you want me?" He laughed mirthlessly. "You don't even have a proper place of residence! You have enough money to support a woman who you don't even love without it hurting at all. You do things just on the spur of the moment. How do I know this isn't just another in a long series of games that you stop and discard?"

Darien's own rage melted in the face of this unreasoning anger rolling off Chris. "Getting married was a mistake," he said carefully. "I've admitted that. But that doesn't mean --"

"Don't. Just, don't."

"But, Chris --"

"No." Chris took a deep breath, obviously trying to rein in his emotions. It wasn't working much. "Even if you believe what you say now, there's no guarantee you'll mean it later."

"Chris, I wouldn't say it if I didn't mean it."

"You mean it now, maybe, and I should be flattered by that."

"Flattered? Jesus, Chris, I just told you that I love you."

"And just how many people have you told that to?"

"Hey, I don't go around telling everyone I love them."

"Why not? You could. And you could bloody well get away with it."

"This isn't about me, is it? You don't want to believe me. You're scared."

Chris stared at him, wide-eyed. Nothing physical stood between them, but it was like the few paces between them were filled with an impassable mountain. "Yes. I'm scared. I've been with someone like you before. I *won't* go through it again."

"I'm not Nathan."

Chris barked out a sharp laugh. "Not Nathan."

"I'm certainly not Simon."

Judging from the second harsh laugh and the scraping of the hand across his jaw, Darien figured that was the one.

"Listen, Chris, I'm not that guy. I wouldn't use you like that."

"What do you know about it?"

"Some. I talked to Hell." He took a step toward Chris. "Please listen to me. I'm not Simon."

Chris shook his head, backing up toward the door. "Perhaps not." He stared at the floor. "But I can't take that chance."

Those words injected ice into Darien's veins. He took another step forward. "Chris…"

Chris shook his head and turned, grabbing the doorknob. "No. I can't do this."

Darien caught his arm as he opened the door. "Chris, don't leave."

The taller man yanked his arm free, then crossed the threshold. "I'm sorry, Darien."

"Chris!" He followed into the hall.

"No, damn it. Stay away."

"But --"

Chris whirled, eyes wild. "Darien, stay the fuck away, or I swear to God I will deck you."

Darien froze, shocked. "Don't do this."

Chris met his gaze. Darien thought he saw something melting, but then the cool exterior was back. "Goodbye, Darien."

He turned, and Darien could only watch his back as he disappeared through the far door.

Chapter Fifteen

Hell found him a few hours later at the beach house. Darien had left the club without saying a word to anyone, but the driver worked for the hotel, so he had probably called back to notify the powers that be of Darien's whereabouts.

Darien sat at the open window, arms crossed on the sill, chin propped on the backs of his hands, watching the stars blink. He only knew it was Hell when the man pulled up a chair and sat beside him. The lavender hair was kind of hard to miss.

"Are you all right?"

"Yeah." He heard movement behind him, signaling the presence of another, but he couldn't be bothered to turn.

Brent appeared on his other side, crossing his arms and leaning against the wall beside the window. "What happened?"

"He left." Darien was surprisingly calm about this. He'd had a little bit of a tantrum on the front lawn of the beach house when he'd arrived. There were a few bushes that had taken the brunt of his rage. But now everything was level. His thoughts were even clear. He wondered if he was in shock. Or maybe Chris was right and what he'd felt wasn't love.

How were you supposed to know?

"He went to the airport," Hell said.

Darien startled, glancing at Hell. But then, it made sense, didn't it? Why would Chris stick around? He sighed and put his chin back on his hands. "That figures."

"Talk, man," Brent prompted. "What happened?"

"I told him I loved him. He didn't take it well."

He heard Hell's little groan.

"I know, I know. I said I'd take it slow. I meant to. But he was dancing with this guy, and I just…" He shook his head. "I lost my head."

"It's not like you to get jealous," Brent pointed out.

"I know that."

"You really think you're in love?"

He sat back, hooking his fingers around the windowsill. "I think so." He turned to look at Brent. "How do you know?"

Brent's lips curved into that self-deprecating smile of his. He glanced past Darien at Hell. "Don't look at me. I had to get beaten over the head to admit it."

"Yeah, but you *did* admit it." He glanced at Hell, then back. "Both of you. How do you *know?* How does anyone know?"

"I don't think that's anything we can answer for you, buddy," Brent admitted.

"I know." He sighed. "I *think* I love him. Really, I do. But maybe he's right. Maybe I'm not capable of it."

"What? He said that?"

Was it wrong that Brent's instant anger warmed his heart a little? Well, he wouldn't tell anyone. "Sorta. He pointed out a bunch of things, all true, that kind of suggest it."

"Like what?"

Darien shrugged. "I got married on a whim."

"People get married for all the wrong reasons. You knew then that you didn't love her."

"No, I didn't."

"Yes, you did. You were just too boneheaded to admit it."

"I've never had a long-time relationship."

"So? When you've got the kind of life we have, it's damn rough to have any kind of relationship."

"I don't own a home."

"Oh, please, that's just scraping for reasons. You'll get one when you need one. You've been traveling solid for, like, seven years. I've thought about getting rid of my two places."

"Oh?" Hell asked.

Brent flushed. "Yeah, I said 'thought about.'"

Darien chuckled. "See? You guys...I can tell you're in love. I could tell before dickwad here admitted it."

"Hey!"

Darien smiled up at Brent, then sobered, shaking his head. "Johnnie and Tyler, Luc and Reese. You all have it. I never have. I *think* I started to with Chris. It feels right."

"So go after him."

"No." This from Hell. "I know Chris. I saw him before he left." Hell's cherub face was full of sympathy. "Yes. You've frightened him."

"I frightened him? He scared the hell out of me."

Hell nodded. "You have frightened him. Which leads me to believe that he *does* feel for you. Very much."

He stared hard into violet eyes. "What do you mean?"

"He's had boyfriends confess love in the past, but he hasn't reacted this badly to any except Simon."

"You mean, you think he loves me?"

"I think he cares for you very much. He wouldn't be frightened if he didn't."

Hope flared, then died. "Yeah, well, even if he does, he won't talk to me."

"Not tonight. Maybe not tomorrow. But he's going to calm down eventually," Brent pointed out.·

Hell nodded. "Chris is a man of reason. He's not accustomed to strong emotions. Once he calms down, you should try and talk to him again."

Darien pushed a breath through his lips. "Yeah. And have him blow up at me again."

"Well," Brent said, pausing until Darien turned to face him. He arched a brow, and it was a little bit too much like Chris's for comfort. "Is it worth it?"

Chapter Sixteen

For two weeks, Darien called at least once a day. He left rambling messages on Chris's voicemail and waited for some kind of reaction, even if it was Chris telling him to shut the hell up.

He'd already made flight arrangements to head to New York at the end of the third week, when Chris finally picked up.

"Darien. Stop."

"Hey, Chris." It was nearly nine at night in New York, so he didn't worry that Chris had anyone with him. He'd *better* not have anyone with him.

"Stop calling."

"Can't do that."

Chris sighed. "Darien…"

"I love you."

Pause. "Stop saying that."

"Why? It's true."

"For now, perhaps."

"For always."

"I don't believe you."

"What can I do to convince you?"

"I don't know."

Darien sat back, staring at the wall above the mirrored dresser in his room at the beach house. An idea that had started to take root in his head the previous week. Hearing Chris's voice helped make it grow.

"Darien, please stop calling. This is not going to work out between us. We're far too different."

The trick was to prove Chris wrong, and his new idea just might do it.

"Darien?"

"Yeah, okay. You're right."

"I...am?"

"Yeah. It won't work like this. You can't let yourself trust me."

"Darien..."

"And any good relationship has to have trust. I trust you, but that doesn't matter, does it?"

"Darien..."

"Okay. I'll stop calling." His heart beat fast. He knew what he sounded like. He knew Chris heard exactly the type of flippant response he expected from Darien. He was taking a chance, but his gut told him he was walking the right path.

"You will."

"Yep. I thought I could make you see it, but I can't. So I'll stop."

Pause. "Thank you."

"No problem." He swallowed over the nervous lump in his throat. "Hey, Chris?"

"Yes?"

"For the record, I *can* be trusted. I've never had a bad breakup with anyone. Even Nicole. Until you."

He hit the button on his cell to end the call.

Oh, shit, was that a mistake? He stared at the number pad on his cell, dying to call back and explain himself. But that wouldn't work. Chris was dead set on not listening to him.

Chapter Seventeen

Faith
That I'll hold you
Faith
That I'll need you
Faith
That I'll be there when you need me to be there
And it takes faith to know I'm always by your side

Darien twirled a drumstick through his fingers as he sat on the floor, back to the wall, letting the music wash over him.

It was a rough recording of a brand-new song. It wasn't perfect by any means. The song would go through a number of changes before they went into the studio and laid down the tracks, but it clearly had a solid foundation to build on.

When the music faded away, Darien opened his eyes.

They were all staring at him. Hell stood beside his keyboards. Brent sat on a stool over the by the recording console, his favorite working guitar cradled in his lap. Luc was beside him on a straight-backed chair, bass guitar face-up on his thighs. Johnnie sat cross-legged on the floor with Darien, facing him.

They were waiting.

Darien smiled and nodded. "I like it."

Their smiles followed his.

Johnnie leaned forward to pat his knee. "You think it'll work?"

Darien shrugged. "Who knows? But I gotta try."

Johnnie nodded. "Good." He pushed gracefully to his feet, holding a hand out to help Darien up. "When do you leave?"

"Tomorrow."

Raw guitar notes drifted in the air. "We're going to change that chorus when you get back, y'know? Not the words."

Darien smiled. "Yeah, I figured you weren't happy with that. It's cool."

"Hey, Hell." Johnnie left him to wander over to the keyboards. They started muttering together.

At the table, Brent was fiddling with the recording console and Luc was pulling out smokes for both of them.

These were his friends, and he'd never felt closer to them.

"Thanks, guys."

They all stopped, looking at him again.

He knew he was being sappy, but he had to say something. "You guys are the best. You didn't even blink an eye when I asked you to do this."

Johnnie chuckled. "It's not every day you hand me lyrics like that. Made my job easier." Johnnie was the main lyricist, sometimes with contributions from Brent. But he hadn't protested at all when Darien had handed them the sheet of paper the other day.

Brent nodded. "Yeah. This is going to be a good one." They all contributed, but there was no doubt that Brent actually ran the game when it came to the music. But he, too, had just followed Darien's lead, listening as Darien used his rough piano skills on one of Hell's keyboards to illustrate the melody in his head.

Darien knew they'd improve on his original thought, and they had. They would continue to do so. They didn't even have a studio date for any real recording, and there was no doubt the song would go through many changes before the final cut.

But Darien had a song now. Something tangible made from an idea in his head. His friends had made it possible.

He swallowed over a sudden lump in his throat. "You guys gave me all sorts of shit about Nicole," he told the chair beside him, unable to look at any of them. "Why's it different now?"

Silence. Then a chair scraped and soft footfalls came toward him.

Luc slid an arm around his shoulders. "You didn't talk about her like you talk about Chris."

"You didn't write a song about her," Johnnie added from where he still stood at the keyboard rack.

"You don't think I'm just obsessed?" Darien asked, chest tight. Because it was possible. It was possible that he was making more of this than it really was, because it was different.

"Yeah, you're obsessed," Luc answered.

Darien's heart fell.

Luc chuckled, squeezing his shoulders. "But, personally, I think it's the kind of obsession that goes with love."

Darien looked up at him. "Yeah?"

Luc grinned. "Yeah. God knows I'm obsessed with Reese."

"True."

Luc's arm slid higher, wrapping around his throat to pull him in for a joking chokehold. "Go with your heart, nimrod."

"All right," he laughed, pushing at Luc. "Let go, asshole."

Chapter Eighteen

A car door shut outside. Darien looked up from his seat on the staircase, watching the front door. Afternoon sunlight made the frosted glass of the three little windowpanes in the door shine.

Footsteps on the covered porch outside, then a knock.

"It's open."

The knob turned and the door swung inward. Chris stepped inside.

God, he looks good. Dressed in a charcoal-gray suit with a pale blue shirt, he looked every inch the lawyer. He'd probably come straight from the office. His hair needed a trim, the bangs actually touching the rims of his glasses. It had been three months since that fateful night at the Weiss, and Darien hadn't seen him once. The sight of him now made Darien's heart swell in his throat.

Chris didn't see him immediately, casting his gaze around the empty entryway, no doubt seeing the equally empty living room to his right. No furniture in sight. Then he looked up the gold carpet of the dark wood staircase to finally find Darien sitting on the top step of the first flight of steps.

Darien smiled. "Hi, Chris."

Chris took an audible breath. "Hello, Darien."

Darien kept his hands folded between his bent knees. "You like the house?"

Chris clutched something in his hand. A CD case. "It's lovely."

"It's mine."

"I know."

"Richard talked to you?"

"Yes."

Good. He'd worked with Chris's realtor friend for a reason, hoping he'd contact Chris even though Darien hadn't mentioned the lawyer other than to say who'd recommended him.

"Congratulations." Chris standing so very still. He looked nervous, although you'd have to know him to see it.

Darien saw it. Breathing over his own rapid heartbeat, he nodded toward the case in Chris's hand. "You got the song."

Chris held it up, glancing at it. "Yes."

"Did you like it?"

Chris opened his mouth twice before he finally got out words. "It's beautiful."

Darien stood. "It's still rough, but I think it came out okay. It was my first shot at lyrics."

"You wrote the lyrics?"

He'd made sure to send a hard copy of the lyrics with the CD, just in case Chris missed hearing them exactly. "Yep. And I meant every word."

Chris's panicked look stopped Darien halfway down the staircase. "Why?"

"I love you."

Chris closed his eyes, shaking his head. "No."

"Yeah. I do."

Chris glanced at the empty space around them. His arm curled into his chest, clutching the CD like a young child might clutch a favored toy. "You bought a house."

Darien slowly descended the last few steps. "Yep."

"Because I accused you of not having a home."

Darien shrugged. "Wasn't that I was *against* it. Just didn't have a compelling reason before."

Chris scowled. "And proving me wrong is a compelling reason?"

Darien scowled right back. "It is when you're using it to keep us apart."

A helpless look passed over Chris's handsome face. He shook his head, staring at Darien. "Why are you doing this?"

"Because I have to. I have to get you back."

"You never had me."

"Not true. I think I did. I think I had you until you got scared and backed away."

"This won't work."

"This has to work. I love you."

"Stop."

"No. I love you, and I'm pretty damn sure that you love me."

"You don't know that."

"Not completely, but I've got a sneaking suspicion."

"And why is that?"

"If you didn't love me, you wouldn't be scared to talk to me."

"I'm not scared."

Darien took a few steps closer. "If you're not scared, then let me touch you."

Chris stepped back. Did he realize he did it? "What?"

"Let me touch you. Let me kiss you. If you can convince me that you don't care about me, I'll leave you alone."

"Darien, stop!" Chris's hand came up, palm out toward Darien.

Darien stopped. For the moment. "See?"

"See what?"

"You love me."

"You're talking nonsense."

"Why'd you come today?"

"You…I wanted…"

"You wanted to see me."

"We needed to get this settled once and for all."

Darien took another step. "You're absolutely right. Say you don't love me."

"This is absurd." Chris's back came up against the wall beside the door.

"Say it."

"Why are you doing this?"

"Because you need to stop fighting this. I need you with me."

"Whatever for?"

"Everything. I want you in my life."

"Until you find someone better."

"There's no one better. Not for me."

"You hardly know me."

"I know enough."

"You know the sex."

"It's more than the sex."

"You don't know that."

"Prove me wrong. Give us a chance."

"I --" Chris shook his head, eyes wide as he stared at Darien. "No. I can't do this." He spun, reaching for the doorknob.

"Chris!" Darien grabbed his arm, spinning him and slamming him back up against the wall.

The CD case flew from Chris's grip, clattering to the floor. The look of fear and longing on Chris's face broke Darien's heart.

Darien braced his hands on Chris's shoulders, pinning him to the wall. "Stop being scared. I'm not Simon. I'm not going to leave you."

The icy demeanor cracked. "Stop."

"I want you. I *need* you. I want to tell the world. Just tell me I can."

Chris's eyes shut, his face crumpling. "Don't." His knees gave out, and he was suddenly a heavy weight against Darien's arms.

"Chris, please. I don't say the words lightly. Please believe me." He eased up, letting Chris slide to the floor, following him down. "You have to believe me a little; otherwise you wouldn't have come." Chris's legs slid flat across the hardwood flooring, and Darien straddled them. He cupped that wonderful, sharp-angled face and kissed the tear that started to roll down one defined cheek. "I love you."

"Darien." Hands gripped high on his thighs.

He kissed Chris's jaw. "I love you."

"God."

He held Chris's head, forcing the man to look at him. The glasses were slightly askew, and tears rolled down those cheeks. The hazel eyes bored into his, challenging. Darien smiled, putting everything he felt for this man into his eyes. "I love you."

"God help me." Chris's gaze darted back and forth from one of Darien's eyes to the other. Searching. Searching hard. "I --" He shook his head. "I can't say that."

Darien smiled, taking heart in the pure emotion showing in Chris's face. "You don't have to say those words. Just don't say no. Give us a chance. That's all I'm asking." He thumbed away a tear that tracked one cheek.

The bite of Chris's fingers in his thighs hurt, but it was a good thing. Chris snarled faintly. "This had better be real."

Darien kissed him, tasting the salt of his tears. "It's real."

"Kiss me."

With pleasure. He would have said the words, but he figured the kissing would do the trick. Chris's mouth opened to his, tongue stabbing between his lips. Eagerly, he sucked it in, drinking in the taste he'd missed so much. One of Chris's hands speared in the hair at his nape, crushing his lips closer. There might have been blood from teeth digging into gums, but Darien didn't care. That reckless, out-of-control thing was taking over Chris, and Darien was going to feed it as much as he could.

Chris's glasses bit into Darien's cheek. With a growl, Chris pulled away and snatched them off, then yanked him back.

"We gonna do it here?" Darien asked, words muffled against Chris's lips.

A hand slid into the back of Darien's jeans as far as it would go, which wasn't far, but it was enough for fingers to dig into one cheek of his ass. "You mind?"

"Nope. I'm yours wherever you want me." He paused for Chris's groan. "But the lube's upstairs."

A little bit of reason came back into Chris's eyes. The hand came out of Darien's jeans and slapped his ass. "Up."

"Yes, sir." Darien jumped to his feet. He held out a hand to help Chris up.

Some of the heat faded as Chris stood, worry clouding over his face.

Darien hooked a hand around the back of his neck and pulled his face close so that their foreheads touched. "I love you. This is real. Must fuck me now. *Stop. Thinking.*"

Chris smiled. A real smile. "Yes. Upstairs."

Nodding, Darien took Chris's hand and led the way up the stairs. He tried not to recall the disastrous results of the last time he'd dragged Chris off. *No, not disastrous. If that hadn't happened, you wouldn't be here.* Well, probably.

Who cared?

They reached the bedroom with its brand-new California king. Bed, nightstand, and lamp were the only furnishings so far in the big room. Darien sat and bent to pull off his boots. The bottle of lube he'd placed on the mattress rolled toward him.

"You have furniture here."

He glanced up. At least Chris was undressing. The jacket was gone, and those gorgeous fingers were unbuttoning the blue shirt.

"Yeah."

"Presumptuous."

"Hey. I figured if I got you up here, sex was happening."

Chris chuckled.

Oh, thank God!

"Good thinking, magpie."

Tossing away his second boot, Darien groaned. "Oh, geez, not that. You're not calling me that."

The shirt was all unbuttoned, open to reveal a swathe of smooth chest and belly. Calmly, Chris unbuttoned one wrist cuff. "It's an apt name for you."

Darien tugged off his polo. "Is not."

"It is."

Darien grumbled, standing so he could take off his pants. "You're just saying that to piss me off."

"No."

Hands on his jeans, he froze when Chris's hand came up to splay across his bare chest. The cuff at his wrist was open, dangling to show off his slim wrist. *God, he's beautiful.* He looked up into serious hazel eyes.

"I don't say it piss you off."

There was more to this than just the name. "Okay."

The hand came up to cup his jaw. "That's *my* name for you. Mine alone."

Warmth spread over Darien's skin, making him tremble. "Yeah. Okay."

"Are you sure about this?"

"I've never been more sure of anything. Really."

"I want to trust you."

Darien reached out and slid an arm around Chris's waist. The other went around his neck, pulling him down. "You can trust me, Chris. I promise."

Time slowed as they kissed, lips fused and tongues twining in a dance of new knowledge and new feeling. They had all the time in the world to simply meld, chest to chest, lip to lip, soul to soul.

Gradually, without stopping the kiss, Chris nudged Darien's jeans and briefs down farther to his thighs. This freed Darien's aching cock, and Chris wrapped those wonderful fingers around it and pulled.

Darien groaned, head tilting back. Chris nipped his bottom lip, his chin. "Beautiful," he murmured, other hand flat on Darien's lower back to keep him upright. "All mine?"

"All yours," Darien sighed without hesitation.

Chris released him and pushed him back on the mattress. He went willingly since he didn't think his knees were going to hold much longer, despite Chris's support. He lay back as Chris took hold of his jeans and underwear and got them the rest of the way off. Moving as though he had all the time in the world, Chris unbuckled his belt and slid his own slacks and underwear off. He must have gotten his shoes off when Darien wasn't paying attention. When he straightened, his hard, leaking cock gave lie to the calm in Chris's demeanor.

Darien sat up, reaching, but Chris stopped him.

"Not this time. If you touch me, I'll go, and I want to be inside you."

Darien melted back onto his elbows. "'Kay."

"Condoms."

"Don't need them."

"What?"

"I haven't had sex since you."

Chris stared at him. "No?"

"No. I'm serious, Chris. I don't want anyone but you."

Chris swallowed. "How can you be sure I haven't?"

Moment of truth. He'd thought about this, but there wasn't anything he could do about it except go on. "I guess I can't. Have you?"

"No."

Darien smiled. "We're good, then."

"Why should you trust me?"

"Did I mention I love you?"

Chris shut his eyes. "Darien, I…"

"Look. Either we do this love thing, or we don't. I love you. I'm willing to trust you. Seems our only problem is whether you're willing to trust me."

Which, of course, was really it. He watched that dawn on Chris. Darien had figured out that it scared him. He hoped against all hope that Chris was willing to overcome that for him. With him.

After a very long moment, Chris nodded. "I trust you."

"Sweet." Darien fell back and drew up his knees, providing Chris with an excellent view of his hole. "On with the barebacking."

Chris laughed. So, okay, if Darien wasn't good for anything else, he could at least make the man laugh.

Then that dark demon grin grew, and Darien recalled that he was good for something else. Getting royally and thoroughly fucked.

Oh, yeah!

He picked up the lube bottle and held it out. Chris took it, but set it back down on the mattress. Darien frowned, but said nothing as Chris climbed up on the mattress between his thighs. Obviously, he had something in mind. When Chris grabbed his thighs and pushed them up toward his chest, effectively raising Darien's ass off the mattress, he figured it out.

"Oh, *fuck* yeah!" he cried as Chris leaned in and swiped his tongue over Darien's very exposed hole.

"That's it, magpie," Chris crooned, shifting to get Darien right where he wanted him. "Talk to me. Tell me you missed my tongue in your ass."

"Oh, man." Tongue played around rim. "Oh, yeah, Chris. Oh, *God,* I missed this." Tongue prodded, stiffened, poking his opening as far as it would go. Darien gripped the spread beneath him, trying to balance in this completely vulnerable position. His cock oozed precum down onto his chest. He babbled on, encouraging Chris, pleading with him.

Chris bit into his thigh, then backed away. He snatched up the lube and poured some in his palm. "Turn over."

Darien whimpered, but obeyed. He'd kind of wanted it face-to-face, but he had to admit that it felt better doggy-style. Chris got in deeper that way.

He was barely in place before Chris's lube-wet hands grabbed his ass, parting his cheeks. No fingers, just the blunt tip of his cock smearing lube with the saliva already there. Darien fell forward on his elbows, bracing himself for the bite of pain as Chris pushed in.

"Fuck," he grunted, mashing his face into the mattress.

Chris paused, waiting for him to adjust. Darien felt the tremble in the hands that smoothed over his ass and lower back.

Once the initial bite passed, Darien needed more. Slowly, he shoved back.

Chris took the hint and pushed forward. "Darien, God!"

It was tight going, but they pushed and pulled until Chris was seated fully inside. The taller man draped himself over Darien's back, hands sliding in the layer of sweat that had broken out across his shoulders and back. "God, Darien, so tight. You feel so good." Kisses along his spine, little nips at the base of his neck. "Want you so much. Need you."

Darien groaned, twisting his neck.

Chris leaned in and they kissed awkwardly as Chris ground his hips against Darien's ass.

"Chris, fuck, do it! Fuck me."

Chris's fingers slid down his arms, finding the hands Darien had bunched in the bedspread beside his shoulders. Their fingers wove together as Chris pulled his hips back, dragging that hot, bare cock almost all the way out of Darien's body. "Darien," he cried softly, and there was pain there. But Darien was pretty sure it wasn't physical pain. It was probably a lot like the heart squeeze he felt himself, knowing that the man he loved was deep inside his body. "Magpie." Darien didn't mind the pet name at all now. In fact, his heart swelled further.

Chris strained above him, going slow, pushing and pulling that steely rod inside Darien, rubbing that spot that ignited the fire at the base of Darien's spine.

Words spilled out of Darien's mouth, but he couldn't figure out what they were. Didn't matter. He wanted more. He *needed* more, and he seemed to be conveying that.

Chris picked up the pace, freeing one of his hands to slide down Darien's chest. He took hold of Darien's cock and squeezed the head.

Darien cried out, arching back. "Chris, *ah!*" He came in Chris's palm, unable to stop. His ass clamped down on his lover as his whole body shook violently.

"Bloody --" No more words. Chris came, hips spasming against Darien. A warm flood filled Darien's body.

Darien slid forward onto his belly.

Draped over Darien's back, Chris slid forward, too. They lay like that for precious moments, simply enjoying the knowledge that they were together.

But idyllic moments only last so long. Darien had to move his leg for fear of cramping. As soon as he moved, Chris groaned, pushing up off of him. Darien flopped onto his side as Chris left the bed, padding unsteadily to the bathroom. *Shit, are there towels in there?* But there must have been because Chris came back with two, one small wet one and a bigger dry one. He used the wet one to carefully wipe Darien clean. Darien watched him do it, smiling.

"Thank you."

Chris's answering smiled was heartfelt. "You're welcome." He tossed the dry towel at Darien.

A few moments later, the towels were discarded and the two of them lay together under the sheets. Daren tucked his head into the bend of Chris's neck, one arm and one leg thrown over the other man, who lay on his back.

"I do love you," he said. "You believe me?"

"I'm trying."

"I believe that you love me."

Arms hugged him. "That remains to be seen." The brush of lips over his forehead told a different story, though. A story Darien was willing to progress gradually this time, as long as Chris didn't shy away.

Chuckling, Darien pushed up onto his elbow so he could see Chris's face. "Come on, Chris, you've got to have faith in me." He let his grin go crooked. "Get it? 'Faith'?"

Chris groaned and punched his arm. "Bad joke, magpie."

Laughing, Darien settled back down. *Oh, yeah, we'll be fine.*

Epilogue

"You don't have to do this."

Chris calmly adjusted his already pristine white collar. "I know that."

Darien glanced nervously toward the door to the little lounge room. Someone would arrive any moment to lead them to their table in the main banquet room. They were the guests of honor at the party celebrating Heaven Sent's first album going platinum. It was a huge deal for the band, something that not all that many bands managed to do anymore.

Chris had agreed to come with him. It was still only a few months since they'd gotten together, and Darien hadn't really seen much of Chris since then. He'd gone back to recording and Chris stayed in New York, but they'd stayed in constant contact. Darien had only gotten back to the east coast twice. He certainly hadn't expected Chris to make such a big step so soon.

The backs of three fingers brushed Darien's cheek, prompting him to turn to face Chris.

Hazel eyes smiled behind the thin lenses of his glasses. "I'm fine." Fingers traced his lips. "I want to share this with you."

"Careful, Chris." Johnnie poked his head between them, reaching up to sling an arm around each of their shoulders. The long, heavy braid of his hair thumped against Darien's side as the singer turned his head to face Chris. The two of them were the same height, both looming over Darien. "When we get out there, you can't let him talk too much. He'll tell a *lot* more than you want him to. He always does."

Darien scowled. "I will not!"

"Yeah," Brent drawled from where he stood nearby. Darien turned to see him leaning up against a wall, turning his lighter in one hand. "There was one time he told a reporter, in detail, about his father's hemorrhoids."

Luc laughed from somewhere close behind Darien. "Then there was the time he almost blurted when Johnnie slept with that governor's wife."

Johnnie straightened, glaring at Luc. "Hey!" He twisted his head to look Tyler's way. "I *didn't* sleep with her."

Tyler just raised an eyebrow, clearly skeptical.

Darien ducked his head. "I don't mean to blurt stuff out," he grumbled. He reached up to grip Chris's lapel, peeking up at the man from beneath his lashes. "I've been good lately, though, huh? I haven't said anything to anyone about us. Honest."

Chris's indulgent smile remained. "You've been very good, for which I am profoundly grateful."

Darien gave Johnnie an I-told-you-so-look.

Johnnie snorted, stepping back from them. "Who'd have thought that fucking his ass would give him some discretion?"

"Damn it." Darien started for his friend, hands fisted, "If you don't shut the hell up, I'm gonna --"

Laughing, Chris wrapped his arms around Darien's shoulders and pulled him so they were chest to back.

Grinning, Johnnie scuttled away, ducking behind Tyler, who rolled his eyes.

"It's all right, magpie," Chris murmured near his ear, loud enough for the others to hear. "We both know you know exactly what to do with your tongue...and when."

Stunned, Darien glanced up at Chris, to see his demon grin pointed at Johnnie.

Johnnie, of course, cracked up. As did Luc and Brent. And Reese. And Hell. Oh, damn, they were all laughing, and all he could do was blush and glare around at his so-called *friends.*

Yeah, his friends. Outside of his family, all of the people who meant the most to him were in this room. Grinning, he settled back into Chris's embrace, reaching up to lace his fingers with his lover's. Including the most important one of all.

"Yeah, well, fuck you all," he grumbled.

"Nah," Luc said, waving his hand, "that's Chris's job."

Teeth nipped his ear gently. "Yes, it is."

Warmth suffused Darien, threatening to tent his suit trousers, but just then the door opened.

A pretty girl smiled at them. "I'm here to lead you to your table."

The others filed out, but Darien made no move out of Chris's embrace.

"You don't have to do this," he muttered. "Last chance. I swear, I understand."

Chris kissed his neck, squeezed his hand. "I know." He unwound his arms from Darien's shoulders, then reached to relace their fingers as Darien turned to face him. "I'm ready to be with you." His smile grew. "I love you."

Darien stared at that gorgeous, angular face, besotted. "Say it again." It was the first time he'd heard the words from Chris's lips.

"I love you."

"Yo, guys?"

He heard Johnnie but couldn't take his eyes from the wonderful man standing before him.

Johnnie whistled. "C'mon, Darien. Sex later, big ta-do and an award now."

Chris bent to brush a quick kiss on Darien's lips. "Let's go."

"Yeah." Darien turned, then stopped and faced Chris again. "I love you, too."

"I know."

⚘THE END⚘

Jet Mykles

Jet's been writing sex stories back as far as junior high. Back then, the stories involved her favorite pop icons of the time but she soon extended beyond that realm into making up characters of her own. To this day, she hasn't stopped writing sex, although her knowledge on the subject has vastly improved.

An ardent fan of fantasy and science fiction sagas, Jet prefers to live in a world of imagination where dragons are real, elves are commonplace, vampires are just people with special diets and lycanthropes live next door In her own mind, she's the spunky heroine who gets the best of everyone and always attracts the lean, muscular lads. She aids this fantasy with visuals created through her other obsession: 3D graphic art. In this area, as in writing, Jet's self-taught and thoroughly entranced, and now occasionally uses this art to illustrate her stories, or her stories to expand upon her art.

In real life, Jet is a self-proclaimed hermit, living in southern California with her life partner. She has a bachelor's degree in acting, but her loathing of auditions has kept her out of the limelight. So she turned to computers and currently works in product management for a software company, because even in real life, she can't help but want to create something out of nothing.

Printed in the United States
207925BV00006B/24/A